The Washington Heights

By

Paul J. Hammond

KCM PUBLISHING

A DIVISION OF KCM DIGITAL MEDIA, LLC

CREDITS

The Washington Heights by Paul J. Hammond

ISBN-13: 978-1-939961-35-8
ISBN-10: 1939961351

Second Edition

Publisher: Michael Fabiano
KCM Publishing
www.kcmpublishing.com

To my parents without whom;

To Alessandra, my Beloved;

And to Wysocki, who lived this scene

as a good man should.

Acknowledgements

A doff of the cap to the two who made this edition materially possible, Nancy Palmer and Michael Fabiano.

Contents

The Washington Heights

Paul J. Hammond

Within this circle of stars,
I keep my voice still.
From my stand on this iron dome,
I see my town turned to other uses.

CHAPTER ONE

ork was the paramount guy in Washington. It ruled all aspects
of the day. A man was measured against how many hours of his
private life he sacrificed, how difficult it was to reach him while he
was working. If he lied, cheated, robbed the nation blind, there was
always a justification to be found in his workload. The question most
people considered too childish to ask was, what purpose did that work
ultimately serve?

For Sterrett Emerson Groves, who could be said to take life easily,
the purpose was clear. It was to pursue the moments of relaxation, the
moments he had free from work with all the more vigor. No mistake,
he was a lawyer, and he believed in good money, a clean name, and
lasting success. He knew the only point to relaxing was to be able to
return to work all the more fired up. But he couldn't help himself. Sterrett lapped up free time as though it were quality beer.

"I mean give up? No way," the girl was saying, her cotton blouse
bunched on top of her like a headdress. "Understand?"

It was a national holiday, the last Monday of the month, the last
day of the month, Memorial Day, and Sterrett Emerson Groves and
the slightly younger girl who was with him were celebrating the end
of cherry blossoms and garden tours, and the start of air-conditioning. They'd left work lunch time and had started out in a restaurant
not far from where Sterrett lived, and had ended up on the sofa in
the living room of the boy's condominium in the heights above
Washington.

"Give up and go back, I mean, to Idaho? Do you get it?" the girl
said, as she flung her blouse to the floor. "I don't have anything there."

Her name was Dinah, a zesty brunette come to work at Guiteau and Garfield right out of college. Earnest and proud, she was quick to color. Her dark brown eyes had ambition in them. But she was still very young for the world she was moving in, her pale skin firm and clingy, her thighs not yet grown to fat.

"I've been tempted to give up. Oh gosh, yes. You made the difference."

Sterrett was surprised that she would admit to his being so important to her. He felt, yes, he made the difference, and he admired the girl for telling him that. But he was smart enough not to say so. Instead he freed the last hook of her brassiere. Her breasts, uncovered, leapt into his hands.

"I thought, you know, Washington wants people to succeed," the girl was saying. "So here I am. I won't go back. No way. This is the place, you know?"

He ogled her bare flesh; the essence of a woman, her generosity, her tender heat, and the ample comfort she had to give were there in her breasts. He permitted himself a squeeze.

"Oh, gosh," the girl said.

Not all women seemed at peace with their breasts. Some complained, Sterrett had heard them, that theirs were too small, others that theirs were too big. Some had "innies" that they were not completely contented with, and other women were modest and super-sensitive and would rather not have their breasts played with at all, not even by young attorneys. A few were quite happy with the bosom God gave them. That seemed to be the case with Dinah. As he kissed her here and there, she permitted herself a joyful, "Oh, oh, gosh, oh," but then went on explaining herself, went on talking.

"And I met you, and you, you helped me with that stupid Xerox machine, and well, you made me feel so welcome. 'Keep on trucking' has to come from that, doesn't it? From feeling accepted by at least one person. Feeling welcome."

Well, that's what he was, the young attorney thought as he kicked himself free of his pants, a welcome wagon hard with desire.

"I mean finally someone in the office was nice to me. You know? Know what I mean? By someone I mean you."

Sterrett ushered the girl onto her back. Then as he pulled at her panties, rolling them free of her feet, there was a silence in the big room and the mood changed a little. The girl hadn't intended the afternoon to get away from her to the degree that it had. She'd intended to get a free lunch, share some talk, and make a new friend, that was all. But she found she liked the boy more than she had expected.

"Don't you think we should use something?" she tried. She was taking pleasure in a way she hadn't prepared for, in a way that wasn't part of her plan, and now she had to find a way to regain control of the situation. "I mean, you know sex protection…oh gosh…"

Sterrett wasn't sure whether she meant "oh gosh" in a dissuasive, anxious sense, or "oh gosh," she was enjoying herself for real in that moment. But it was a moot point for "here I come" became the boy's only thought, endlessly repeated in his head as they rocked together on the sofa. Dinah bore him up so tenderly that his face grew solemn, and he couldn't help bellowing a little.

A pause followed, that postcoital happiness between two people lying like damp rags in each other's arms. Then the girl wrestled out from under his weight, sagged against him on the cushions of the sofa, and sat up. "I have to go." She looked round at the boy, gazing down at him from over her shoulder. She spoke fussily to herself, "Mr. Klocker's expecting me back at the office."

"What?"

"I have to get back to the office."

Sterrett laughed, surprised. "It could have been better for you, is that it?" He reached out to her, clutched her leg. "Come on, kisses, Dinah. Kisses."

"Will you please let go of me?" the girl said. "I have to go to the bathroom." She pushed herself up from the sofa. "Where's it at again?"

"It's there, down the hall." He watched her as she went round and scooped up her bra, her panties, her various other items of clothing that were strewn like clumsy confetti across the living room. Then she made for the bathroom. Her movement, a swaying of buttocks in the dusty light, made her petulant mood easier to tolerate. She disappeared, and he could hear the door to his bathroom open and shut. He flopped back down on his sofa.

He wanted calm after sex, that's what he liked, calm, the warmth of another close at hand. It was the only time feeling something for someone made any sense to him. He liked the dreamy being together with a woman, that languid afterglow, exhausted, intensely gratified. They'd had it, but then the girl had broken that spell for the sake of work. Incredible, he thought.

After the span of a couple minutes Dinah came back into his living room.

"It's almost three," she said, brandishing her wristwatch, showing Sterrett the time. With her hair full of static and her skirt askew on her hips, she had a thoroughly frisky appearance.

The boy sat up. No, she wasn't bad, he thought. He didn't care that she was a frontier girl from the University of Idaho, that she was an ordinary secretary. He liked her better for that, not to any contractual degree, no, but well enough to want to hook up with her again. He started to speak, wanting for once to tell a woman how good she'd made him feel, but thought better of it. Graveling his fingers through his hair, he said simply, "How 'bout sticking around?" Their eyes met, his blue, hers brown, eyes dividing a mutual perplexity. "Why rush off?"

"I have things to do. Mr. Klocker is working today on the Orange-U-Glad merger and I'm sure he'll be asking for me. It's not that I want to go back. I have to."

"You don't have to. It's an observed legal holiday," Sterrett said. "From sea to shining sea, and all across the Nation, it's a day for relaxing." He needled her good-naturedly, "Have fun for once..."

The girl stared at him. "That's a theme with you, isn't it? Having fun."

"Fun in your life instead of all the time worrying."

Did he understand a thing she said, her wrinkled brow announced he didn't. "A woman cannot 'have fun,' Sterrett. She has too much to do. She has to better her fortune in life by any means possible. Thank you by the way for lunch."

Sterrett Emerson Groves hopped to his feet. He stood there encamped in the middle of his living room, exuberant, naked, bare belly gleaming with sweat. "Have fun," he sang out louder than before. "Come hang with me and be my love."

He came over to her. Held her by the waist. Dinah pushed against him, pushed weakly, and let her eyes close, forgetful for a moment in the imperishable desire that united them, a desire of one for the other. She let herself go, kissing him.

"It's late," she said finally, not wanting to be free of him, but pushing him away because it was what she knew she had to do, using both hands to push him away. "And oh gosh, you know, I think you should get dressed." If she was being hard-assed that was fine because it would pay off. "It's the middle of the day." She kicked at the boy's underwear. Sterrett reached down and stepped into the tartan boxers.

"I didn't expect this," he said, maneuvering as a good lawyer should. "I didn't expect this to happen. I don't do this, first dates like this, but it's like we've known each other forever. Do you know what I mean? It happened because it was natural between us and because it was meant to happen. Some people call it destiny. And destiny is defined by its ineluctable quality…"

It was a speech. The young attorney was making a speech. Dinah struck a pose then and asked, "Oh gosh, we're not going to argue about it, are we?"

She was suddenly fed up with the situation, an apartment not her own, a place she wanted to get away from once she'd decided to get away from it. She was angry with the young attorney too, for being the way he was, at once manipulative and inexplicably attractive. "I admit I'm not sorry at what happened," she told him. "I'm grateful, you know, that you made the effort. I am grateful for that."

Touchy, Sterrett thought. This was what was wrong with secretaries, their thin skin. It was the reason he had to remember to avoid dating them; they were too afraid all the time of doing something wrong. He watched the girl as she put a hand out to steady herself against the wall, slipping on her high heels. Not used to them perhaps.

"A person has got to make the most of every day," she explained, and with her shoes on and her leather bag in hand, she was ready to go. She knew she would be one of the few secretaries in the office that holiday afternoon, but that was the point, she wanted to stand out. "You have to make the most of each and every day."

"What does that mean? Make the most?" Sterrett rebuked her, "You're a secretary."

"You have a real nice apartment," Dinah answered primly. Then she put her hand on the knob and swung the door to the apartment open, put a foot out into the brightly lit hallway. He wanted nothing from her except what he wanted for himself. It was going to lead nowhere, and it wasn't what she planned. "I envy you your wonderful apartment," she said. "And the fact that this is home to you."

"This is making the most to me." He grabbed the girl. Kissed her on the lips. This time Dinah slapped him, not with all the force she might have, but it was a gesture clearly identifiable as a slap. Instantly the worry came to her that she'd overstepped herself and if he were at all vindictive, she'd just then risked if not her job, her peace of mind at work. She wanted to leave right then before things got worse. She hurried off to the elevators and batted at the call button.

"What the hell's wrong with you?" Sterrett said, rubbing his cheek, following the girl.

"I don't know." Dinah backed into the steel carriage as the door slid open. She reached out and pressed "L" for lobby. "Maybe it's me and I expect too much."

Sterrett didn't have anything to say to that, and all he could do was watch as the elevator door slid shut. He listened as the elevator descended. He went back into his apartment. Shut the door, rested his back against it, arms folded tight on his chest. He opened the door again and peered into the hallway to see that she was gone for real. Closed the door with a slam. "So much for that."

There were no signs left in his living room, no impress of the girl's body on the sofa. No crumpled tissue, not a single odor, nothing of hers, not even lipstick stains on a glass. Nothing was left him but the stinging red mark where she'd slapped him. Nothing left him but the feeling that she'd left.

He went to the balcony, threw back the curtains, and put his face to the view out the sliding door. He shut his eyes, and a moment later, opened them wide. Washington was all before him, spread out under the afternoon haze like some rugose invertebrate lying just below the surface of the salt tide.

He'd been the ingenuous one. The girl had turned him inside out, telling him how kind he was. He'd believed it, and for a wonderful moment, he'd bought into the idea that Dinah from Idaho was a forlorn bird, lost in the immense city, needing his help. He'd bought into the idea because that was how he wanted to see himself, as a good man who knew how to help young secretaries get oriented.

But this secretary, this hick chick who worked for Corny Klocker in Mergers and Acquisitions was markedly different from most of the other secretaries he'd brought to his apartment. She'd turned the situation upside down. She'd done it smartly, too. He didn't want to dwell on it. It only made him frustrated. As a rule, he didn't like to be frustrated with women. There was no point in being frustrated with a woman. But the more he thought about it, the greater his resentment grew at what had happened.

Not on account of the slap. It took more than a slap to upset him. He was a bigger man than that. No, it was because he'd made an effort, opened himself up to the girl, and given her, Dinah, all of what he had to give, and gotten back a lecture on knuckling down. Giving and not getting what he wanted was like not giving in the first place. If he didn't get anything back then there was no real exchange, and part of the pleasure of sex was that exchange, two people caring for each other in that very moment of pleasure, caring enough to make sure that that moment was, well, extremely pleasurable.

Sterrett went over to his liquor cabinet, thirsty now. The cabinet was one of the few things he'd kept that had been his father's, a heavy piece of furniture in tawny oak. He turned a key and opened the glass door. He took the bottle nearest to hand and poured himself plain straight whisky. Then he went over to the one big armchair he had and sat down. He couldn't sit for long; the girl had put a bee in his bonnet. He switched the whisky to his left hand and caught hold of the telephone on the side table, then dialed his office. He was put on hold a sec' and then he reached his own secretary.

"Everything okay, Suzy?"

"No one's asked for you," was the woman's reply. "If that's what you mean. Is that what you mean?"

"Sir Simon call at all?"

"No, Sterrett, so far no."

"Okay, that's a relief. What about the others?"

"No, I think now the only one working on the fourth floor is Mr. DeMurphy. Everybody else went home and didn't come back. Except Patty Johnson, she's here. And me."

"Natch."

"Natch," Suzy echoed.

Patty Johnson was Mrs. Patricia Johnson, Guiteau and Garfield's office manager, a hyperactive soul without whom the firm could not have gone forward a single day. Seen filling every doorway of every office during emergencies or important deadlines, she was a robust little Tony Robbins, hurtling around heartily restoring the partners' faith in themselves whenever that faith flagged. She practically never left the building except to change into a different pants suit.

"Well, listen." Sterrett stroked his cheek with the back of his hand. "Make the most" was still ringing in the space between his ears. "Okay, maybe I'll drop back into the office for a couple hours." Down in the garage, he had a bicycle he rode to work. The bike got him downtown faster than if he went by car, and if he really applied himself, sprinting through red lights and snubbing his nose at traffic, he could make the Guiteau Building in ten minutes. "I can be there practically now."

"What's the point of that?"

"I don't know. What do you mean?"

An uncertain pause along the phone line, then Suzy said patiently, "I'm going home soon."

"Right away?"

"Not right away," Suzy said. "In twenty minutes."

"All right. I got you." Sterrett hung up.

The shower stall a refuge, Sterrett Emerson Groves stood under the steaming hot water much longer than normal and used abundant soap, careful to scrub his loins clean. After the shower, he shaved with unhurried, meticulous strokes and after shaving, he went into his bed-room and put on a fresh pair of boxer shorts and a T-shirt. The glass of whisky had opened his stomach, and he went into his kitchen hungry. He was a milk and cookies man from way back. That was comfort food to him, and he sat down at the kitchen table, the cookie jar by his elbow, and he dipped an oatmeal cookie in the full glass of cold milk before him. "Make the most," he urged the slowly dissolving cookie. "Go on, make the most of yourself."

And when he saw his oatmeal cookie was good and soggy, he slopped it into his mouth. He drank the milk, full as it was with cookie pulp, drank it down in big gulps, cold milk filling his belly, enjoying himself as he let a little milk slobber down his chin. Almost a holiday in itself, being able to eat like that. He wiped cookie crumbs from his cheek and got to his feet. He licked the corner of his mouth. Cookies were as good as whisky. But he couldn't take them together. He'd tried once, dipping graham crackers into a tumbler of scotch whisky, but it was too much of a good thing. Cookies went with milk. Scotch was best neat.

He took the dirty glass and put it in the sink. He put the cookie jar back on the cupboard shelf and left the kitchen, went into his living room, to the balcony's door. He thought this was what he liked, being alone. He quite simply did not want to be in love or feel anything like love at that stage in his life. He wanted to be perfect before he let himself be loved, a perfect person, sure of himself, sure of his worth. So he was doing fine; he was eking out his destiny the way he should.

He looked at his watch. It was a little past five o'clock. What to do if he didn't go into work? See a movie, he wondered, or stay home, watch television. He stared at the hall closet, Ping, go to the driving range. Too hot. Go to a bar. That sounded best. Washington in summer was a town of hard drinking. Participate in that, Sterrett thought. Prove how much he could take. He went back into his bedroom and got dressed for the bar.

He didn't wear jewelry on his wrists, just a watch. He didn't tan himself in parlors or dye his hair the way many of the other lawyers did. He found in the dark suits, the wing-tip shoes they all wore, an oppressive sameness, a uniform. In order to avoid being just another one like the others, Sterrett flouted the dress code for an associate at a law firm by sporting extremely ugly neckties. It was not possible to do as the U.S. president did, forgo the necktie entirely and wear the open collar. A law firm was a serious forum. Instead, Sterrett made his statement by eschewing the regimental or the red or the blue power tie, favoring wide, inelegant ties hand-painted in Vermont or ties of cadaverous colors, or simply ties with paisley designs.

Where he was going, to hang out in a bar, no tie was required, and a pair of blue jeans and a button-down shirt were sufficient. Standing before his mirror, he couldn't help admiring himself, an agreeable face topped with his messy crown of short-cut blond hair. Essentially, it was his father's in the long, aquiline nose and the softly cleft chin, and his mother's face in the clear coloring, the blue eyes, the usual filial mix. He touched his nose. If it were smaller, he could have made the motion pictures. It was a face he knew women liked.

It was his underarms that caused problems. He tended to sweat too much from his underarms, and they became somewhat daunting. He had tried all brands of deodorant—spray, roll on, powder—and not one among them made a breach in the faintly rancid odor. At best he could neutralize the stinkiness with a combination of roll on and baby powder. His sweaty underarms sometimes made intimacy a thorny issue. With Dinah it hadn't been a problem; she hadn't said a thing about his armpits.

He was dressed, and he was ready to go, but first he went out onto his balcony. His balcony was the first thing he showed visitors to his apartment. It was the first thing he'd shown Dinah. He was as proud of the view as if it were his own creation. The balcony faced south. It took in an angle of downtown Washington and all of Georgetown's denser village. He could see the river and the Virginia heights beyond it. It was a view to the heart of the mightiest city on earth.

Sterrett clasped his hands together. He raised his eyes. "Berwick, give me strength." It was a prayer to keep him from drinking too much. Sterrett knew he had that one problem. He prayed to his father, who had also been a heavy drinker. He hoped the old Army tanker was up there in the sky and could hear him and would help him out for once. Sterrett left his apartment and got into the elevator. He went down to the lobby, thinking, on the other hand if his father left him alone and let him get drunk, maybe that was better.

His favorite bar was the Lucky Key on Wisconsin Avenue. It was within walking distance from his apartment. Next to an Orange-U-Glad convenience store, the Lucky Key was a former Chinese restaurant turned late night strip club. There was a banner over the entrance that read, "The hip grindingest girls in D.C."

Sterrett didn't go there for the girls because the girls that danced there weren't the kind of girls he'd ever want to date. He went there for the atmosphere. The Lucky Key had avoided the gentrification that had taken over that part of Wisconsin Avenue in the last fifteen years. There were no ferns, no cutesy lighting effects. They served beer at the Key, yes, but only domestic beer, and the bar had the blessing that the only music played was what the girls danced to. The television was an old RCA and it was never turned on, except to see whether it worked or not.

Sterrett Emerson Groves had tried, and kept trying, to make friends out of his colleagues on the fourth floor of the Guiteau Building, Jacques and Hugo, Bird and Walt. They were lawyers his age, Jacques DeMurphy a little older, pretty much from the same educational and economic background as he. But all that sameness only made things worse. It made for envy of the little things that made them each different, each envious of the things the other had more of.

The other lawyers at work reacted to Sterrett in particular, always trying to diminish him because he was smart and didn't have to work as hard as they to achieve the same results. Sterrett knew his importance at the firm, but he didn't know any longer how to react to the others outside of competing with them. He didn't know how to make friends.

The folks he rubbed elbows with at the Lucky Key, off-duty cops, sales clerks, building contractors, were people he had nothing in common with and thus people he didn't have to compete with. They were like friends to him, a substitute for friends, what Sterrett liked to call his "chumlings." He was attracted to his chumlings because they seemed to be honestly who they were. Two off-duty cops, his best chumlings, were already there, sitting under the ceiling fan along the bar, bottles of beer before them. It looked as though they'd been sitting at the bar for some time. Gooch saw him first, called him over.

"Now here's a real son of a bitch," the cop said, grinning. From Kentucky, he'd served fifteen years with the MPD and had seen plenty enough mayhem on the stale city streets. His fervent goal was to be noticed by a superior officer and put behind a desk in an air-conditioned office downtown.

Sterrett came along the bar and sat down next to the younger of the two policemen, Deterisi. Dave Deterisi winked at him and said, "Hello, sport."

"What are you guys doing?"

"Whatever we're doing," Gooch said, "We're not doing much of it."

Sterrett stayed at the Lucky Key until late. It was the height of his day in terms of plain human relations, his sitting with Deterisi and Gooch and listening to their stories. It was enough to share a little space, to have a laugh, and drink his fill. No one talked insights and no one talked about feelings. There was no confessional moment among the men beyond the usual gripes. Sterrett for his part wasn't afraid of feelings. It was that he found feelings often betrayed a man, let him in for ridicule, left him too vulnerable.

He was content to drink. That was what made him happy. He thought about telling the two cops about Dinah, what the girl had said to him, "make the most," but he decided to keep quiet. He left the bar to wind his way home just as some of the customers in the front stood up and began singing "We Are the World." It was the end of the last strip show for that evening and that was what they sung.

CHAPTER TWO

The day after a legal holiday, Washingtonians were sure to come into work half an hour earlier to prove how heartfelt their commitment to the work ethic was. Their cars filled the bridges into town with traffic, car upon car, and in each car one man or woman was already on a cellphone talking to a client, doing business. There was no sense in resting. The evil done in the world was done by people who did not rest, by men and women who did not find joy and comfort among their fellows.

Sterrett had a different point of view, the product of conscious reasoning; he had before him the example of his father, Lieutenant Colonel Berwick Groves. The harder Berwick applied himself in the field, the worse off he was as a human being. Often he returned home from a mission, physically battered and emotionally depressed. There was no happiness in being a soldier.

Berwick's last mission had been as a peacekeeper in the Balkans. That mission eventually cost him his life; within a year of coming Stateside he was diagnosed with leukemia from the radioactive dirt of Kosovo. No one worked harder at keeping peace in the world than the Pentagon, and no one paid a higher price than its officer corps.

Sterrett was a teenager when his father died, and yet he took Berwick's death philosophically. His mother was shocked by his lack of tears at the grave site. She feared Sterrett was suffering from some sort of mental breakdown, a fear not put to rest when he quoted to her a phrase Berwick himself had repeated often, from the Ionian poet Anacreon: "War spares not the brave man, but the coward."

His mother's fears were allayed only when Sterrett graduated law school. By then he had ceased confiding in her. He knew she'd be worried if he told her that what he'd taken away from Berwick's death was an idea of life in total opposition to the work ethic. He made the equation that the harder one worked, the heavier the price one paid.

Sterrett wasn't a shirker however. He didn't lie low. He was careful to work as diligently as he had to, to get to the next level. But hard work, he felt, was for those who had no other resource. Sterrett relied more on God-given qualities, his athletic bearing and his good looks. He had as well a talent for arguing at length and brilliantly upon things he was perfectly ignorant of. That gave him an edge he might not have enjoyed otherwise. This advantage of his was not always appreciated by his peers.

But he'd won the goodwill of the senior partner at Guiteau and Garfield, Vincent Jorrigo. Vince didn't need another grind at his side. He wanted someone who could speak to the issue at hand without being heavy handed, someone who could glide with the client through the client's many moods and still keep a certain humor. He'd chosen Sterrett Emerson Groves, the best possible associate to help manage one particular client, a leader in the field of waste management, Sir Simon Psora.

It was Tuesday. Sterrett sat at his breakfast table with a mug of coffee. He drank his coffee without milk, without sugar. He liked bitter best, bitter made him smile. That was all he had time for, some coffee. He'd have something more filling at Lemke's before going into the office.

He was running late, that didn't worry him, late was normal. He dared anyone to say anything to him about it. He was going to be late, and if the senior partner wanted to yell at him for it, that was fine. Sterrett sat at his breakfast table, mulling over the things he should have done that he hadn't.

Memorial Day he should have gone to visit his father's grave at Arlington National Cemetery—that was something he should have done that would have cost him nothing. It was a question of going down Rock Creek Parkway and across Memorial Bridge, a forty minute bike ride from his condominium's garage to the Visitors' Center parking lot. It seemed the holiday had been designed for that, to remember the war dead, and not for wasting time fucking a secretary.

He got up from the kitchen table. He went into his bedroom. He got into a white shirt, a gray pinstripe suit, and put on a thin, green tie. He was proud of the tie because it was very ugly. He'd picked it up at a yard sale in Wheaton. The tie was the exact color of his own snot, not his normal snot, but his snot when he was sick with the flu. It was made of a slick, synthetic material that added to the blatant authenticity of its atrocious and uninviting hideousness. It was sure to elicit protests from his secretary, and even the senior partner would be annoyed. When he was in a bad mood that was what Sterrett liked to do, annoy others.

He went into his living room and sat down on the edge of his sofa. He slipped on his burgundy wingtips, tied the laces. He looked at his watch. He had been a little too long in the shower, and perhaps a little too long shaving, certainly way too long in the kitchen, letting himself feel lazy. He had one other thing to do. He went out onto his balcony. He clasped his hands together. He peered into the heavens. "Berwick," he said. "Give me strength."

He lingered there a moment more. He had never talked to anyone, how he felt about his father, about his father's painful, early death. It was his secret how he felt, and he deemed it inappropriate to expose his secret to facile solemnities. It was unwise to diminish their disruptive force by giving his hidden emotions too much expression. He had not even talked to his mother, how he felt. He believed she deserved not to worry.

He stepped back inside and crossed the living room to the vestibule, checked himself in the large, oval mirror that hung there. He'd bought it at Ikea, as straightforward a piece of furniture as the Swedes could manage. But the mirror was in truth a tricky surface, slippery in its effect. It never seemed to reflect the same person.

Sterrett looked the same—same nose, eyes—and yet he was never quite the same Sterrett. There was always a surprising element to spoil the sought-after perfection. Today it was his hair. It stuck out in spikes from behind his ears. He licked his fingers and pressed his hair down, and struck a partnership pose. He was reassured then, the person he saw in the glass, a young man with that infallible look of self-confidence and success proper to a top Washington attorney.

Then he was out in the hallway, waiting for the elevator. A woman appeared. She appeared at the door of an apartment several doors down the hall from his. She came down the hall towards him. She was wearing a bedraggled-looking wool sweater and held an unfiltered cigarette between her fingers.

Sterrett knew the woman well. He often opened jars for her and helped her with her furniture, moving chairs from room to room when she wanted. He knew the woman had her good days like everyone else, and her bad.

"Good morning, ma'am."

"Who's there?" she asked, looking right at him. "Who you?"

Sterrett answered, "It's me."

The woman put her lips to the damp end of her cigarette and puffed and puffed, her eyes among so many wrinkles, quite alert. Then she tapped the cigarette ash into her hand and dropped the ash into a pocket of her shapeless sweater. "Ah, you. Don't you have work to go to?"

"Yes, and I'm late."

"My husband..." the old woman started to say, but the elevator was there and Sterrett got in. "I know all about your husband," he told her as the doors closed.

He went down to the garage, where his bicycle was parked. His suit jacket buttoned, sunglasses on, Sterrett paused as he came out of the garage on the bike, then he dashed into traffic. The trip was a swift one going down Wisconsin Avenue, slipping past the lights, and after the Social Safeway, Sterrett stood on the pedals, grinding his way up the short incline past the row of shops, Starbucks, a vets, a liquor store, then Ignazy Kunin the tailor's, to reach the Georgetown Library at the intersection with R Street. He held up there, dabbed the perspiration from his lips. Let a Metro bus go by.

He felt strong and fit for how little time he spent in the gym. He knew too that no one helped the strong and the fit; they had to make their own way in the world. "Make the most" meant that, making way in the world without the benefit of other people, and it wasn't something to be proud of. He had that chip on his shoulder. The fact that he'd had to make it on his own was proof he was uncared for.

He propelled himself through Georgetown, down to M. He crowed like chanticleer riding the leafy streets, not so much happy maybe, as fully energized. "Cock-a-doodle-do," he crowed at passersby.

The bicycle hadn't been originally his idea. His insurance company's stark unwillingness to insure him after his last car accident made it an inevitable choice. In any case, the D.C. Department of Motor Vehicles had suspended his license, too few points, to the point that he had no points at all. Rather than go through the mortification of having to take driver's ed again like some weedy juvenile, Sterrett bought himself a Wind Wrangler Criterium. Now he circulated on spoked wings with twenty-one speeds.

Turning left on M Street, he swung out in front of a taxicab, riding his bike more like a hellion than any angel, forcing the cabby into a skid. The cabdriver leaned out of his brown Chevy. Sterrett caught some of the words the cabby was spewing forth, an unusual string of accented curses, dogs and dung and wanton mothers flung at his fleeing back. Changing gears, he crossed Rock Creek to the Guiteau Building on the corner of M and 24th Streets. He jumped the curb and chained his bike to a "No Parking" sign. He took off the metal clip that held his pants leg in place, and went hurrying round the corner to Lemke's Dairy on Pennsylvania Avenue.

Like every weekday morning, Lemke's that morning was thronged with well-dressed, well-scrubbed youth, men mostly, mostly lawyers taking eats before going to the office. The floor underneath the tables was a herd of upright briefcases. Waitresses hurried from table to table, making comments on their customers to each other, "that one's cheap," "this other one, watch out, he has claws." The place had an informal, shabby air that the younger generation of professionals appreciated as authentic.

Ed Lemke, the seventy-five-year-old proprietor was there every day, a faded, wheezing presence sitting on a high chair by the door. He had been an assistant manager for the Washington Redskins in long ago days, and the walls were shingled with photographs of former players from Larry Brown to Pete Wysocki, with pictures of fans and hangers-on, including three U.S. presidents. The most prominent photograph was of Sonny Jurgensen in a large wooden frame above the cash register. There Jurgensen, his arm flexed to launch the ball, had written famously, "To all my athletic supporters."

He was late, late; the other Guiteau and Garfield associates were already gone, and Sterrett sat at the counter instead of at their usual table. Liz, the waitress who worked the counter, came up to serve him a mug of coffee. Sterrett ordered scrambled eggs. He held the mug in his fist. He took short sips and made gently appreciative sounds, slouched against the counter. Then he opened the small notebook he carried, concentrating on the language he wanted to use to boost the model sanitary landfill his client was proposing to build in Washington. "The garbage dump, reinvented," that was the phrase he wrote down in the pad.

It was important to find the right language; the dump was going to be a big dirty hole in the ground with all the plastic bottles and all the plastic bags and all the tons of paper Washingtonians consumed, piled in with rotting apple cores and old lettuce. It was going to be like any trash dump anywhere, but it had to sound better, a model sanitary landfill, so as to sell it to the Department of the Interior and to Congress.

The client, Sir Simon Psora, was offering a lot of money for the lease of fifty acres of public parkland, an oval of grass and some trees immediately to the south of the White House. It was an area of no particular usefulness, other than it was where the Zero Milestone marker stood and where the National Christmas Tree was located, put up once a year and lit by the president, enjoyed by millions.

Sir Simon, known in the media as the Greek Dustman, was tempting the federal government with lots of money at a time when cash-money was what the federal government needed. More, he was tempting the administration with his idea, that the sanitary landfill be an American showcase. He wanted it to be something the president of the United States could point to and say, this was why he was proud to be a citizen, the way Americans dealt with waste.

The woman was in her twenties, an associate like he was, but at another firm. She was sitting on the stool next to him, her legs crossed. She had her personal financial report for that month spread out on the counter, and she was studying her quarterly from the Liddell Growth Fund. Prompted by the sounds Sterrett was making as he drank his coffee, she introduced herself, "My name's Kara. I'm with Collazo Torresola Blair and Coffelt."

"Uh huh, Guiteau Garfield," Sterrett said distractedly.

He was concentrating so hard on the client that he couldn't remember the word for the small metal implement with two or more prongs used for taking up and eating. He could think of a lot words to describe it, but he had drawn a blank as far as its name was concerned. He stared at the scrambled eggs and bacon on his plate, and then looked over at the woman.

He said to her, "Can I borrow your, uh, fork. Mine fell on the floor."

The woman handed her fork over and said, "You keep it."

He ate his eggs helter-skelter. Liz came over and said, "How about some dessert? Cool cherry cream? Nice apple tart?"

"No, I'm late."

He left Lemke's. M Street was lined with trucks unloading merchandise. Sterrett got to the Guiteau Building and went in, through the lobby, took the elevator to the fourth floor. It was nine o'clock, and the elevator was crammed as if for a college prank, noisy and sweaty, so that the day's exertion was already palpable. That was the feel of the city in the morning, the reason the city existed, to give people a place to go, to unite them in making the city feel dynamic and alive.

The first thing that struck anyone getting out of the elevators on the seventh floor was a concave screen painted gold with "Guiteau and Garfield" spelled out across it in big, red enamel letters. Turning to the right, there was a foyer with deep leather couches, couches for the client in a dark chocolate color. There were steel lamps, a couple Benjamin fig trees, a very low, glass-topped coffee table with magazines strewn across it. Over by the far wall, there was an espresso machine and cups and sugar, all the comfort and coddling work-afflicted corporate heads and politicians needed so as to feel at their ease while waiting for their attorneys. The magazines were travel monthlies and sports featuring women in bikinis.

That was where the firm's red carpet for the client was, the seventh floor. On the fourth floor, where Sterrett worked, the welcome mat was the size of a post-it. Turning to the right, after the bank of secretaries, came the paralegals in cubicles, and then came offices. Going down a corridor, brightly lit, but gray in overall tone, there was an open space, a phone, a worn-out sofa, and then more offices, and at the corner a small conference room with a no-nonsense view of a parking lot.

Sterrett's office was at the end of the corridor. The first thing he did heading for his own was to poke his head into Jacques DeMurphy's office. DeMurphy was a "jp," one of the clique of associates and junior partners Sterrett was not quite in with. A Harvard Law graduate, bright and pampered, Jacques DeMurphy was above all hard working, the hardest-working young man in the firm.

"Morning, Jack," Sterrett said. He wanted to make friends, at least for the sake of his career. "How are you doing?"

"Ah, why the hell do you say hello to me all the time?" DeMurphy asked.

"Why? Because I like you."

"You want to be like me, that's it." DeMurphy had been at his desk since seven thirty, and his shirtsleeves were rolled up and he already looked unpalatably hot and bothered. "But I'm part of a rare breed. You're just a brownnose."

Jacques DeMurphy got up every morning at five o'clock. He'd been getting up at five for so long he no longer needed an alarm clock. He got out of bed, careful not to wake his wife. He went downstairs to the study, closed the door tight, and spent one hour at the piano, practicing scales. He didn't know how to play the piano, except for scales, but he knew scales very well, perhaps better than anyone.

After piano, he got into his running clothes and went jogging around the block, rain or shine. He lived in Chevy Chase where the blocks were enormous, among the biggest residential blocks in the country. Home, he showered and had breakfast with his wife and children, spending most of his time behind one of the three different newspapers he read each morning, the *New York Times*, the *Guardian*, the *Hong Kong Daily*. He left his house at seven sharp, giving his wife the most passionate kiss of the day, petting his dog, urging his children to be good children. For despite his inability to relate to them, DeMurphy loved his children. He drove to work in his car and generally got to the Guiteau Building before most of the partners.

All this was admirable, and the associates knew this was his daily schedule, because DeMurphy told them it was. And the associates, Sterrett included, envied him his capacity for successful self-promotion. His Facebook page for instance opened with quotes in his praise coming from people as diverse as a major corporate client to his cousin in New Jersey complimenting him on his choice of wine for Christmas dinner. A big man physically, his chin a double chin, Jacques DeMurphy had only just turned thirty-two, and already he sat uneasily on his hemorrhoids.

Sterrett looked round the man's office. He smiled. He was the only one of the associates who really made an effort to fawn over the junior partner. Knowing how much he annoyed DeMurphy, Sterrett persisted, despite his own better judgment. "I hope you have a good day there, Jack. So if I can do anything for you, let me know. I'm always ready to drop whatever I'm doing."

"Fuck off," was the junior partner's shrewd retort, and Groves took to his heels, full of relish in his heart that at least he'd done one good deed that morning by pissing off a Harvard grad.

Walt Gdyap and Bird Mallet shared one of the big corner offices, and both were there, busy as beavers. Bird was huddled forward in his chair, his face inches close to his computer screen. Walt was on the telephone, going back and forth over the floor. Next to their office, another one of the associates, Hugo Humphrey was in agony over some contract or other, his groans audible over the din of copy machines and the clack-clack of keyboards.

Sterrett made his way to the bottom of the corridor, an area for the secretaries, cubicles arranged under a grill of skittish fluorescents. Each secretary's desk was a highly personalized tract behind the chest-high partitions, marked not just by family photos pinned everywhere, but by select, idiosyncratic items. Suzy, Sterrett's secretary, was from Scranton. A staunch fan of the Pittsburg Pirates, she had a piggy bank on her desk, a ceramic head, resting on a pair of black ceramic cleats, modeled to look like Pittsburg's Neon Flores. Every time someone asked her to do something that wasn't precisely part of her job, pick up lunch for instance or take a shirt to the dry cleaner's, that person had to drop a penny through the slot in Flores's big round china head.

"How are you, Suze? Have a good time yesterday?"

"I went home and rested."

"Mail come yet?" the young attorney asked, leaning against the partition. The secretary reached into a box marked "SEG" and handed Sterrett his pile. There was a subscription renewal from *Court to Court*, the magazine for lawyers who played basketball, a commercial postcard advertising sunny vacation homes in Cancun, Mexico, and a cheerful and personally addressed letter from a credit card company offering him more credit in return for more debt. Sterrett read this last letter through a couple times without really understanding what it was getting at. Then he wandered into his office and dumped it, along with the other mail into his wastebasket.

Sterrett's was the standard type of small back office, with a window facing another building, the headquarters of the National Retirees Association. A service alley ran under the window and separated the two buildings. The office itself had room enough for a desk and a swivel chair, a file cabinet. Files were piled upon files on top of the cabinet, more files on top than inside. On his desk, piles of paper were piled up under his computer keyboard, and Post-its dripped from the edge of his computer screen, old technology and new technology overlapping.

The desk was made of real wood, an impressive relic of an earlier generation of legal thrall. Its drawers were dark, dusty, mysterious recesses. They had not been emptied, really emptied since day one and contained stuff from other lawyers long gone, old business cards, rusted nail cutters, jammed-up staplers, sheaves of carbon paper like funeral veils, spools of inked ribbon for typewriters whose manufacturers had gone out of business, an infinity of paperclips, old unpaid parking tickets. There were other things in those drawers that remained to Sterrett unidentified objects, never touched, never brought out to the light of day.

He himself had but a few personal items on his desk, a photograph of his parents together, a Baltimore Orioles mug full of pens and pencils, a packaged set of golf balls with the 1st Armored Division's logo. The photograph, an old Polaroid, showed his father and mother waving good-bye to him from the platform at Union Station as he was leaving for his first year at college. It was the image of a sharply painful moment in Sterrett's life, not because he was leaving the warm embrace of loved ones, but because it marked the specific moment he had discovered his father's sickness.

His school learning hung on the wall behind him, a reminder to himself and to others what his personal choices had been. There was his diploma from St. Furban's School, a swank private high school in Washington. There was his BA degree from William and Mary, his mother's alma mater, and his law school degree from Georgetown. This last, his most gainful academic venue, was nailed to the wall in a splendid gold frame.

His learning promised great things, and indeed Sterrett Emerson Groves was sitting at his desk, full of concentration, reading the morning newspaper. There was a lot to inwardly digest, the front-page story for instance. It was a frightening account of the newly minted terrorist organization Zafar Junayd, operating in Turkmenistan. According to Pentagon sources, Zafar was made up of radical Kizils supported by the ayatollahs, part of Tehran's effort to destabilize the Caspian Sea region. It cast a shadow over the news, the world's end as close as the length of a tightly wound turban.

Sterrett read the article full of uneasy yearning, wishing to be part of that Army task force shown walking the tarmac into the maw of a big east-bound Galaxy aircraft. Thinking as he always did, he should have joined. He had had the chance, and if he only knew himself then as well as he did now, he would have made that choice, for fighting appealed to him. It was his father who'd dissuaded him. It was out of respect for his father that Sterrett was now an attorney.

His father spoke against joining the military with unassailable authority. Colonel Berwick Groves had joined the Army out of college, taking the soldier's oath during Vietnam. Yet Berwick never did get to see Vietnam, neither its lush mountain jungles nor its fertile Delta. He trained in tanks and went on to see the rest of the world, or at least as much of the rest of the world as it was possible to see from a gun turret. His tanks worked the Wall in Berlin and pounded the Zone in Korea. He got to traverse his 120mm smooth bore in the first Iraqi war.

Berwick and tanks were built for each other. Anytime there was a riot on television or unrest somewhere or even some lying politician stirring up a crowd, Berwick would say, "send in one Abrams with a good crew, and clap hands, your problem solved." He had the 40th Armor Regiment's motto, "Better Treads than Dead," tattooed on his arm, much to the embarrassment of his wife.

His last field command had been as the leader of a battalion in the Balkans, part of the KFOR peacekeeping force sent into Serbia in 1999. He returned from that mission two years later to tell his son, to warn him and persuade him to stay out of uniform. The Colonel's complaint was something so fundamental it didn't need to be explained. The problem was the Army wasn't about the individual fight anymore, and if it wasn't about the fight, there was no space for individual honor. If there was no honor, there was no benefit in fighting, and a man was better off doing something with less risk and better pay, like the Law.

Those were bad memories. The young associate was tired of bad memories. He was tired of the past always pulling him back. It was the reason he'd pretty much cut off all contact with the rest of his family, his sisters, his mother, his cousins. He didn't want to hear about the family's problems, and he was totally cold to the family's history. He didn't want to bear that burden. It was burden enough being who he was.

Sterrett turned the *Post*'s pages 'til he came to the sports section. Baltimore was last in the standings. The associate was an old enough resident of Washington to be a Baltimore Orioles fan, old enough too, to remember the last time the Orioles were exciting. Now all the excitement on the diamond was in Montreal with the Expos, Steve Zampi and his way with batters.

Sterrett moved a little to the left to get the full blast of the air-conditioning coming out of the vents in his ceiling. He tossed the newspaper onto his desk. Time to get to work, he thought. But before he could actually do anything productive, his secretary, Suzy, appeared in the doorway. Sterrett said, "I'm busy. Go away."

"Your phone's off the hook."

Sterrett glanced over at the newspaper. Lifted it. Peeked underneath it. He'd knocked the receiver on its side. Suzy gave him her usual look and said, "If I were you, I'd put a little order in my life."

"It's him, isn't it?" Sterrett asked.

"He's over some place in Europe."

"No, I know that…okay. Line two?"

Suzy turned out the door. She gave him a stiff nod. "The point is I'm not your mother."

Sterrett made a quick gesture, shooing his secretary out of his office. "Sir Simon," he cried into the phone as though with enthusiasm.

The Greek Dustman was calling from his luxury suite in Monte Carlo in the independent principality of Monaco on the Mediterranean coast. Groves had seen pictures of the hotel room on the man's website. It wasn't a bed and a bath, like an ordinary hotel room, but an entire apartment—living room, dining room, a small personal gymnasium. Sir Simon Psora was in Monte Carlo recovering from a nervous breakdown. That was the big secret that Washington was not to hear about.

Sir Simon Psora was a businessman who never stopped working. His website showed him up to his elbows at his desk, showed him with a hard hat overseeing a future landfill, showed him engrossed in a meeting with the board of directors of Unfragrant Bin Systems, the company he'd started twenty years before, a company that was the number one for solid waste management in the entire world.

The website showed him busy first thing every morning and busy until the late hours of the night. What the website didn't show, and his Facebook account failed to mention, was the amount of cocaine Sir Simon Psora had had to consume to keep that level of energy going, to keep that busy. What the website didn't tell the visitor was that the man had finally gone off the deep end and now took long, hot baths in piles of half-eaten fruit and lobster shells.

He was there in Monte Carlo under the supervision of a team of doctors and therapists, trying to detoxify and return to a somewhat presentable state, trying to shake the mental breakdown off him. His personal physician, Dr. Jawat was sanguine; the cure was time.

Sir Simon's work involved making money off of waste. It involved waste management and the creation of new sanitary landfills. Unfragrant Bin Systems was busy creating new landfills because that was what the world needed. Not just the model landfill in Washington, at the Ellipse, but landfills as far away as China, where Unfragrant Bin worked to build environment-friendly recycling centers and trash incinerators that created "green" energy. One of the latest photos, taken six months before his collapse, showed Sir Simon standing at the Great Wall, shaking hands with one of Mao's nephews, who was a vice president for Unfragrant Bin Systems, China.

Sir Simon Psora continued to run that greasy and colossal enterprise from his hotel room in Monte Carlo after his breakdown, and he received countless calls daily from all those who had involvement in his on-going projects, and often they called him simultaneously. But he was a changed man. It was a terrifying situation; he had lost faith in landfills and incinerators. Society's attitude towards waste was all wrong. Sir Simon had grown convinced rubbish and dust and waste and dirt should be integrated as such, that people had to learn to live

with and to love their trash, not hide it away as though it were a shameful thing.

And confined to his room in the finest hotel in Monte Carlo,
Sir Simon felt only truly blissful when he eased his carcass down in
a tubful of refuse from room service, a little warm water to float it
in, and had a telephone at his side. Yet he was not so bananas that
he didn't think lucidly too, when it came to his money. His specific worry was that the U.S. government would take advantage of the
momentary confusion at Unfragrant Bin to raid his bank accounts
and scrutinize the way he did business, which was not always the
legal way.

He felt he had to move his money out of U.S. bankers' hands, that
was his most urgent concern, and the development of a landfill on the
Mall offered him the perfect chance to give his money legs. It would
shield the movement out of the country of great sums. What made the
deal delightfully foolproof was, in fact, federal involvement, in the
form of the lease with the Department of the Interior. That would pre-
clude too close an eyeball on the part of the Treasury people for fear of
jeopardizing a deal the administration wanted. Sir Simon wasn't so far
gone that he couldn't see the irony; the sanitary landfill, a model way
of dealing with trash that he now personally repudiated, was the only
way for him to keep intact a great part of the enormous treasure he had
in various U.S. banks and institutions.

It was for this reason that Sir Simon loved to talk on the phone
to his lawyers in Washington. For when Sir Simon's illness kicked in
and the fearful interior struggle was on between his rather inventive
financial scheme to safeguard his interests and his murky notion that
trash was good, the only person who seemed to listen, to listen calmly
and appreciatively, was Sterrett Emerson Groves.

"I'm here in the harbor, the perfectly lovely little harbor at Monte
Carlo, Groves," Sir Simon was saying. "It is going very well. Absolutely, I think it is."

"Yes, sir." Sterrett frowned but tried to make his voice at least
sound supportive. "I'm sure you're having a good time."

"Here in Monte Carlo, you can get things done. Why not over
there?"

"Well, sir, we are getting things done. Frankly, it's 'Landfill, Ho!'
here in Washington."

"I will tell you why," Sir Simon went on saying. "Because every-one is waiting for everyone else to get started there in Washington. No one does." The Greek Dustman was getting heated. "No one does because no one wants to take responsibility."

"No, actually, sir, the Bureau of Land Management has agreed to the terms of the gross lease, where the government is required to pay insurance costs and expenses, utilities and such for the maintenance of the surface area of the site…" Sterrett had to close his eyes, bored with his own droning on and on. "Which will remain in the hands of the National Park Service, and it's now only a question of…"

"Ah, I have another call," Sir Simon said.

Birds in the trees, small birds were singing for the heat outside Sterrett's window. He was aware of the birds singing and only that for a moment. He rested his hand on his breast, to suppress an impulse to cry out. What Sterrett hated more than anything was people who didn't listen when he spoke, and next to that he hated being put on hold. He would have slammed the phone down but for the fact that Sir Simon Psora was the firm's wealthiest client. If Bill Gates was the richest man on the trash-laden planet on account of ever new computers, Sir Simon was the fifth richest on account of old ones. He was a genuine, solid-gold member of the ruling Caste.

The Caste was that self-sufficient, tightly related, though not necessarily consanguineous, international set of Midas-like souls. Sir Simon was a member indubitably, though born poor, into a Greek-Cypriot family that lost everything when the Turks attacked his village in 1955. Simon Psora's parents left Cyprus, took their child to England and to better opportunities. As a youth, growing up in Brighton, Simon worked very hard, doing the physical labor he sometimes bragged of as having made him particularly durable, digging ditches, sweeping streets.

By chance he met and courted and married the beloved little sister of a dentist whose practice included the south of London. The dentist killed himself and left all his money to his little sister. This gave Simon Psora the capital to start a trash-hauling business. He began trading in recyclable glass and aluminum. He began buying land and managing solid waste on a large scale. It was for sorting out the problem of over-flowing trash bins in the city that the British queen, always an astute judge of merit, honored him with a title. He'd gone on to vindicate the monarch's shining trust by expanding to the United States, where he was represented in legal matters by Guiteau and Garfield.

"I'm so dreadfully sorry, Groves," Sir Simon said. "It was my son with some crap about, oh I don't know. What is it you were telling me?"

"That most of the lease is done, that's what I was saying, sir. Mr. Jorrigo and I sat down with our tax guy and we've put in language that Ms. Progg has reviewed and temporarily approved of, wherein most of the tax burden and royalties owed by Unfragrant Bin will carry over to the year in which the lease terminates. The ground lease will be considered terminated, legally, when the last net pound of trash goes into the landfill, or at the end of thirty years, whichever comes first..."

"Wait one moment..."

Sterrett was on hold again, a button blinking in the array of buttons on the trash man's bath-side phone.

There were times when Sterrett Emerson Groves, far from wishing to be as rich as Simon Psora, simply wanted to chuck the Law and go live in some exotic place, like Mexico for example. There he wouldn't let himself be put on hold; he wouldn't even have a phone, not even a cell. If someone, anyone, no matter how important or wealthy wanted to talk to him, that person would have to come down and stand there and say what he had to say to Sterrett's face. For the time being, however, the young attorney had to content himself with holding the receiver slack in his hand, limiting his impatience to little noises at the back of his throat.

"Groves?" Sir Simon came back on the line. His voice was hesitant. "Groves?"

"Yes, sir."

"I am fed up with these people calling me. Why don't they see that the future is going to be smelly, and the future is going to be stinky. Now why is it people don't see that?"

Sterrett reassured the Greek Dustman. "The sanitary landfill here at the Ellipse won't smell at all, sir. Your very own lab technicians have assured us of that. You know that new bacteria they developed, what's it called? Flagellatus something? Well, that's going to eat up all the odor..."

"No, no, Groves. That particular bacterium is going to make the site smell worse." There were faint chuckles coming over the line. "A real stench."

"What?" Sterrett was surprised at that, the first time he'd heard it. "Are you sure, sir?" He knew the client was nuts, but this was a new manifestation. "We have extensive documentation that elaborates with graphs and pie charts the degree to which the bacteria in question will serve to diminish and otherwise wipe out all unfavorable smells and…"

"Worse, make it smell worse," Sir Simon shouted into the phone. "The way it should smell."

Sterrett muttered epithets. When Psora began with "the way it should smell," it was a sign the phone conversation was about to degenerate into a fruitcake's tirade, incomprehensible in many of its points to the young attorney despite his having heard the same lecture over and over again. Sterrett could only pray for another call on Psora's phone line. He dropped back in his chair, Sir Simon's voice pouring out relentlessly from the receiver, "Our whole society here in the West is built upon a false assumption of purity, of cleanliness, of being close to godliness for that reason. It is a misbegotten belief I myself until very, very recently, Groves, believed in. And profited from. Oh, yes, absolutely. I was a man in conflict with myself, with my own deepest urges. I repressed my real desire to be stinky. No more, Groves. I am a changed man." Sir Simon paused, added with diabolical relish, "I encouraged my chief scientific engineer to come up with a microbe that would innumerable times multiply the natural malodor caused by decaying waste. He succeeded. Absolutely. And that is your *Flagellatus paraculum*."

"I don't believe it," Sterrett couldn't help saying. "Have you told Mr. Jorrigo this?"

"Jorrigo? Vincent Jorrigo? No. He's a Turk, isn't he?"

This too was new territory, Sterrett thought. He answered, "No, sir. Mr. Jorrigo, he's your attorney."

"I know who he is, Groves, and I know too, that he's a Turk. I don't like Turks. That's why I want to deal with you. Only with you."

"Mr. Jorrigo is from here." The young attorney fumbled with the receiver, sat up, and spoke as clearly as he could, "He was born in Rhode Island."

"No, Groves. I've met him, you know," the Greek Dustman snapped back. "Do you know what the filthy dark-skinned Turks did to us? They came and burned our villages, raped our mothers and sisters, and killed all of our farm animals. Our dogs. I won't deal with Turks."

And after a few more desultory exchanges, the conversation petered out, and Sterrett dropped the receiver into its beloved cradle. He sat back in his chair, stretched, and yawned. The one good thing was that that phone conversation was in effect all the work he planned to do that morning. That was his main job, to keep in contact with the client, and to keep the client abreast of developments. He'd done that. Now he could finish the morning paper.

Sterrett plucked the *Post*'s Style section free from the mass of papers on his desk. He leaned far back in his seat. He had time to kill before his next coffee break. He breezed through an article about a new restaurant opening in Bethesda that specialized in corn dogs and read part of an overly long article about the best walks in town.

He put the paper down. It was impossible to read the paper in peace. Every day was the same, the man called, the man ranted, every day he was worse. But this new revelation, the precious germ, the miracle microbe that was going to make the site, the landfill, smell more like roses than roses did, was a kind of booby trap. They were the boobies, the lawyers, the politicians, all of Washington. He contemplated the fact, and then dismissed it. He was no scientist, but the firm had hired a scientific laboratory to do tests and the tests had come up confirming what the Unfragrant Bin Systems lab rats had claimed: the bacteria was going to make the trash dump smell like Chanel Number 5.

He picked the newspaper up again, started to read the comics. He slapped the paper down with the rustling of inked pages. It was something he should mention to Mr. Jorrigo, but then again, he was just an associate. It was up to the lead attorneys to make sure all such claims were verified, not up to him. It was definitely something that would slow down the approval process, now so close to conclusion, mentioning doubts about *Flagellatus paraculum*, and the deal itself might fall through.

If the deal did fall through, all the parties concerned would be sore upset with Sterrett Emerson Groves, the president of the United States included. If all that time and money trying to make the sanitary landfill a reality were for nothing, well, it was time wasted, and the purpose of work was not to waste time. If the landfill were left the way it was, "undone," he would be named with the blame, not Sir Simon Psora, that was for sure.

Sterrett sighed a sigh expressive of his willful disburdening of that responsibility. It was in any case most likely that Sir Simon was bluffing, crazier than ever. The one thing to be said in the Greek Dustman's favor was that he had the courage to change how he looked at life. He had the guts to stand in direct conflict with how he'd lived up until then and put his sanity at risk, and that was to be admired.

Sterrett pressed his lips together, made a convinced pucker reflecting upon it, yes, Psora was a man to be admired despite all. That done, Sterrett retrieved the *Post* and turned to what was happening in Washington that week under a rubric in the middle pages of the Style section. There was *As You Like It* at the Folger, a famed dance company performing at the Kennedy Center, food tasting in Adams Morgan, and so on. His eye alighted on an event, a lecture. A lecture would be nice, put things in perspective. He thought about Dinah, and making the most, and felt suddenly inspired. He swung for the telephone, called Suzy. He told her, "Get me two tickets for this lecture at Georgetown University."

"Sterrett, you know, I have real work to do."

"It's on Friday, Friday night, Healy Hall. Use my MasterCard. You got the number. Two tickets, can you do that for me?"

Suzy hung up on him.

CHAPTER THREE

Sterrett hated talking on the telephone. He'd decided that long ago; electronic communication of all types, including the internet, all that fussing over Twitter and Facebook, put him in a bad mood. He hated talking to someone whose bodily reactions he couldn't witness first hand, whose smells, always the most revelatory thing about anyone, the sweat on the brow, the stink under the arm, he couldn't take note of. He had to guess that his secretary understood what he wanted. She would do it he was sure, but to be extra sure, he pushed aside his intercom and leaned across his desk. He shouted through his partway open door, "That's Friday night, Healy Hall, Suzy. Dr. Cheung. Two people."

The problem was he couldn't shout through his door loud enough for Dinah, the girl from the sixth floor, in Mergers and Acquisitions, to hear him. That was a pity. It would have been simpler that way, and more to Sterrett's liking. He gritted his teeth, then dropped his hand to his telephone, to call Dinah and ask her out, ask her if she wouldn't like to come with him, walk hand in hand across the greensward to gray, gothic Healy Hall and be enriched, intellectually. He was going to be stubborn about it; they weren't going to have fun. He was going to show Dinah just how goal-oriented he was.

That was why he didn't like the telephone, it encouraged him to think through what he was going to say before speaking, and that, for Sterrett, always ended in disaster. He was best improvising, speaking off the cuff. He didn't call her anyway. It was too soon. He wanted to give Dinah time to feel some regret she didn't hang with him all day, Memorial Day, so that when he did call her, she'd jump into his arms, cry out, "at last, thank god, you called." He wanted to be there for that. He decided when he was ready, he'd go over to Mergers and Acquisitions and ask her in person.

He waited 'til the middle of the week. It went against his determination to remain noncommittal in love as in politics, but the girl piqued him. Not the plain fact that she'd said "no" to him, but the fact that she had said "yes" in the first place, had come up to his apartment after lunch, had had sex with him on his sofa, yes that was what intrigued him. Because she'd said "yes" to sex and then afterward had said "no" to hanging out with him, as though he were not worth wasting time with. It was that rejection that made Sterrett determined as he had never been before to make the girl say "yes" again.

He made plans. Normally he didn't plan his dates but simply let them happen. That was the essence of romance for Sterrett, that spontaneity. But for Dinah, he set up a really spectacular evening, starting at seven thirty with the lecture, a lecture by a famed, book-writing professor, a man of prominence, a man who had made the most of his hard little clump of knowledge, Dr. Ted Cheung. Then they'd go to F. Scott's for dinner, a cozy scenario that would end with a taxi ride up Wisconsin Avenue to his apartment. He'd put new sheets on his bed and bought a brand new toothbrush, left it in its wrapper just for her. Women couldn't resist a new toothbrush to use.

Mergers and Acquisitions, on the sixth floor of the Guiteau Building, was the fiefdom of the humorless and overbearing Cornelius Klocker, Esquire. Klocker had come to Guiteau and Garfield from Chicago, and he was enthusiastic about big companies. He was enthusiastic about big companies getting bought out by other, even bigger companies.

But what made him positively joyous was leveraging the takeover of a big company by a handful of people who had no real managerial capacity. When Corny Klocker had something like that, something that daring in hand, he went thrashing up and down the hallway like a boar in a thicket. The only one who could calm him down when he was that excited was Patty Johnson.

Sterrett Emerson Groves felt uncomfortable going to "M and A." The lawyers there were more like smooth legal impresarios than lawyers. There was a feel of the hustle along the corridors on the sixth floor and a whiff too of uninhibited instinct, of the cruel, shark-like impulse sanctioned. He had heard tales, too, of wild parties where clothes were torn and unutterable folly was committed, parties to celebrate a major merger, parties that spilled over from "M and A" to engulf and devastate other office suites and even other floors.

Sterrett considered the sixth floor an alien world, as intimidating as the surface of Mars. Now he was there, and he worried about making a fool of himself. The receptionist seemed to be positive he was making a fool of himself. She asked him what he wanted in an unnecessarily derisive tone. When, a bit affronted, he told her he was a lawyer, she told him they were all lawyers there, it was a law firm. Well, he wanted to see one of Mr. Klocker's secretaries he went on to say, and the receptionist answered that with, "I'll call her." Not at all like the fourth floor where everyone was amiable and chatty. "Don't bother to sit down," she added.

Sterrett sat down anyway. He dropped his clasped hands between his knees. He rubbed his hands together and worked hard to let his anxiety show, waiting for the receptionist to offer him coffee, a drink of sparkling water, a soda-cola. But she didn't pay him any mind. Dinah appeared. She was wearing a baggy dress of a kind of dingy brown color. The dress made her look like she'd been sick. She had on a pair of glasses, too, unfashionable, bulky frames pushed high up the bridge of her nose.

"Hi," Sterrett said, getting to his feet. "How are you?" He tried to keep himself in a strictly formal mode, but he felt his mouth too full of saliva. "I wanted to see you."

Dinah didn't answer. She glanced at her watch.

Panic overtook the young attorney, his underarms percolating their familiar odor, a faintly pepperoni-pizza smell. What was it he was doing? He was violating one of his most fundamental rules, never pursue a woman. It wasn't for him a harsh rule to live by. Modern women pushed themselves forward without hesitation if they were interested, and plenty were interested in him, so that he didn't have to be there with his tickets in hand like some kind of dweeb. But he was there, and he suspected Dinah knew she had the capacity for making his fate that afternoon, whether he was to be happy or sad.

"So, Dinah?" And then another doubt came over him—was this the same girl? It didn't seem the same girl. She acted tired and at the same time distinctly on edge, ready to turn on her heels and fly from him. Nothing left of the self-possessed and provocative girl he'd made love to in his apartment. Kiss her, he'd have to kiss her to be sure she was Dinah. "I was in the elevator and I said to myself why not go on up and see how she is. Not that I thought anything was wrong with you, but to be sure that in fact and considering the way things went, you were…"

"Yes," the girl interrupted him. "I'm fine."

She squinted at him through her glasses, a pair of reading glasses not really hers at all, but a pair she'd borrowed for the occasion from another secretary. Peering through them left Groves a blur to her. "I have to get back." She smoothed her hand along her dress, her hand gliding the length of her thigh, a gesture that revealed a certain shapeliness, the woman beneath the dress. "What is it? Because really, I have a lot of work to do."

"Making the most?" he asked. He made that sound rancorous, and he covered it immediately with a cough. He was there because he was a gentleman. He was there to prove he wasn't a total asshole if that was what she thought; he was not there to mock her.

"I thought Friday night, you know, we could go see a lecture together, there's this lecture at Healy Hall, at Georgetown University," Sterrett told her. He showed her the tickets. The receptionist was snickering at him under her bleached facial hair. "Dr. Theodore Cheung is going to discuss differential access as regards to the historical applications of the 14th and 15th Amendments."

Dinah gave him a blank look behind her thick lenses.

"After we can go for dinner."

Dinah tossed the tickets back at him. "I never heard of anything so boring."

She knew what he was after, and she had no intention of being a source of satisfaction to the boy. She kept him at bay, wearing the borrowed reading glasses to make herself totally less attractive. For though she liked him, she wanted to resist her desire to like him. That was her true strength, her power to resist having what she wanted unless it was a part of her long-term plan for herself.

"I'm sorry," she said. "Friday, I have to stay late. The Orange-U-Glad, I have the Orange-U-Glad merger. Thank you anyway."

He took the elevator but didn't get off at his floor. He rode the elevator down to the lobby of the Guiteau Building. A drink was what he needed. A drink would dispel the mood upon him. A drink was a drink, that was irrefutable logic. Logic was the thing that defined him. He was a man defined by his own logic, a well-defined man. He walked round to the Pennsylvania side of the building, leaned his shoulder against one of the support columns, heavy concrete columns that held the Guiteau Building's overhang in place. He could see up the avenue as far as the bronze horse and rider on Washington Circle.

Sterrett had quit smoking, otherwise it was a perfect moment for a cig', but his father dying the way he had, made Sterrett an uneasy smoker and finally he quit. He was going to lean there for a moment, and instead of having a smoke, he was going to practice mindfulness. Mindfulness was a new form of contemplation he'd read about. The president himself espoused it, and now Sterrett was going to try it out, even though he had only an imprecise notion of what it was. What he really wanted to do was to go and have a drink, but he needed to think about it first. It was a difficult task to justify leaving work so early.

Other than free time, work was all he had; it was a positive force in his life, and he did what he did because he felt he had something to prove. But prove to whom, he wondered. No one cared for him, and he cared for no one, not really. That wasn't anything tragic. With so many people in the world, what did it matter if the only person Sterrett could manage feelings for was himself? There were so many sainted, moral leaders, so many caring people that if he dropped out from their number, he was sure it wouldn't matter in the least.

Tires made a drum-thudding sound going up Pennsylvania Avenue. Not many women ever walked along that part of the avenue, as there were few restaurants and no shops. A group of tourists passed on their way into Georgetown. Tourists brought money to the city, but there were too many of them. Too many tourist buses, too many airplanes bringing too many strange people, dirt from the buses, dirt from the planes, dropping like dew from the mountain of the sky. Too many foreigners. They were changing the feel of the city.

A balloon man came sauntering by. He called to the tourists on the Rock Creek bridge. "Make the children happy," he cried out. "Make the little ones happy. When the little ones are happy, everyone is happy."

Sterrett watched as the balloons, in many different shapes and colors, bobbed on their strings. The only thing that made Sterrett close to being what was called happy was drinking. He was not ashamed to acknowledge it, and if anyone asked him what he thought about drinking and getting drunk, he would tell them, he thought it something in the nature of a virtue. Since he had the power of not getting drunk, his getting drunk was caused by his voluntary desire to be happy, therefore it was a desire for the good. That was his moving principle.

A slight buzz, that was life to him at its best, that brief, mellow half hour before too much hit him, before he became dim-witted. He liked the taste of beer on his palate, liked the smell of the barroom. It made him happy to see the tap pulled low, the beer flow out, a frothy, liquid sunshine. It made him feel at home to lean against the bar and listen to the improvised talk, talk that meant nothing to anyone, but was in its own way more real than all the legal palaver he himself dished out every day.

He saw Hugo Humphrey coming down the street, walking in that "Hey I'm a flagpole" way most Washingtonians had. Hugo was digiting on his cellphone. He lifted his eyes to Sterrett, and putting his phone away, he slowed over.

"So what's doing, Sterrett?"

Caught out doing nothing in plain sight, Sterrett said, "I'm taking a minute of mindfulness, You know, the world around me?"

Hugo smiled. "Want a smoke?" He took a pack out of his jacket pocket. He offered the pack to his brother associate.

"No, thanks."

They stood out on the sidewalk and talked.

"Tennis, you play tennis?" Hugo asked. "I thought we could go and hit the ball around sometime."

"I'm more into golf," Sterrett answered with a shrug.

"Okay." Hugo stood with one hand in his pocket. His face was blurred by an exhalation of cigarette smoke, but his eyes blazed up sharp and clear. He said, "What's up?"

"Depressed."

"Depression can be good."

"Lucky you," Sterrett said. "If you find something good about feeling like crap."

"I am lucky," was Hugo's retort. "My family makes me feel lucky no matter what happens at work. That's what it's all about, the family, right? A family gives stability to a man's career."

"A family?" Sterrett said. "It's what people who can't stand being alone say. I got away from my family as soon as I was old enough."

"Really? I love my family. Nothing has any real meaning to me outside my family." Hugo proceeded to go into the facts of his wife's hectic and immensely problem-filled life, into the facts of his two kids, problem-filled, them too, despite being geniuses. Sterrett had to say in all honesty, "What's your point? I mean, that's what a family is all about, nothing but problems. Right?"

"I find if you don't try to rationalize everything, it's easier," Hugo said.

Sterrett rubbed his chin. "Easier? Yeah, well, maybe you're right. Easier is what we're after."

Hugo Humphrey finished his cig'. He tossed it into the gutter and went back inside the Guiteau Building. It was a balmy afternoon, not at all humid, the sun peachy and warm. So Sterrett stayed outside a little longer. Mindfulness, no, he was tired of all the cleverness, and he was tired of work. He simply decided to say "no" to the world and all its worries.

He went back up to his office. He moved stealthily, spider-like, but Suzy was busy at the phones, too busy to notice him anyway. He went into his office and shut down his computer. He put a few files away, left his tan, soft-sided briefcase where it was. He snuck out of the fourth floor, down to the garage where his bicycle was. He went direct and he went swift, up Wisconsin Avenue to the heights above Georgetown. He chained the bike to a "no parking" sign and pushed through the door of the Lucky Key.

It was a Thursday afternoon, late in the afternoon, but the bar was practically deserted. There were three beefy-looking men in identical, cheapo suits sitting at a table and one old soak sitting alone at a small table near the bar. Well, being alone in the company of other loners attracted Sterrett Emerson Groves at that particular point in time, and he took a stool and sat down at the bar.

The beer tasted cold, very cold, too cold to have a real taste. The cops weren't there that evening. No chumlings to talk to, no stories of gore, of wickedness to listen to. He looked over at the old soak who was rubbing his hands together watching a scrawny woman with wayward, overlarge tits strip up onstage. The women at the Lucky Key were not all scrawny. The fat ones generally came on much later in the evening.

Thinking it through Sterrett realized that when he was there in that bar, and it could be any bar, drinking, he felt protected from the suffering in the world. Protected in that way was half the pleasure in drinking, the feeling that whatever was happening to other people, he was safe. Safe like that was the only way he could think things through. He needed to think the thing through, this strange hurt that was growing in him.

He sat thinking and drank his beer and considered the rings the bottle left on the wooden bar, and drank again. Thinking maybe he did drink too much, okay, that was his biggest flaw. Maybe he wasn't so brilliant a lawyer after all. There was nothing wrong with drinking and nothing wrong with not being brilliant that drinking couldn't help. He guzzled his Bud, sat staring at the overlapping rings on the dark bar.

Then he studied the bottle, held the emptied bottle out before him. A beer like a blossom. He took out his pen, the one his mother had given him for his law school graduation. Looking at the brown glass, at the bright label, he jotted it down in the notebook he kept, "the emptiness at the beginning of something good." It was written in hopes that what he was feeling wasn't self-pity.

He was sure she did want to go out with him, Dinah. She simply didn't want to acknowledge it. Women were perverse like that. He was afraid of them, he knew it, afraid of their unexpected reactions. It was maddening. What disadvantage was there to admitting she'd been in his apartment, he wondered. He wasn't important enough to her, that had to be the answer. She'd used him, outrageous insult to his pride. He disliked her for that. She was driving him to have strong feelings.

He could take the issue to court and prove that Dinah from Idaho had been his lover, albeit for only one afternoon. He could put her on the stand and make her talk. She had been with him and had enjoyed herself. They had made the most of their libidos together. But no, he realized, if you really liked a girl, you didn't take her to court. It didn't matter in any case. She was only a secretary. There were secretaries galore in Washington. Washington floated on a Sargasso Sea of secretaries.

He ordered another Budweiser, and when it came, he tugged at the bottle. Closed his eyes a moment. The beer came out like snowflakes. It basked in his gullet. It steamed in his brain-pan, and filled him with courage. Courage was what he needed. Work was antithetical to that. Work defeated the brave spirit.

Sterrett called to the bartender and had him pour a scotch, just one, not the blended stuff, but the real deal, the single malt, a little Auld Reekie with ice. He stirred the drink with his finger, watching with pleasure how the ice bobbed round in the coppery liquor. He took the tickets out of his pocket. Ted Cheung, the man was no slouch. He had published books. He was an industrious, well-respected university professor, an expert in whatever text there was to be an undeterred expert in. Who wouldn't want to hear him, Sterrett asked himself. Healy Hall would be packed.

He finished his scotch. One scotch was okay, if another followed, he'd be in trouble. He would save getting hammered for tomorrow night; he had nothing else to do Friday. He could go to the lecture, better himself, by himself. But no, he had two tickets. Well, he thought, he could invite one of the strippers. Find a stripper free for Friday night. He knew one or two of them well enough to give it a try, a noble cause, the cultural improvement of strippers. He called for the bartender. He wanted to leave.

One of the men in the cheapo suits came up to the bar. Sterrett knew exactly what the man did for a living. The vice president's house was nearby, in the fenced-off grounds of the Naval Observatory. These were the men who protected the Veep, men in loose, cheap-looking suits. Their cheeks were lined from standing on tarmacs, their eyes were like hard gems from sitting in the freezing cold staring into the night, guarding the entrance to some pampered, government official's house. Sterrett wasn't intimidated however. He leaned in front of the man, and waved the bartender to him.

The man in the cheapo suit said to him, "Excuse me. I was here before you."

"Wanna bet he'll serve me before you?" But when the bartender started to take the other man's order, the young attorney bristled, "Hey, I was first."

"What you want me to do?" the bartender asked. "These guys got to go back to work."

"So what?" Sterrett let go a little of his self-control, finding something like pleasure in letting go. "What the hell does that mean? I'm always at work."

"It means wait your turn, son," the man in the suit said.

Words, patronizing words that had a strong effect on the associate from Guiteau and Garfield. He squeezed out his knuckles and presented them to the Secret Service agent, ready to go to fisticuffs. For that was the one thing Sterrett missed about the way he was, a little fight now and then. Men didn't fight in his social circle, lawyers didn't, they competed. They competed in well-equipped ways: tennis, golf, racquetball. A flying elbow in basketball was as bloody as it got.

The men, the women in his social circle liked war, too. But not in-the-field kind of war, more the bloodless pose of war, the language of war, the tough speech. They took satisfaction in other men killing mutual enemies in far-off places they didn't even know how to locate on a map. Some of them, lawyers who'd become politicians, lawyers who'd become national security advisors, already had a role in waging war, present wars, and future wars if they got that lucky. War meant wealth and prestige, and that was what the men and women in Sterrett's social circle were after.

But the violence Sterrett missed was not the chaotic hysteria of war, but something much more personal, much more fulfilling. It was violence with fists. He was proud for instance of the comeuppance he'd given a real estate agent a year back, a fight over parking spaces when Sterrett still had his car. It was a question of settling what was just. In any case, there was great solace in getting the better physically of another person. Being quick with his hands made Sterrett feel like he knew one thing more than the next guy.

That the next guy in this particular instance was probably a little quicker with his hands than he was, and was certainly armed, didn't deter the young attorney in the least. He kept badgering the man in the cheapo suit until the bartender had to intervene. He pulled Sterrett aside, physically pulled him by the sleeve of his jacket, and pushed a fresh beer into his hand. "This is on the house," he said just to keep him quiet.

His head dropped forward, and he found he was drooling. Some of the drool adhered to the wool of his suit, but drooling made him feel better. The bartender came round and made him clear off the stool. Sterrett could tell it was late. The twins had finished stripping. They were not really twins, that was clear from how different they looked. Now Ginger came out to close the night, swinging her hips to the strains of T-Red's latest. The bartender told Sterrett he'd had enough and it was time for him to go home.

"Go home," the barman said.

Sterrett obeyed. He always obeyed bartenders. Bartenders ruled. He paid his tab and was sure to leave a tip for the drinks and a tip for the girls, the way he always did. He pushed through the door, staggered heavily across the sidewalk. He was surprised to see how dark it was outside. It was night outside. He'd gone into the Lucky Key when the sun ruled the heavens. Now the stars were out, shining like pasties above the land.

It took him a few minutes to decide what to do. It was late, but not that late, not so late that he couldn't still find a bar open somewhere. He tried unlocking his bicycle, but he got nowhere with the combination, so he gave up on that. He tried to hail a taxicab. He stepped to the curb and his cheeks swelled like Dizzy Gillespie's. Through his fingers came a high-pitched sound. The taxis passed him by. Well, he wasn't so drunk that he couldn't walk. He was feeling too gloomy to go to bed, too gloomy to sleep. He walked right past his apartment building. It was too early to call it quits.

There was little traffic along Wisconsin Avenue. A few empty buses went by, a couple cars. There was no one on the sidewalks. The Georgetown Library was dark. Down the block, a homeless man had bedded down for the night in front of the Lutheran Church. Sterrett was pretty steady on his feet. It was an easy walk.

Then he was on Key Bridge. He wasn't sure how he'd gotten there; he'd been wandering, block after block of two-story brick houses, going zig-a-zag through Georgetown. Key Bridge was a well-lit place made of vaulting sandstone arches. It led into Rosslyn, Virginia. Sterrett had no desire to go into Rosslyn, Virginia. But he did like the fact of being on a bridge. He went to the middle of the bridge. The night air was fresh, far better there than the sticky, sooty air that pervaded the streets of town. Cars went by. Sterrett slid along the railing until he could see the muddy waters of the Potomac in full flood.

He had the two tickets for Friday night's lecture secure in his hand. Why did the girl vex him so much, he couldn't savvy the reason. She was no prettier than the other secretaries, maybe a little brighter, but in a secretary being bright, that was more a defect. Better in bed, hard for him to say, a good lay, okay, but Sterrett was sure he could find other girls as good on the couch. Dinah, well, she'd been able to see through him, that was it, to see that there was more going on inside him than just having fun. That there was more to him, otherwise she couldn't have dared to say what she'd said. She'd said it because she saw deep within him and knew its opposite to be true, that he did add up to something.

He sighed. He closed his hand around the tickets, precious paper that promised admittance to hear Ted Cheung speak. He crumpled them in the ball of his hand, and then let them drop into the river. He watched the tickets go whimsically through the air only to disappear above the dark, swirling water. Make a change in the way he lived. He had to start applying himself, take on more responsibility. Go to bars only on weekends.

Someone honked going by, kids rallying him from a car window, "Go for it, man."

That was encouraging, and in a flash, Sterrett was standing up on the metal parapet with his shins braced against the top railing of the bridge. He thought, looking down, he'd go right into the Potomac. Not a jump or a leap, but a dive, palms joined just as if he really knew what he was doing.

Go for it. Follow Berwick, he thought, follow where the colonel led even in the grimmest of valleys. His father had been so strong, how could one not follow him. Seeing him in his mind's eye, Sterrett wanted to go with him, protected by that strength, comforted by those arms.

Sterrett peered down at the river, a tenebrous and undulating body. It was undulating pretty fast. To feel it stream around his clumsy limbs, covering him, flowing under him and over him. Try it. Then another chance, a start-over as something more durable than a human being, like a cockroach maybe. Or maybe he'd survive it. Try it at least once, the relief after if he made it.

He thought of his father's favorite phrases, catchphrases, and they all had to do with sacrificing himself for his country, but towards his later days, Berwick grew afraid of what his country had become. Sterrett knew because he heard this as a constant complaint from his father. His father didn't shrink from death; more it seemed to Sterrett that Berwick cottoned to it, for the colonel's fear was of being constrained by his country to do something he would be ashamed of doing as a soldier. To serve honor or to serve his nation's leaders, which to choose when they diverged in the quality of goodness, dying for Berwick was a perfect release from that conundrum.

Self-sacrifice was his father's obsession, not Sterrett's. Not that way, Sterrett realized. That was not the way to be. He had to take his father's strength in a different direction. But which way, he wondered as he swayed on his feet, swayed high above the river's path. He didn't know what was missing, but some element was missing that would tie everything in his experience together and give him the answer. He had an inkling, but it was no good, whatever it was that escaped him, escaped him.

A car passed, kids, more drunken Virginians.

"Kill yourself," they yelled at him.

Sterrett started laughing and got down off the bridge.

CHAPTER FOUR

Things came to a head the second week of June. A meeting was held in Guiteau and Garfield's main conference room on the seventh floor of the Guiteau Building. It was a meeting to decide once and for all whether to finalize the ground lease for the site or to continue with more meetings without coming to any agreement. A sanitary landfill on the Ellipse would prove profitable in the long term for the federal government and stand as a prize embellishment for Washington, D.C. That was what Sir Simon Psora argued through his attorneys at Guiteau and Garfield. Sir Simon's company, Unfragrant Bin Systems, would not only pay lavishly for the leasing of the ground, but would pay the government a percentage on each ton of garbage processed at the site so that the Feds would make cash money on their own refuse.

The government, the Department of the Interior's Bureau of Land Management, was represented by attorneys from Melody Hogan. The government officials were publically full of fears and concerns, hand-wringing over issues as diverse as environmental impact and historical context. But the appeal of profit was strong, and the idea too, of doing something remarkable for the future, something that would show how much the incumbent Administration held waste management to heart encouraged the president himself to compel the director of the Bureau of Land Management, Ms. Antonia Segreen, to get the deal made. The president wanted a trash dump behind the White House; he was eager to show that "not in my backyard" was a purely Republican attitude.

Neither of the principals was there. It was all to be handled by the attorneys. It was now early afternoon, an hour when blood sugars ran low and heads were drooping, lawyers dressed in somber woolens and bright silk cooped up since eighth thirty. The conference room was a tad too warm, and there was the breath of unhappiness as the agreement, important to all parties, could not be reached.

Vincent Jorrigo, the senior managing partner at Guiteau and Garfield, was pacing back and forth over the carpet. He had on pleated charcoal pants held waist high by braided leather suspenders. He wore a white cotton shirt and an off-white tie, part of his dandy look. He had two looks, dandy for meetings with other lawyers, somber and plain, almost Puritanical for meetings with clients. His jacket rested across the back of his chair, and one of the pockets of his suit jacket bulged with a half-empty bottle of Pepto-Bismol.

Vince was short and thick-shouldered, but a man who had aged well, with only a few wrinkles round his black, searching eyes. He kept his curling hair combed back, with always one dark coil sprung lose, hanging roguishly above one eye. He was of mixed race, an African American with a heavy influx of Portuguese blood from his father's side, fisher's blood, as much fish oil as blood. He considered himself black, but he could out-white any white man, for he had acquired enough stiffness in his manner to be perfectly at home in the predominantly Anglo-Saxon culture he had to move in.

Raised in Millwood, Rhode Island, he was a graduate of East Providence College and subsequently of Yale Law School. As an undergrad, he'd been the leader of a clique of hardy, Marxist intellectuals, had studied Herbert Marcuse and Frantz Fanon, had marched at the South African Embassy in Washington. Fluent in Portuguese, he translated into prose the revolutionary verse of Angolan poet Marcello Soko for the University Press. Vince was nothing if not painstaking, and he pursued his radical ideals deep into his first year of law school.

And that was how Vince saw himself, as someone who had weathered life, whose struggle deserved particular attention, always pursuing the most hazardous course and in the end winning. Coming to D.C. to clerk for Justice Allardyce was an eye-opener. For the first time he felt the South near, Dixie, the Land of Cotton, and working in Washington, he could sit down and face that fabled land across his desk. That was what first encouraged him to stay in Washington, not the fact of power, but the challenge of being black and standing out, being as loud and proud as he wanted in the face of race hatred.

Vince easily adapted to life in the nation's capital. Times changed rapidly, and just as his Marxist ideals had withered away, so did his perception of prejudice, his concern with minority rights. He became one of them, the hurried lawyers whose single wish was to serve in the aggrandizement of wealth, of prestige, of privilege.

After a stint working at an over large firm where he was one of many interchangeable attorneys, Vince moved onto partnership at Guiteau and Garfield, a mid-sized LLP that handled a select group of corporate and political clients. All the same, he continued, as he had in college, to rebel against too much success. Playing poker, rather than celebrating the Commune, had become his way to resist losing what was special about him.

All eyes were on him now. Vincent Jorrigo felt it and drew himself up. He brushed his one lock of hair back from his brow. Turned his back to the room. Bent to a painting hanging on the wall, an oil showing tall-masted ships battling before a desert port. He wiped his lips and then clasped his hands behind him. He could see himself at the helm, giving chase to Barbary pirates. It would certainly have been easier sailing than trying to make a deal with the government. He raised his head from the painting and rocked back on his heels.

"We're just pissing in the wind."

"Vincent," Celia Progg said. "Language like that."

"Making water if you prefer."

The attorneys round the conference table nodded in agreement at that, making water was better. They were there for a piece of public land. It was stretched out upon the table, fifty acres of grass and of tall trees, that part of the National Mall situated behind the Executive Mansion, an oval area officially known as the Ellipse. It was a natural choice for a sanitary landfill. Already undergoing revamping as part of the "Make it. New. Washington!" project, the Mall still offered way too many plain, empty spaces for tourists to get lost in. The landfill at the Ellipse would fill up an otherwise wasted space and stand as a landmark worthy of the Mall's other landmarks. There was nothing more historic than trash.

Psora's company, Unfragrant Bin Systems, already had a ten-year contract to collect the trash produced by the federal government's many offices in Washington. Unfragrant Bin had been hauling that trash on trucks on a daily basis to a distant landfill in West Virginia, but that site was close to being filled and the cost of dumping there had tripled. Building a landfill on the apron of parkland immediately behind the White House would significantly cut the operational costs to the government. That was a substantial argument.

But Celia Progg, the lead attorney for Melody Hogan, was mildly pigheaded. "The Mall is a precious resource, a precious national resource. Yes, it needs to be spiced up a bit, but I'm not convinced yet," she argued, putting emphasis on the adverb. "Director Segreen is not yet one hundred percent convinced the Mall is where a trash dump should be."

"Not a trash dump. Let's be clear," Vince said, coming down the room. "The word derives from the Old Scandinavian, 'trask,' torn, in the sense 'torn away and useless.' 'Useless' is the fundamental adjective." He stood behind his chair, leaned his weight against it as though it were the wheel of a trim schooner in a dead calm. "My client, Sir Simon Psora, is out to prove that trash is not useless, but profitable. It can produce energy for instance. And by the way, let's call it a landfill, a sanitary landfill. There's a night and day difference."

"Whatever you call it, it's a park, a national park, the Mall, and it belongs to the American people, Vince," Celia said. "The American people want their natural resources preserved. They don't want their public parkland ruined with a lot of trash. Also they don't want it used to the profit of one private individual."

"The American people want their resources to be used wisely," Vince insisted.

"Wisely for all."

"Wisely is as wisely does. Do you have to argue all the time?"

"Yes."

Sterrett Emerson Groves was sitting to the right of his boss, neat and clean and bathed in seriosity. He was in mild agony too, irritated by the fruitless give-and-take between the two lead attorneys. Unlike the other, older attorneys, Sterrett found no joy in their little game, the game they'd been playing throughout the negotiations for the landfill, the teasing one-upmanship that ensured that the negotiations would go on and on into infinite billing hours.

Sterrett had never liked the conference table, that whole scene, trying to work out differences by sitting down with a large group of people. There was no rest to be had from the endless talking, and he had to pretend to be interested in what the others had to say, that was what galled him the most. Most of his peers had nothing interesting to say; they merely rehashed what had been said already, waiting like everyone waited in Washington, waiting for someone else to decide the issue.

Sterrett grew impatient. He touched his hair. He picked at his nose. Shifted in his seat. He had gotten to work late, too late to go and have a real breakfast at the diner. He hadn't even had time to finish his one donut in the office, and now from his stomach came the rude threnody of hunger. Vince turned alertly. Sterrett smiled up at his boss, as solicitous a smile as he could muster. He laid a hand on his stomach as though to say, not my fault, it was my digestion.

Vince stared down at him. He said, scathingly, "Well, Groves, you have something you want to say?"

In moments of anxiety it was always best to take an aggressive stance. The young law associate bolted from his chair without a word. His chin raised as he turned his nose against the stale air of the conference room, he strode up to the big picture window. Stood there a moment and snorted, grunted. The room fell silent, the room waited to see where this was going.

Sterrett gestured at the window, a view of the city that took in the monuments, the Mall. "Look outside, look," he beseeched them. "This town was nothing more than a swamp when George Washington came here. All of that, nothing but swampland. Oh, well, a few Indians here and there, an old rotting farm, and lots of nothing, a wasteland. But there was a vision in one man's head, a vision people were ready to make sacrifices for, at Valley Forge for instance, to make that piece of land out there the seat of the free world…"

Every other lawyer, whether from Guiteau and Garfield or Melody Hogan, turned in their seat to listen. There was a refreshing consciousness that here before them was a bold voice, young Sterrett Emerson Groves waking up the class.

Sterrett was not talking tediously and to no purpose. He was arguing in his barefaced way for the Department of the Interior to stop its foot dragging. "Look, there, ma'am," he said, addressing Celia as though he were about to sell her a new vacuum cleaner. "See that streak of different-colored marble? There, out there, on the Washington Monument?"

Celia rose up in her seat.

"Construction stopped at that line in 1856. Construction stopped because the builders grew afraid, afraid of the future." Sterrett thrust his arms out, made his appeal vivid, universal. "They lacked the will to face the future in 1856. They grew afraid of progress at 150 feet. Do you see it?"

The gathered attorneys got to their feet. They nodded. They could see the sun stark upon the elongated shaft of the Washington Monument. They could see where construction had stopped on that adored landmark, the different-colored stone, and they knew the story was true.

"Was it marble they lacked? Look at it and ask yourselves," Sterrett went on. "Not of marble. There was plenty of that. Was it man power? Not of man power. There were thousands and thousands of able hands dying to work. What was it then? Not the Civil War as some texts will tell you. No, construction stopped well before the Civil War began. What then did they run out of? Money? That's only part of the answer. I'll tell you. What they ran out of was the courage to get the thing done," Sterrett said. He waited a few seconds to let his words sink in. "It took twenty years for Congress to put up the funds they needed to finish the Monument. This was to commemorate George Washington, the first president of the United States. This was going to be the standing symbol of the Father of our Country. That's this city for you. Without vision, without the courage to get that vision realized, nothing gets done. Nothing goes forward. And we have to go forward or else we slip more and more back. And we can't let this nation slip back, can we ma'am?"

Ms. Progg wasn't a particularly vain person. She wasn't touchy or quick-tempered, and after all the young attorney had the facts right, that was what mattered, and too, Celia didn't want to seem unpatriotic. She pursed her lips and for the moment, withheld comment.

"Then let's agree to this lease," Sterrett Emerson Groves said, coming back over to the table. "Please, ma'am. We've put everything in there that needs to be in there, everything the government wanted. There's no point to this endless discussion. Let's agree, okay?" There was impudent passion in his voice, an urgency, but it tallied well with what was there before them, a deal that had taken perhaps a little too long to come to fruition. "Let's agree. Please, I beg of you. Enough talking."

The lead attorney from Guiteau and Garfield watched, he listened too, to his associate, a mere associate deliver a peroration worthy of a Clinton. He himself was not good at speeches, and he was impressed. When he heard "George Washington," Vince knew that Groves was on the right track. But he felt it incumbent upon him to ask, "Have you finished, Groves? If so, come over here and sit down. Sit."

He waited for his associate to do as he was told and return to his place at the conference table. Then he pulled out the bottle of Pepto-Bismol he kept in his jacket pocket. His stomach didn't really bother him; he simply liked the taste and the soothing texture of the pink liquid.

"Well, Celia," Vince pursued after taking a swig. "Groves has hit the ball out of the park, that's what I think. The ball is therefore in your court, so to speak."

"Why thank you, Vince. The fact is that the Bureau of Land Management wants a little more. Price is the issue. Not the future of American civilization," Celia said, glancing over at Groves. She shoved a strand of her short blonde hair behind her ear, shoved it there, tucked it in so that it would stop brushing against her cheek. "I want to be clear on that. We too, we want to agree to the lease contract, and yes, and we want to sign the lease once we've agreed to it, but no, we think the price per square foot is still too low considering the location of this landfill, too low for us to agree to it. That's my client's concern. That's Director Segreen's concern."

"Price?" Vince said. "Like Groves pointed out, this far into the game, money's going to stop the thing? No, I think we can find a compromise on the per square foot."

"Well, Vince, the one other issue is the odor. That's more Congress's concern than the Department's. But it's an issue."

Guiteau and Garfield attorney Jacques DeMurphy had spent hours upon hours researching the landfill process. He had immersed himself in the techniques of waste collection and disposal. His notes were fanned out before him, almost as many pages of notes as there were pages in the lease contract. If there was any merit to the lease contract in complex, practical terms, it was, in Jacques DeMurphy's mind to a large extent Jacques DeMurphy's doing. He decided to make himself known.

"The odor problem has been solved by the use of a bacterium Sir Simon Psora's lab technicians have developed," DeMurphy put in. He didn't stand up or anything, and he spoke with great poise compared to Groves. He was a big man and he didn't need to be showy. "The bacterium is called, it's called *Flagellatus paraculum*. This bacterium feeds off the methane gas produced by decomposing solid waste and converts that substance to a starchy syrup. The landfill will smell like maple syrup."

"Maybe the maple syrup in your house," Celia said.

The Guiteau and Garfield junior partner frowned. Didn't like his "house" brought into the argument. He consulted his mass of notes; a very systematic man, Jacques DeMurphy wrote down everything, everything he was told, something he'd learned to do as far back as elementary school, something that had always put him at the head of the class. "No, it says right here, and I quote, 'like pure maple syrup.' That's what Dr. Heidi Cooper says. She's the head of research and development for Unfragrant Bin Systems."

"Here's my suggestion," Vince Jorrigo said. "Perhaps we can offer the government a share in the patent for this revolutionary bacterium." Still standing, he nodded at DeMurphy. "Are we sure about this bacterium?"

"Yes, totally. I spoke to Dr. Heidi Cooper personally. She's an esteemed microbiologist, you see? A graduate of Cornell University. She told me this *Flagellatus paraculum* will change the whole solid waste management picture. Not just for this site, but for landfills all over the world."

"So the copyright will have tremendous financial value," Vince said.

Sterrett Emerson Groves leaned forward in his seat and studied Jacques DeMurphy a long minute. He thought about saying something, repeating Sir Simon's words to him the week before. But it would only serve to draw the meeting out further. Since Sterrett didn't have any facts or figures to back up what Sir Simon had told him re: *Flagellatus paraculum*, it would merely serve to make him look stupid. No, he didn't say a word, but he did shake his head at DeMurphy in a sad, disenchanted way.

Jacques DeMurphy wasn't fazed by that. He chalked it up to jealousy, knew Groves was totally ignorant of any of the working details of waste management, knew he couldn't tell the difference between a trash compactor and a compact disc player, and was sure he had no idea whatever what *Flagellatus paraculum* was.

"There will be a windfall profit to the Bureau of Land Management from marketing that bacterium to other landfill sites across the world," Vince went on to say. "That's appetizing to the government. Am I right, Celia?"

"My client would want a guarantee."

"Listen, we'll do whatever it takes to satisfy your client, understand? My client wants to make your client happy. Whatever it takes." The attorney was pleased with himself; finally he'd gotten the woman to make a specific demand on behalf of her client. "So, Celia, tell me, which sort of guarantee does the Bureau of Land Management want?"

The Melody Hogan attorney took no time fielding that question. "Written."

Vince smiled at that, a smile something in the realm of forbearance. Building a model sanitary landfill within spitting distance of the White House would require something extra on the table, over and above the patent for some strange new wonder bacterium. Something special would be required. He'd suggest privately to Celia that if her client, the director of the Bureau of Land Management, approved the lease, the director would receive as a thank you, something nice and personal, an arrangement just for Antonia Segreen.

"Why don't you and I go to lunch and discuss what needs to be done?"

"Dove and Rainbow?" Celia Progg answered, retrieving her bag from the floor. "You and me. We can discuss the details."

"Lemke's is nearer," Vince said.

"Nearer is not always better. The Dove and Rainbow makes fresh."

Vince conceded that fresh was better. He looked forward to lunch, not so much for the crisp romaine or the chunky tuna fish, but because the two of them alone, they could hash out a deal the way it had to be hashed out. He hoped that Sir Simon would have no objections to hiking the price a few cents per square foot; it had to be done. The pot had to be sweetened. There was money in the budget for it, and in any case, that would have to be handled by his associate. Sir Simon Psora wouldn't talk to anyone else, and Groves could convince the Greek Dustman to go along with practically anything. Well, Vince was happy to have someone he could rely on.

"You gentlemen hold the fort until we're back," Vince said. Trained in gallantry towards the opposite sex, he ambled over and held the door of the conference room wide, accompanied the stylish, sylph-like Celia Progg down the corridor. Their voices mingled with other office sounds as they reached the bank of elevators.

The conference room drifted on the tide of the late morning, momentarily becalmed. In the moody silence, a shifting of chairs, a cough, a pen scratching idly on a margin of paper were the only sounds. Then a few of the others got up, stretched and scratched, made a beeline for the bathrooms. Secretaries came in with fresh-brewed coffee. A small group, including Sterrett Emerson Groves, all men with good bladders, pulled their chairs around as the luncheon platter was brought in, piled to the ceiling with sandwiches from the Armenian deli on the ground floor. There were potato chips and ice-cold soda-cola too.

The secretaries passed out paper plates and plastic forks. But the attorneys had no need of plastic forks. Demolishers of many a buffet, many a Bar Association banquet, they used their hands, and soon round the table played the bucolic sound of chewing, of soda slurped from cans. Neckties loosened, there was the dignified moment of appetites sated, men and women attaining to dormant attitudes.

"That little homily of yours, Groves, about the Monument? It got us out of stall," one of the attorneys said musingly, his jacket unbuttoned, hands clasped upon his lardum belly. "It's amazing what words can do. I'm always amazed."

Another of the lawyers at the table made a vague gesture. "And he's right, too. Courage. Got to have it. The Chinese have it. Do we?"

Jacques DeMurphy stewed in his seat. "Groves and his malarkey about the Washington Monument? That was what broke the deadlock? It was my elucidation of the efficacy of *Flagellatus paraculum* that changed the course of the discussion, not Groves's ridiculous little performance," Jacques cried out. He turned to Sterrett Emerson Groves and said excitedly, "You don't know. You don't know anything about anything."

The others were feeling way too relaxed to fuel any clash of egos, who was better than who. They ignored the bilious DeMurphy. They talked idly about Washington, the city they lived in, its beginnings as a muddy, malarial town.

"What if the nation's capital had remained in Philadelphia?" someone asked, shaking a can of soda cola, drinking down the sugary dregs.

"They moved the capital from Philly because of too many riots. You know, after the Revolution?" another said. "The protests, farmers and such. The veterans of the Revolutionary War protesting for back pay. Scared politicians is why there's a Washington. They went looking for a place it was hard to get to."

"Ah, that's the reason for the Beltway."

"I like living here," Sterrett said.

"Because you're not from here," Anne Marie Smith said, joining Sterrett at the window. A junior partner at Melody Hogan, she was one of Celia's protégés, an urbane blonde, attractive in a dark blue dress.

"But I am from here," Sterrett answered. "And I like it here."

"What's so good about it here?" Anne Marie challenged him. "As opposed to New York. Give me a list."

"Well, look." Sterrett waved his arm at the Washington Monument visible above the trees, at the blue sky beyond it, mirroring itself across the sheeny-brown ribbon of the Potomac. "'The River of Swans,'" he asserted.

"I don't think there ever were swans. I haven't ever seen any. I haven't even seen a single duck, not in six years. Maybe one." Then she said, no longer teasing, getting to the point, "I thought you were wonderful, the way you spoke. Not what you said, okay? But the fact that you spoke from the heart."

"I did," Sterrett said, thinking that was a feeling that gave one a sense of purpose, being praised by people one barely knew. That filled the soul with warmth, absolutely. But it was also important to be modest, so as to gather round more praise. "But all I did was finally say what everyone knows."

"No, tell me, Groves, what does everyone know? What was the substance of what you said that was so goddamned stirring?" Jacques DeMurphy, up from the table had come bounding over to the windows to give his Guiteau and Garfield colleague grief. "That the Washington Monument was built in two parts? Every tourist knows that. Tell me something I don't know."

"The shaft is 555 feet high."

"I think he spoke from the heart and made it clear," Anne Marie put in. "What we need now is not discord, what we need now is the desire to get this done. I think it struck a chord in Celia. She tends to dig in her heels and…"

"Him? The heart?" DeMurphy said. "Hah, no heart there."

Sterrett didn't like the junior partner, but he simply chuckled and started back towards the table. That irritated DeMurphy to no end. He turned to the Melody Hogan attorney, "Let me tell you one other thing, so you'll be warned, Anne Marie…"

"What Jacques?"

"He doesn't like women of letters. Only secretaries."

"You mean he's a snob in reverse?" Anne Marie asked. "I don't mind that." She caught up with the young associate and slipped something into his hand, muttered softly as she did so, "The Body of the Law."

Sterrett looked at the piece of paper as he went and sat down on the facing side of the conference table. It was Anne Marie's business card. On the back she'd written in bold script, "Call me. I really like you."

The door opened and the two principal attorneys appeared, Vince looking as though the carrots in his mixed salad had really done his eyes some good, and Progg too, looked satisfied, happy even. The two didn't enter the conference room. They stood in the doorway, discussing some further particular while the others, unwilling by a single breath to disturb a dovetailing of interests, kept still.

"All right, we'll put that in writing, and I think as to the price, that will be acceptable to the client, we'll run the numbers, but I think we have a deal," Vince said with great vigor, purposefully speaking at the top of his voice so that everyone who was listening could hear. "And then we can get you a final draft of the lease agreement, one that both sides can sign, so that when the time comes, we're ready to go." He came back into the conference room to fetch his briefcase, to take with him too, the half-empty bottle of Pepto-Bismol he'd left there on the table. He slid the bottle into his pocket.

"Meeting over?" someone asked.

"Meeting over," Vince said. "Oh, and Groves, I want you to call Sir Simon first thing when you get back in your office, fill him in on our progress today."

The other attorneys brushed their laps and stood up. One of Land Management's attorneys went to the window. One of Unfragrant Bin's attorneys joined him. The future was all before them. It was only a matter of time. They would bring wealth to town, make Washington more appealing, working to make the city a better place for people like them to work in.

One of the men put out his hand. The other took the hand offered and shook it, both hoping they'd soon come to terms. It was not the last meeting. They'd see each other again. The lawyers followed each other out the door. The river of the day was at ebb tide, the conference room full of shadow. The last man out closed the door. A Styrofoam coffee cup, a scrap of over-doodled paper were all the signs left.

Five of the men went together to the bathroom, one in the stalls, three at the urinals, one, Jacques DeMurphy, washing and washing his hands at the sink. He was pointedly silent, devoutly believing like all stupid souls that his silence would be noticed. He considered Sterrett Emerson Groves an unalloyed slacker and felt that his silence at the sink would be understood for what it was, as censure.

"Not the Groves we've always known," the man in the stalls called out.

The young associate was incredulous, "What are you talking about? I was in rare form today. I pulled in the Washington Monument, for god's sake."

"No, I mean treating poor Anne Marie like that," the law colleague at the urinals said.

"Huh?" Sterrett asked, looking up from the business at hand.

"She practically lay down before you," the other lawyer said. "The old you would have laid down a rap like nobody's business. I don't recognize the Groves I see beside me."

"I don't care," Sterrett said. "Is that what bothers you? My love life?"

They called out to him in amazement, "Yes. Of course."

"Let us now enjoy vicarious pleasures," said the Guiteau partner coming out of the stalls. "We rely on your lusty adventures, you know?"

"Yes, the secretaries all complain, but in vivid detail," the man at the urinals said, as he flushed and zipped. They huddled at the sinks, where DeMurphy was washing his hands to the wrists.

"He took her card though. Did you see? He's got her card. Maybe he'll call her. Maybe they'll go out, and will he tell us about it?"

"We'll have to hear about it from one of the secretaries from Melody Hogan," one of the other partners said. "You've got no sense of loyalty, Groves."

They gathered up their briefcases, in good humor. Jacques DeMurphy had kept his peace throughout. They saw there was steam coming out of the junior partner's ears and fire from his hairy nostrils. But he was like that, moody sometimes, and perhaps he was still focused on *Flagellatus paraculum*.

Balled-up paper towels littered the floor around the wastebasket. The men went down the hallway and clustered around the elevator, their briefcases slung in front of them. When the elevator came, they got in, shoulder to shoulder, the five of them, standing rigid. The three partners got out on the fifth floor, and Jacques DeMurphy got out on the fourth. He wheeled round in time to see Groves still in the elevator.

"What's your problem?" DeMurphy called out. "Why can't you act like the rest of us?"

Sterrett Emerson Groves waved at him as the doors closed, riding that elevator all the way down to the lobby of the Guiteau Building. It wasn't as far as the elevator could go, for it went all the way down two basement levels still, but it was as far as Sterrett wanted to go. The lobby of the Guiteau Building was faced in gorgeous white marble, modeled on the bathrooms of the bar at the Ritz Hotel in Paris, with an ample spread of brass in the doorknobs and lamps, in the brass-mounted Directory.

The names on the Directory of the Guiteau Building included people of renown in Washington, a former vice president, two retired congressmen who now worked for the armaments industry, a former deputy attorney general, an ex-White House staffer more often on television than in his office, the usual roundup of the unwilling, men and women from all over America unwilling to leave Washington, butts too comfortable where they were.

Sterrett was feeling grumpy despite the praise, despite the amiable jibes. He'd been cooped up in the conference room too long, too long surrounded by lawyers. His love life, the others at the firm admired him for his love life, not for his bold action in speaking up, not for his rhetoric. That's what he added up to, that's what his life added up to, the life of a droll seducer. He wanted to stretch his legs, let his feet go pounding down the pavement. He wanted a drink. He pushed on through the doors of his building onto M Street and went out, happy to be free of the others.

He held up then, put his briefcase down on the gray pavement, swept his shirt cuff back and looked at his watch. He could go out to the Army-Navy Country Club and play some golf. He had a lifetime membership, courtesy of his father. Golf was one thing he was willing to work at. It never bored him. But he realized he'd never get out there in time. He had to bike home first, then change clothes, get his clubs and take a taxi out to Arlington, an hour, an hour and a half, and then he'd have to wait for a slot. He thought about the papers on his desk, his computer full of files that he had to read over. It was all too much for him.

Doltish DeMurphy was right. Sterrett knew nothing about solid waste disposal or the mechanics and technicalities of sanitary landfills. He had no intention of reading up on that sort of stuff. It bored him, garbage and how to get rid of it.

So he hesitated: go back up to his office and work on copying out his notes from the meeting, or go out to the Army-Navy Country Club and knock the ball around, or simply go to a bar, have a drink. That was the issue, turn the moment to good, the better use depending on the foremost exigencies of his mood. He wished he could be as meticulous and persevering as DeMurphy was. He wanted to be as convinced that the work he was doing was of such importance that all his life could be given over to it. He admired DeMurphy, envied him that conviction, and didn't see why the junior partner should hold a grudge against him.

That decided the issue, his perplexity over his colleague's blanket animosity. Figuring out the why of that sort of human behavior was what mattered most to Sterrett, and that could only be done, that philosophical musing, over a cold glass of beer. Plus it was hot outside, too hot to go back to the office, too hot for copying out his notes, drops of sweat by far outracing lucid legal arguments. Too hot for nine holes.

He looked up. He found he'd been walking east along M Street and now he crossed to Washington Circle. Pennsylvania Avenue at that height was a wide and relatively unremarkable street, surrounded by hotels, university buildings, and squatty offices. The young attorney shifted his briefcase to his other hand as he went by the Bristol Hotel. He stopped a second to peer inside. It was too early and there was no one in the lounge, the bar deserted, the lights of the bar dimmed. He continued on down the avenue, going against the current, a harried crowd heading for the Foggy Bottom subway.

Where to go, which bar? He wanted a bar with the right atmosphere for thinking. He was not looking for a bar to have fun in.

"Let me think," he said as he swung round, looking up and down the avenue.

It was not an easy task in Washington to find a bar to think in. There was a university bar nearby, but it was too noisy, and on the north side of the avenue there was an upscale bar, far too stuffy for thought. Sterrett reached the corner of 17th Street, held up at the light, and then mixed in with the crowd of people. He put his sunglasses on. The faces around him were mostly office clerks and middle-aged bureaucrats. As many worn-out faces as he ever wanted to see. They were tired people, pushed back by the traffic, suffering the start of the day silently, their eyes raised for the sign of the man walking, the green light to go. Yet even when the green light came, they hesitated.

Down 17th Street, the Corcoran Art Gallery, a pagan-looking building, stood where once there'd been a famous racetrack, where Andrew Jackson's ponies used to vie against Nick Biddle's, where waist-coated civil servants went to pass an afternoon wagering over bales of Oronoco tobacco. That Beaux Arts building echoed in part the oblong outline of a racetrack. But lions, and not horses, guarded the gallery's entrance. There were no bars down that way, down 17th; all the way down to the river, there was nothing to drink but water.

Sterrett crossed into Lafayette Square. A solitary chess player sat at a park bench in the square, playing an absent Fischer King. A pair of girls passed in daisy dukes. Sterrett turned to watch them. He watched the pigeons fly up as the two girls passed, the pigeons making a wide turn of the park to come back to the same spot, always coming back to the same spot, a turn around the park and then back to the same spot, always the same spot. Pigeon poop in chalky loops across the pavement.

He passed under Count Rochambeau whose bronze finger pointed southeast, to where the doors of the Old Inebriate Grill brimmed open, and now Sterrett knew where he wanted to go. He hurried a little now, grown quite thirsty, heading for the intersection of G and 15th Streets, and he bumped into other people, coming the other way. He said perfunctorily, without bothering to slow down, "Excuse me."

Then he bumped into someone who bumped back. It was a woman big as he was. Sterrett pulled himself together. He experienced a moment's confusion.

"You have not made attention your friend," the woman was saying to him. She was awkward looking, big forehead, big shoulders, big knees, but not entirely unattractive. Her eyes were beautiful eyes and her hair, hanging lush and wavy to her shoulders, was a richly dyed gold. "You have not been careful."

"You walked right into me," Sterrett cried.

"But I'm not sorry." The woman smiled. She produced a card case and opened it and took out her calling card. She presented it to the associate. Printed on hard paper was, "Ellen Berman, President. The Consolidated Bank of Rockville." The name Berman was well known in Washington, and her bank was one of the few to have endured and prospered during the general decline in local banks.

Sterrett, glancing repeatedly at her card, said, "Well, I won't be bullied."

"No one's bullying you," Ellen Berman replied, a little astonished to hear him say it. She looked the young attorney up and down. "That tie. Abhorrent," she said.

"My tie's my business," Sterrett answered, putting the banker's card in his pocket. He walked around her, walked on down the street.

"Call me. I'd like you to call me," the woman said.

The bar he was reaching for, the Old Inebriate Grill, was there and he started for it, definitely deserving a drink. He slowed then, let his hand come to rest on his heart. He was always going into bars. He had to stop going into bars.

The next few days there were several more meetings, in the offices of Melody Hogan and in the conference room at the Guiteau Building. A bump-up in the lease price per square foot was agreed to, nothing extravagant, nothing close to the actual market price of leased property in Washington, but enough so that no one could point and say the government was giving the ground away. New language regarding the copyright revenue from the methane-eating bacterium was initialed, and the lease was considered doable.

Fine points had to be settled. Sir Simon's attorneys agreed that Unfragrant Bin Systems would pay for the removal of several items of statuary from the Ellipse. The Butt-Millet Memorial and the statue dedicated to the Boy Scouts would go into storage in a government facility in Landover, Maryland, while the 2nd Division's flame-skirted sword would be transferred to stand between the Haupt Fountains, part of the German-American Friendship Garden.

The Secret Service stepped in and demanded that all personnel involved in the development of the sanitary landfill be identified and vetted for security purposes, from the architect to the backhoe operator and including the lawyers of both firms. The lawyers of both firms balked at this, crying an invasion of privacy. A volley of memos followed between the lawyers and the Secret Service, and then there was a hearing scheduled with a federal circuit judge so that the question of the lawyers going through a background check became an issue on its own that would take several weeks to settle.

There was too, the problem of taxes and royalties. Unfragrant Bin Systems claimed the subsurface rights to the site at the Ellipse and would therefore have to pay the taxes and maintenance costs on that, including paying royalties on any natural resource found at the site and subsequently sold by Unfragrant Bin Systems, such as sand, oil, water. The problem was to establish what was considered surface and what subsurface, and to determine to what extent these surface rights too, were to be considered taxable to Unfragrant Bin.

On first glance an easily resolvable question, for surface was surface and anything under it was sub, as any sixth grader knew, it required precise legal and contractual definition. Skip Toomey and John Silva of Melody Hogan sat down with Cliff Lemberger and Sissy Bateman of Guiteau and Garfield, and they sat down every day with hardly a single break until they came up with a formula that was satisfactory to all parties.

Then there was bellyaching over at the Department of the Interior. The Secretary of the Interior, Dr. Thomas Morrow, called Director Segreen into his office to chide her for going too far, too fast in her negotiations for the landfill. Morrow, formerly the president of Syracuse University, was diminutive in stature, a stern, professorial type with a towering forehead and an unkempt brown beard. Known as "Silent Tom" among the other members of the Cabinet, he had to make extra efforts to impose his will on his department.

He was particularly harsh with Segreen. He told her that before any lease could be signed, the nittle-pickers and environmentalistic naysayers who had already begun protesting in a loud, disrespectful manner against the proposed garbage dump had to be placated. Secretary Morrow told Segreen he wanted the thing to be achieved tactfully so that the members of the Senate subcommittee concerned with the site would see that the people were in fact for it.

This delicate task was given to Sterrett Emerson Groves. It was given to him under pressure from Director Segreen's lawyer, Celia Progg, pressure the Melody Hogan attorney put on Vince Jorrigo. For Progg rated Groves a salesman, more salesman than lawyer, a more persuasive voice than any of the lawyers in her camp. Vince finally agreed. He called Sterrett Emerson Groves, to his face, the P.T. Barnum of law associates—praise indeed.

Praise was fine, but what it meant in practical terms was that for the next couple weeks Groves had to work as hard as he ever had, talking on the phone to members of Congress, fielding questions from a mish-mash of citizens' groups, reading virulent letters sent in by environmentalists. Now Sterrett could be found where in the past he was least likely to be found, busy at his desk. His computer was always on. His trash basket was full. His eyes burned. He was too tired at the end of the day, going home on his bicycle, to go to the Lucky Key and see his chumlings. He was too tired for beer and whiskies. That was the purpose of the work he did; it kept him from drinking.

CHAPTER FIVE

Dinah Solatoff wanted to live on her own and by herself, but there was nothing affordable for rent, no apartment of any decency where she wanted to be, which was in Georgetown, so she had to rent a room in a group house, in a section of town called Burleith, cottage-like houses in the back-behind of Georgetown University. The house was in the middle of the block, like the others set back from the street. It was different from the other houses on the block in that it was painted a different color.

She felt capable of living with others, though she was used to students like the ones from her own college, self-consciously bookish and quiet, and she was not entirely ready for Georgetown University students. She lived with three exuberant girls who were never home or were home all at once with a large crowd of boys. But she had a room to herself, a room with a front view of the lawn and the street, and the rent was exactly what she could afford. The college girls considered her their maid, in the sense that as messy as they left the house, they knew Dinah would clean it up.

She had been in Washington since before Christmas last. She'd left Idaho without qualms, leaving her family and the woodsy life along the Snake River. Her parents had come to Idaho during the Vietnam War, longhairs with a lifestyle out of a big book called the *Whole Earth Catalog*. Every problem that came up was solved consulting the *Catalog*. Her mother fortunately was a good enough potter to make the family money and keep them fed and clothed and warm in the howling winter. Her father was a substitute school teacher, working here and there, on and off. What he liked to do best of all was to get high.

Dinah studied hard, was intelligent, and her mother had given her the chance to go to university, where she majored in art and architecture. Though she was quite good as a colorist, she found the technical side, draftsmanship in particular, difficult, but she stayed with it because she dreamed of living in a well-planned house one day, rather than in a house shaped like a Quonset hut and made out of apple crates and pieces of fallen timber. She definitely would have no shells, feathers, wind chimes, or "Peace" flags hanging or flying from any part of the house she would one day build for herself from her own plans.

After graduating from the University of Idaho, after a summer breaking up with her college boyfriend, a lifeguard in a resort complex on Lake Coeur d'Alene, she came east, came down out of the clouds in her first airplane trip and landed, elated to be in Washington. She spent six months working at a real estate agency downtown before landing a job as a secretary at Guiteau and Garfield.

Those first six months were the unhappiest months she'd spent in her grown-up life until then. The work at the real estate agency showing people apartments she herself could never afford to live in was humiliating and the pay was too little for her to quit. Every morning she had to take the bus. Every evening she had to take the bus home to Burleith. Her life revolved around that. She knew it was not a lasting situation, but she knew too, and worried, that temporary situations could be for a lifetime.

She met Mrs. Patricia Johnson in a gym she went to once a week downtown near the real estate office. It was her only luxury, going to the gym. Mrs. Johnson went every evening, and apparently it was the only time she took off from work. It was clear to Dinah that Mrs. Johnson had a side to her. Dinah didn't mind, and the woman wasn't aggressive. She found Dinah attractive and they talked. Patty Johnson was impressed by the way Dinah carried herself, the fact that she was an orderly person. As soon as there was an opening at the firm, and one came up in Mr. Klocker's office, Patty Johnson called her and asked her to come to work.

It was not Dinah's intention to remain at Guiteau and Garfield indefinitely. She was an optimistic enough person to believe that her plans and dreams could come true over time, and her plans included her wanting to try something more than being a secretary. She wanted to get her master's degree, advance beyond her simple college training. But Dinah was a realist and she knew she would have to stay where she was for some time more.

She was confident however, confident overall. She liked the East Coast. She liked the pressures of deadlines and the formality required by office life and all the things she'd been trained to avoid, all the things hippies hated, the uptight world of money. She saw right away that she had an advantage over many East Coast women because of her good looks, her pleasure in being a woman. Eastern women seemed uncomfortable in their skin, and it showed. By the time they were in their twenties, they were all fat and dowdy and seemed only to think of slimming down and being sexy. Mountain women were born sexy, born with the wind in their hair and the moon bursting from their fingertips.

Dinah wasn't afraid of men. She didn't feel at all inferior to them, and she knew how to take them, treat them like kings as long as they were of any use. Men always bent over backwards to be kind to her, or at the worst, bent over backwards to be their predictably stupid selves. She let them buy dinner if they wanted and she let them pat her ass, too. It made most men feel like they were in control, and Dinah enjoyed men who enjoyed that illusion.

It was the women who made trouble, who resented her. She disliked the women her age she'd gotten to know in Washington, disliked her roommates, disliked them with energy. Ever since the day they came to earth, they'd had whatever they wanted from their parents, all the good things in life. They were set to grow into careers and claim their rightful place in the world. They were tough-talking women, acting tough from the inside because it was easy for them to be tough inside when everything was given them and think that was real life. Survivors of a lousy life appreciated how much inside was tender and how desperately that tenderness had to be protected.

To Dinah protecting that little bit of tenderness meant limiting the amount of sleeping around she did. Her roommates screwed different guys on a weekly basis and thought that was the coolest thing in the world. They wanted to be like the guys, fuck whatever moved. Dinah didn't want to be like the guys. She knew she had to prize herself as a woman, and that meant keeping a tantalizing distance from men, making it hard for them, rather than easier.

She understood too well, coming from a big family, the consequences of promiscuity. She was there because her father and mother had gotten horny, coming out of a dope fog. It was a very simple concept, so simple that there was no need for a philosophical explanation of parenthood. People came from people, that was about as absolute a truth as there was. Considering how difficult it was to get along, it was amazing there were so many people in the world. Yet there was no clear explanation as to what kept them together.

She went to work at Guiteau and Garfield on the bus. She didn't mind not being able to afford having a car. That was one notion she did share with her parents, that the automobile made people fat and lazy, made the air sooty and unbreathable. It drove her crazy to see one person to one car. She liked the bus not only from a public transport point of view, but also because on the bus, she could squeeze her eye and take a peek at people around her, see what made them tick, their faces. It was only when the bus was late, when it was raining, or when some drunk got on that Dinah wished she had a car.

There was a Metro bus that stopped on Reservoir Road. It took her to Dupont Circle and she walked south to M Street from there. She adored walking among all the people walking to work. There were more people walking the sidewalk on New Hampshire Avenue than had ever lived within the city limits of Garcia, Idaho, where she grew up. She loved the fact that there wasn't an open meadow or a mountain peak within sight. Though New Hampshire Avenue did have trees and there were birds in the trees, it was a street shaded in the way a city street was shaded, in a grimy, bedraggled way, and the birds in the shade trees were the usual dirty birds.

Every morning she got coffee and a sticky bun from the Armenian joint at the corner of the Guiteau Building. She liked the foreign feel, marveled at the way the two brothers who ran the place talked to each other, using a rapid, alien tongue. What a trip, she thought. She wanted to learn Armenian, or any new language, and when she had the time, she'd go take some Berlitz course. That was the great thing about Washington, so many things you could study. Then she would travel, once she had enough money, travel to all the breezy corners of the world.

At Guiteau and Garfield, Dinah worked for Cornelius Klocker, an attorney of some weight. Klocker had been an assistant district attorney in Chicago before coming to Washington, and his reputation for being a tough negotiator who got what his client wanted was widespread, and his phone calls were always worth listening to. Klocker liked to remind people how brilliant, how tough he was. His favorite retort was, "What do you think, I got beans for nothing?"

Dinah had a desk in an open area between the offices of Corny Klocker and Deborah Takahashi. It was a midweek morning and she was at her desk, thinking about Sterrett. That Sunday she'd gone to church, to the Presbyterian Church on P Street, the Protestant church nearest to her, and she'd thought about the whole forgiveness scene, and thinking how she'd treated Sterrett made her cringe a little.

He'd been nice to her, and she knew that she'd enjoyed herself and had let herself go, willingly, and that it wasn't his fault if she felt it wasn't the right thing to do, after. She liked being hard-assed sometimes. But Sterrett had taken it okay, for instance, her slapping him, and she admired him for that. Plus he hadn't taken more of her than she herself was willing to give. Her quickness to intimacy had come from the fact that it had been a long time since she'd been with anyone.

She was at her desk, pondering this while at the same time efficiently copying word for word what Corny Klocker had jotted down on a bunch of cocktail napkins, his observations during an airport meeting with the CEO of High Leaf Bakeries. As she worked at her keyboard, Dinah couldn't help smiling, thinking about Sterrett and his very romantic idea, the two of them sitting in an auditorium listening to some old fart speak.

It wasn't a question of being bored, which surely she would be, but boredom was tolerable at times. It was the way Sterrett assumed things, took for granted that she would want to go to that lecture because he was the one asking. Dinah agreed with what CEO Bahman Trunkajar had said to Corny Klocker in the lounge at O'Hare, his angry words fighting off the takeover attempt by the Orange-U-Glad Corporation. If they're trying to put their hands on you, make them suffer for it.

But she reasoned there was no sense in making the boy suffer if she had to suffer along with him. She'd been sitting alone in her bedroom night after night for several weeks now, and she was bored with that and that kind of boredom was the kind that was not tolerable.

She wasn't completely without friends in the city, and she sometimes hung with a couple of the other secretaries at Guiteau and Garfield. But her immediate best friend was a waitress, an African American girl named Barbara, who liked chic and flashy eyewear and bizarre hairdos. Barbara worked as a waitress at Lemke's Dairy, around the block from the Guiteau Building. One day serving breakfast, talking idly, the two women found they had certain things in common, both strangers to Washington, both artists at heart, Barbara already a somewhat accomplished sculptor in that two of her pieces of "found art" were in a local show for charity.

But it was their differences that made them fast friends. Barbara had an open, spontaneous, and playful manner that got her good tips where she worked. She had been married and divorced and had recently ended an engagement to a sales executive. She'd made many mistakes in her life but was eager enough to go on making them as long as she learned from them and had some good loving in the bargain.

Dinah wasn't interested in good loving and she wasn't interested in fun. That was the chief difference between them. Dinah's immediate goal was her own apartment, and then grad school. She planned to get where she wanted slowly but surely, by hard work, but by any means necessary, without any hectic detours along the way. Dinah wanted to dispose of her life along the best plans possible. Barbara told her that the worst thing that could happen was to make plans because to discover who she was, she had to live day to day. Dinah already knew who she was and what the limits of her character were. She had had her trials and had come through and was calm deep inside.

Now Dinah was thinking of calling Sterrett, of making that telephone call over to the fourth floor and agreeing with him that they should go out again. Make up for lost time and go out, let him take her to dinner. She was about to dial him up when she turned to see Molly Dearden standing next to her desk.

"You scared me."

Molly was studying to become a paralegal, and in the meantime she filled in at the firm wherever she was needed. The last couple weeks she'd been working reception on the sixth floor. She'd come over from the reception area with a phone memo. She wanted to be there to catch Dinah's reaction. She said, with a twinge of envy, "Mr. Jorrigo wants to see you."

"Are you kidding?"

"At the Outhouse no less."

"Oh gosh, should I go?"

"You have to go," Molly said. "He wants to see you."

"I'm not ready for that."

"I'll cover for you here," Molly assured her.

Heat filled the street. It lay heavily on Dinah's small shoulders as she went down M Street, dressed in a pale gray blouse and a long gray skirt. She was unsure she was dressed nice enough for a meeting with the senior partner. She'd hardly had time to refresh herself with a dash of perfume, a little blush. She touched her neck, bare, no pearls, no gold, and her earrings were the glum old baubles she'd bought at a department store. At least she was wearing her good belt, black patent leather to match her shoes.

She decided she needed a quick smoke first, digging through her purse as she went down the block. She found the fresh pack of Marlboro Lights and tore the plastic wrapper free, broke through the silver foil with a fingernail. The wrapper made a ghostly appearance at her feet and then floated away.

Cigarette between her teeth, she raked through her purse for her lighter or for a stray book of matches. She was always tossing things into her purse. She found business cards and packets of saccharin, but no light.

"Never when you need it."

She stood on the sidewalk, a coarse strand of hair grazing her lips, intent on her search. A man appeared from a store in the middle of the block. He looked her up and down and offered her a complimentary match.

"Thanks," she said. She took a quick trial puff and focused on the tip of her cigarette.

"No problem," the man said. "My name's Jason. What's yours?"

"Thank you for the light," Dinah said and walked away, her legs snapping up the hard pavement. The man tucked the matchbook into his back pocket. He had customers waiting for him at the cash register, but he lingered at the door to watch the girl make for the end of the block.

The headquarters of the National Retirees Association was a long, low, unadorned building from the 1950s. It cast its shadow over that corner of M Street and over 24th Street, too. Vincent Jorrigo had his offices right next to it, on 24th Street, in a three-story house in a row of three-story houses that formed part of an old neighborhood by and large long ago demolished.

The other members of the firm called it the Outhouse and considered it an unjustified extravagance, especially since the firm itself paid the mortgage. But for the senior managing partner, having his office in the row house gave him the right distance from the petty resentments and politicking of his colleagues in the Guiteau Building.

Dinah left swirls of smoke behind her as she came up to the Outhouse. It had been a difficult morning—first the calls, Klocker's broker calling every ten minutes panicked with the falling price of gold, then Klocker's mostly illegible cocktail notes to decipher, and then Molly Dearden telling her it was her big chance, going to see Vincent Jorrigo. It was unnerving how pushy other women could be, Molly telling her to be sure to make herself as desirable as possible. Dinah was suspicious of people who gave her advice, no matter how caring they acted. There were those who used caring to make sure everyone felt the same way about things. But she knew Molly was right, it was her big chance, and she was nervous, too.

She gaped at the narrow, three-story building. It had a musty, crusty, old-fashioned look with its peeling paint and dreary windows. It should have been torn down like the others, she thought, the old things always hanging on long after they served a purpose. The two windows of the second floor were flung wide open. The curtains, which she saw badly needed cleaning, clung to the sills as if ready to jump. It was a façade that said quite distinctly, "Thus passeth away earthly glory."

But she didn't care how old-looking the building in which he worked was, it didn't matter; Dinah had a personal thing for Vincent Jorrigo. If she'd been a little more girlish and giggly, it could have been called a crush. She took a final drag on her cigarette. If Molly were right, and she usually was when it came to gossipy matters, Vince Jorrigo was coming out of a long drawn-out divorce and he was looking for female companionship.

Dinah didn't mind depending on a wealthy older man to better live her kind of life, if that's what it took. Lawyers were a soft touch when it came to gifts. That was the key with them, gratitude. She was determined however, not to let the little innocence she had left be leeched away. It was the only way to do more than just survive in the world. Already and despite herself she'd let Sterrett touch her too deeply.

She tossed her cigarette into the gutter and then walked quickly to the front door of the Outhouse. Pigeons stirred at their roost on the roof's ledge. A couple loose feathers swam past the windows of the Outhouse. Fraudulent doves, Dinah thought. She stood at the door, her shapely figure flashing in the brass plate, "Guiteau and Garfield. Attorneys at Law." She buzzed at the buzzer. There was a click-click, and she pushed her way in.

It was pleasantly cool in the Outhouse, a relief, and she sighed, an asylum from the aggressive stickiness of the street. Kimmie Albright, the receptionist, was nestled under a cone of light, her long black hair loose around her shoulders, her feet visible under the desk, one shoe off. The shoe sat on its side, an abandoned high heel. There were flowers in a vase on the desk. They were yellow irises, slightly wilted despite the air-conditioning.

"Kimmie," Dinah said in a friendly way.

The receptionist, a poised Mississippian, raised her eyes to ask, "Oh, Dinah?" They knew each other from lunch, the secretaries and receptionists tending to hang together over salads at the Armenian deli. "Are you here already?"

"Here I am."

"Coffee, Dinah?"

"No, no thanks." The Mergers and Acquisitions secretary leaned against the desk and peered over the computer screen to make eye contact with the receptionist. "So Mr. Jorrigo wants to see me. Here I am."

Kimmie dropped her eyes to her keyboard. "It's a desk, not a railing." She added, "You'll have to wait. He's busy."

Dinah drew herself up. She expected a little more conversation, but it was clear Kimmie Albright had nothing else to say. Dinah went over to where there was a rug the color of old salami spread out in front of a dustless fireplace, where there were a few uncomfortable ladder-back chairs. She sat down and crossed her legs and waited.

There were magazines on the table by the chair she was sitting in, but Dinah didn't feel like reading magazines. Magazines and newspapers were for people without thoughts of their own. Dinah was too full-up thinking about herself for any casual reading. But she reached over and out of flat impulse hauled a copy of that month's *People* magazine to her, rested it on her knee and began flipping through the scatterbrain pages, mostly pictures of news personality Sandra Hoop interviewing herself, even while interviewing others, always herself, her experiences, what she had to say. But she did look quite fash' in that one outfit, what she'd worn to the Oscars.

Dinah turned her eyes to the mirror hanging above the chimneypiece. In it she caught a glimpse of Kimmie Albright, fingers trotting at the keys of her computer. She guessed at her hostility, and what it meant, for the senior partner had seen Dinah, picked her out, perhaps during a conference and had a real interest in her. What that meant was that Dinah had been noticed, and she was pleased because it meant her plans were the right plans.

Vincent Jorrigo was at his desk on the second floor of the Outhouse. He had his checkbook open on his desk. $4920 was his current and available balance. He had his salary coming at the end of the week. Half of his salary went to his wife, his ex-wife. The rest was destined for credit card bills, insurance and finance payments, expenses at the Tahoga Yacht Club where his boat was docked, at the Little Falls Country Club where he was a member in good standing, for the bill at the River Club where he often ate lunch and dinner. When the dust cleared, he'd be lucky if $4920 was still his total current and available balance. In any case, $4920 might be enough to get him a seat at a run-of-the-mill poker game, but it was way too little for the Bitch.

He slapped the checkbook closed. He tossed it into his desk drawer. Closed the drawer. Put both hands down on the draft of the ground lease for the sanitary landfill at the Ellipse. It was a thick volume, paper upon paper, the paper consumed to arrive at this final draft enough in and of itself to fill half a good landfill. He had Sir Simon Psora to count on; the firm's billing for more than a year's work ran to over three million dollars. He personally could put his paws on thirty percent of that, but only once the contract was signed and the landfill was under way. That was a pretty good stake.

He reached across his desk, picked up the photograph of his cabin cruiser, the *Arabella*—10 meters with two 250 hp. engines, a flying bridge, and teakwood interior. His Hemingway dream from years back, the boat was practically the only thing of value his wife had left him free and clear. He'd brought it up from Florida and kept the boat at the Tahoga Yacht Club, at dock on the Washington Channel. Using the boat the way he did, he had to pay for extra services, and he needed to have work done on the hull, and that meant dry dock for a couple weeks and extra, out-of-budget expenses. He really had no choice but he had to play cards, couldn't manage not to.

The photo of the *Arabella* was taken by his wife from shore, when the boat was brand new, not tied to a dock, but barreling along at full speed off Loggerhead Key. What a precious thing it was to have the freedom to drop hawsers and ride the waves to where you will. But the boat sat at the marina, and he could barely afford the fuel to keep its batteries charged. The *Arabella* desperately needed paint, new fittings, too. He had never expected that there would be a time in his adult life when he couldn't afford new fittings for his boat.

He knew he had to play, that was the only way out of his situation. He had to end his losing streak. Rest was deadly. Rest from the game meant a player lost his feel, and no matter how much he knew about playing poker, his hands turned cold with rest and he was like a beginner. Vince had been in a losing streak since Abraham Lincoln's Birthday. No, since the Capitals lost to the Flyers in the conference finals. He'd lost $34,000 on that series. It had seemed like it was going to be the Capitals' year.

He hated to lose, but losing had its charm. He couldn't very well lose at the practice of the law, that meant his reputation, and in Washington reputation was life. But he could lose at cards and still be admired as a card player if he lost enough and in a way that made an impression. Losing brought with it an intense feeling of self, of being what a man really was, abjectly alone while at the same time connecting him with greatest mass of people possible, because the masses were losers. Losing justified a man's struggle, his continuing to struggle. Loss was what life was about, and feeling sorry for himself when he lost gave Vince a strangely sweet feeling. That was a sickness Vince was afraid he was ailing into, and he had to play his way out of it as soon as possible.

He put the photo of the *Arabella* back on the desk. Stared at it some more, a truly fine boat, a marvelous boat, a Chris*Craft of a quality they didn't make anymore. He couldn't sell it if he'd wanted to.

Kimmie buzzed him on the intercom. "Ms. Solatoff is here."

"That's fine," Vince said absently.

"I'll send her up? Is that fine for you?"

"Thank you, Kim. I said, fine."

The stairwell, Dinah could have scaled it with her elbows, it was that narrow. The second-floor landing was as dark as perdition. Some daylight filtered in from an open door, and there was a breeze, like warm breath coming down the corridor. Dinah paused. She'd climbed too fast and for a second felt dizzy. She tugged at her bra.

"Mr. Jorrigo?" She made the most noise possible approaching, pushing the door all the way back before feeling her way into the senior partner's office.

"Dinah Solatoff?" Vince asked. He got right up from his desk. Cocked an eye, she was indeed quite pretty, with nut-brown hair, an hourglass figure, and clothed in somber colors, a girl of good taste, a good choice, too. "How are you, and I'm so glad you could come over and meet with me."

Dinah for her part gave way to a modest smile, and she kept her voice neutral. "I'm very pleased to meet you, sir. I think we met once when you came over to Mergers and Acquisitions to…you know… talk to Mr. Klocker." She came hesitantly into the office. The carpet felt tacky underfoot, and there was dust in the air, and the dust was not just settled on every object in the room, but moved, endlessly adrift as well.

"Mergers and Acquisitions," Vince said, as he came forward and they shook hands. He knew he had to be careful not to make their meeting seem more than it was. He was attracted to the girl, but only in a general way. Young girls were seldom as satisfying in bed as the popular imagination made them out to be. "I hope Corny's treating you right?" He turned back to his desk. "Come, come on in and sit down, won't you?" he said.

Dinah walked around, busy drinking in the senior partner's office. The bookcase had books, but they were not the usual legal tomes, not like, say the books in Corny Klocker's office, but rather old dog-eared books of philosophy, a few novels, their authors only vaguely recognizable to her. Many books on boats and boating filled the shelves. One central shelf was given over to someone named Marcello Soko, more than a dozen copies of the same hardback book. Dinah lingered there.

Vince, at his desk, wanted to say something, tell the girl about Soko, who he was, tell her too, about that book, still the only prose translation available in the U.S., a book that still sold some copies per year. But he thought, no, he'd keep quiet about that. She wouldn't be interested, and in any case, the Vincent Jorrigo who had done that translation was no longer the Vincent Jorrigo who sat at that desk. Marcello Soko himself was a specter, a poet no longer read in his own country. Books in themselves had to seem like odd junk to the young secretary.

But Dinah was no fool. She had good eyes too, and saw "Jorrigo" along the book jacket's spine, the senior partner's name followed by, "Soko. Avenida da Liberdade." "This is by you," she said. She rested her finger on the spine, tapped it. "You wrote this? How wonderful."

"That's by an Angolan poet of the 20th century," Vince said. "It's mine in so far as I did the translation, only the translation. He wrote the poetry, revolutionary poetry. It's left-wing stuff, anti-imperialist poetry of the sort that might even be considered illegal these days, you know, inciting terrorism. It's the kind of poetry no one would dare touch today."

"I think poetry's important," Dinah said decisively.

"I keep it more," he replied, "to remind me what life's business is."

"Oh gosh. What is it?" Dinah asked, as though afraid to be told.

"The business of life is to be understood."

"I never thought of that. Wow."

"I didn't say it. Someone else did."

He was able to see Dinah was a bit anxious, perhaps even a bit excited to be there with him. He wanted to put her at ease, but not so much so that she got ideas beyond his own ideas. His own idea was to go to the Gala, and be there with a young girl as pretty as any man could want, and show off. It was a very simple idea, a boost to his ego.

"This is a favor I need from you, that's all. A small favor."

It was way too hot to sit down. With the windows open to the weather, heat came in from the street, heat, dust, noise. For another thing, Dinah was too nervous to sit down. A favor, she thought, no one ever asked her a favor, and what favor could she do for the managing senior partner of her firm, she wondered. A sexual favor sprang to mind, but it didn't seem to be the context for that.

"Mrs. Johnson recommended you to me," Vince said. He was bucked to one side of his chair, legs crossed. From time to time he massaged his earlobe in a reasoning way. "She's an invaluably good judge of character, I think. And if she says you're someone of quality, then there you are. So you have to thank her."

Dinah was even more perplexed than ever, and that was what finally brought her to sink her bottom down into the big leather chair. She didn't get comfortable in it. She sat perched, a bird ready to fly off at the first blatant sign. Though he was middle-aged, Vince had a presence. He was a little overweight, but attractively so, not some skinny Johnny. His face was not overly good-looking, nor was it effeminate in any way, but it was the face of a man who pampered himself, who knew the value of careful vanity, and this intrigued the girl. It meant to her that he was interested enough in others to be interested in how he appeared to them.

"Mrs. Johnson told me you come from out West. Is that right? Though I'm not a traveler and have never been farther west than Houston, I hear it is quite nice out there."

"I'm from Idaho," she said. "The Gem State. That's where I live, or I mean lived, a small town, you know up in the hills near the Snake River? Garcia, very small, oh gosh, not even two thousand people in all. But I think really, one of the most beautiful places in the entire world. But then Washington, well, it's quite beautiful, too. I can understand why once you're here you never leave." She realized she didn't know anything about him and asked the senior partner, "Are you from here?"

Vince smiled, helplessly smiled at the girl's freshness to town. He said, "No one ever asks that question."

"I'm so sorry…I didn't mean to be nosey."

"No, what I mean is everyone here is from somewhere else." He wasn't skilled at small talk, that was clear. "I'm from Rhode Island. I believe they call it the Ocean State. The last person who asked me where I was from was a U.S. Customs agent." He composed himself at his desk. Loose ribbons of conversation from passersby came in through the open windows. City noises, music from passing cars. Vince went on, "The reason for my calling you into my office today, well, I'm glad to hear that you think poetry is important. And art, painting that kind of thing?"

"Art? Yes, of course, I like painting. As a matter of fact I majored in art at the University of Idaho. I like architecture, too. How did you know that?"

"How did I know that? Let me ask you this, then," Vince said. "Do you know what this is?" He took an envelope out of his desk drawer. He used a pencil to push the envelope across the clear space of his desk to Dinah. She reached out and took a look. "Mr. Vincent Jorrigo, Esquire" was handwritten in royal blue ink across the front of the envelope, at the return address corner, "From the Office of the Director of the National Gallery of Art. Washington, D.C."

"It's a request for money," Dinah said, somewhat disappointed. He was merely seeking her advice as a secretary. "That's what that is."

"You don't get penmanship like this on a simple request for money. Open it for me, will you?"

The secretary pulled a heavy card out of the envelope, and she began to read out loud, "'The Director Dean Richards joins with the Consolidated Bank Corporation of Rockville to request your participation with guest in a Grand Gala in honor of Jean Dubuffet's monumental sculpture, *Hommes En Fracs*." She looked up at Vince. He nodded encouragingly. Dinah read the next line, "The Grand Gala will take place Monday evening at Seven o'clock the 21st of June. Please present this invitation at the Constitution Drive entrance of the National Gallery of Art, the East Building. Formal wardrobe required." She sifted out a much smaller card. "There's also this, an 'RSVP' form…How many people in your party…Amount of donation you're making…There's a check list. Gosh, $100 is the smallest number."

"Should I go?" Vince asked her. "I hate these affairs. I've been to too many. I'd rather not go."

"If you don't go, you're missing a great opportunity."

"But if I do, I'm an opportunist, going against my not wanting to go."

"If you're an opportunist and you are, and you don't go," Dinah argued playfully, "it's worse. It's you acting in bad faith. Bad faith is a no-no."

"Bad faith?" Vince chuckled. "What are you talking about?"

"I'm pretty much right out of college." Dinah permitted herself a little more horsing around, she was that excited to be talking to the senior partner. She said, "I know a lot of stuff like that, philosophy, history." She jumped up from her chair and went over to one of the open windows. The view was mostly cars zooming by and a few people. She got serious. "I studied Sartre," she said. "Bad faith is when you act in a way that's not really who you are. Oh, well, you do it because society constrains you or because..."

"Are you finished?"

Dinah realized she'd gone too far.

"Sorry," she said. "Oh gosh, really."

She went and sat back down in her chair, feeling chastised. But she smiled too, pleased with herself. He had noticed her for sure, her backside, she knew her backside was as good a view as the view from any window.

"Will you listen? Now. This firm has contributed $5000 to the Gallery's Acquisitions Fund. That means I probably should go, and I will, but I hate going to these things alone. Hate it, Dinah."

"Hate it?" Dinah made a frown. "You shouldn't hate anything."

"Hate. It," Vince replied. "So what this means." He pointed to the envelope in the girl's hand. "Is that you will be 'guest.'"

"Me? Go with you? Is that true?" She absorbed the idea quickly, took it to heart. It meant for one thing, she would need new clothes. That meant spending money. She had very little to spend. "Formal wardrobe means what?" She placed the invitation on top of the envelope, placed them both on the edge of the desk. She sat on the edge of her chair. "I'm going to be your date?"

"That's why you're here," Vince said grandly. "Yes, no? You don't have to. But I'd like you to."

"Thank you. All right, of course," she said. She had to keep herself from clapping hands and bouncing up and down in her seat. "I'd love to."

"I think you'll be right at home at this gala. You'll be perfect."

Dinah couldn't stop beaming, giving out a cheek-to-cheek smile. But going to a gala was going to involve some sacrifice, and she was aware of that. She would have to buy a really nice dress. She'd seen one in the small shop in the Galleria mall. But where was she going to get the money for it, that was her worry. She tried thinking of that and of the other practical elements involved, rather than of the whole big deal of going to a big event with a man as important as Vincent Jorrigo.

"Good. That's one thing settled," Vince said. He didn't mean to sound as though he were going down a checklist for the day, but he was. The next problem to solve was to get accounting to put together a comprehensive and up-to-date billing for Sir Simon Psora. He rose, came round his desk.

"Good," he repeated, rubbing his hands together.

Dinah got the hint and stood up and let him escort her to the door. She had several questions to ask him. But she thought to wait until later, when they had more time to themselves. It was after all the middle of the working day. She asked him, "Should I call you and we can discuss any details, you know like transportation, and stuff like that?"

"I'll take care of everything," Vince answered, thinking, here was a girl who was truly dangerous, for it was difficult to tell how much of her thinking was as good-natured as it seemed. She wasn't dumb and she wasn't jaded. It made him worry whether he could handle her. "Don't have to do a thing. I'll call you."

She walked down the hallway. She went down the stairs. She went past the receptionist and out the door. She was on the sidewalk, and then it hit her for real, she was going to a party.

Dinah's most immediate plan was to get Vincent Jorrigo to take her seriously enough as a woman not to want to have sex with her right away. She wanted him to have to court her, buy her presents, take her to dinner a couple times, the whole nine yards, and then maybe she'd consider sleeping with him. Maybe after sleeping with him a few times, she'd consider becoming his girlfriend. More than that was thinking too much ahead. She marveled that in such a short time she'd come so far. Not just because Vincent Jorrigo represented success and class, or because he was attractive, but because she liked him well enough to hope her loneliness was at an end.

CHAPTER SIX

She told Barbara about it a few days later. Barbara came over with pizza. She brought a friend, Kate Goodwin. Kate carried a bag with a six-pack of light beer in it. It was the end of the week. The house in Burleith was practically empty, with two of the three students who lived there gone home for the summer. The one other housemate was off to Rehoboth Beach with her boyfriend.

They were sitting in Dinah's bedroom on the second floor. The door was open and the air-conditioning was wailing away at the window. Dinah had T-Red playing in her CD player, but the volume was turned down and only his rhythm section was audible. There was one chair in the room, a rocking chair, so the three women sat on the floor, cushions spread out, eating pizza and drinking beer. Dinah told them about how Vincent Jorrigo asked her out, the game he played with the envelope, and how excited she was and how she knew to hide it. They were all in tears, laughing, and for Dinah it was for a moment like she was a little girl again.

"I didn't want to scare him, you know, jumping up and down."

"It's a difficult thing for a grown man," Kate said. "For them to show they have an interest in you. They worry about their image. Especially if they're divorced."

"Especially if they hold a position of power like he does." Barbara, whose hair that evening was a jazzy burst around her head, pulled her big-lensed glasses low. "I mean, now are you sure he's not after your body and that's all? So, once you go down that road…"

"I don't feel like it was a mistake," Dinah answered. "Saying yes. You know what I mean? I trust him, I do. I like him enough so saying yes feels right."

"No, why should you care? When do you get a chance to go to a big party like that?" Barbara said. She let out a snort, adding, "I mean there's a whole lot of men out there. Young lawyers out there, but who are they, they think they're so hot. They come into Lemke's and they need to be slapped the way they act. So all I can do is smile. I got to keep my job for now. Let's hope Di', you got yourself something better than that."

Then Dinah told them about Vince Jorrigo, described him. Described the color of his skin, a crisp brown color like singed paper. Described his features, his dark eyes, the way his hair rippled. Described him the way she'd seen him the day before, in his dark blue suit, perfectly fitting, with a white shirt and a bow tie. "It wasn't a plain bow tie…"

"No?" Barbara offered. "What'd it have propellers?"

"It was a deep, saturated salmon color, and he had the nicest leather loafers I've ever seen, Guccis. They had the green and red stripes of Gucci across the vamp. You know, like this. Very nice."

"White man," Barbara said admiringly. "Is no competition to any African when it comes to style."

"But he's strange," Dinah said. "I'm used to men, but I mean I can tell he likes me and all, but he's never, you know, quite there, when you talk to him you got only half his attention."

"Thinking about his wife?" Kate suggested.

"He has a wife and two children, but he divorced about a year ago," Dinah replied evenly. "His wife's well-off because in addition to the money she makes as an attorney, working in Boston, she inherited a substantial amount from her father. I know all about it. Kimmie, his secretary, told me."

"You must be very aggressive," Kate said. "With divorced men. They're lazy at heart."

"Lazy men, that's what this town is full of," Dinah complained.

"No, Kate is right. You got to take a chance. Ask him over here… Wait a minute, Di', listen to me…of course he'll say no. But then he'll ask you over to his place. You got to say yes. Don't play the unvanquished virgin on him. No, I know you do. But divorced men, married men, they are all thinking the same thing and they don't want war game strategy. They want conquest and that's all."

Barbara went on to explain about her latest boyfriend, who was a lawyer at the firm of Cermack Zangara. She'd gotten to know him from when he came to see one of her sculptures at the charity exhibit. He flirted with her and Barbara upped the ante.

"I called him a racist pig, because he was patronizing. It worked," Barbara said. "Well, they all are. Racist."

"You think?" Dinah said. "Vincent is black anyway and they all work for him and they all seem to respect him all the way."

"I bet in his own way he is too. Vincent? I mean what black guy's named Vincent? He's a wanna-be white, I bet." Barbara made a face, pooh-pooh. "No, they're all racist those lawyers, they feel bad about it, and so anyway the point is I used that and my lawyer fell for it. You know, me saying you think you can flirt with me because I'm black? Now I can't get rid of him even if I wanted to."

"Do you want to?" Kate asked.

Barbara told them her lawyer boyfriend had a wife, no children, but a young wife who worked as a doctor. She was very jealous, and he was constantly being paranoid about it. One time, he'd made Barbara hide in his closet, like in the movies, and it turned out to be just the refrigerator making hubbub in his big old kitchen. Plus he liked to make her watch dirty movies while they were doing it.

"That's revolting," Dinah said.

"It is," Barbara agreed. "But what can you do? I really like the guy. He's got the knack." She laughed and hugged herself and repeated it, "He's got the knack."

"My ex-boyfriend, Eric," Kate began, not wanting to be left out, "he was way into drugs…"

And she told a long, dismal story about her high school sweetheart and how he stole jewelry from her parents and how he was always in trouble with the police and always lied to her about where he'd been and then got hepatitis. She'd stopped seeing him and had hooked up with a sweet guy who worked at a supermarket. But her old boyfriend still called her, threatening to do stuff to her. Dinah was pleased Barbara had brought Kate over. It made her realize that what made the big difference among them was the ability to choose. Neither Kate nor Barbara had much luck with men because they habitually chose the wrong type.

They had a good time, talking. Kate was on a diet, so she said, but she ate all of her pizza and part of Barbara's. Dinah finished what the other two didn't touch, picking the anchovies off of Barbara's Four Seasons pie. They left the salads, iceberg lettuce and croutons, in clear plastic containers, untouched. But as for the light calorie beer, it was all gone in a flash.

Dinah knew there were plenty of beers in the refrigerator, practically the only thing in the refrigerator, and she went downstairs and brought up an armful of bottles, and they sat around on the floor, drinking and talking long into the evening. When the dark of night came, they decided to go for a drive around town.

"Hit the bars," Barbara said. "It's Friday. Got to celebrate. Got to."

"Celebrate what?" Dinah asked. She had planned to do some laundry and clean the kitchen, which the Georgetown students had left full of dirty plates.

"Surely, celebrate your promotion from secretary to boss man's lover girl," Barbara said. "That's significant benefits, that promotion."

"You should come out with us," Kate urged her. "You really, really should. We'll have fun, very much so."

"I don't know." Her financial situation wasn't so good that she could go out whenever she wanted; she didn't have money to spend on drinking. "I have to get into something first."

Barbara and Kate went out to the car. It was light out still, and they leaned against the fender and waited while Dinah went into the kitchen and did a few plates, and then went upstairs and got changed. She put on tapered jeans and a halter top, white sneakers. She got out some spangled bracelets and put those on. She checked herself in the mirror. That's what she liked, the streamlined look, like a tight little locomotive.

When Dinah came out the house on S Street, she, Barbara, and Kate flung themselves into the car and drove around for a good hour, probing the town for action. Nothing happening in Adams Morgan, nothing in Woodley Park, only lightning bugs in a hullabaloo above the lawns. Nothing was going on in Dupont Circle.

Barbara, bored driving around to no purpose, parked on a side street in Foggy Bottom and the girls settled down in the car and opened a bottle of Mateus and then passed around a joint. Dinah didn't like the smell of marijuana. It was one of her hang-ups left over from living in Garcia, Idaho, with zonked-out *Whole Earth* parents. Marijuana was what the adults smoked, and the whole thing disgusted her.

Plus Dinah wasn't by nature a big talker, but smoking dope made her talk, and she had no desire to talk about all the things that she was thinking about. She left the others in the car and headed off on her own for a walk around the block. She was drunk. Drunk, she tended to brood, and she liked that better than being giggly and conversational.

She was ultra-hungry, too. There was an Orange-U-Glad in the middle of the block, next to the Bristol Hotel. She was on Pennsylvania Avenue, the west end where it was a relatively unimportant street, surrounded by churches and residential buildings. She went by the hotel, its big windows pouring out buckets of light. It was late, but there were still people in the lounge, yawning, talking, ready to turn in, ready to go out on the town. She liked hotels for the variety of faces.

She went into the Orange-U-Glad store. She was quick, that was the key. Not to linger and draw attention. Most of the time the people on the late shift were inattentive, sitting behind the register, dozing to the tune of the television. By the time they focused that she'd come in, she'd already taken what she wanted. She did a circuit around the candies and cakes, grabbing Twinkies and a bag of potato chips. She came around to the counter and asked for a pack of Marlboros.

"Lights or regular?" the man behind the register asked.

"Lights, soft pack," she answered. When he turned his back, she cached packages of Slim Jims up under her blouse. She glanced sideways at the video camera. The man turned back with the cigarettes. He was a tired man in an orange apron. Printed across the apron in dark blue letters was, "Orange-U-Glad."

She thanked him, paid for the cigarettes and snacks and walked out. Always sure to leave as though forgetting something, and then, outside, always the first few steps, a purple tension along the shoulders and down the spine, luscious pearls of sweat. Then into the shadows quickly with her surreptitious joy.

She ate the Twinkies and a few of the potato chips, sitting on the front steps of a row house, watching the other girls in the car, dope smoke leafing out of the windows. She didn't feel even a bit of guilt. It was something she'd started doing as a little kid, something her parents encouraged in her, ripping off the "Man." Her father's biggest dream was to figure out a way to steal gas direct from the pump.

Dinah only or almost only stole food. She first stole food when there wasn't enough food to go around the table in her house, and then even when there was enough, she kept on. It was something she felt she had a right to do in a nation so overfed, so super-paranoid about the smallest crime. She had a right to eat. That's what she'd say if they ever caught her. They never caught her except once when she was a teenager. But she'd learned several new techniques on the 'net and it was her luck to have excellently nimble fingers.

There was a crackling sound. She sprung up, a cockroach on her potato chips. She bent low and squinted, the place was full of them, coming out of the ivy, coming up from the damp. She walked quickstep away, towards the car. It was dark along the street, dark in front of the two-story houses that had been the homes of the working class when Foggy Bottom was a real neighborhood. The gasworks, the brewery, the flourmill, all torn down, students and professors and bureaucrats in the now quite expensive houses. It was the idea of professors that scared her a little.

"What you bring to eat?" Barbara asked.

Dinah got in the car and tossed the Slim Jims into the front seat.

"Great, I love this shit."

"I am so famished."

"Ready to go?" Kate Goodwin asked. "Should we go to Warty's or try someplace else?"

"Let's drive around some more," Barbara said.

Dinah turned her face to the window. She wasn't with them yet, but she felt comfortable enough not to have to pretend or be amusing. They went back downtown, first to the Old Inebriate Grill, a ritzy tavern a stone's throw from the White House. At the Old Inebriate, they had martinis, the best martinis in the city made by Debbie in the backroom bar. They sang "Yesterday" for her because she was leaving the Grill to go and live in California. Then they went to the Sign of the Whale. The Whale was an aging yuppie bar, full of men who in the

1980s had been single and had had money to burn, who could only go out now with their wives' permission.

The girls had beers and camped around, talking over the music. A couple men came up to them, and the girls brushed them off, making jokes among themselves that the men didn't understand. Dinah stood apart a little ways down the bar. One of the men gravitated to her. He was full of banter.

"You look lost. My name's Geoff. Can I throw you a drink?"

Dinah showed him her bottle, still half full.

"Well," the man said. "When you're done with that one?"

"You're too old for me," Dinah said. "So go away."

There were people who mistook hostility for a kind of playfulness. Geoff grinned. "I like your attitude." He pushed closer to her. "What do you do?"

"I don't do anything that's your business."

"Well, that's great. Let me find you something." He explained his business to her, essentially monkey business. "I believe you have the finest rack I've ever seen."

Barbara and Kate saw there was trouble brewing, and they knocked back their own drinks and hustled Dinah out of the Sign of the Whale. They didn't drag their feet and got right to Barbara's car, got in and drove to Georgetown. They parked in a garage near the Canal and went up Wisconsin Avenue to Warty's. Barbara expected to find her boyfriend there, a lawyer from Cermack Zangara, but instead she was met by a group of lawyers from Guiteau and Garfield.

"Hi, I'm Hugo," one of them said, coming up to Barbara, recognizing the waitress from Lemke's, but not recognizing Dinah, a secretary from the sixth floor.

"We're from Guiteau and Garfield."

"You're all married, aren't you?" Barbara said, laughing.

"We're lawyers."

And the lawyers invited the girls to sit with them at a booth, join them for a round of sex on the beach. After that one round of shooters, they had the waiter bring them another round, this time watermelon shooters.

"Too much," Bird Mallet cried. It took him a few sips to empty the shot glass. "It's too much."

"It's like some kind of grassy knoll," Hugo Humphrey put in.

Mallet's eyes gleamed. He got the joke. "Too many shooters," he said.

The bar was full of smoke. There was music and the noise of pick-up lines being exchanged, and kids were dancing in the empty area between the booths and the counter. Dinah kept to herself pretty much, and she kept quiet about working at the same firm as the young attorneys. She kept quiet about Corny Klocker and Mergers and Acquisitions. She preferred to hide behind her beer and keep her eyes open.

"Is that true?" Barbara asked Hugo.

"Of course, of course it is. It's called the Old Stone House because the first weed smoked in America was smoked there. That was back in 1765. That was the thing that led to the Boston Tea Party. They called it tea back then. Full of stems and seeds. The world turned upside down."

And Kate was telling Walt Gdyap the story of her life, "When I was little, we had those plastic plates you used to get for free at the filling station? I had three brothers and I was the only girl, so they got all the cool colors and I got pink. Can you imagine? A pink plate to eat my string beans off of. My brothers were like, 'Pink, means you stink'…I hate pink."

He hadn't seen her, she was sure, but Dinah spotted Sterrett over at the bar's long wooden counter, and she was trying to decide what to do about that. Jacques DeMurphy was resting his behind next to her, and he was going on and on about a germ. He seemed very gassed up about it, and while he was telling her about *Flagellatus paraculum*, he inched closer to her and began trying to gift wrap her in his arms.

"Leave me alone," Dinah had to say at last.

"You have to be like that fellow in the deodorant commercial," the junior partner told her. "Say, 'no sweat' to the world."

"You're beginning to piss me off," Dinah answered, squirming out of the booth to get away from him. Barbara leaned forward and said to Jacques DeMurphy, "Leave the girl alone."

Warty's got louder. It was a loud, lively place, crammed with college students and hip young professionals. It featured well-chosen music, and the waiters were all working on their MBAs, and the bartenders were witty and mixed and poured drinks like acrobatic wise guys. It was exactly the kind of bar Sterrett avoided. No chumlings, no, it was too full of people who smirked rather than people who burped.

Sterrett Emerson Groves had been there on the bar stool since after work, since after seven o'clock. He hadn't moved from his stool in a long time, not even to go to the john, and now he showed the bartender his empty bottle. He said, "One more."

The bartender asked, "Same?"

Yes, Sterrett nodded. He hadn't seen Dinah come into the bar with the other girls, but he had seen the other associates. He waved at them, but they sat in another area. Sterrett felt not at all sorry for himself, sitting there alone. He was sure nothing could get to him, with his tie so brazenly ugly and his suit so spaulding gray. He unhinged his fingers from the warm, empty bottle he was holding on to and took a swig of his newly uncapped beer.

Jacques came over, bored with the girls at the booth. He sat down next to Sterrett, shifting his weight so that he was comfortable. He snapped his fingers.

"Once again," he boomed at the bartender. "Him and me."

He chose to sit with Sterrett not because he wanted to make friends no, but because he considered him the most satisfactory of the group to tease, by far the touchiest in terms of pride. An unearned pride, for Jacques considered Sterrett a fake and a slacker. He wanted Groves to smart before that fact, that he considered him a fake.

Sterrett for his part was suffering a lapse in his usual high alertness, looking like the beer bottle in his hand was the only thing holding his eyes open. But with someone he knew sitting down beside him, surprised it was Jacques, he made the effort and began expatiating at length about his father, the one person really dear to his heart.

"I haven't visited him in a long time, I mean at the cemetery," Sterrett explained. "He was given a military burial at Arlington about eight years ago, yeah, eight. There were close to a hundred people there, officers, but enlisted men as well. Some of the officers, and I mean full colonels, actually cried. The Honor Guard gave loose with blank rifle shots and a bugler from the 40th Armored Regiment put his lips to a really moving rendition of 'Taps.'"

"Listen to you," Jacques DeMurphy chuckled. "Stuff no one cares about."

Sterrett ignored that, wanting to say what he had to say. "My father died, you know, leukemia from the ordnance they used against the Serbs. That was it, the air, the dirt, the water in Kosovo was full of depleted uranium particles. My father told me. The Army denies it because they won't take the responsibility. My Mom wanted to make a stink with, you know the Pentagon about it, but after Berwick's death she was too worn out."

He held the beer bottle close and studied the label. He told that story a lot, and telling it like that to someone who didn't care or who only pretended to care was healing to Sterrett. The indifference of the world before death, it was something worth underscoring. Death was not of permanent interest to anyone. Life was, that was what Sterrett liked to hold on to.

"My father knew. He faced it…I was always crying as a child or fighting, getting into fights, my way of trying to get attention. My father had all the attention. He was a military professional, and he deserved attention. He believed in that, bend a man to you, he always said. Get a man angry enough and you have his attention for life. He was right, 'cause I think about him all the time."

"Just maybe, my advice to you is, you shouldn't drink so much," Jacques said. He stopped Sterrett from lifting his bottle to his mouth. "You're a drunk and you drink too much."

"Let go."

"Perhaps I will," the other attorney said, leaving his hand where it was. "Perhaps I won't."

Sterrett tried moving his arm. Jacques was strong and he held him to the bar. Well, Jacques was a junior partner, and that higher status surely gave him extra strength. Sterrett kept trying, but it was no use, and he clenched the bottle of beer, afraid it would burst in his hand.

"By the way, buddy," Jacques went on. "I do not give a rat's ass about your father or the fucking story of your fucking life. No one wants to hear that shit."

"Let go, goddamn it." The associate had no idea why the junior partner had it in for him. They had been close to being friends, working in part with some of the same clients, Sir Simon for example. But it wasn't unusual to find prominent and even powerful lawyers whose bullying manner came not so much from practiced arrogance as from a natural inability to know how to behave with other people.

"Will you let go of my arm, please?" Though the blood was whistling in his ears, Sterrett tried putting his frustration politely, "I'm saying please."

Jacques ignored that. "I can tell you right now, you, you better stop bullshitting all the time. It looks bad for the firm. You're bad for the firm."

Sterrett warned the other man, "If you don't let go of me..."

"What'll you do, buddy?" the junior partner asked. He was using all his weight now to keep the associate from raising his arm, from taking a drink of his beer. His face however, began to show the strain, and with the sweat on his cheeks and his eyes popping out of his head, Jacques DeMurphy looked like a fat-assed fiend.

And Sterrett saw how simple the thing was. He used his free hand to shove at the junior partner, shove him backwards, and he shoved him right off his stool. Then with mocking serenity, Sterrett tipped the beer to his lips and drank his fill from the bottle.

"You're nothing but a faker," Jacques shouted. "Admit it."

The other Guiteau and Garfield attorneys craned round in their booth to give their complete attention to their two colleagues. Hugo got up from the booth, and he looked like he was going to butt in, but Barbara held him back. Sterrett hopped down off the bar stool and had to take a moment to gain stability across the floor.

"A faker and a drunk," Jacques taunted, grinning to see Sterrett cockle on his legs. "Look at you, Groves. I feel disgust that we work at the same law firm. Dis-gust."

Sterrett was used to being drunk and he was used to being wobbly on his feet so it was no big deal, and without further to-do, he punched Jacques, a single hard right to the stomach. Then Sterrett took his stance, and he moved forward and hit Jacques again, a fake jab with his right and then a cross to the junior partner's jaw.

Jacques DeMurphy stood rooted where he was for a tick-tock of seconds. There was silence throughout Warty's. Then the Guiteau and Garfield attorney went ker-plunk to his knees, and very suddenly, he let go a thick wad of vomit, tossing all the cookies he had in him.

Bird Mallet and Walt Gdyap hurried over from the booth; Hugo Humphrey was there too, and they helped the attorney up off the floor, more intent on checking how badly he was bloodied than in any way going after Groves. They took the junior partner over to their table where they wiped his dirty face with a napkin. But they stood by helplessly as Jacques DeMurphy went on to weep with humiliation and pain.

The bartenders had been too busy serving drinks to react to the scuffle and since it had ended quickly on its own, they let the incident go. So Sterrett Emerson Groves stood where he was, legs trembling, proud that he'd taken care of things. What he'd learned from his nation's leaders, men of success, was that it was best to strike first, pre-emptively.

Then he was out on the street. He wasn't sure how it had happened. He was looking for the men's room, perhaps he was coming from the men's room and he mistook one door for another and he was out on the street. He went up Wisconsin Avenue, stretching wide his wings, soaring across the pavement, making rusty noises, caw-caw. He flapped his arms, trying to stifle the hankering he had to throw up. Suddenly feeling caw-cawful.

"This is the boy you were talking about last week? The one you liked. Him?" Barbara asked. "Holy Shit."

"When I first met him," Dinah said. "He was kind of cool, and he had interesting things to say, you know about living here in Washington."

"Yes, he's an excellent conversationalist," Kate put in.

The girls had followed Sterrett outside. They'd had fun that evening, had met some new faces, but tomorrow was a workday for them, waitresses started early. But it was also that Dinah insisted they make sure the boy didn't have any further misadventures.

"Looks like he'll survive," Barbara said.

"Gosh, he shouldn't be left alone," Dinah answered.

Sterrett flapped his arms, went a few more steps forward, then had to lean into a big white building, the GAP store, leaning his shoulder into it as though the store and the entire street, the entire neighborhood had listed to one side. He wrapped his arms around his stomach and tried to hold on tight. He felt his stomach was spinning topsy-turvy away from him, and the tighter he tried to hold on, the faster he seemed to lose a grip of his digestion. He had to bite his lip to keep it down.

"Does he get drunk a lot?" Barbara asked Dinah.

"I don't know him that well."

Dinah was there, Dinah and two other girls. He stared at them. They were there staring at him. He waved at the people staring at him. That was why he preferred being alone. Feeling awful was better done alone, and being alone he could feel awful and yet feel good. Another person would get in the way of that. Other people got him confused. Wanting from him all the time. Sterrett knew his getting drunk was a way of not feeling anything, whether people were there or not.

But no, he hoped he wasn't that far gone. He hoped he wasn't that drunk, and to prove it, he moved on his feet, moving not agilely, not all in one motion, but like an old man, building on different joints and different muscles, so that he staggered forward, staggering like that over to the girls, and then sat down on the sidewalk. Barbara, when she stopped laughing, said to Dinah, "Let's get out of here. Want a lift?"

"We should take him home, no?"

"I'm going the other direction," Barbara said. "Wherever he lives, I ain't going there, you know?"

"I can't just leave him like that."

"Sure you can," Barbara insisted, and she turned her back on that scene and started walking down to M Street, to the garage where she'd parked her car. She confided in Kate Goodwin, "I've never seen Dinah give a shit about anyone like that. Not since I've known her."

The truth was Dinah was shocked by Sterrett's outburst, his violence in the bar. It made an impression on her. For Dinah prided herself on being able to tell what sort of person a person was. But the young associate was hard to classify. He had seemed to her an ineffectual man. He had seemed to her too docile with his good looks, with his soft eyes, eyes too blue for him to be a jerk. Yet he was a jerk. It was a conundrum. It intrigued her.

Sterrett sat with his arms round his knees. He looked woebegone, tanked unto sickness when Dinah Solatoff came up to him. She rested her hand on his back and asked him, "Are you all right?"

Sterrett leered at the girl. "I know who you are."

Then he took a metal trouser clip out of his jacket pocket. He showed the clip to the girl. "Don't have a car. I came…bicycle…twenty-one speeds…"

"Put that thing away."

"'I want to ride my bicycle, I want to ride my bike,'" Sterrett started in singing, waving his bicycle clip in the air. "'I want to ride it…'"

"Quiet." Dinah put the kibosh on Sterrett's crooning. She pulled at him. "Come with me," she said, and together they went up N Street and then took 35th Street north. The clock tower of Georgetown University rose before them, lofty as a dunce cap above the tinned rooftops. Dinah went ahead. It agitated her to have him so close. She turned around and there he was. She marched on, and could hear him, following her. It was distressing that she couldn't find a way to just leave him; she was too conscientious for her own good. She was too attracted to him.

She'd been purposefully avoiding him the last few weeks. She was okay not seeing him. Not seeing him, she found she thought of him only early in the morning that half hour half-awake when her body had that gorgeous longing in it. Otherwise, outside of that sexual context, and working, she was too busy, not seeing him, to think of him except sometimes. But when she saw him, now that she was near him, it was too much for her to deal with, without wanting to be near him and not lose sight of him again.

"Wait," Sterrett said. "Wait for me." He was trying to think the thing through how he'd ended up there. One minute he was in Warty's and now he was out on the street, walking up a long, uphill street full of trees. Across the way was the Convent of the Visitation, nuns. "I got to rest a minute." He remembered the fight, punching DeMurphy. He'd actually punched a junior partner in the face. "I was within my rights, though. Where it's a question of 'jus naturale' or the right of nature in, you know, human affairs. I won't have hands laid upon me…" He clasped his head with his own hands as though not to let any other stupid ideas escape from him.

"Come on," Dinah said, clapping her hands together. "Gee. Gee."

She shepherded him up the block to Reservoir Road, grabbed him by the tie and led him to her house on S Street. She was anxious to get the boy inside. She didn't know what she'd do with him once she got him inside. There was the possibility she would put him to bed and leave it at that.

"Please keep your voice down," she told him as she led the way up the stairs to her bedroom.

Sterrett followed her up the stairs. They went in Indian file up the stairs. He followed her in through the door into her bedroom. Suddenly his heart was going nuts. Here he was with Dinah Solatoff and now he had the means to get back at her for making him feel inadequate, by making her feel inadequate. He could make comments about her place for example, her bedroom, which in the weak light of the ceiling lamp seemed a kind of rental dump.

His idea was to make her feel sorry for having ignored him, but then he realized what was the point of that, if he was there in her room. She wasn't ignoring him at all, and yet he wasn't sure what he was doing there. He wasn't sure what he was going to do now that he was there. He thought a horrible thought, that Jacques DeMurphy had in fact been right, he shouldn't drink so much.

"I guess I should go home," Sterrett said as he sank down on her bed. "Where are we? I mean, whose room is this?" he said it, knowing perfectly well, not being utterly stupid, whose room it was.

"It's my place. Welcome."

Dinah thought, why not, why shouldn't she, she was there that night to make merry and celebrate. There was no reason, the boy in her room, why she shouldn't have some fun. She was always running away from fun. Not that no more, she decided. She needed a little sex; a little sex would tide her over until her big night out with Vincent Jorrigo.

Dinah dropped down on the bed, and Sterrett promptly hopped to his feet. "I need to walk my bladder through the system," he said. "You know what I mean?"

Dinah got to her feet too, and led him down the hallway. "It's that first door on the right. The one with the little teddy bear. Close the door when you're in there."

"Sure."

A stuffed bear hung by a length of red ribbon tacked to the door of the bathroom. The boy went in and sat down. He sat there for a while, on the john, hands between his legs. He found bitter humor in his situation; here he was all right, but he was too drunk to take advantage of it. But too, he felt guilty. Dinah had saved his ass, otherwise he'd probably be wandering around the streets still, and he might have even gotten into trouble. He owed it to her to stay. He needed to sober up a little more, just enough. At least the desire to throw up had passed, and his stomach felt okay. It was his head, still accusing some dizziness.

He flushed and got to his feet and went over to the sink. He opened the faucets full blast and let the water run, leaning over the sink to gaze into the mirror. His face, veiled by the steam from the hot water, had a surprisingly fresh look to it. He washed, dried his face on the one towel that didn't have lace sewn around it, and swung through the bathroom door and went to her room.

Dinah stood up from the bed. Without thinking about it, she put her arms around him. He felt right in her arms. She held him and they were both unsteady on their feet, and the moment, long enough to fill her with the fear that it would fade, faded and they stumbled apart.

He gave her a smile, and she blushed knowing what that smile meant to her and said, "Stop that. Take off your shoes and let's lie down. I'm dogged."

He began to remove his shirt, but his arm got tangled up and his head was stuck. Dinah helped him. He was not a self-unmade man. He had to have help to get undressed, and Dinah undid his tie for him, so that he could get his shirt over his head, and she undid the laces of his shoes and unbuckled his belt for him so that he could take off his pants. She slipped out of her clothes, too. Draped them over the rocking chair she had in a corner of the room.

She slipped into bed so nimbly that all Sterrett saw of her was the pale orbit of her bottom. She drew the covers to her. The air conditioner was on and it was chilly in the room. He nestled his head against the girl and fell sound to sleep.

When he opened his eyes again, he had an arm around the girl and he didn't think he could disentangle himself without waking her. He flopped back on his back, thinking that she was a secretary and had been easy to take to bed the first time around, and now that he was probably in love with her, he couldn't have sex with her because he kept thinking how easy she'd been the first time. Then on the other hand, how extraordinary, a miracle really after all he'd been through, he realized, that he was actually in bed with her.

But he thought the best thing would be to get out of the room as quietly as possible. He wanted to get out of the bed, get his clothes, make the living room, make the front door, out into the night. Dinah had the air conditioner going strong, and he was pretty confident he could slip away without her hearing him. He wanted to slip away; he felt it was the right thing to do, to show the girl that it wasn't only sex he was after. But the girl stirred, her feet seeking his feet underneath the covers. Sterrett kept very still.

She sighed, curled her fingers around his arm, strong fingers for a girl, and her hair spilled across his chest. He tilted his head forward and could see down the pale chub of her breast, a nipple. Sterrett vacillated, looking down, looking away. The persuasive power one wakeful nipple had, and his hand moved slowpoke under the sheets. The girl's eyes opened, and she asked, "What are you doing?"

He answered her by putting his lips against her mouth. They kissed the long kiss and then disappeared under the sheets. Resurfaced. Underclothes flew away like storm leaves. Dinah became soaked in his sweat, his smell filling her lungs, and she eased back and drove him on with the softest and most nuzzling sounds he'd ever heard. Every bone in Sterrett's body shifted with small pops of delight. Every nerve was scrubbed clean by the penetrating resins of ecstasy, and his muddled brain glowed with a stainless clarity it had not known in a long time.

Afterwards, they lay flung apart in the kicked-away sheets. Their knees touched, nothing else. They slept like that until morning.

They slept, dreaming they each belonged to the other.

They slept, resting in dawn's angle, before leaping free, one from the other.

Dinah was already half-dressed when Sterrett woke up. It was a quarter past eight, and she came in from the bathroom, her hair wrapped in a towel. She had on a pair of gym shorts and was getting ready to go work out. They didn't talk much, just a "good morning." They were awkward for a long time, and Sterrett flung himself out of bed and got busy getting into his clothes. It was Saturday, and that Saturday, with the sanitary landfill hanging over him, it was going to be a workday. Bent low, sitting on the edge of the bed, tying his shoe laces, Sterrett made a private frown, staring at the girl blow-drying her hair before the dresser mirror. He felt she was snubbing him for some reason.

"How did you sleep?" he asked her.

"What?" She turned off the dryer.

"You sleep okay?"

Dinah turned the hair dryer back on. Sterrett stood up, a solemn figure dressed for the office. "I can't talk to you while that thing is going."

"I said, I slept fine…"

"I wanted to talk about us."

Dinah held the dryer away from her. "What?"

"Listen," he said, trying not to shout. "We can go on seeing each other like this, right? Because that's what I want." He told the girl what he really wanted to tell her, his teeth clenched, his words issuing as though at dear price, "I really care about you. I really like who you are."

Dinah put down her hair dryer and came over to him in her bare feet. All she had on were her shorts and a sports bra. Sterrett looked down. Her bare toes were as small as berries.

"I like you, too." She couldn't resist in that moment humbling him a little. "But, well for me, Sterrett, no, I have to concentrate on my future."

"We have a future. Being together is a future."

"Being together isn't enough," Dinah said.

"I don't mean just being together, I mean more than that." He added impulsively, "You and me, making the most of the two of us."

Dinah laughed at that.

"Oh, well…" she said. "In that case."

And she saw, his blue eyes betrayed him; he was hurt, hurt in his pride, his argument not a winning argument. Well, she thought, he had feelings after all. She leaned up and brushed her hand along his cheek, conscious of her own desire to love. "It's nice to be with you, I like being with you, more than I thought, but it's not enough." She was negotiating for more, more from him, but for all his brilliance as an attorney Sterrett didn't seem to catch on.

"We can have good times," he said, "and then let's see what happens. That's all. But give it a chance."

"I told you back when we first met, when we first went out together, over lunch remember? I'm here to work hard, to make something of myself. First I want my own apartment, that's my number one priority, then eventually I want to buy a house. That's my plan. A house of my own." The idea of a plan was a good reason to keep her distance from love. Washington was a City of Plans, born of a plan laid out by Pierre Charles L'Enfant. A plan was a good reason. "All the rest, well, if it is not part of my plan, I have to put it on hold. I'm not interested in doing anything different from what I've planned for now. I want to stick to my plan if you don't mind."

"Who's stopping you?" Sterrett cried. "I'm just saying, why don't we give it a try?"

"Is it so difficult to understand? It's the one area a man and a woman can agree on, you know. Having property. That's what I want."

"Okay, but what I mean is…"

"What you mean is what?"

All this time, they were standing close to each other, so close they could feel the riled heat from each other's cheek. Sterrett reached out to her. He reached his arms round the girl. She let him, but then held back from a reconciling kiss.

"I avoid entanglements, normally," he said loud enough to cover his discomfiture. "But I really like being with you. I know you like being with me."

But Dinah didn't trust that sentiment, liking and being liked. Life changed what there was to like.

"What I really want…"

"I know what I want," Sterrett said.

"I'm not disputing what you want." Dinah pushed free of the boy. She wanted to feel love and to be told that she was loved. She wanted the boy to show her he was not just thinking of sex all the time, so that she could trust him to mean what he said when he talked about wanting to be with her. But she was glad the boy didn't have the courage to tell her that he loved her. It gave her an excuse, an excuse she could give to herself. Armed with that excuse, she could keep to her plan without feeling she was acting against her own heart.

Her plan meant she wanted a car, a house, a vacation home, in that order. She longed to possess, to be a proprietor. She thought of Vincent

Jorrigo, that might be her path to proprietorship. She wanted to focus her energies on that while she still had something to offer.

"I'm saying who's going to look after me if not me? Can you buy me a house? I don't think so. Tell me if you can."

"You want a fucking rich man." He couldn't help himself. He couldn't help talking to her, sneering all the way, "The American Dream, isn't it? Get what you want. Make the most. Blah, blah, blah. All that crap. Make sure you don't care a thing for the people around you. I got it. Okay. Great. Money, huh? Who would have thought that's what you're really about?"

"It's not only about money. You have to work hard, Sterrett. That's what I'm talking about. Money is the way to, to measure that, how well you work, how hard you want that success in life."

"But working for what? What's the purpose, that's what I don't get."

"Success so that people respect you, and so that you can have your own house, it's one of the things that matters the most to me."

"Your own house? That's what you're living for? I'm living to enjoy this life while I've got it."

"Maybe in time," she said earnestly. "You'll figure it out."

"I want things," Sterrett said, "to be the way I want. Or else I can do without them. I can do with you. Just fine without you."

He went down the flight of stairs, feet noisy all the way out the front door. Dinah went to her window and looked out at him through the panes, watching him march down the street. He was going away, but she'd been around the block enough not to believe everything a man said in a moment of hurt.

CHAPTER SEVEN

The days passed the way unhappy days always passed. Happy days passed quickly, but universally unhappy days went by much too slowly, unhappy weekends slower than anything imaginable. That Saturday, after working the morning in the office, Sterrett went to the gym and played pickup basketball all day. He played good, aggressive ball with an eye for his teammates, passing when he had to, sacrificing himself for the pick. He stayed on the court at Yates Gym for a long time, winning.

But he played too much for the shape he was in. He was getting too old to hold the court so long. He was thinking these were his last years playing basketball competitively. There was no way to know how getting older felt until it happened, crossing over from strength and promise to the dead end of aches and chronic pain, and what was worse, to too much knowledge about one's own limits. Sterrett realized he'd have to move on to a low-impact sport, a sport like golf.

It took him forever to get home on his bike, going uphill the back way. He passed close to where Dinah lived, going up 37th Street passing through Burleith. He was tempted to stop by her house and knock. She was far from being the only pretty brunette in town. Well he could make a goodly list of her faults, and he could omit a couple and still have a nice list to show her. Yet Sterrett would have never thought to treat her the way she'd treated him, callously and without regard.

He was a lawyer, and he had done her a favor from the start going out with her, and she'd thrown it back in his face, as though she were the one with the top ten percentile at Georgetown Law, and as though she were the one everyone envied for a close working rapport with Vincent Jorrigo, as though she were something more than just a woman who worked at a law firm. That was Dinah's problem, she was arrogant and egocentric and that came from pure, unadulterated, backwoods ignorance. Arguing it through in his head as he labored on the pedals, slipping low through the gears, he went on, well past where she lived.

Home, he had a long shower. He had a shower even though he'd showered at Yates. He had a shower and then he wandered around his apartment for a while. He flopped down on his couch and then got up and flopped down on his bed. He read part of a magazine. He got up and turned on his computer and then turned it off immediately, bored ahead of time.

He boiled water, that always soothed him. He boiled water and put two hot dogs in it, and he had hot dogs and an unheated can of beans. He ate like a hobo, sitting in his kitchen, cold beans and hot dogs. He looked at the clock over the kitchen sink. It wasn't even eight o'clock.

There was a night game on the television, the Orioles losing against Detroit. Sterrett let out many imprecations. That was the good thing about being the fan of a losing team, of a team like the Orioles that lost consistently and well, that it was a guaranteed outlet for rancorous swearing. When Digger Graves struck out for the third time, Sterrett turned off the television. He decided to go out, go to the Lucky Key and sit with his chumlings and the other duds goggling at the skinny-assed stripers. He started to get dressed. Sitting on his bed, putting on his socks, he fell back onto the pillows and he fell asleep.

Sunday was likewise never-ending. Clouds were seen in the area for the first time after two months of categorically head-splitting sunshine. Clouds seen over Washington, and people looked up and scrutinized them as though they were UFOs come from some distance to save humanity from extinction. There were children, albeit very, very young, who had never seen clouds. They tugged at adult arms, asked their parents what those large and puffy balloons were up there in the sky. They asked in the cute way children had. But for all the clouds, the promise of rain didn't come off.

Sterrett was feeling too beat up from basketball to go out Sunday. He wouldn't have gone out even if it hadn't been humid as hell. He had no real friends to go and hang with, other than his chumlings, and he didn't feel like a bar. But without a bar, without the office, he had no real destination, and in any case as the commercial said, he deserved a break. He turned the air-conditioning on high, and he lay back on his sofa in his underwear and watched television all day. For dinner he ordered from the Chinese takeout, ate steamed dumplings and fried rice. He washed it all down with three or four beers and fell asleep watching reruns.

Monday came, and then the day after was Tuesday, and then by Wednesday Sterrett Emerson Groves was feeling his oats once again. It happened that a girl came along he liked, but that their personalities clashed too much for them to get beyond a couple good times in the bedroom. He felt Dinah had been especially hard on him, but he wasn't going to be a baby about it.

Wednesday morning he was in the hallway of his apartment building. He was bent over a golf ball, dressed only in his boxer shorts. He rehearsed the motion a few times, his eyes darting up the hall. Then he took his shot. "Tok" went the ball, and it traveled down the carpet. At the last, its course altered and it came to rest, "tok-tok" among the other balls, all well behind the empty stadium cup.

Mrs. Mandelstam appeared. She stared at the balls clustered near her doorsill. She went out to the middle of the hallway. Sterrett nodded at her.

"Morning, Mrs. Mandelstam."

"You're not permitted to be playing games in the common area."

Sterrett spoke loudly enough for the woman to understand, "It's not a game. It's golf."

The old woman held her cigarette high, pinched between her fingers, the usual homemade job, misshapen and droopy; the smoke that issued from it had an acrid odor, like pipe tobacco. She said, "You should be playing this out of doors. Not inside an apartment building at eight o'clock in the morning."

"Yes, ma'am," the young attorney said, lining up another ball.

"And I hope you didn't think I am such an old woman I don't notice underclothing is all you have on. You should be in underclothes in your own apartment, not here in the common area."

"I need to blow off steam," Sterrett said.

"You're too young to need any steam," Mrs. Mandelstam scolded him brightly. She was having a good day, sharp as tacks.

"I'm going to quit my job at the firm. I want to hit the circuit, play golf for a living. Professional players earn a lot of money."

The woman eyed Sterrett doubtfully, then came tramping up the hallway. She dropped her cigarette into the pocket of the ill-fitting flannel vest she wore. Then she elbowed Sterrett out of the way, reached for the putter with a steady hand.

"May I, please?" she said.

Sterrett smiled, full of gentle tolerance for the old woman and her tetchy ways. Mrs. Mandelstam took a position alongside the ball. She was already bent over by arthritis, so she didn't have to make much of an adjustment to her stance. She swung at the ball and sent it down the hallway, sinking it cleanly into the cup, "tok-a-pok."

She stood a moment, leaning against the club. The ceiling opened to an expanse of warm blue sky, and the worn gray carpet took on the vivid freshness of a well-tended green. Then she dropped the club into the young attorney's hands. "Putt to win," she said.

Sterrett was in an easily defeated mood during that period, despite all his oats, and he could only wheeze glumly in response. Mrs. Mandelstam explained, "I learned to play in the resorts, when my husband Ossie retired. He was a fantastic golfer. We used to go to all the big resorts, to the Catskills summers where his family used to go, and in the winter, to Florida. I much preferred Florida. No family but the two of us there. Once we tried Arizona, but there were too many cowboy hot shots out there."

"You must have been pretty good."

"I was very pretty. My husband wrote me letters, how beautiful I was."

"I enjoy hearing about it. Right now, I have to get dressed."

He really did have a lot on his plate that day, and he'd gotten zero sleep, thinking about things. He was in the middle of getting the Ellipse settled, and he had nothing but garbage on his mind, and he already counted on being late to the office.

The woman stayed put as Sterrett gathered up his balls and the plastic stadium cup and took his putter and went back into his apartment to go and get ready for work. He could hear Mrs. Mandelstam roam up and down the hallway. She had with her one of the letters her husband, an insurance executive, sent her. She was reading it out loud.

Sterrett had no idea whether the letters were any good because they were in a language other than English. But the sound was pleasant.

They had been neither of them, very good-looking. Sterrett had seen photos of Mr. Mandelstam. He always stood in the same way, feet close together, his hat in his hand. He was an ordinary man as bald as Bald Mountain, but something in their lives had filled them so much that he wrote an overflow of sentiment Mrs. Mandelstam had long ago gotten by heart.

Sterrett was running late, that was undeniable. He put his clubs, his balls back in his hall closet and went into the bathroom, and had a quick shave using a disposable safety blade. He didn't have the time for a shower. All he had time for was to roll some deodorant under his arms and splash some soapy water around his loins. He stood in his bare feet before the bathroom's full-length mirror. He held himself to be essentially a reserved person, if not in some way downright shy, always less a presence than what by his father's brash standards was required.

He fidgeted under that critical eye, his father's, and the father seeing himself as inadequate as a father, dishonored by a losing battle for love, in the end blamed the son, the son inadequate as a son. The son blamed the father for not having tried to understand him better. They had never bothered to go beyond blaming each other. They confided in each other, but they never wanted to talk about the difficult things between them. In the end grief simplified things and furnished its own resolution.

Clad in his stiffest two-piece suit, still standing at the mirror, Sterrett worked his tie into its knot. It was a tie that for its sumptuously garish colors would have blinded Cerberus, Hell's howling, three-headed Doberman. He'd bought it and spent a lot for it, in a store in Friendship Heights. His father had once berated him, that what he wore to work was as much a uniform as if he were in the Army, but Sterrett had the tie to prove his father eternally wrong. He wasn't like the other lawyers; the tie told it all, and he would make partner by being unique and indispensable.

At that hour when the associate, Sterrett, was getting into the elevator, taking his time going into work, his boss, Vincent Jorrigo, had already broken into a sweat and was sweating gloriously. Not sweating from some legal problem too Gordian to disentangle, for he was dressed in white shorts and a white polo shirt. Not sweating as so many of his colleagues were that morning, from going up and down city streets, no, Vince held a racquet in his hand and he was playing tennis.

He was playing tennis on the tennis courts at Rose Park. They were clay courts shaded by tall oaks. Single-family houses, some of them old, some of them brand new, faced the high hurricane fence that surrounded the courts. Beyond the courts was a softball field and at the corner, a church of merlot-red stone. It was Georgetown and the whole was a well-heeled, relaxed atmosphere, immersed in the freshly unwrapped tranquility of early morning, a scene as secluded as was possible in a public area of a big city.

Tranquil, it was a tranquil scene but for the loud, intermittent arguing on the near court where Vince Jorrigo was playing against Ellen Berman, the banker. They got up a game against each other every time it occurred to them it was a while they hadn't played together. When they played, which was about once a month, they played only one match, all they could take of each other. For they were fairly matched in skill and argued almost as much as they played, fairly matched for stark stubbornness. They enjoyed the arguing however, always a pre-amble to doing business together.

Ellen Berman was a tall woman, tall and physically intimidating, that was the first thing most men noticed about her, that and her long golden locks that would have made a medieval Swede envious. What she had that the careful man noticed first about her, what she had that was truly formidable, was an abundance of hard knowledge about human behavior. It was there in her eyes, that cynical and mesmerizing gleam flashing from beneath tawny lashes. Ellen Berman had gained that knowledge distributing more to those who asked for more. She had developed a sense of style in the way she handled all the more her bank had, a style some called regal and some called roughshod. The fact that she was only thirty-five years old, younger by far than most of the national corporate leaders who came to borrow money from her bank was to many men the most frightening thing about her.

The Consolidated Bank of Rockville was the biggest bank in terms of deposits in the state of Maryland, and Ellen Berman was the president of the Consolidated and one of the most influential women in the Washington-Baltimore metropolitan area. A Democrat, she'd given money to the sitting president's first presidential campaign, a sufficient amount to merit being appointed U.S. ambassador to Liechtenstein for two years, a job she held without difficulty while at the same time working as hard as possible to the profit of her ever-expanding bank.

Ellen was also a top-seeded amateur when it came to almost any racquet sport. She'd won local championships in squash and badminton, racquetball, too, but it was at tennis that Ellen had made her name, having won several USTA National Pro-Am tournaments. She loved tennis more than any other pastime, and every year she spent a fortune to attend Wimbledon with select members of her family.

Ellen, like Vince, was wearing white that morning, a white skirt and a white sleeveless blouse, and she swung one of her tennis collectibles, a small, oval laminate racquet strung with yellowing catgut. Tad Davis, it said. The racquet's handle was dark and dirty with age.

Vince was no unhandy athlete either. He'd served on the varsity tennis team at East Providence and had won his own goodly share of trophies in his youth. But he didn't play for the pleasure of playing the sport anymore. He played in pain most of the time, had been playing with a bad back for years. It was that he liked the narrowly focused and almost pointless struggle there on the court, that was why he still played tennis. It was something not completely in his control that brought him close, almost as close as poker, to the divine in human affairs, to chance.

The two were into their second set. Vince had won the first. It was hot on the court despite the early hour. The players were slow on their feet, but they showed no inclination to yield, neither one nor the other. It was Vince serving. He plied an expensive carbon-composite racquet that had been purchased already broken-in by former tennis great Pete Sampras. He was stooped forward, two balls in his fist, ready to put down his opponent. Ellen on the other side of the net assumed a pose, brandishing her racquet like Artemis her huntress's spear.

Vince began the slow arcing of his body, and snap, he served the ball.

"Out," Ellen Berman cried.

"All things are possible. Except that that ball was out," the lawyer said.

"That ball was out. Trust me."

Vince frowned but he didn't say a word. He readied his second ball to serve, bouncing it off the clay. He bounced it once, twice, then clutched the ball, leaned back, his features compressed, his kinky hair shooting out as he rose up, like the rays of Apollo's crown.

Then his cellular went off, ersatz Isaac Hayes filling the air. The attorney broke his stance at the baseline. "Ellen, two seconds. Two."

Vince went over to his equipment bag, and with his racquet tucked under his arm, tossed through the bag. Towels and sweatbands were flung to the ground. Finally he found the clangorous cellphone. He looked at the number then at a smoldering Ellen Berman. He assured her, "It's an important call."

Up and down the court he went, walking with abrupt halts as though before depths only he could see. He was talking to a dentist, Dr. Clarence Dunne. The dentist was known by the nickname Curveball. The nickname was a way to keep his real name from getting bandied about too much. It was a sign of belonging as well, of being part of a special community of poker players. Some players swore by nicknames and aliases, others like Vince, felt their first name was enough.

Curveball was trying to round up players for a poker game to be played in the next few days, and also to spread the news that Frank Mavis, a professional gambler affectionately known as Half Price, was coming to town at last. Some years he bypassed Washington on his way north, but this year he'd be in town a full week. He was coming up from Nashville, bringing his nephews, his pretty niece with him. He'd hit D.C. in about three weeks, so it was best to get ready. He was going to be hosting a big game in his Road Quest motorhome.

"The Bitch then?" Vince asked, impatiently. "The Bitch?"

"That's it. You'll need to put together $30,000 to sit at that game, Vince," Curveball said over the phone. "$30,000 for the Bitch."

"Not a problem," Vince answered. "You let me know the details?"

"I'm working on it," Curveball replied.

Everyone had a way to get beyond their daily limitations. Curveball for all his cruel, depraved hand with the drill, for all his sloppy use of novocaine when it came to his patients, was as sweet and reliable, as fussy and conscientious when it came to cards as if he were Hoyle's most devoted handmaid. He knew the who's who of the city's top card players, knew who to put at a table with whom. He was the man with the connections, and he could always be relied on one hundred percent to find, to organize the best high stakes games in town. He did most of the players' bridgework too, for a discount.

"And what were you saying, this other game? Saturday night?" Vince raised his head to see Ellen Berman with her ears burning. He turned his back, walked all the way down to the bottom of the tennis court and said, "Ah, no, not Saturday? I get you. So Monday for sure. But why not Saturday?"

"Do you want me to confirm?" Curveball said. "Mark you down a place?"

"Yes, yes. As long as they're…are they people I know?"

"It's being put together by a pop singer."

"A singer?"

"Sure, but I can tell you, I'll be there and it's going to be some of the guys you know. It's Monday because Monday the singer doesn't sing."

"I'll be there. Trust me. I'll be there. Thanks." Vince stood a moment gnawing on the phone. He was relieved. Though he felt sorry for her, sorry to disappoint her, Vince was relieved that he had a perfectly good reason to unload Dinah, the secretary from Mergers and Acquisitions. Inviting her out had been an impulsive move; he'd seen her over at the Guiteau Building and had asked who she was and had thought to take her out to the artsy-fartsy gala. But then Celia made a scene when she heard he was taking a young secretary to the Dubuffet thing. It was a jealous scene that clarified an otherwise uncertain situation.

"I haven't got all day," Ellen Berman was saying. "Let's go."

"Two minutes." Vince repeated, "Two minutes more." He showed the banker two fingers.

He held his phone in his palm and tapped out a call to the office. He asked for Groves and got Groves's secretary. Groves's secretary told him, with apologies and imprecise excuses, that Sterrett Emerson Groves was not at his desk yet. Vincent Jorrigo left a message, expressing at the same time the hope that Groves would eventually overcome any impediment he was facing and arrive in one piece behind his desk. Then Vince tossed the cellphone back into his equipment bag and resumed his place at the baseline.

Ellen Berman held her racquet, moving rhythmically, moving side to side. She nodded, was ready, and Vince came to the line and nailed the ball hard enough that it touched up a cloud of dust well inside the service box. The banker didn't budge. She said Stentor-like, "Out."

"That ball was in," the attorney shouted.

"Out."

Vince brushed aside a wayward lock of his hair and wiped the back of his neck, nervous movements to better compose himself. He didn't want to insist in contradicting the banker. It was never good to contradict a banker. So he let the thing go, but he knew as well as he knew anything that he knew in the entire earthly world that his serve had been in. Both balls had been in.

He moved over to the far side of the baseline and served a ball he knew Ellen could return, and they played on like that. Vince played, no longer quite as concentrated on the tennis ball. He was thinking about cards, thinking this was the year he was going to win a big enough pot so that he could stop playing poker, win enough so that he could ease up working, too.

He wanted to ease up working, not because of the work itself, but because he was growing increasingly tired of the people he had to work with. He was tired of being nice to clients. If he could work as a lawyer and do it without having to be nice all the time, he would have, but he couldn't. So the only alternative was to take a vacation. He thought of that year as the year he would win enough to take the *Arabella* and go for a sail somewhere, leave the firm to its own devices for a couple weeks.

While Vince was daydreaming of his big poker win, lobbing the furred yellow ball at the banker, his associate, Sterrett, was up on the seat of his bicycle, his soft-sided briefcase strapped to the aluminum rack. It was a perfect day for it, a ride into work. He held up at the intersection of Whitehaven Street and Wisconsin Avenue, perched forward on his Wind Wrangler watching the flow of traffic the way a man might watch the riding sea. Then he got up and churned the pedals going downhill through Georgetown, cutting round the back streets, wheeling in and out of traffic.

He felt intensely free on his bike, all his natural disdain for ordinary mortals awake in him as he pelted through the crosswalks along the avenue, scorning the lights. Flabbergasted pedestrians, in harm's way, were sent scrambling for the curb. Sterrett grinned broadly. Many a middle finger was sent flying his way, many the Anglo-Saxon curse curdled his ear as he passed. He could handle that; he knew not to overreact. More, he enjoyed the curses.

He liked pissing people off. Having to behave with so much probity and propriety within the confines of the practice of the law, it was an extreme pleasure to be able to be rude on the streets. A superior person, an attorney bound so rigorously by rules should be able to be a little rude from time to time, Sterrett thought. But once he hit M Street and crossed the creek, there was only smooth riding, and the young attorney sailed like a little angel into the Guiteau Building's garage. He chained his bike to the looped rack.

Hector, the valet, came up from the lower level of the garage. His short-sleeved shirt hung loose outside his belt. He came over and shook his head at the associate. He said, "You don't have the money for a car, brother?"

"It's a Wind Wrangler Crit. It's got a carbon fiber frame," Sterrett said. "With titanium dropouts."

"It's a coat hanger," the valet said. "Man, I could hang my coat on it."

They went up to the sidewalk together. Sterrett thought to ask, "Where you from?"

"I'm from Nicaragua."

"How long you been in the U.S.?"

"Five years. I been here five years."

"You speak pretty good English. Are you married?"

"Yes, a girl from my town," Hector said.

"That's nice. Hispanic girls are nice, aren't they?"

"Like all women." Hector slapped at the air.

"Okay," Sterrett said.

"Don't worry. Your coat hanger will be here, brother."

Sterrett was late getting into the office, not so late that anyone would notice, but late enough that he had to skip eggs and bacon at Lemke's and he had to skip getting coffee, too. The elevator wasn't crowded, a few people from the public relations firm on the third floor, one or two lawyers from the lobby group on the top floor of the building, no one from his firm. The elevator smelled faintly of armpits, his armpits.

He got off at his floor and went with his big feet plodding down the hall. He could see the top of his secretary's head. He aimed for that.

"Can you get me a cup of coffee from the kitchen, Suzy, and something substantial to eat?"

"There might be one donut left." Suzy nodded at Neon Flores. "Maybe I kept one for you. Maybe I'll bring it in with your coffee."

Sterrett plunged a hand into his pants pocket and then brought out a penny. He looked at it in case it was a collectible penny, then dropped it into the slot in the home-run hitter's slotted head. Then he started for the door of his office.

"I also got a message for you." Suzy held out a slip of paper. She held it high over her head. She waved it back and forth. "It's from Mr. Jorrigo. He wants to see you."

"What? Now? I just got in."

"You just got in and boy, I had to talk fast why you weren't here."

"My bike had a flat." He shrugged. "At the Outhouse?"

"Not the Outhouse. The tennis courts over at Rose Park," Suzy said. "He's playing tennis. Your serve, my serve, that kind of thing."

"Tennis?" Sterrett shook his head. "Well, if he's playing tennis he can wait for me to get there. Get me some coffee too, Suzy. I need five, ten minutes for myself."

He let himself down in the snug chair at his desk. Patted his desk, his one true friend. Drummed his fingers on its surface, a beat that kept him from thinking for a full minute. Then he picked up the phone and called the office of the City Council member for the Southwest Ward, Curtis Bayard. After a brief wait, the councilman's secretary put him through.

Sterrett had to fix a date for the Neighborhood Advisory Committee hearing on the sanitary landfill and he wanted to know when was best for Bayard. They talked about sometime the next month, after the District Council had voted on whether to approve the landfill or not. Since the site was on federal land, the council had no real say in the matter, but as Bayard explained somewhat apologetically, there was the District's perception of its own sovereignty at stake.

Sterrett was sympathetic, or at least made himself sound sympathetic, to the complaints about D.C.'s lack of self-determination. In truth he didn't care less whether the District had statehood or not, and if anything thought it just as well not to have to pay to send a congressman and two senators to the Hill. But Sterrett reassured the councilman that the landfill would have nothing but a positive impact on the District and would in no way compromise the city's ability to deal with waste in its own sovereign way. They rang off with a tentative hearing date for the middle of the second week in July.

In the meantime, Suzy had brought in coffee and a powdered, jelly-filled donut, Sterrett's favorite. He thanked her with a smile, an unusually tender smile as though he were truly, honestly, deeply grateful. So few people were nice to him, he was grateful when Suzy was.

Rose Park was on the other side of the bridge into Georgetown, a five-minute walk from the Guiteau Building. He didn't mind the walk. What irritated him was the fact Vince couldn't simply call him and tell him what he wanted on the phone. He wanted Sterrett to be there, had a need to tell him whatever it was in person. It was an imposition. It was certainly going to be some trifling detail involving the sanitary landfill.

Sterrett crossed the Rock Creek bridge, peering over the low stone wall into the creek. It was fairly clear water going over the rocks, and the sand had a golden hue. Sterrett could see among the sumac bushes and tall tangle of ailanthus where some vagrant had built himself a shelter out of old crates. There were the cars rushing along the parkway below, and joggers went by on the paved path, three women, ponytails bobbing behind them.

At the Georgetown end of the bridge stood a row of freshly planted trees, saplings with pale green leaves. Farther on, there were some gingkoes shading an area of grass along the high bank of Rock Creek. A brick walkway led through the trees and wound its way to the tennis courts of Rose Park. Sitting on a piece of cardboard at the entrance to the park was a woman with a shopping cart. A big hand-written sign was fixed to the cart, "My teenage son the Victim of illegal wiretap by FBI. My house taken away by lying Courts."

"Got a smoke?" the woman asked looking up at Sterrett.

"Don't smoke," the young attorney replied. The woman told him to go screw himself. It struck him she was hostile because she had no other response to offer. She could say all sorts of shit and no one minded because vagrants were different, a different culture.

People who hadn't the self-respect, that was the way they lived and how they ended up beggars. They deserved it, hunger and poverty and all. Of course, that's how he'd end up if he continued like he was doing, drinking so much. It was secretaries. Their fault, dating them. He worried how much would be left of him if he continued giving so much of himself to every lonely secretary around. That was what was ruining him and skinning him down to nothing.

He saw the high green fence and the tennis courts, two courts side by side. The far court was empty, on the near court, two people, a man and a woman were battling it out over a net.

"Mr. Jorrigo." The associate waved.

"Wait. Will you?"

"Okay. Sorry." Sterrett let out a force of breath. Ellen Berman, that was the woman Vince was playing against, the banker Sterrett had bumped into a little more than a week ago. It wasn't a crisis, no, but the young attorney moved off, keeping to the sidewalk, to the shade of the trees, a little distance from the courts. He was thankful now he hadn't given Berman his card, a smart move. Now if they were introduced he could pretend not to know her. Smart, that was how to do things.

"Play the tiebreaker?" Ellen asked. She came over to where Vince was standing at his equipment bag, towel in hand, patting his cheeks. "Double or nothing?" She glanced through the hurricane fence at the young man waiting among the enshrouding shadows. Squinted at him, even as the boy turned her back to her. "What do you say?"

Vincent agreed, but said, "I can't take a whole morning off, Ellen." He paused. "Give me two minutes." He pointed at his law associate. "I have to talk to Groves there."

"Groves?" Ellen asked. "Is he a lawyer?"

"Yes, Sterrett Emerson Groves. He's my number one son, so to speak."

Vince bent down and fetched his half-empty bottle of Pepto-Bismol from his bag. He took a swig. Wiped his filmy lips dry. He pushed through the gate. When he signaled to him, the associate came up the sidewalk to meet him.

"I've been talking to Councilman Bayard, you know to set up that hearing with the neighborhood," Sterrett declared, wanting right away to show the senior partner how busy he was. "Sometime in early July is when he wants to do it. After the City Council..."

"That's fine, Groves. Not what I want to talk to you about," Vince said. "I've been impressed by your work so far." He used the towel draped around his neck to pat the damp under his chin.

"We work well together, I think," Sterrett pursued.

Vince studied the young attorney with critical attention. Groves had a good-natured face that too, because of the big nose seemed child-like and was therefore a trustworthy face. Not a leader, not a pathfinder, but a man willing, he could see Groves was a smart man willing to be of use, not one of these modern grasping, avid types, too slippery to rely on. He was not mean-spirited or callous. A follower, good, perfectly loyal, and an honest young man, stubbornly wanting to be of service.

"Didn't call you over here to talk about trash," Vince said. "So don't let's go into that now. I frankly have had enough of Sir Simon."

Sterrett made eye contact and then gave a glance over at Ellen Berman. The Consolidated banker was standing close to the fence, massaging her wrist. She looked doughy, sticky and doughy, like big people looked when they were tired. Sterrett said to his boss in a low voice, "I don't think you should say that, sir. All things considered, he's one of our best clients ever."

"Look Groves, I know you're Sir Simon's pet, but I think I do know how to handle my clients. And I don't want to talk about the..."

Sterrett shook his head. He didn't think of himself as Sir Simon's favorite, his pet, though it was true the Greek Dustman did call him practically every day, confided in him, too. "Okay." He decided to do a little flattery, see if that put the senior partner in a better mood. "I was watching you, sir, and I think you can beat her, but it's better if you go ahead and let her win. That's what she wants. Not just to win, but for you to let her win." Sterrett didn't quite know and if asked couldn't say how he arrived at this perception. He saw it, that was all. "Women are like that. They want to be right whatever it costs."

Vince Jorrigo brooded over that an instant, impressed by Groves, impressed and relieved to have found someone so young who thought in the same embittered and calculating way he did. It was certainly what he was already doing, letting Ellen win. She was one of the few clients, her bank was, who paid all fees and billings on time and in full. But it was tough going. He didn't like to let anyone win, especially if there was money at stake. He felt in an odd way reassured by what Groves had to say, reassured he was doing what had to be done.

"Well, maybe you're right, Groves," Vince said. "Now I wanted to talk to you about something else. Something that has just now come up."

Sterrett nodded, looked over at some trees, looked back at the senior partner and said, "Uh-huh." The senior partner's tone was an ominous one, and the associate had a thing or two where he knew he'd screwed up.

"First, Jacques DeMurphy is leaving the firm. He takes with him some important contacts. He told me he's leaving the firm because of you."

Sterrett nodded.

"He was a good lawyer."

"Sir, I believe that every individual has that inalienable right which is not only guaranteed by our Constitution, but is part of the very fiber of this nation, and which is inherent in the definition of freedom itself, to react if another lays hands on you or in any way interferes..."

"What Groves? What is that you're saying?" Vince clasped tightly both ends of the towel that hung round his neck. His voice became shrill, "I can't imagine how you thought it was a good idea to beat up another attorney in a bar, especially an attorney, a junior partner you work with, but that's your business. My business is to run a law firm. A law firm depends on its reputation. I can't have my lawyers notorious as barroom brawlers. You're a loose cannon, now, what do you think I'm going to do?"

"That's an unfair question, sir. It wasn't my fault."

"I'm not a judge. But I do pass sentence."

Sterrett's body blistered with the strain, and he began to sweat, sweat soaking out his armpits, sweat stinking up through his shirt, through his jacket. But though the associate was suddenly governed by a furious desire to strike out at the world, he didn't react other than sweating. He stood there, ready to take it, nobly, like a good soldier in need of a good deodorant.

118

It was just that he had never been fired before, and he didn't think he deserved to be fired now. If he got into fights outside of work, on his own time, that was one hundred percent his own business. He didn't understand how it mattered otherwise. He kept his smarts however. He spoke calmly, knowing the calm man was always in the right, and he said, "The work I do is the only thing I should be called to account for." Then he added with enormous dignity, "I know the work I do is good work. You told me so yourself, sir."

Vince took a step backwards. "We all work hard at Guiteau and Garfield."

"If you'll excuse me saying so, sir, Jacques DeMurphy is not the kind of lawyer who can put a deal together. Anyway, I won't accept being fired. I won't. Not for this. I worked too hard on this Ellipse thing."

"But listen now," Vince said, raising his voice. "Listen, instead of letting that temper of yours get the better of you, Groves. Listen, I hate quitters. It's a category I can't stand. If Mr. DeMurphy wants to quit, fine. Am I all stomach and no guts?"

"No, sir."

"In conclusion, I'm not going to fire you."

The young attorney couldn't help it; relaxing, he let out a burp, an ugly little gassy burp of relief. "Oh, I didn't think you would, sir," Sterrett said, eyes fluttering. "I mean I'm glad you didn't." He put his fist to his lips to prevent any further burping. "Excuse me," he said.

"But you have to promise me. Stop this fighting of yours. It's not the first time." Vince bobbed his head reprovingly. "You understand? It's reputation that matters. I care about you, about your career. I want to see you make it. All right?"

"Yes, sir."

"Now the other thing," Vince said. Ellen Berman was stomping around with her racquet, waving it with uttermost irritation. "I'm coming, Ellen," Vince yelled at the banker.

"And I'm waiting," she yelled back.

"The other thing is a favor I'm going to ask you. Dinah Solatoff. Do you know her? She works in Mergers and Acquisitions. From out West, I think. Mrs. Johnson hired her."

"Dinah, the girl who works for Mr. Klocker?"

"Somehow, I don't know, I ended up inviting her to this social event at the National Gallery. She's quite pretty, I guess that was why."

"Nothing wrong with that, sir," Sterrett said, cringing at the thought, he and Jorrigo dating the same girl. Thank goodness he'd gotten out of that fast.

"Whatever the reason, as it turns out, I have another commitment that same evening. Something I can't say no to. So listen, will you do that for me? It's for the unveiling of a newly purchased work of art, very important event, all the best people will be there. At the National Gallery, this next Monday."

"Do what?"

"Kim will bring you the invitation. Will you take over for me? Make sure Dinah has a good time? She's a secretary but she's okay, if you know what I mean."

A swell of biting insects passed over them and tumbled away. Sterrett swatted at the back of his neck. "No, sir," he said flat out. "I'd rather be fired."

"That's strong words."

"She's not my type, that's all," Sterrett said, adding, "Where I go and with whom, after work, well, I think that's all my personal business."

"I'm not asking you to put a ring on her finger, Groves."

"But you invited her, sir."

Vince started back towards the courts. "Listen," he snapped, "There's more to being a good lawyer than good arguments."

"If I want to make the most of myself?" Sterrett commented bitterly.

The senior partner reached the gate in the high fence and passed onto the tennis court. "I'm not asking a big sacrifice from you." He shouted after his associate, "You owe me this favor. You know it."

Sterrett, feeling imposed upon, didn't go right back to the office. He stayed in Georgetown, found an empty stool at Warty's. He had just ordered a second beer about the same time that the last game between Vince and Ellen ran up to 40–30, and Ellen put a nice spin on a return across the net, and the ball dropped short before Vince could get to it.

"It wasn't my day today," the latter was explaining as he pulled his white cotton shorts high up his waist. He said it with sarcasm, too. "I seemed not to be able to get my serve right."

"A bet's a bet," Ellen said.

"I didn't forget, Ellen." He padded down the acre of clay to his equipment bag. "I didn't forget."

"Just saying."

They bet $200 on the match. Ellen wanted to go for $300, but Vince wanted to discipline himself. They often bet money when they played, small amounts, never more than a couple or three hundred dollars. Vince disliked losing small amounts of money however because it was the small amounts that seemed most real to him. But more than a question of money, he would have liked very much, very much to have won that morning for the sake of breaking his general and ongoing losing streak.

"You cheated too damn much today," Vince said.

"Cheaters are losers, we used to say when I was a kid," Ellen Berman told the attorney. "I won, and ergo, I am not a cheater."

"Ah, a banker's logic."

But Vince thought about it while he was putting away his racquet; his law associate Groves was a genuinely perceptive young man. He granted him that. The banker didn't merely want to win, she wanted the lawyer to let her win. It was like a courtship, where the stronger party showed he could be defeated by the weaker. Vince had to show he was willing to be defeated.

He modulated his derisive tone. "Look, Ellen, I played badly, that's the truth of it," he said. "You...no, you played an excellent game. Today you were in excellent form. This town needs more players like you."

"Why thank you, Vincent. That's very nice of you to say."

They collected their things, leaving as they always did a couple balls on the court, a tip for the gods of play. Like all successful people, they were both superstitious.

They went down the block, dancing on sore feet to the banker's car, which was parked along 27th Street near a sign that said "No Parking Anytime." On the metal sign there was the ideogram of a tow truck. But the banker's car was still there after four hours and there was no ticket under the wiper, no boot on its wheel. Berman's personalized tag read, "Bank Shot 2" and was well known to District officials.

Vince Jorrigo took some trouble getting into his seat. Once he got strapped in, Ellen Berman repeated what she'd said before, this time with her hand out, "A bet is a bet."

Jorrigo made a show of removing his wallet from the pocket of his tennis shorts. "You know, Ellen, I can't forget the days when even a hundred seemed to me to be all the world, and then some. Having that much to spend, I mean."

"Do you have the money?"

"I don't have it," he said plainly. He put a finger into the inner fold of his wallet where there was only a ten and a one dollar bill. "I don't have $200 on me. Can I owe you?" He let the woman see his discomfort. He let her see the desert, the grievous desert that was his wallet. "I don't have it."

"Pay me later. When you have it."

They were friends so it was natural for them to have nothing else to say to one another as they drove along, heading for lunch at the River Club. The air from the interior vents stirred the hairs along Vince's bare legs. Ellen felt contented, knowing that the lawyer knew she'd won cheating and had given in so easily, and without much fuss, to that reality, that she could win cheating if she wanted. To make it right, however, she said, after weighing her words, "Vince, you played well, too. It was the bounce of the ball. Nothing to blame yourself about."

"Yeah, I gave it my best try anyway." He then took the opportunity to say, "Now, Ellen, let's talk about that loan to Sir Simon…"

"It's important to you?"

"If it comes through now, now as in this week, Ellen, it will convince the congressional subcommittee that's up there right now weighing the merits of the landfill that the landfill is workable."

The result was that the Consolidated Bank of Rockville announced some days later that it intended to finance the lease and development of the sanitary landfill at the Ellipse to the tune of $120 million and was ready to advance Sir Simon Psora a personal line of credit for $9,000,000. So that now all that was needed to achieve the dream of a model rubbish heap at the Ellipse was a signed lease for the site from the Bureau of Land Management. Vince Jorrigo was pleased with himself despite losing the match. It was the client who was important, and the client could have no reason to complain. Though it wasn't his game, he knew that in Washington, tennis was as good a way to get things done as any meeting.

CHAPTER EIGHT

The girl stepped clear of the door as he came up S Street. She'd been waiting for him, supposing him the type to be on time. He told her six thirty, and she was perfumed and prompt at her doorstep. She supposed too, that he'd pick her up as any normal boy would, in a car. She had hoped for a nice car, a big car, but even a compact would have been better.

"Funny," she muttered, as he peddled into sight. "Very funny."

Advancing a couple steps up the walkway, Dinah tried hard to keep herself in check. She'd made a great effort to be ready on all levels for that evening, overcoming a more than understandable bitterness. Watch out if a woman complained. She'd complained when Vince told her he wasn't going to take her to the gala event at the National Gallery and protested even louder when he told her his stand-in was Sterrett Emerson Groves. Vince remonstrated with her for being ungrateful. Chewed her head off.

She couldn't explain to the senior partner that Sterrett Emerson Groves was the very last person she wanted to go to the gala with. She couldn't draw a picture for him, but Sterrett was the one person that put all her plans at risk. He was anathema. She had vowed, and was damned and determined not to let herself get involved with him in any way, anymore, anywhere, and here he was being thrust upon her.

"Very funny," she cried watching Sterrett coast up to her. "I bet you're drunk too."

"You try pedaling in a tuxedo."

"It's the very last thing I would want to do," Dinah said. She smoothed a hand along her thigh as though to iron away this added humiliation.

"It's a joke." Sterrett got off the bike. He rested it on its side on the front lawn. "It's not mine. I stole it. A rusty old girl's bike." He took a stance, legs apart, head to one side. He found Dinah as far-out stunning and desirable as any goddess, any goddess in any man's pantheon of gorgeous, celebrated goddesses. "It's from the garage at my condo. It doesn't belong to anyone."

"Neither do I," she said, returning his look.

Her preparations for that evening had been enormous. She fitted, only just, into her perfectly close-fitting dress, a silver satin dress that was worth as much as all her other clothes put together. Faux diamond earrings hung in a cascade from her ears; a cross studded with faux diamonds lay starry at her breast. Her hair had taken painstaking hours at a shop, swept up in a real 'do on her head, held in place by two sterling silver hairpins, heirlooms from Russia her grandmother had left her. She was going to make that low-down heel Vincent Jorrigo sorry, and she was going to make Sterrett Emerson Groves sorry too, show them both that a woman did have control over events no matter what men did to the contrary.

To start with she was going to go for the boy. "What an idiot you are," she said to him. "A bike? You show up on a bike?" She wanted to put her hands in her hair, but didn't dare touch a single strand. Instead she stomped her foot. "What a damn moron. A drunk, my date's an idiot and a drunk."

"Hold on, I'm not drunk," Sterrett said. "I meant it as a joke. I'm just joking."

"I can't believe it." Dinah had her cellphone out, trying to figure out what number to call for a taxi. "I can't believe it. The one thing I wanted from you, and you show up like this. Everything is a joke to you. How romantic."

"Come on, Dinah. You really think I'm going to take you to this gala on a dinky bicycle? I don't even have helmets. I called a limo, it'll be here any minute." He repeated it, "I called a limo."

He was flustered. He thought she'd find it funny his arriving on a bike. He had not expected her to be the way she was, taking everything he did so seriously.

When the limousine arrived, they got in on different sides, sat in the back not touching. The chauffeur's eyes, from time to time, rose to the rearview mirror to get a curious look at nothing happening. The two nicely dressed young people didn't argue. They sat quietly, each trying to outdo the other in the degree of fake smiles they dished out. The ride was unendurable.

Sterrett wanted to tell Dinah how beautiful she looked, that was all that mattered to him. He realized he should have told her that first off. But he resisted telling her, for the girl seemed in total possession of the moment, sitting there in her glittering dress, her legs crossed, mouth shut in the backseat of that cool ride.

But truth was, Dinah was balanced on a tear. She passed a glance at Sterrett, a handsome but hopelessly inconclusive boy. The evening that seemed to promise so much was already edging to disappointment.

It was a gentle night for Washington, with a nice breeze and a plugged-in sky, and the beautiful people swept up the shallow steps from the courtyard into the National Gallery's East Building, a modern building set down among some trees. Culture was curiosity, and the curious were most of them from Washington's professional class: lawyers, doctors, university lecturers, and so on. But there were many people there who simply had money, more money than curiosity. There were car salesmen, real estate developers, and there were restaurant owners and fund managers. There were politicians. They were members of the Caste and they came to the gala not quite knowing why, trusting that they would seem curious enough to be considered cultured.

Sterrett was at the curb in front of the building. He let Dinah get out of the car on her own, and he paid off the chauffeur, telling the black-capped driver in a loud voice not to wait. Dinah, in turn, ignored the boy totally. In her eagerness to enter the hall and rub elbows with society, she spanned the stone treads up to the National Gallery's main hall two at a time. She swung round only once for a last super-sham smile in his direction.

The young attorney tilted his head to one side and watched her go up those steps. The movement of her body, thighs that had once been his, that sultry rhythm once part of his touch, he kept his eyes glued on her. Her legs and full bottom moved him. Well, he shook that off, and then hit the steps himself, and came into the hall, into the airy central hall of the National Gallery's East Building.

He looked around him, seeing as many notable and virtuous faces as he ever wanted to see. Platinum Record rapper/musician T-Red had come with his girlfriend, Sandra Hoop, and since many of the gala guests were fans of the TV news show *Sandy Hoop is Here* there was a noticeable hubbub around the couple.

Republican Senator Roger Simmers of Texas, a possible candidate for president, had noisily forced his way in. He quickly got lost in the crowd. Poet Leonard Between Dogs, also uninvited on account of a presumed offense to the National Gallery's director, was there with his muse, Washington heiress Booboo McLean. A Cheyenne of the Tongue River Reservation, Leonard Between Dogs was clearly recognizable for his shock of black hair, which he rarely combed in any way.

He had recently come out with a new book of verse, *The Wind River Shore*. Critically acclaimed for his first book, *To My Brother Plenty Horses and Other Poems*, he went on to real resounding, national fame with his verse play *The Trail of Broken Contracts*. He had earned a Golden Globe for the screenplay of *The Trail* as performed on PBS. Fame had had a contrary effect on him. He enjoyed himself less and less and complained about living in Washington and talked more and more about returning to his people in Montana. A man presumed by many to be the most exasperating celebrity in town, he showed up with Booboo to make fun of the event wearing a T-shirt, Bermuda shorts, and flip-flops.

Sterrett made for the buffet table. The Dubuffet Buffet Gala was a business opportunity after all, a chance to talk away from the office and the conference room, a formal way to be informal. The buffet tables were at the hub of this relaxed but shrewd sociality.

There were all sorts of goodies up for grabs on the tables, from pigs in a blanket to caviar, drinks too, a stadium-sized punch bowl full of sangria surrounded by flutes of champagne. The name of the champagne was Springfest, a domestic brand from the hillsides of northern Virginia. It had a sweet taste like the night, rich with effervescence. Sterrett lingered there, moving along the table, noshing, and listening, too.

Two men, elders of the Caste, loitered backs to the buffet table. They were waiting for their wives, who were busy talking to Sandra

Hoop, trying to get tickets to her television show. One man was the chief operating officer of a major international bank and the other was a prominent energy executive. The energy executive said, "No, Patrick, I think you're wrong about that."

"I'm not wrong, Barry. This guy Dubuffet is French and he's surely a Marxist Communist. And we're promoting him financially?"

"Not to worry, the man's dead and buried."

The Dubuffet sculpture recently acquired by the gallery had a small, windowless exhibition room all to itself. People came into the spot-lighted room from the buffet table, savory tidbits held to their lips, and the wall-to-wall carpet of the small exhibition room was covered with crumbs. The crumbs formed a circular pattern at two feet distance around the sculpture.

Hommes En Fracs was a black and white painted-resin sculpture about nine feet long and five feet high, a masterpiece of Dubuffet's late period. The title was arbitrary; there was nothing representational about the work. It was harsh in aspect but had a certain playfulness too, and unlike much contemporary sculpture, it showed a meticulous craftsmanship in execution. It had been acquired from a private collector in Lausanne, in Switzerland.

The chief patron of the event was the Consolidated Bank of Rockville through its chairman, Ellen Berman. She appeared at the gala in a stately, trailing evening gown, her neck a-drip with pearls. She looked slightly ridiculous, a bit too matronly for how young she was. But her good cheer won her through as she stopped to talk to everyone, everyone without exception. She shook hands with men of business and with politicians and bussed the air around their wives' cheeks. There was an allure about her, the same fascination that an elated and unpredictable animal, a rhino for instance, might generate.

But she was not so heavy-handed and pushy as she seemed. Art was her way of showing she had a liberal, an enlightened side to her. The gala served her both to sweeten her image and also as an inroad to an otherwise exclusive social circle. For now Ellen Berman was positioning herself to move in on Washington. That was what the city was made for, for people to move in on it, and Berman was going to be the one.

She was in the exhibition room, peering intently at *Hommes En Fracs*. It seemed to her the title was meant ironically. She had insisted they call the Jean Dubuffet something more precisely English and descriptive like *Winter*. That was what she saw in the work, thin, winter clouds suspended among eternally frozen branches. The gallery's director, Dean Richards, had gently reminded her that they were constrained to call it what the artist had called it.

"I still believe," Ellen Berman said, turning to Antonia Segreen, who was moping about in the exhibition room with her, "*Winter Scene* would have been a more fitting title than what he's got there. What do you think, Toni?"

Segreen, the director of the Bureau of Land Management, wasn't sure how to answer that question. She was a civil servant. Art seemed to her overblown in importance, and anything foreign, anything that needed interpretation, she called pretentious. Segreen turned to her attorney. "Anne Marie, you speak French, right? What about that title?"

Anne Marie Smith was there, delegated by Celia Progg to represent Melody Hogan. The young attorney liked dress-up affairs, but she'd already been to two that year. Both times she'd ended up feeling out of place and miserable. Fluent in French, with a solid background in both law and art, Anne Marie had a lovely physical presence, too. Celia took advantage of that, using her as a stand-in for parties and events she herself couldn't attend. Now Antonia Segreen kept the Melody Hogan junior partner close, relying on her good judgment to avoid looking foolish.

"What does it mean in English, Anne Marie?" Segreen insisted.

"Basically, 'Men in Black.' *Hommes En Fracs*, it's sarcastic."

"The wrong approach," Ellen Berman said. She gazed at the sculpture, seeing something different in it this time. Not a winter scene, but the rush of water over dark stones. That pleased her. She was getting the hang of it. She had one sure consolation that evening, that in the National Gallery's presentation brochure her name as a board member appeared first, even before the artist's. Berman felt she had earned that distinction.

"What do you think about this?" Ellen now asked Anne Marie, seeing she was, culturally speaking, the most competent one in the room. She glanced at a slip of paper she held. "I open with this, 'welcome supporters of the arts. Welcome my fellow…'"

"No," Anne Marie said. "'Good evening' is the best way to start, these people are fond of getting to the point."

"So just, 'Good evening'? Maybe so," the banker said. She peered out into the main hall; the ground floor was filling up with guests. Women much older than she moved together in small islands, like Jonathan Swift's Laputa, sailing round the bunched coast of their wealthy husbands. Wealthy husbands were a dime a dozen. Then Ellen Berman spotted the boy, Groves, Vince's young and obnoxious associate. She zeroed in on him with her big eyes. Turned to Antonia Segreen and asked, "You, Toni? What do you think?"

"'Good evening.' I always begin with 'good evening,'" Director Segreen answered. "Or else, sometimes, simply, 'ladies and gentlemen.'"

"Really?" Ellen asked.

Anne Marie didn't know what to do with herself. She felt awkward being there, always alone at these functions, always cosseting some client. She stared at the sculpture and then stared out at the great hall full of people. She was overcome by a dizzy sensation, an effect of the cocktail she'd had or more probably the sight of so many diamonds. "'What a wonderful evening,'" she said. "Open with that."

"Oh, yes?" Ellen asked. "You think I should open with that, 'What a wonderful evening'? Yes, I think I will. Good idea, Anne Marie." The banker put her hand out, an importuning gesture. "Come with me," she said to the lawyer. "I want you to meet someone."

Anne Marie shook her head. She didn't want to meet anyone she didn't already know. It wasn't so much out of timidity, but that she was sure whomever the banker introduced her to would bore her, and that was her big fear, being bored. She said, "I'm hungry." She pointed to the tables.

"Help me out, Toni," Ellen said to the director of the Bureau of Land Management. "Don't you agree? Anne Marie must mingle."

"Mingling, I don't know," Director Segreen said. "But a woman should never be seen eating at the buffet table. She should pick one piece of food, a spring roll, say, and walk around with that all evening. Taking very little bites now and again. No more."

Ellen grabbed Anne Marie by the arm and pushed her out of the exhibition room. Pushed her along until the young Melody Hogan attorney gave in and made the effort to be sociable. The banker slipped around the crowd like a cat and Anne Marie had to follow. They stopped at one point to shake hands with a woman Ellen

Berman knew from other events, a dowager a little older than Kirk Douglas.

"I love your earrings, Ellen," the woman said.

"This is your son? How do you do?"

"A gaga, a gaga," the middle-aged man muttered incomprehensibly, and in truth he had no idea how he was feeling or what kind of an evening it was. He had flown in from the Middle East that morning, a career diplomat on Zoloft, his face as though he were wearing an unfinished mask.

Ellen finally spotted her target.

"Come on," she told Anne Marie. "There he is."

"I know him."

"So do I," Ellen Berman cried, and she launched Anne Marie forward as though she were a javelin. "Go speak to him."

Sterrett had wandered into one of the exhibit rooms. It was tepid and airless, and the only sound was the hum of the lights. There was one painting on display, on loan from a Spanish museum, an immense oil, cavaliers and cardinals and the livid, distended Christ brought down from the cross, bodies vibrating with supernatural intensity. Sterrett liked the overlarge noses, the cold, astonished eyes, the austere faces transformed by revelation. He stood before the painting for a long while. It made him happy.

Taking big gulps of the Springfest champagne, he thought about Dinah. He decided he should try to learn from her. He decided he too would start using people, manipulating them so that they would like him, and then he'd ignore them. It seemed to be the way to be. Being good, a good man and that got no one anywhere, people would only walk all over you.

Well, he was mulling these things over when he looked up and saw the lawyer from Melody Hogan, Anne Marie Smith, standing there right in front of him. Looming behind her was Ellen Berman. Sterrett was ready to run off into the crowd. He was sure that the banker was about to dish out some lecture or other about good manners. But Anne Marie reached out her hand before he could make his move.

"So how are you? I didn't expect to see you here."

"I'm fine, fine I guess," Sterrett said.

Ellen, satisfied with the benevolent work she'd done, gave handsome young Groves the peace sign and then excused herself, leaving the two young attorneys alone.

"Isn't all this art horrible?"

"Look at that thing, what the hell is it?" Sterrett agreed. He hitched up his pants and pointed to Alexander Calder's huge sheet-metal mobile *Whirls Apart*.

"It's art and it moves," Anne Marie said, laughing. "That's the last thing I want, pieces of sheet metal spinning around on my ceiling. I mean then it's a fan."

She had on a simple satin dress of a lush jacaranda color, suitably revealing for the occasion, and despite the slightly stiff way she walked, she was, he had to admit, soft and perfumed and slender as a ribbon of silk. He told Anne Marie Smith he was glad they were all part of the same team. What a wonderful project it was, building a sanitary landfill. The whole world envied America for its waste management. He went a bit overboard, for he was that agitated. The woman saw it, and she saw in it a chance. The very fact that he was there was a sign, and she had seen him in action and knew he was a winner, the kind of man she wanted by her side as she scaled to the heights in Washington.

"Not a team. We're more than that, a body, Sterrett, one body, you and me," Anne Marie said coyly. She brushed her hair from her cheek and clung to him. "A body that acts like an individual to achieve a certain goal."

Sterrett believed that all a woman wanted was all he wanted, a little companionship for the duration of the party, share a few drinks, some good sex after. He had consistently believed that of Dinah, and he had never been able to see beyond that. At times, having fun was all there was in the world.

Dinah was keeping as far away from her date as possible. She was there to show off and to win people to her side, not to feel weighed down by the boy. Sterrett was suffocating, almost gloomy, like she owed him simply because they'd had sex together. If she owed him, she owed him because he'd treated her with more patience than she treated him. She'd treated him the way Vince had made her feel, like trash. But that was why she wanted to avoid Sterrett. She didn't want gloom in her life that night. For once she wanted joy and laughter. The

Dubuffet Gala was a tonic, and she felt she had worth as a woman, so many eyes upon her.

She was in the small room where *Hommes En Fracs* stood, wanting to see what was what as far as art was concerned, having been raised in a household where art was considered of vital importance. That was one of the virtues of being raised by hippies, they had a high respect for the arts. Her mother had framed many of her favorite album covers from the Sixties and Seventies, Beatles, Yes, Zappa, and so on, nailed them to the walls of their cabin. Dinah's father, an awkward but lovably nostalgic longhair, did spontaneous painting, using his fingers instead of a brush when he was high. One large work that he'd done on peyote hung over the fireplace in the communal lodge in downtown Garcia.

Dinah studied *Hommes En Fracs* from several different angles, standing as close to the work as she could without bumping up against it. Its abstract life made her own struggle for emotional balance seem vitally important.

"What do you think of that piece?"

He was tall, handsome the way few politicians were, a truly rugged profile, a mass of reddish brown hair combed back from his low brow. He spoke clean of any boorish slang or backwoods accent, a smooth customer with deep-set, gray eyes.

Dinah was cautious. "Do I know you? I've seen you on television."

"You are indeed right." Then he put out his hand. "I'm William Coote, Republican. I represent the 9th Congressional District of Minnesota."

"Dinah Solatoff."

"Well, Dinah, by goodness, I'm glad to meet you."

"I like it," the girl said, turning back to *Hommes En Fracs*. "It's art for the people, you know? It helps people understand who they are. Like a mirror."

"That's the most intelligent thing anyone's said to me all evening. I am a congressman, you know."

She found him a relief after all the gloomy and self-focused people she'd run into so far. She had begun to question her belief that the rich lived well, for the rich people at the gala all seemed either thoroughly annoyed or thoroughly pleased to be thoroughly annoying to others. The ones not annoyed were drunk. The ones neither annoyed nor drunk, trying perhaps too hard to have fun were probably gay. Coote was markedly different, not some old guy, but stimulating, interested in talking about something other than himself. He told her all about Dubuffet, his "art brut" and his fascination with children's art, with visceral beauty. They walked round the sculpture slowly. Coote explained to her that a politician had a responsibility to understand the culture he navigated in, and that culture wasn't Facebook and it wasn't Justin Bieber.

"People seem afraid of art. Most of my colleagues are content to let America wallow in ignorance. We want to wake this country up. Art is a form of consciousness. Shouldn't we all be a bit more conscious of what's going on in our world?"

Dinah became enthusiastic. She'd never heard anyone talk like that before. She told him that she wanted to be some sort of an artist herself, that her ambition was to study at the Corcoran School. "I do a little drawing, you know? I think I have talent, but…"

The congressman spied out his wife, who was spying on him from among some potted palms. His wife rarely came to Washington and so he felt he owed it to her to pull the conversation with Dinah Solatoff short. He told the young woman, "Here's my card. You call me during the week. We'll see what we can do for you as far as getting you into the Corky goes."

The director of the National Gallery, Dean Richards, stepped up to the dais where the band was busy rocking Vivaldi. He signaled the musicians to bring to a close their playing. Then Dr. Richards waved for both the president of the Consolidated Bank and the director of the Bureau of Land Management to join him on the dais. Ellen Berman took an eminent position in front of the piano. She had a strong, reboant voice, and when she began speaking, the people who'd been shuffling around restlessly during Dean Richards's brief introduction came to an excited stop.

"A year ago the director of the National Gallery of Art told me that before he retired there was one contemporary sculptor that he wanted in the worst way for this gallery. We have Henry Moore, and we have Giacometti and of course we have our Calder." Ellen Berman indicated the mobile that hung from the high roof beam. "But Dean told me he wanted a Jean Dubuffet. So I called the caterers and arranged this splendid evening for him, and oh yes, there was a multimillion dollar piece of sculpture involved as well."

The crowd laughed and applauded. Dinah appeared, close to the dais; she was clapping briskly, her arms raised. Sterrett, way in the back of the crowd, taller than many of the guests, fixed his eyes on the girl. The absolute desire to retch was growing strong in him, and his head was spinning, spinning like Calder's *Whirls Apart*. It wasn't the domestic champagne. It was Dinah, what a show she was making, how stupid he'd been to think that a secretary would have any but mercenary values. He turned to Anne Marie. He smiled at her and boldly put his arm around her waist, felt her hip rest against him, and then turned back to watch the speechifying.

"Next Dean tells me he wants a Niki Saint-Phalle, but I'm a prude about that sort of thing…" Ellen Berman waited, to let the laughter go on a little longer. "But seriously," she resumed, looking round the hall. "What a wonderful evening this is. I want to say this, I'm flattered and honored that so many came tonight, that so many of you took time off from busy schedules to be here tonight. Work is what pays in this town. But art can be hard work too, and sometimes those of us who keep this town working, have to step back a moment and give some time to art. As the National Gallery broaches this new century, it's important that we as members of this city's most important corporations and foremost institutions lend the gallery our fullest support. Art goes hand in hand with free enterprise. It flourishes where free enterprise is prevalent and dies when tyranny is the rule…"

Berman coughed into her hand, two throat-clearing coughs. There was a very faint sense that she was making a political speech. Expert ears in the crowd caught it, and a few murmured approvingly.

"What we need today," the banker went on. "Is a willingness to commit ourselves to the artistic welfare of this city, the city we love. For by improving the quality of Art in Washington, in the Federal City, we are improving the quality of the free marketplace, not just in America but in the world as well. That is why I'm here tonight. That is why we're all here tonight. We must show our support for these, the decisive, creative acts of corporately affiliated men and women without whose efforts we return to a selfish and savage state, and become slaves to violence and ignorance. I trust you will show your support tonight." She folded up the piece of paper she'd been consulting. She took on a tough air. "My job, you see, is to make sure that after all is said and done, you girls and boys pay up." Gratified laughter was succeeded by hearty and prolonged applause. "Give to the National Gallery of Art. Thank you."

After her speech, people took the opportunity to corral the banker, to congratulate her. They pressed in on her from all sides, like giddy children, to show they were ready and in earnest, rich people wanting to give of themselves in communion with an emergent personality. The mayor whispered something in her ear. The Speaker of the House of Representatives squeezed the woman's arm and someone else pinched her bottom, exclaiming, "Never have I been so proud to have money in your bank."

The drinking got heavier. The few celebrities, the doctors and lawyers, and various philanthropists began leaving, leaving the floor to the regular, gala habitués. The odor of sweat now permeated the East Building, and up on the stage the orchestra was doing its Bee Gees tribute. The men loosened their bow ties and joined the gowns on the marble floor as the rocking beat affected them like it was youth time again.

The champagne had run out, and Sterrett and Anne Marie were over in a corner, drinking the fine Sangria punch put together not by the caterer, but by the director of the National Gallery himself. Dean Richards, an aging cool cat, had learned to make the wine punch during long vacations in the Hamptons. The secret was to add three teaspoons of Pernod. It made the punch bitter, but no one seemed to care at that hour.

The young attorney had been in Anne Marie's company pretty much all the time. They talked about the Law, the marvel that was the Law, and the ability of the Law to rise above every other profession in that it was the Law itself that conditioned society. Sterrett wasn't bored by Anne Marie, however. He kept his arm around her, and he was pleased to see that she drank almost as readily, as avidly as he did, a born enabler, he thought. She drank down the blood-thick punch without showing any outward sign of being in any way affected. She did not slur her words when she spoke, and she spoke a lot, moving from the Law to the issue of billing fees.

They moved to a secluded corner of the main hall, where there were few to see them, and Anne Marie let Sterrett kiss her. She spoke to him then, not about the Law or about fees, but about romance. Then she put her hand on his leg, and squeezed his leg too, and it was driving him nuts, and he kissed her neck and he was enjoying himself and yet he was suffering a little. Suffering because his blue eyes kept homing in on Dinah over in the middle of the hall.

Dinah was moving from group to group, smiling so disarmingly that even the women noticed her. Every old moneyed geezer in the National Gallery came round to coo over the secretary and sink his thin lips to her hand. Sterrett couldn't blame Dinah if she sought her own self-interest. But he did blame her for being so happy and thrilled about it.

Hommes En Fracs was finishing the evening largely ignored. The gala-goers who were curious enough to gaze upon the angular sheets of painted resin and try the game of extracting a meaning from them now passed the exhibition room by. The sculpture was revealed for what it was, a pretext for throwing a party. A security guard came in. He turned off all but one light in the room. Then he took a position in front of the Dubuffet, a gunslinger ready for a showdown, man versus work of art. With one swift gesture, the guard popped his dentures out of his mouth. He lisped at the sculpture, "This is the real me."

Out in the main hall, the orchestra had started to pack up. The strings were the first to go, the bass fiddle waddling down the stairs to the concourse level, blocking the way for everybody else. A couple of the horns were undecided, but the piano player had no problem playing for free. He indulged himself, playing Sinatra tunes. There was a sing-along crowd round the Steinway, an informal and intimate ingle in the grandam hall.

Outside, the East Building of the National Gallery of Art glistened like a knife's edge. People emerged, the men with their bad knees, limping, the women with their sensitive feet, waddling arm in arm. They crossed the cobbled plaza and limousines pulled up to sweep them away.

"Has she become too big for Rockville?" a woman asked.

"Her bank is the only one I trust," another insisted. They were following their husbands, who'd gone to the corner to hail cabs. "I keep my diamonds there, at the branch in Bethesda."

"But why all this art boosterism? Has she got a hidden agenda?"

"I think her agenda is pretty much right out in plain view," the first woman said curtly.

"Did you notice, I think she's tinting her hair. She used to be grayer."

"I had a good time, but what I want to know is what she's up to."

The Honorable William Coote, the Lion of the Longworth, put Dinah Solatoff in the limousine. His wife had already gone home, and Coote felt the evening still had an inning left to play. He got into the limo himself and told the driver to go to the address the girl gave him. The driver was a former Army sergeant, and he'd been working for the congressman two years. While he was driving with the politician in the car, he listened to Top Forty, but with the radio turned down low, so low that all he heard was a constant, metallic jangle, very soothing, like cow bells in a distant valley.

Dinah rocked back in her seat and kept herself physically close to the congressman, close enough to give the impression she was a willing body. For some reason he had gotten into talking about baseball. Dinah didn't mind baseball, but she was from Idaho where baseball was considered a sissy sport.

She sat looking out the window, looking at the lights of the town, listening to Coote talk. They passed through Freedom Plaza, Brigadier General Casimir Pulaski up on his bronze trotter, the White House nestled round the next corner. It was one thing to imagine these things happened, and not believe they really did, and another to live it for real. She was living it for real. She had to keep heart. A congressman was better than a lawyer. It would more than make up for getting so rudely dumped by Vince Jorrigo.

"Don't you think it's late in the day to talk baseball?" she asked.

"I just think, this could be their year. They have a couple good hitters. All the Twins need is a healthy pitcher." Then he slapped his forehead and chuckled. "Of course. I'm sorry. My wife says the same thing."

They were coming up Pennsylvania Avenue, going into Washington Circle. The Congressman tapped the driver on the shoulder. "Stop here, Ralph. Stop here."

The driver pulled over to the curb near the World Bank. It was a deserted area, no pedestrians and few cars, the one car there was Secret Service, and they would recognize the limo's congressional plates. Congressman William Coote said, "Go for a walk, will you?"

The driver acquiesced and got out. He looked at his watch. "I'll be walking about fifteen minutes. That all right?"

The answer was a gruff, "Okay."

Left alone with the congressman, Dinah was persuaded to have sex with him. It was a little disorienting. They talked very little during, and right after, Bill Coote called for his driver.

Sterrett Emerson Groves stepped clumsily out of the boxwood where he'd gone to take a pee. He stepped onto the sidewalk and looked around him, everyone gone, the street empty. Behind him, the National Gallery rose from the warm ground, casting its shadow upon the silent night. Traffic lights all the way up Constitution Avenue changed in sequence, beacons across a dim and dusty wasteland. He knew the history of his town, knew it was President Truman's doing that downtown Washington, unlike the Loop or Midtown Manhattan, unlike the downtown of most any great national capital had no bright lights.

During the last year of the last world war, the amusements found along Pennsylvania Avenue—bars, clubs, strip joints, and burlesque theaters—had so disturbed Truman that he initiated a project called Operation Clean Town. The scope of the project was a ten-block area from the White House to the Capitol. The goal was to guarantee that no honest bawdy of any kind would flourish in the area. The result was that more than sixty years later, downtown Washington was no more alive after sunset than Nagasaki after the Fat Man.

Sterrett went up the corner, not a taxicab in sight. He cursed, went clomping down to the next corner. A horn blared. Sterrett jumped round, not expecting to see anyone he knew. Expecting some kind of harassment. His fists closed tight, he was ready with some choice words.

"Anne Marie," he said instead.

She pulled to the curb. She sat at the wheel of her huge, high-riding sports utility vehicle. She had the window down. "Come on, I'll give you a lift wherever you're going."

He glanced up and down the street. There were no cabs. There was the cosmopolitan hum of the night and Anne Marie with her hand patting the seat next to hers.

"Get in, Sterrett."

He felt compelled to do so. She used a commanding voice, and Sterrett was willing to sacrifice himself to a commanding woman that evening. He got in and got comfortable, ready for whatever it was the woman wanted of him.

"I live on Wisconsin Avenue near the Social Safeway."

Anne Marie ignored that. She asked, "Hungry?"

She told the young attorney she for one was quite hungry and they agreed that there was nothing open at that late an hour, no decent restaurant within a mile's radius. And Anne Marie told him she had plenty of food in her refrigerator. Plenty of things to eat and to drink. So it was only logical for them to go to her place, and they did, being both of them highly logical people.

She was a swift, two-handed driver on the straightaway. She advertised it by rolling down the avenue so as to make every light. They went onto Rock Creek Parkway, heading north along the creek's bed, the watercourse falling to one side of the paved road. Up ahead under the lamplight, a pair of crows were picking at the stringy remnant of some furred animal. The crows took to the air loudly, caw-cawing as Anne Marie barreled past. Sterrett watched them make for the safety of the overhanging branches.

Turning up the off ramp to reach Connecticut Avenue, the sport utility vehicle was forced to stop its plunging ways, forced to wait for the light to change near the grounds of a big hotel. There, waiting for the light, Anne Marie and Sterrett monkeyed around with each other. Then away again, over a bridge and a left onto Newark Street. That's where she lived, her hidey-hole as she called it.

It was an impressive house for such a young attorney. Room after room, two floors and a basement, a pool in the back, and everything was neat as a pin, shiny and polished and in place. The only thing, shoes were everywhere, abandoned in pairs. Anne Marie was apologetic. "I hardly ever, ever have the time to pick up after myself."

She kicked off the shoes she was wearing. She mussed her hair, went and put some music in the CD player, the popular jazz singer

Johnny Vettore, and right off began to execute a very comical strip-tease in front of Sterrett Emerson Groves. Nothing unclean or vulgar about her, Anne Marie was graceful in movement and seemed to know what her long, lithe limbs were capable of. She stripped right down to the fuller brush between her legs.

Then they were in her bedroom, and the next thing they knew, they were together high above the bed, gone out the room, through the sky, off the roving earth. She hugged him to her, told him how much she loved him, and Sterrett exhaled to make the point he was done.

Lying on the bed afterwards, they could see through the window, the moon dangling low over Cleveland Park. There was an oncoming line of clouds, and they talked about the possible change in the weather, summer getting wet. They laughed over that turn of phrase. While Sterrett was thinking he didn't want to screw up the moment by saying anything more to her, Anne Marie raised his hand and placed it upon her breast. Wanting to touch, wanting to be touched, that was the true indicator of humanness, because it presupposed a state of solitude from which an individual sought redress by another individual in a willful act of comprehension.

Wanting to touch and to be touched. It was so fundamental that upon touching, Sterrett judged, society based the whole of its moral structure, who can and cannot touch one, whom a person loved, whom one hated. Sterrett felt compelled to say something that would sound like love, a winning phrase. All he could think of in that moment was, "I really like your breasts."

"I can tell," Anne Marie said. "Let's eat."

And they went into the living room, and the woman had Sterrett open a bottle of chilled white wine, a Rastignac, as though they hadn't had much to drink already. She stole back into the kitchen and brought out leftovers from one of her firm's parties, a rainbow of caterer's delicacies. They sat at the coffee table in the living room, the lights low, and ate lobster tails and warmed over asparagus and other tidbits. A couple candles were burning here and there for effect. Anne Marie put on some light piano jazz. They settled back in the sofa, their glasses full in their laps, their feet close.

"I bet you think I'm somewhat trashy to have you like this?"

"What do you mean?"

"When I'm here, alone, I'm not necessarily happy, but I'm secure." She took a long sip out of her glass. "It would be nice however if there were one man in the world who gives me the same sense of security I have here, without me having to be alone. Do you get what I'm getting at."

"Yes."

"Oh please, you tire me with that shit. I know underneath, you're a real proper bastard," Anne Marie said. She finished her wine. Got to her feet. Swayed above him. "Give it to me like that. It's no sin. A good fuck is what you have when you have nothing else. I'm in love with you, but a good fuck…If you're not in love with me…" She stood over him and said, "Don't say a word to me."

Sterrett didn't know how to answer that. He said, "Is there any more wine?"

"I have refrigerators full," Anne Marie cried joyously.

They had sex again, this time on the carpet, and Anne Marie fell asleep on the floor and the evening pretty much petered out like that. He didn't know why he didn't go ahead and fall asleep too. Instead, Sterrett got to his feet, found his pile of formal attire, and got dressed as best as he could.

He carried his shoes in his hand and went to the door, drew the door open, stepped out onto the porch. He was quiet in every movement, but the porch creaked, the steps creaked. He turned and looked up at the living room window, but no light came on. He'd call Anne Marie later and tell her something like he had to get to work early that morning. Work was the best excuse, that was its main purpose.

He came out onto the street. His look was disheveled enough despite his wearing a tuxedo that a police cruiser slowed to have a close gander at him. Sterrett walked down Wisconsin Avenue towards his apartment building, recalling as he went along, all the outstanding nights he'd wasted in his life getting drunk, hanging around at horrible parties, going home with women he cared little for. But whether he cared for them or not, making love to a woman gave him that exuberant feeling of having proved himself. It was something a man never ceased doing, even if he wanted to; he lived in relationship to women.

He hiked the mile downhill, feeling mixed feelings about the night, though on the whole he judged it had gone pretty well. He would not tell Anne Marie about Dinah; she didn't have to know about that. He would tell Anne Marie that she was the first woman he liked enough to want to see on a regular basis. He believed the woman represented a need in himself he'd long passed over. She would help him change the way he lived. He finished reasoning this through, and he was in his own bed, undressed and asleep just as dawn was gathering over the gold-leaf pinnacles of the Temple of Latter-Day Saints.

CHAPTER NINE

The evening of the Dubuffet Gala, Vince Jorrigo had a poker game to go to. The game had been organized at the request of a well-known jazz musician, Johnny Vettore. Vettore was in the D.C. area to sing a couple songs and stride around the piano at Blues Alley, a club in Georgetown. He was there for two nights and he didn't start until Tuesday; Blues Alley was dark on Monday. Johnny Vettore contacted Curveball, and Curveball put the game together in the same hotel where the singer was staying, in Old Town.

Vince didn't like to travel across the river and into Virginia. Virginia, it was like driving headlong into the past, all its putrid guts and putrid southern glory, Robert E. Lee, Stonewall Jackson and that ilk. But to break his losing streak, he'd go wherever there were cards to play. He was dressed in summer's version of his dandy look, a pale cotton jacket, pleated pants, an open collar on his tattersall shirt, and now with his face perfumed with a manly tonic, Vince Jorrigo was driving his vintage, British-made sports car over the 14th Street Bridge into Old Town Alexandria. He went slowly, with the cloth top down, going slowly for the sake of his companion and her hair.

Celia was riding shotgun, hoping to be Vince's good luck piece for that evening. She wore dark slacks and a tight-fitting blouse, a mock fifties look, as though she were a heedless teenager, expressly unlike the image Celia projected in the conference room or before a judge. The tight-fitting blouse gave her a chance to show off her slight bosom. Long, beaded earrings, folksy and cheap, added to the effect.

"It's a mid-level kind of game, the opening ante is only five hundred dollars," Vince said.

"Only?" Celia said, raising an eyebrow. She'd ended up loaning him $10,000 to play with, the condition being she'd get to go along. She'd led a protected life and had never been to a poker game, though she understood the rules. "You better win, right? I gave up on going to tonight's big gala for this."

"It's poker," Vince replied, beginning to get testy. "There aren't guarantees."

"No, I know what poker is. I was joking." She could tell, he was much more anxious than she'd seen him for a long time, and she left him alone. She didn't need him to be cross with her. Celia rested her arm on the door and leaned her face to the whooshing breeze. She took in the passing scenery. Heron broke from a sandbar at the southern end of Mason's Island, moving slow wings close to the startled eight of a university shell. Celia watched as the birds flew downstream, towards the Memorial Bridge. Birds of good fortune, she hoped.

Vince knew at least two of the players who were going to be there, regulars in Curveball's circuit. Sky King was a news anchorman, the star personality of a major television network. Promptly at seven p.m. weekdays, the man's white-bread image gave legitimacy to the flat screen and offered reassurance against incalculable events, keeping vigil over living rooms and bedrooms for a full half an hour. But for all that Sky King was a sharpie at cards.

"Who else?"

"Curveball of course."

"Ah, yes Curveball," Celia scoffed. "A game of poker wouldn't be a game without Curveball. He can't be reliable with a name like that."

"He's a dentist." Vince was on the parkway. He was looking for the exit onto Washington Street, heading for the Ambassador Hotel. "And this singer. Johnny Vettore. I don't know him. But he's got a name. It's his game tonight." He downshifted and made a right onto King Street, and then took the ramp into the hotel's garage. "He plays jazz, you know."

"He had that one album," Celia agreed. "He's good. There are better singers. But he's got style. You have to have an ear."

"When we're playing," Vince was telling Celia as they walked down the hallway to the singer's hotel room. "You have to keep quiet. No kibitzing and if you have to move around…"

"You know, if it weren't my money you're playing with, Vince, I'd walk home right now. I wouldn't even bother with a cab."

Vettore's room was a large suite with all the curtains drawn and the television on, but mute. Not everyone was there, but the game was going to get underway anyway. Vince Jorrigo shook hands with Curveball and with Sky King, and he introduced Celia to them in a very low-key way, didn't mention she was a lawyer like him. Vince didn't want her mixing with the others. He didn't want to dilute any positive influence she might bring him. The woman didn't understand that it wasn't a game, but a serious enterprise, playing poker, as arduous and risky as scaling Nanga Parbat.

Two of the players were new to Vince, and one of them he disliked right off the bat, a young man who called himself Steve. He was tattooed and pierced and as snide as his manners were poor, one of the new generation. He was there to make money, that was his game. He kept talking about it too, money. He wasn't passionate about risk, about the fall of the cards. He was the new generation, vipers coming up from the ground, men and women who would do anything to be on the winning side of the money.

"Hello, hello," Johnny Vettore sauntered into the room, pushing back the sliding doors of the bedroom. He had a greasy, altar boy's face. He wore a gold watch, but no other jewelry, and wore a tie, a thin pearl gray tie with a pattern of small black lozenges scattered across it, as ugly, Vince thought, as anything his law associate Groves might want to wear.

The game was into its second hour when the poet Leonard Between Dogs came knocking at the door with his girlfriend Booboo McLean in tow. He apologized right off for being late. He'd been over to the National Gallery of Art at the gathering for the Dubuffet, and he apologized too, for the way he was dressed, for the bright shorts and the flip-flop sandals, his formal wear as he explained.

"I was supposed to go to that," the news anchor said. "How was it?"

Between Dogs was busy settling Booboo McLean on the couch, getting her comfortable with Celia's help. Booboo was young, and Booboo was unused to drinking, and she needed to lie down. She needed to close her eyes.

"Very clubby," Leonard Between Dogs told Sky King. "The food was good though, and they were serving champagne like there was no tomorrow. I left before Dean Richards got up to speak."

"They kick you out?" Vince asked. He knew the poet from court; his firm had defended Leonard Between Dogs a number of times in nuisance suits filed against him by various individuals and private organizations he went out of his way to offend or to slander. At cards, however, the poet was the very model of decorum.

"Dressed like this? They wouldn't dare."

Celia was thrilled to meet the "Robert Frost of the Plains" as one reviewer had called him, and she said so. She knew his poetry, and to prove how much of his work she knew, she went right ahead from his most famous poem, "'Their finality lying, in that Dakota moonscape, suspends the breath. If I could reach my hand, through that frozen veil, my warmth here in this room passing to them, would it be enough to make them cry out, wakened one last time?'" She paused. "Such devastating words."

Vince turned in his chair to look at her. He had never heard Celia get so worked up about anything that wasn't strictly part of the practice of the law. It surprised him. She seemed to go drippy over nothing. Johnny Vettore saw it too, and he was a little jealous the woman wasn't fawning over him. He was a singer after all. Vettore urged the poet to sit down with them, and the other players made room round the table and the game resumed with fresh money in the pot.

They played until well past two o'clock in the morning. To her credit the only sign of boredom Celia showed was when she took off her earrings. She sighed a little and put her earrings away, then played with her cellphone. But she recouped her interest after a while and seemed overall to enjoy herself. She tried desperately to pepper Vince with all her good joss, but it was not much use.

When the smoke cleared, the attorney wasn't the heaviest loser, that honor belonged to the host, to Johnny Vettore. The big winner, naturally, was Steve, and he was smug about it, and he toted up his winnings out loud. Vince for his part, had won some good pots. He wasn't the kind of player to count every chip, but at one point it looked like he had more than $40,000 stacked at his elbow. That was the end of his streak of bad luck and trouble, and he should have been elated. If he'd stopped there and then, he would have had his stake for the Bitch.

But Vince's reasoning told him best to play on, that it was only logical, his losing streak over, he'd win more and more. The result was swift but it wasn't unreservedly disastrous; hand after hand, Vince went down to the table and was swept away by better hands. But the game came to an end sooner than expected, due to the fact that Sky King got a call on his cellphone, some piece of breaking news, an intrusion of the big world outside.

And then Booboo McLean woke up and wanted to go home and that broke the spell definitively. The next day was Tuesday, and everyone had to work. Johnny Vettore, the singer, walked them to the door of the hotel room. Despite his losing a good amount of cash, he told them all, "Good bye, good bye," singing it in his easiest voice, "Good bye, good bye, my friends. And thanks."

Vince had lost only half of his stake, about $7,000 of the $14,000 he'd brought to the table. He should have been happy it didn't go worse, but the lawyer didn't think in comparative terms. He didn't owe any other player money when he pushed up from his chair, but he came out of the game as much a loser as before.

He didn't owe anybody at the table any money; he did owe Celia Progg. They stopped at the Bistro Marseilles for a late dinner. They didn't speak much at the table. Celia had passed on going to the Dubuffet Gala to go see Vince play poker, thinking to see Vince win thousands, to celebrate afterwards with a cascade of champagne, hoping finally to be able to play lovers in bed. She hadn't planned on sitting around eating watery eggs benedict with Vince brooding, pathetic and brooding, and not even making an effort to seem romantic or upbeat.

"You took about $7,000, am I right?" Celia had to say. "I know I am right."

"I didn't lose it all if that's what you mean," Vince said, using a piece of toasted bread to sop up his egg yolk. "But I'm wiped out at the bank."

"You can give me $5,000 of that then. Owe me the rest for later."

"Come on," he told her. "I'll write you a check for later."

"You need help, Vince." She lowered her eyes. "No check. I want cash." Celia decided the cure had to be harsh; rub his nose in it. "And I don't want a check later. I'll take $5,000 in cash now."

He pleaded. He was a pleader by profession, and that's what he did, but he did it with a little too much pain to be convincing. "Celia, come on, you can trust me, won't you please trust me for the next couple weeks?"

"I gave up a society evening so I could go and watch you throw my money to the wind, and I can't say I'm particularly ecstatic about it," Celia said. "It's not the money itself. It's you, Vince. You do realize you have a problem?"

"Me? I'm fine."

"You? Fine? Oh no. You're not fine by a long shot, you."

They argued all the way out Maine Avenue to the Tahoga Yacht Club. Arguing was a way for them to communicate affection one for the other without actually having to say anything truly affectionate. It was a good excuse to invite Celia on board, and they argued some more over a little red wine, and argued all the way into bed. They were on Vince's Chris*Craft, arguing over his gambling and whether it was a problem.

He admitted it was a problem, from the point of view of losing, but he admitted it and Celia found that admission good enough reason to give him a hug, and then they were down in the forward cabin. They lay down together, Vince and Celia hugging, lying together on the big bed in the cabin of the *Arabella*. They lay down together for the first time, the way two lawyers would. But their energy had been drained away with all their arguing and they lay in bed and fell asleep, the healing roll of the Potomac keeping them in each other's arms.

They were wary of each other waking up the next day. They made small talk over coffee, and over coffee, Vince peeled off ten one hundred dollar bills and placed them into Celia's palm, a tenth of what he owed her, but a good start, as Celia herself said. Happy to be off the hook as far as having to be tough with him, she confessed she'd slept very well in his bed.

Encouraged, Vince told her he knew where and how to win back all of what he'd lost. He started to tell her about the Bitch. But she stopped him short and began to insist he pay her back all of what he owed her. She was getting worked up again about how cards and poker were all he thought about. So Vince changed the subject. He talked about the sanitary landfill.

It was complicated enough that Celia forgot about Vince's gambling problem for the moment and listened attentively as he explained. Capital Landfill Development Partnership was the entity that would be responsible for the construction and the operation of the model sanitary landfill at the Ellipse. Sir Simon Psora would be the general partner, his son Kid Psora, a limited partner. The other limited partner to share in the money made by the Capital Landfill Development was a shadow company known as Stinky and Smelly Limited. Stinky and Smelly Ltd. had its corporate headquarters in the Principality of Liechtenstein, high in the mountain fastness of Vaduz.

"It's going to be where the real money is. You can have a part of that, if you want," Vince said. He was driving up 14th Street, taking Celia Progg to work, to her offices on Connecticut Avenue. "Groves is writing up the language. A participation in Stinky and Smelly Ltd., it's going to work as a kind of safety net for me. For you too, if you want it."

"I see." There was the droning of traffic all around them, and then a truck's backfire. Celia glanced out the car. They were at a red light, at the intersection of 14th and F Streets, near the National Press Club building. Along the sidewalk, vendors slumped in bored poses before their wares. Sunglasses and umbrellas, wristwatches from China, and inexpensive CDs were laid out on plywood tables in a jumble of counterfeit name brands and faked logos.

"Do you see for real? Do you understand? This is a real chance. Through this corporation in Liechtenstein, we'll be off the radar. Any tax-free money Sir Simon makes with this landfill, we'll make."

"That's generous of him. Are you sure it's an offer you want to accept?"

"The truth is he's gone off the deep end. He has no idea what's going on," Vince said. "He takes baths in coffee grinds and rotten tomatoes."

"Really?" Celia gave him a skeptical look. "Cherry tomatoes or fried green?"

"You should worry. You're signing a contract with him."

"He's that far gone?"

"His son's okay, though. So what I mean is, I can profit from the upside. All I have to do is paper it over, and what I'm saying, Celia, listen to me, we'll go in it together. Consider what I owe you as an investment."

"Vince, we'll talk about it," Celia said. She looked down at her lap. "I'm not really expecting you to pay me back. I care about you, that's my problem. I care very much for you. Tell me this, how many IOUs do you have scattered around town?"

Vince was not at all shy admitting he had quite a few IOUs outstanding, some going back two, three years, most with friends and various colleagues, not big amounts of money, but money he'd borrowed and hadn't yet paid back. He seemed proud that he had that many friends willing to loan him money. He seemed content to have lost that money playing cards, as though he'd done something socially worthwhile losing money.

Celia was shocked. A window had been flung wide. His whole attitude, that shocked her even more. She wanted to know who these friends and colleagues were. Vince tried to mollify her. Everyone borrowed money; it was what made the nation's economy grow. They argued about that all the way into Farragut Square, where Vince let Celia out at the curb. There was a flashing morning pace to the street, businessmen hurrying past watches on display, and droves of tourists on their way full speed ahead to see the Mall and its museums.

"I want you to promise me you'll stay away from poker for this month."

Vince gave her a nonplussed expression, what was she asking. But it was a moot point; he wanted, anyway, to save all his poker juices for the Bitch. That was all he cared about, the Bitch. It was his game. He said, "I promise. No poker for, well, let me try two weeks."

"You promise."

"I can try two weeks to start with."

Celia on the curb stooped low, leaned into the car, and Vince, at the wheel stretched his neck and they kissed, a peck of the lips. She gave him a sigh, too, a consolatory and forgiving sigh before disappearing down the sidewalk.

She was right, of course, as women always were. What he needed was cash. He would have to study a way to get cash, as in fact at that moment he had none, except the little left from Celia's loan. There was one way that Vince knew of, which was drastic. It was a way to get money. It was a way without too much hassle. It didn't involve banks. It didn't involve cards.

Vince had made his reputation on being methodical and dogged, and for the sake of being methodical, he spent the next two weeks trying to exhaust all normal, sane means of raising cash money, every opportunity available to him before going to what was drastic. He went to his local bank, the Dalecarlia Bank in Spring Valley. A small loan, he told them, to repair his boat, but the bank turned him down. They weren't uppity about it, on the contrary. It was just that there was already a refinance on the *Arabella*. It was at about 120 percent of the boat's present market value. They told him, amicably, he'd have to repair the hull out of pocket.

He didn't feel depressed by that refusal; it confirmed his particular opinion of banks, that they only lent money to happy people. Of his next step, Vince was also confident of failure. He called his ex-wife and asked her to loan him some money. He told her about the hull of the boat she'd hated so much. It leaked he said, and each morning he found himself closer to sinking, anymore and he risked going down with the ship. His wife knew him too well. She told him to sell the boat; she advised him to sell. The very last thing she was going to do was to lend him money. He told her he'd pay her back within the month. His wife called him a fabulist and hung up.

There was no leakage problem with the hull of the *Arabella*. It needed paint but otherwise it was quite watertight. But in Vince's social circle cash money was seen as a shameful thing to admit needing on a personal level, that was the problem. If he'd revealed to his wife his fear and agony in that moment, then she might have loaned him the money; if he'd pleaded, begged, and prostrated himself with tears in his eyes and his voice broken by a chance sob, she would surely have staked him. But he couldn't be frank in that way. He couldn't go and tell his wife how desperate he was, that would have made him feel too scummy, too much like some poor, pathetic panhandler, and he couldn't sink that low. So he was trapped, thinking of money. He was as close to being without hope as he had ever been in his life.

He dropped meeting with Cornelius Klocker and the CEO of High Leaf Bakeries. He dropped taking the time to patch up a turf battle over in tax law between Sissy Bateman and Cliff Lemberger. He even dropped the work he was doing, hammering out the final details on the development partnership with Sir Simon Psora, turning it over entirely to Sterrett Emerson Groves. He dropped it all to dedicate himself to getting the cash he needed to sit at the Bitch. He even scratched at lottery tickets. But when he'd found no cash to find, he went ahead with the drastic option.

Though storm clouds, thick and lumpy with moisture, covered the sky to the north, from Philadelphia to Boston, Vincent Jorrigo left his office and took a cab to Union Station, outward bound to New York City. He got to the train station early and walked around. The noise of the hall excited him. He walked to the center of the Head House, turning slowly. It was a bath of random voices, of people rushing to board a train, of people weaving in and out of the shops or lingering in refuge from the morning's humidity.

Vince wandered down a corridor full of tiny boutiques and began to notice the objects on sale, reminded by a particularly sumptuous display of chocolates in gold boxes of how he used to stare as a child of relatively poor parents, into the shops along the main street in Millwood, Rhode Island, feeling the emptiness that a well-stocked store represented to him, as if all his senses had been stripped and piled high on the storekeeper's shelves. Touch and taste and smell taken from him, a birthright he'd have to buy back at the store owner's price.

He checked his watch again. It was twelve minutes past ten, and he had a train to catch in twenty minutes. But he enjoyed the feeling of not being able to do anything but be idle, a feeling that only train stations and airports afforded him. He went down another corridor of shops and came to a dead end before a store loose with Secrets, its display window full of white foam and pink surf, as though a wave of lingerie were breaking across the glass.

He fought against it but couldn't help himself, and Vince stood a long time at the display window, seeing if he could imagine Celia Progg in bright satin, her bitty white breasts tapering against the sleek material, if he could picture the hair below, a thick, rough mat behind the frilled panties. He found he could indeed imagine her that way. He could adore the Melody Hogan attorney dressed that way. Adoration, admiration too, both her racy little body and her splendid mind, Vince was startled to think of it, Celia, an adorable lawyer in only underclothes.

But that's not what women wanted, a man who adored and admired; they wanted action. They wanted love. Love itself the prime mover of so much grief was not what Vince considered the foundation of reasonable behavior between two people. Pity was a much more reasonable emotion. Pity was what he got from Celia, what tied them together, her pity for a colleague, he was sure. Be content with that, he thought.

By ten thirty he was on board the Acela train outward bound for New York City. It was a three and a half hour trip with stops at Baltimore, Wilmington, Philadelphia, and Metro Park, New Jersey. He got to New York's Penn Station right as the storm clouds burst. Though the rain tried to hold him back, clasped him for a moment in its shimmering fist, Vince broke free and made his way to the skyscraper that housed the offices of Hidell Kennedy and Stone.

Vince Jorrigo had come to see an old friend, a classmate from Yale Law School. He was dressed not in his usual dapper way, but somberly, a stark white shirt, a cold blue suit, slightly damp along the shoulders, a blue bow tie. He was coming in the middle of the work-week, with his hat in his hand. He came with the hope of a friendly reception. He came, remembering those moments in law school when the course of one's life depended simply on surviving the winter and the friends one made.

So Vince stood, full of poise and confidence, in a puddle of his own making on the forty-second floor of the polished glass building on the Avenue of the Americas. He said to the receptionist, "Ray Wilbur. He's expecting me."

Some attorneys became very rich simply practicing law, some, very few, not many. These ones who became rich were the trial lawyers who'd won a couple spectacular court cases. Very few of these stayed rich for long, unless they retired early. Staying at the focal point of the media circus, in the center ring was expensive.

The few smart ones turned their name over to a batch of younger men and women and went and sat their butts down in a comfortable chair out in Aspen or in Cape May. They let their money grow in the hands of competent investment brokers. They went off to teach at some college or other when they were tired of sitting around. But these were a handful.

The majority of attorneys were not rich. Many of them were smart, many competent, and they were the men and women who did a fair and honest job representing their clients and an admirably steadfast job getting their fees paid. They did not however cause The Donald's combed-over heart to engorge with envy. They struggled, and at most, became affluent, lived house and garden lives.

Then there was that type of lawyer many people in America swore to, well-heeled, supercilious, greedy, inordinately wealthy. They were not so many as to represent the mass of attorneys. Enough of them around and that was why the average American swore to them. They appeared in court and they were on the streets, and they generally hung together, generally seen in big cities at tony restaurants. Average families, one in five, had at least one relative who either worked for this type of attorney or who had gone to school with this type of attorney.

But this type didn't become wealthy at the practice. They were lawyers of course, practicing lawyers, yet their source of wealth was not the Law. It was confusing of course, these were men and women who became wealthy in other ways, and the practice of the law was merely a semblance.

Ray Wilbur was such a one, and not only was he wealthier than most of the affluent clients he stood beside in court, he was extremely powerful, a man even the eggheads up Riverside Drive feared. Most of the truly wealthy attorneys in New York, Washington, and Los Angeles had become powerful through double-dealing or through illicit connections or through lobbying. Those means were too squalid for a high-minded man like Wilbur. He betrayed no one's trust, and he didn't get his fingernails dirty with influence peddling.

He had made his billion dollars the way they should be made, lending money at exorbitant interest. He was choosey of course, not widows and orphans, Wilbur lent money only to the famous and to the mighty, to men and women ravaged by their ambitions. He had been doing it for years and had an organized way about him that pleased and comforted the forlorn souls who came to him. He had a staff too, ready to help. The loans were done quietly, and even the collections were done with tact and discrimination albeit sometimes with punishing force. There had never been any story leaked to the Press, and if once and a while a welsher had got beaten to a pulp, that event never made the evening news, was never even seen on YouTube.

Money lender as well as attorney, 3ʳᵈ Degree Mason as well as a member of the 5ᵗʰ Avenue Presbyterian Church, a descendant of a First Family, come to the country on a wooden tub with square sails, Wilbur carried himself as though all that tradition, all that intrigue, all that education was nothing compared to his own personal cleverness. Cleverness that translated as power, power that meant his will was done.

Though many feared him, looked upon him as a force to be reckoned with, Wilbur was not omnipotent. He too was made to fear others, demurring before those higher up in the Caste. He was able to use his accumulated power only in the direction he saw as important, that was to make his law firm the supreme law firm of the world.

For the rest, in his social life for instance, he was a bust in bed, a boring conversationalist, a whiner when it came to silly, daily mishaps, a shirker when it came to giving others a hand. He was above all quite thrifty with his own money. He wore tailored suits and expensive shoes, but that was because he had calculated the overall cost of doing so as being on the credit side in terms of impressing people.

His light, badly cut hair was parted to one side, as it had been in law school, and his eyes were the same hazel-colored, observant eyes with a healthy dash of something sinister. Vince went to shake hands, but Wilbur took a step backwards. He didn't like to be touched, that was something Vince had forgotten.

Wilbur said, "Look at you, old man."

"Yes, it's been some time."

"You look great, Vince. Look at that stomach."

"You haven't changed either, Raymond."

Wilbur, in reality, looked several years older than Jorrigo. His face was the way New York faces were—puffy, gray skin. He had some flab going, nothing like the lean and limber whiz kid Vince remembered from law school. Vince thought, well, he could understand that time had changed his friend, taken away the pimples, the biceps, replaced them with wrinkles and flab. He too, was flabby where once he'd been trim, he was honest with himself about that at least.

They left the office and went down to a restaurant on the first floor of the office building. The Village Inn, four diamonds in the Triple-A guide, was entirely nondescript, a smoked-glass door on the ground floor of the building. From the windows of the restaurant it was possible to see the marquee of Radio City Music Hall. But the empowered who ate there kept their eyes on their peers while at the watering hole, and the Rockettes went ignored.

The empowered who ate there, ate there because they were confident no one else would come to eat there, the prices too high and the food mediocre. Tourists crashed the place by mistake from time to time, and were sure to be given a table near the restrooms, and were sure to leave wondering how one greasy cheeseburger with a serving of limp fries could cost $60. More often, people seen every day on television were seen at the Inn: financial pundits, commissioners, network anchors, talk-show hosts, lawyers. The mayor ate there at least once a month. It was a very "in" place made all the more bearable by dim lighting.

The two men sat in the HKSer's regular booth. For the first few minutes, Wilbur did all the talking. He sat talking in his deep baritone, his lecturing tone. Vincent Jorrigo was content to listen, sipping at his martini cocktail. Not himself alone, that was a relief, he wasn't the only chump in the world. That was how Wilbur made him feel, telling him sob stories there in the quiet corner of the Inn. Telling him how many people there were in Manhattan who needed money revival and who came to him, Wilbur, with a flood of tears and went to their knees, explaining themselves, trying to seek pardon for their sins when it wasn't to him they should go for that, but to a preacher.

Vince was zoomed in, thinking about the Bitch, and all he wanted to know was whether he'd get his money. He was ready for anything, ready to promise anything to get his stake for the Bitch. He had no interest in Wilbur's sanctimonious charade. He would have cried out, "money, are you going to loan it to me or not?" had he thought it seemly. Instead he continued to display his control, his patience.

"These are people without a moral compass," the HKS attorney said, wielding his own drink, a gin and tonic full of ice. "I have no interest in them. They dug their own graves." He let go a bland smile. "I'm not referring to you by that. Not you, Vince."

"Fine. I know. But…"

"But nonetheless, it's universal, isn't it, being human? We live in the personal lives of those around us. We are all a party to what is done by others, as others are a party to what we do. So I have to be careful when I lend money. And generally I know what my clients are after, what they're dragging me into. I don't lend money to drug users, unless they've got property and I don't lend money to anyone under twenty-one."

Wilbur spoke in a normal tone of voice. He was not embarrassed by what he did and felt no fear of the censure against usury. He himself found great amusement in the tales he told. Needing money was the result of a choice a man made. Needing money was reparable one way or another. It was just a question of being in good grace with the right person.

"And you?" he asked. "What are you come crying about?"

"But I'm not the type to cry."

Vincent didn't tell the whole story of why he needed the money. He needed to borrow money, using no other collateral than his reputation. Wilbur told him okay. He had his ways and he knew what was behind the money. He'd heard all about Vince and his losing streak.

"You've become something of a Jonah, haven't you?"

"No." Vince closed his eyes for a second, annoyed, and then asked, "Where did you hear that?"

"From Larry King that he'd heard it from Mo Segal at Duke's. Some players won't even sit down at the table with you."

"You're going too far, Raymond."

"It isn't important," Wilbur answered. The three things that were important were the interest rate on the loan, the expiration date of the loan, and above all the collateral. The collateral was the thing that interested Wilbur above all other things. "We're oldest of friends, aren't we?" he concluded. "I can give you whatever you want. I'll do it gladly."

"Good. I appreciate it."

"But as I say, I need some form of security. You do see that?"

Vince had no assets that weren't otherwise committed and therefore they were of no use to the other lawyer. But it wasn't a sticking point. Wilbur always knew where to find his security. It was decided over steak sandwiches that the collateral would be Vince's share in the firm of Guiteau and Garfield. It was not a surprising choice. Vince didn't own anything else of value, not the Outhouse, the mortgage being in the firm's name, and his cabin cruiser was already financed out the whazoo.

But Vince Jorrigo's partnership share in the firm, that was a rich taking, for it meant Hidell Kennedy and Stone, not as yet established in Washington, could control Vince's position and begin to take over the Guiteau and Garfield client list from within, without having to try to steal away a client here, a client there. Stealing clients from rival firms was hard work and bound to be fraught with unnecessary difficulties.

"You can remain as senior partner for a few years," Wilbur explained. He took out a pack, shook out a cigarette, and lit up. He took a long, savoring puff, indifferent to a sign to the left of the booth that ruled, "No Smoking Under Penalty of Law." "You don't have to leave the firm. But what I'm asking is that you bring in a couple of my attorneys and they take over. Let them come in and take over. Let them manage the firm."

"You know I won't do that," Vince bridled. "It's my firm. It'll cause incredible confusion for one thing, and that's not good for a law firm."

"I know that, Vince." Wilbur nodded. "But what else do you got? I want you to transfer your partnership in the firm to me." He raised his hand against any immediate objections. "You agree to that, but only if you otherwise welch."

"You know my good name," Vince said. He grit his teeth, meting out a properly unamused expression, a touch of disdain, to show that he was a man not to be taken lightly, even by loan sharks. "I pay my debts."

"Then no fear, and we're in accord, me with you, you with me. It's easy."

They were interrupted by a visitor to their booth. The visitor had a hard-set face, a native New Yorker of about fifty-five years old. Like Ray Wilbur, he was a regular at the restaurant. The man pointed to the sign on the wall near the booth. He said, "No smoking means no smoking."

Wilbur shifted his cigarette to his left hand and took a drag, exhaled, sending the smoke ceiling-wards.

The man didn't move. He waited. No one else in the restaurant paid them the least attention. "I got all day," the man said.

Wilbur took a couple more quick puffs and then dropped the cigarette into his water glass. It extinguished with a hiss. He settled back in his chair. "See you around, chief."

The man gone back to his table, the lawyers got down to brass tacks.

"I can have it for you by this afternoon, early tomorrow morning," Wilbur said. "Are you staying the night?"

"At the Belvedere."

"Okay." Wilbur was careful to make sure the attorney understood what he was asking. "I calculate interest on your kind of loan at a daily rate of twenty-five and five-tenths percent to the entire sum, compounded day per day. Since you're a friend and an Eli too, twenty and eight-tenths percent for you."

He surveyed Vince over the top of his sandwich. He was interested to see that he took the "day per day" language in stride. His old classmate was a tough cookie, as he expected him to be, or else he was an idiot.

"Okay. You understand when I say compounded, day per day? I do it that way, since a greater part of the people I deal with don't live but day for day."

"I do," Vince said.

Wilbur nodded. That calm meant Vince had urgent need of the money. It wasn't going to be some small sum either. Vince Jorrigo was the type of man who got agitated over small sums of money, but kept his head with big numbers. He was the type who calculated his dinner check to the penny and fretted if he had to pay too much, but wouldn't bat an eye at dropping $10,000 at the roulette wheel. Not the way Wilbur had the habit of looking at the world; he was frugal on all fronts. Money wasn't recreation for him. He didn't care about diversions, games, and pastimes. He didn't care about his reputation or what people thought of him. He was that serious, self-sufficient type of man who hung on until he got results.

"I can wire the money to an account of your choosing, anywhere on the planet and for that there's no fee, whether it's a bank in Switzerland or in Washington, D.C., or as I'm estimating you want,

I can have it brought to you in cash. For that there's a five percent service fee."

"I need it in cash."

"No problem, old chum. Of course listen, Vincent, you and I… no, hear me out please. I want to talk to you not only as a friend, but as a man reasonably acquainted with human nature." They had been friends once, Ray Wilbur comprehended that, but all that was left of that friendship was a vague notion, they'd shared the same law professors. Any feelings beyond that were ephemeral things. "This is gambling money, isn't it? You know, I quite frankly don't approve of gambling. It's a deplorable habit. I for one don't gamble. Gambling was once at the margins, okay? Something to keep the low-life type of man busy. Now it has now become so much a dominant aspect of our culture…"

Vince raised his hand. "Enough of the soapbox. All I need is $60,000."

"$100,000, at least that if no more, Vince. To be sure you won't be coming to me again and again after that."

"I just need my stake."

"A number I like 'cause it's easier to calculate compound interest on it, so $100 thou', huh?" Wilbur hated human contact, found it something greasy, another person's body, but he reached out now across the table and pushed at Vince's arm with the tip of his finger. "Come on, let me loan that amount. I think $100,000 is for you."

Vince shook his head; he felt virtuous doing so. Yes, he was borrowing money at an exorbitant interest rate, but he was limiting himself, he had control. Back and forth and finally they settled on $80,000. Vince didn't need that much but he wanted his old friend to be happy.

"But listen, twenty and eight-tenths percent daily? That's impossible."

"I'm not a Pez dispenser. Money has a cost. That's what I charge, you know when there's no solid collateral."

Vince got to the point. "You can't tweak it for me?"

Wilbur chuckled heartily. "You want bank rates…go to a bank."

"Okay. Okay."

The waiter came by and set a fresh gin and tonic down, taking away the dirty glass. Ray Wilbur glanced up, "Thanks." He took a sip of his drink. "The secret, Vince, is to pay back as quickly as you can. It's not at all impossible. There are people who do it every day. Quick money gets paid back quick." Wilbur went on, explained in a more engaging tone of voice, "The first day of the first week, I leave you alone. But the first day of the second week, I give you a call, 'cause you're you, and see how you doing, are you ready to pay up. Toward the end of the fourth week, that's when I send my man in to collect. My man's no ruffian, he's a lawyer, like me, like you, and he wants to take whatever you can give him..."

"I know how you work."

"You know how I work?" Wilbur got huffy then. "Don't like that. No, no. You can't know how I work until you owe me money. Once you owe me, you owe me. Me. Got it straight now?"

"Okay. All right. Do I have to sign something?"

"See? You don't know how I work. A piece of paper doesn't make this money mine. You make this money mine."

The waiter came up to them again. "How was the steak sandwich?"

"What's that Zuckerman is eating that looks so good?"

"That's a Savoy truffle. Shall I hold you a plate, sir?"

"Not for me, Bob. For him." Wilbur nodded at Vince. "He deserves a sweet."

CHAPTER TEN

*W*ork was the paramount scam, and the world was done wrong by those individuals who did not relax their hold. To compete with those devils, to save the nation from their immodest enterprises, required that good souls forego pleasure, forego love, for pleasure brought only satisfaction, and love weariness, and the weary and the satisfied had to have rest. Rest was honest, and rest was healing, but rest was not a profitable enterprise, and love itself was not the same as work.

This was the second most important lesson Sterrett Emerson Groves learned that summer, that love was not the same as work. It was not a lesson to be learned by midnight study or to be downloaded from a 'puter. It was improbable that any high school teacher or any college professor, any institutionally trained educator of any sort would know enough about life to teach that lesson, or be willing to teach if they knew it. It was a lesson to be grasped with the hand and with the heart, through the rough of experience.

They hadn't been together a full month, Sterrett Emerson Groves and Anne Marie Smith. It was a bit more than two weeks, but it was the Fourth of July weekend and they decided to celebrate being together anyway. They celebrated it with cake and candle Friday evening, and then early Saturday morning, they drove out to Middleburg, Virginia. Anne Marie did the driving. They went out Route 50 in her SUV, all the way out to the town at the foot of the Blue Ridge Mountains where they'd booked rooms in Deek's Tavern.

After checking in, they went exploring the backroads in the car. Anne Marie was drawn to the whole hunt country trip. She went for dark plaids and rusty horseshoes, tea and scones and stuffed heads on the wall. Sterrett was less inclined to imitation English, but he put a good nose on it. In the end he had a fairly good time, too.

He enjoyed it when they went and visited Festival Vineyards, a few miles south of Middleburg, where Springfest champagne was made. They passed a good hour in the converted barn, tasting the champagne, and the Riesling and the Gewürztraminer and the Sauvignon Blanc the winery produced, tasting the grape jellies and jams too, the slices of ham. They passed another couple hours lying side by side in the meadow overlooking the orderly rows of vines, talking and half dozing, with the luscious summer at their feet.

Anne Marie had changed him, Sterrett had changed enough to concede that. He'd acquired friends for one thing, Anne Marie's friends, just the set he himself had always avoided, young up-and-coming lawyers, some with families. They were chatty. They were achievers, and that's what they chatted about, their achievements.

Sterrett's insecurity, his feeling of being abandoned to his own devices, these elements of his character plagued him less. He had been resisting success because a truly successful man was more likely to attract his peers to him, and therefore was more likely to be loved. Being loved, the responsibility of that had always made Sterrett nervous.

Anne Marie soothed his fears, made his life comfortable and easy and above all normal, giving him affection and a social context wherein no real thinking was needed, outside of work. Choices were made, of course, where to go on weekends, what to wear, whether to buy a new cellphone or not. Sometimes a little thinking was needed when one's career was in question, whether to accept a job offer at another firm.

But thinking about things that had to do with how one lived or why one did what one did was not the way to get things done. It was in some ways an ignorant way to live, that was Sterrett's suspicion. But there was an advantage to ignorance, always a great advantage to being ignorant. It precluded doubt. Anne Marie repeated it to him on occasion that he wasn't a serious person to have doubts about his own success. It didn't seem to be the thing to do in Washington, to have doubts.

He discovered that he did live better that way. He discovered that if he tried not to think in a philosophical way about his life, he gained in self-confidence. He found that if he believed in success, and only thought in terms of achieving success, success would be his. He knew that of course already, but it was Anne Marie who made it possible for him to think that way. Anne Marie told him he should be earning more money too, and he agreed. He agreed emphatically, and he decided to start pushing himself forward, that was the direction to take his life.

They had a wonderful lunch Sunday at the Tavern, baked oysters and breast of pheasant with a bottle of white wine, and evening, they sat on the grass and watched the fireworks. That night in their room the only problem they had to face was that the four-poster bed creaked something awful when they made love. But they slept like angels afterwards, with the window open and the cool country air coming in and no mosquitos.

Monday, they drove back into Washington, stopping for lunch in Upperville, stopping to look at lawn furniture in the little town of Aldie. Anne Marie told him it was the best weekend she'd ever had, and Sterrett told her he was glad. Anne Marie poured love and attention on him, and he was feeling as close to happy with a woman he didn't love as any man could.

And so during the final leg of their return drive home, Sterrett, feeling comfortable with the girl, feeling confident, made the mistake of trying to be honest too and explain to her how he felt. Anne Marie thought he was kidding. But no, he told her that he rarely if ever spoke to how he felt. He never opened up to anyone because he considered it a form of conceit to talk about himself, and he was much too intelligent to be conceited. But he told her, in sincere tones, that he was as happy as he could be without being in love with her.

The woman was startled. She was driving, and she was so startled that she had difficulty keeping her eyes on the road. She'd been raised on the popular concept of love; love was all, totally all. Love and more love, that was what made people happy, and there was nothing that couldn't be achieved with love. More, it was impossible that he not love her if she loved him. It was because he willfully resisted love, the way he willfully resisted success that he could even imagine he was happy with her without loving her the way she loved him.

"Maybe it's because I am enjoying at this time my own amount of success at the firm..." she tried to explain her own happiness, trying to hold back the waterworks. "But I can't do it without adding that I love you."

She went on to elaborate her idea of love, and she tried to do it without getting too heated. But she began to raise her voice as he kept saying no to love, and she began to get teary-eyed at the steering wheel, and finally she rebuked him, and through her tears, she insulted him, telling him it was because he was a depressive that he couldn't love, telling him it was because he was an idiot that he couldn't fulfill love's equation properly.

Sterrett answered back with what he believed, still believed about himself. "Love is not what keeps people together," he told her, turning in the passenger seat, turning to face her. "It's fear that does that job."

"Are you afraid of me?" Anne Marie asked aghast.

"In a way," Sterrett said. "Yes. Not of you as you. Or you as a woman…" And the whole thing became explosive when he went on to profess what a man should never profess to a woman, that he preferred being uncared for, unloved, that was what made him, Sterrett claimed, in the end free, a free man. "But it takes courage, that kind of freedom."

Anne Marie pulled over abruptly and turned off the ignition. They were on Route 50 coming through Seven Corners. She unlocked the doors of the car and told him to get out. Sterrett tried to laugh it off. He pointed out that he didn't speak Vietnamese and therefore would be at a total loss wandering around that area. She told him to get out. He didn't and she sat in the car, at the wheel, white as a sheet. She drove the rest of the way home and every time he tried to say something, apologize or whatever, she raised her hand and said, "Quiet. Be quiet."

In her circle, whatever was the problem, it was always best to take a course in it. Or if it was too much of a problem, it became pharmacological. Anne Marie herself was taking a drug called Tlaxcalin, a tranquilizer. Sterrett found out about it that very evening when they finally got to her house on Newark Street. His hateful stubbornness drove her upstairs to the bathroom where she gobbled up a couple of the pills. He followed her to the bathroom. Caught her with the pills in her shaky hand.

"What the hell are you taking?" he said to her.

"When you're upset, it's the best thing," she told him. "You upset me a lot. A lot."

"I don't like your taking pills."

"Then please don't ever give me your idea of love again. I beg you."

Sterrett had trouble understanding how a theoretical discussion could be upsetting. He was talking philosophically, and he told her he was too fond of her to ever want to hurt her feelings. Anne Marie told him to be quiet; she was too wired to speak any longer. She took four pills from the orange bottle of Tlaxcalin, and after that she got in bed and slept like a doll.

That Wednesday, hunched over his desk, a long, bifurcating vein standing out on his forehead, Sterrett himself craved nothing less than the possession of a couple hundred milligrams of Tlaxcalin. But he was not suffering over love, he had more important things to get hung up about. Anne Marie and her pills, he didn't take that seriously. He didn't care less about how much he'd upset her. That was her problem. He had a sanitary landfill to pitch, and the best he could do to tranq' himself was to sharpen and resharpen a number two pencil.

He was preparing his notes for the hearing with the Neighborhood Advisory Committee. The NAC was one of those ineffectual, watered-down administrative institutions the District of Columbia was built upon. Ward Councilman Curtis Bayard was going to preside over the hearing, and his opinion was the only opinion that in any way might matter one way or the other at that late date in the development of the sanitary landfill at the Ellipse.

But there were many ranged against the landfill, and they had made their cause known in the press, on television, and throughout the net, and had demanded a public hearing. Sterrett was busy therefore with ruled paper and pencil trying to put together words that would convince these coltish citizens to change their minds. He was looking forward to it, a kind of baptism of fire. It was going to be the first time he took on a lead role at the firm, and it was a role that had a political twist to it. Thus not for the first time, but for once for real, Sterrett began to dream Washington's big dream. Chin raised to the stale air coming out the vents, he began to think about politics.

Sterrett was struggling however. "Neighbors and concerned citizens, fellow lovers of the environment..." Every time he started to get beyond, "As many of you know, the site at Ellipse is nothing if not..."

the lead broke, and finally the young attorney muttered, "A pain in the ass."

He took the pencil and nuzzled it into a small plastic sharpener. He screwed it round and round and then took it out and blew on the lead tip. Lead dust flew up. Then he began writing, "As you all know it was Sterrett Emerson Groves who taught Torts to be civil. So it is a known matter of fact that he brought the first bench to Washington and told a judge to sit on it..."

"No, no." He tore that page from the pad, crumpled it up, and shot it in the direction of his wastebasket.

He would be pitching to a cranky crowd of men and women, people either extremely ignorant on the subject of trash, and therefore passionate about it, or people informed to the hilt, well beyond what he knew. He knew that most of the landfill would be made up of rubbish, non-decomposing waste, and such debris as came from the construction of various new government buildings. Federal offices in Washington produced 40 tons of trash per year per employee. By hauling that rubbish to a park not 300 yards from the Washington Monument, the government would save 90 percent of the overall cost of disposal, somewhere around $66,000 per federal office employee.

His experience taught him numbers and such, specifics were good in a court of law, where whoever had the heaviest amount of favorable documentation won. He however had to redirect the opinion of the general public, persuade them progress was good, show them the sanitary landfill was progress. He had to present the dump in a favorable light, how mounds of paper, mounds of plastic bottles, mounds of greasy rags could be formed into three marvelously green and contoured hills, indistinguishable from the hills nature herself formed. The landfill would assuredly offer a bucolic background to the White House, as long as one didn't inhale too deeply.

Sterrett tried to boost that aspect, sell the folks the enchanting image of a green way to be. Trash could furnish an image too, of serious work being done, the kind of work that put an entire nation on the move. That would appeal to many. Simply put, great nations produced, progress itself required, lots of trash. The sanitary landfill at the Ellipse would be the concrete and visible measure of America's greatness as a consumer nation. True, it was a dump visible to tourists from the world over, but it would therefore be an extraordinary means to promote America as the one nation offering real solutions.

It was rhetoric that worked, "the one nation offering real solutions." He'd put it in the client's mouth at the appropriate time, a phrase inviting applause. Then Sterrett sat back in his chair. He drummed his pencil against the pad before him, drumming in step with his thoughts. He sat, gazing at the wall, then he began doodling. He stared down at the sheet of paper.

D I N A H

was there at the dead center of his doodles.

He balled that up and dropped it to the floor. He was getting good at wasting paper. He started again, writing on a fresh page, "Friends and neighbors, concerned citizens, America is a great nation..." How many times had that formulation been used in a speech he wondered. His telephone rang, and he tore the receiver from its cradle. "What?"

It was Anne Marie on the telephone.

"'Vulture up to?'" she asked in the amusing way she used. Right off, he could tell she was trying to be lighthearted, had already forgiven him for Sunday night.

"Nothing. I'm working on my speech."

"That's today isn't it?"

"At noon." Sterrett pulled his sleeve back and there was his watch, telling the time.

"You're always doing things at the last minute," Anne Marie said. But she laughed into the phone saying it.

"I got two hours."

"What about this evening? You coming over?"

"Of course, baby." He'd stayed away Tuesday, sleeping by himself in his apartment. He needed to regain a certain control over his situation, that was all. He didn't want her to think he was acting out of spite, staying away from her just because they'd argued. He said, "I'll see you tonight."

"Good. Then I think I'll invite Kiki Farquhar and her husband. We can barbecue, is that okay?"

Sterrett spent more time at Anne Marie's house in Cleveland Park than in his own apartment. He was at the point where he had almost as many underpants and socks there as he did at his place on Wisconsin Avenue. This was in part due to the fact that Anne Marie had a swimming pool in her backyard. She'd bought the house several years earlier at a good price. She came from a wealthy family, and her father, an investment banker, gave her the down payment.

It was a big house, and for all the rooms it had, there were never enough rooms for all the things Anne Marie did. She used one bedroom as her study, and one bedroom as her music room where she practiced the flute and her singing. In the basement, she had an exercise room, fully equipped for everything from Pilates to tai chi. Anne Marie loved to give parties, too. She had her friends and colleagues from Melody Hogan over at least once a week for barbecues. Now that she had a real boyfriend, she let him run the barbecue.

It was a house that Sterrett liked. He liked the house quite a lot, perhaps if truth be told, even more than he liked Anne Marie. He liked the wraparound porch in particular. It reminded him of the porch he had when he was a real little kid and they lived on base at Ft. Bliss. It was the house that made up for those moments of dissatisfaction Sterrett had, those times he wished things had gone differently between him and Dinah, the times when he wished he hadn't shown up at her house on that bicycle the night of the Dubuffet Gala.

He thought about Dinah more often than he should, that was pretty clear. Not so much because he liked her better than Anne Marie, for he suspected women were all alike once they were in a relationship, but because she was someone he didn't have to say a word of explanation to. Dinah knew who he was, what he was, how he felt about life without his having to go into words. She knew it, because she saw through him as easily as if she'd been studying him for a long time. The difference between them was, it made him laugh being the way he was, but Dinah seemed to take a more serious approach, not necessarily disapproving, but certainly wary. He was curious how she was getting on. He had heard the rumors she was dating a congressman, and Sterrett hoped she was doing the right thing, though it was true congressmen made very good money.

"What? A barbecue?" Sterrett said to Anne Marie, trying to keep from groaning. "Tonight?"

"I think it would be nice, yes. There's all that meat in the fridge."

Anne Marie exhausted him, even when she wasn't talking of love, she exhausted him. That was the downside of the house on Newark Street, that it was a house full of chores, and Anne Marie liked to delegate those chores to him. She was a junior partner after all, and she worked harder than he did and made more money than he did, and she spent more money than he did, and theirs was consequently a relationship based on earning power and the fact that the house was hers, which made Anne Marie the boss. She had the strategic advantage too, of having very wealthy, caring parents who were always glad to lend an interfering hand, bossing him around too, something Sterrett could only stand by and endure.

Weekends were the most difficult time. Sterrett was a law associate, and he could afford to take Anne Marie to eat crab in Annapolis or venison in Middleburg, to Harvey's restaurant, downtown, to have baked Alaska, but airplane tickets for two to eat at Morton's of Chicago, in Chicago, or to see a Hollywood premiere in Hollywood, and do something like that every weekend was completely out of his range. Anne Marie offered to pay, she had no problem, but Sterrett had his pride, too. He had to find a way to earn more money. But he was terrified of the idea; he was already working harder than he'd ever thought of doing.

"That means I'll have to pick up charcoal," Sterrett said into the phone.

"Oh yes? Well, you can manage on your bike, one bag, can't you?" the Melody Hogan lawyer said. "I'll buy dessert coming home. Also remember, if we're having guests, the pool needs to be chlorinated today...I love you."

Sterrett hung up hard. He bailed from his desk and went out into the hallway. He said to Suzy, "Anne Marie calls again? Tell her I'm out."

"Out, okay," Suzy said.

"She's likely to call again in about twenty minutes, you know, and go, 'Vulture up to?'" He shook his head.

Suzy watched him. "She's your girlfriend."

On the southwestern side of the city at the corner of G and 22nd Streets was the Pathfinder Middle School, and in the Pathfinder Middle School was the auditorium where the NAC hearing over the sanitary landfill was to take place. The school was a solid building, solid in the way of the 1950s, reddish brown brick giving the impression of being bomb-proof. The auditorium was likewise a throwback to earlier school days, a large drafty hall, the seats, folding seats, the stage flimsy as cardboard; a sad hall the way big drafty halls were.

By the time Sterrett got there, it was full of people, neighbors, environmentalists, local businessmen, a slew of the curious come together to question the turning of 50 acres of the Mall into a garbage dump. They'd come together with some urgency, but in a responsible way. In a way that also guaranteed some news coverage.

Celia Progg from Melody Hogan greeted him at the double doors of the auditorium. She said, "We were waiting for you."

He said, "I couldn't find a taxi."

And his heart leapt up as the doors opened, a crowd, a real crowd. There were placards and shouts from protestors. There were shouts from community leaders, too, solid waste disposal encouraging the active participation of all elements of society, the essence of a relevant democracy. Sterrett marveled. This was grass roots. This was where he wanted to go.

Some of the crowd were seated, some stood. Many people carried signs. The signs were cut out of cardboard, and some were painted to resemble a Christmas tree. Progg led Groves down the aisle to the long foldout table that faced the crowd, and he had a chance to read what some of the Christmas trees had inked on them, "Save the Tree," "Keep Xmas Christian," and "Don't let International Jewry destroy our Tree," and more preposterous things, too.

The Melody Hogan attorney explained in a whisper, "Our biggest adversary, that group, they're dedicated to preserving the site of the National Christmas Tree."

Sterrett had his notes and plenty of supporting documentation in the soft-sided briefcase he was carrying. He had prepared himself by and large for environmental complaints, the toxic odors, the explosive threat of methane, and most of all, the problems concomitant with ground water pollution; he'd learned all there was to learn on impermeable lining. He said, "What's the National Christmas Tree got to do with it?"

"Oh, they'll tell you," Celia replied.

He gave a shrug and reached over to shake hands with the Blast Garnet architect Ian McMinn, AIA. McMinn had come toting a rendering of the site as it would look once the landfill was completed.

"This is Ward Councilman Bayard," Celia said. "He's going to oversee this meeting."

Groves smiled.

"We've talked on the phone," the Councilman said.

Curtis Bayard was a graduate of Howard University's business school and a former furniture store owner who had turned to politics after his company went bankrupt. He was a better politician, as it turned out, than he was a businessman. Diligent and painstaking, his deficiency as a cutthroat businessman proved his main virtue as a legislator in the form of his concern for the welfare of others over and above any personal benefit. He was there as the moderator, giving all voices their chance to be heard, trying to draw a balance between the "pro" and "con" landfill forces.

Sterrett put his notes in order. It was a nervous gesture. He didn't really need them. Everything was down pat in his head. He introduced himself to the hall as representing Sir Simon Psora. He began, "Neighbors, concerned citizens, my fellow Washingtonians. Trash is a problem. But as Sir Simon Psora so often says, this country, the United States of America has always been a Nation with real solutions to offer…"

It was as if the steam pipes in the old building had all at once burst. They wouldn't let him finish, the crowd shouting at him what he couldn't quite catch, chanting phrases he didn't understand, all while agitating their homemade tannenbaums and cardboard bats. Sterrett was buffaloed. But Bayard raised his hand and asked for silence.

"Quiet down."

Sterrett cast a dismal look on Celia sitting to his right; "Help, I need somebody!" his fretful countenance said. Progg gave him a cranky grin and returned to her electronic tablet, busy updating her website profile. Sterrett looked over at Ian McMinn. The architect pretended to have trouble biting his nails. So Sterrett took a deep breath and improvised. He didn't want to screw up the whole public relations aspect of the meeting, because that was all this was.

"If you want to," he said. "I can start off answering questions. If you like that better."

A man rose up from a large group all wearing T-shirts with "No Landfill" on them. They were most of them residents of the District, some of them Hill staffers, some of them bank clerks, some lawyers, young and old, of all races, all of them against putting a waste dump where Unfragrant Bin Systems and the Department of the Interior seemed to want to put it.

"My name is Ron Lenzini. I'm the Neighborhood Advisory commissioner."

"Yes sir, what's your question?"

"Well, we're against the landfill," the man said and sat down again.

The young attorney assumed he was against the landfill because it was a landfill. He went with his modestly researched ecological rhetoric. But the man stood up again and said, "No, we don't care about all that." He passed his hand over his crowd and they all booed and cheered . They were softball players, members of a league, lovers of the burly aluminum bat and the oversized pill. They were angered by the fact that the sanitary landfill was going to take away two of their best playing fields. They were willing, so they claimed, to go to court over the issue.

"I don't know," Sterrett began.

"'Don't touch our field,'" someone jeered.

"I think we can work with the Department of the Interior…what you think, Ian, couldn't there be room down the south end there for at least one softball field?"

"Yes, yes," Ian McMinn said, getting up from the table and going over to the architectural rendering. "We can level these trees here. We move this area around, that's all." He used his pen to indicate the where of what he was saying on the scale drawing. "See? The baseball players can play over in this, around here, that's an area going to be untouched when construction is complete. Do you see?"

"No, I'm not sure I do see." Lenzini shook his head, but he sat down then and grew thoughtful, as thoughtful as league softball players got.

Then there was the muster of politically active students from Georgetown University and American University and George Washington, too. They sat slumped low in the front row. A couple of them wore T-shirts with Che Guevara's hairy and heroic image plastered across it, a couple with Bob Marley. They were not from Washington. They were college students with a vision of how society ought to work.

"We're concerned students," one of them got up to say. "And we're concerned that this garbage thing is going to impose restrictions on us. Okay? On our tossing the Frisbee around for instance. Yeah, it's no joke."

"Sit down," one of the softball players yelled. The softballers were hostile to the Frisbee players, since they were reckless kids and often spilled over into an ongoing game, ruining a run or crashing into a softball player trying to field a ball. The students often brought dogs with them who also got in underfoot of a game. It was annoying and there were other shouts, back and forth, voices raised in free exercise.

Amid all this, near the back of the hall sat an aged African American couple. They had come to the Pathfinder Middle School with some fear in their footfall. They lived in a modern apartment complex near the Southwest Freeway and were afraid of robberies in broad daylight. The man was a retired bus driver, a clean, round face lined with worry, his big hands at rest on his knees. His wife was dressed in an elegant if somewhat dated manner and carried a very big purse.

They listened attentively to all that was said and were mainly concerned that the Mall, the parks surrounding the Mall, should remain leafy areas for the sake of the beauty and health of the city. That was their concern, the city itself.

"What we'd like," the woman said, holding her purse before her like a Viking shield, "is to have more time. I can't believe anyone would think this is a good idea. I'd like to have more of these meetings and I'd like some assurance that these meetings, well, if there is an objection, this dump will be stopped."

Because they were old and black, they were listened to with attention by the pro-refuse panel that sat at the foldout table facing the auditorium. They were listened to for the sake of appearances, and certainly not heeded.

Sterrett smiled condescendingly on the couple. "We will have plenty more of these meetings, I can assure you. And if there is a problem we'll hold up on going forward until that problem is resolved."

That was a lie. He had no choice, but to lie. He was used to stretching the truth at a conference table or on a conference call, and he had lied once or twice, little white lies, and they were lies made to other lawyers, but Sterrett had never lied publically to people who were not lawyers. But now, he was being forced by circumstances to lie. There was no intention of delaying, postponing, or abrogating in any way the landfill at the Ellipse just because of a few private citizens. But Sterrett didn't want to say so. He saw it made everything go easier if he lied. He saw it made people more content to be lied to.

There were environmentalists at the meeting, plenty of them. But they were all too well-meaning, too polite, with way too much respect for the democratic process. Had they been more like the other groups, more aggressive and rude, they would have agitated at least one protest sign and gotten themselves heard. They would have shouted what they had to say, would have jumped up and down.

The environmentalist had brought no signs at all, but instead a box-load of expert documentation gauging the negative impact a landfill would have, the general territorial degradation and health menace incurred by storing decomposing solid waste in the heart of an urban area. They knew they were right, and they were right, but they sat there in their seats all of them, waiting their turn, knowing they were right.

The Tree people were indeed another kettle of fish. The Ellipse had been the site of a National Christmas Tree since the second term of Franklin Roosevelt when some Civilian Conservation Corps loggers up Oregon way sent a jumbo fir down to Washington as a gesture of thanks. Many retirees who didn't have the money or energy to erect a tree of their own in their apartment relied on the National Tree's splendor and warmth during the holidays; otherwise they would be unable to participate in the spirit of Christmas.

The mouthpiece for the Tree people got up and explained this. He was a spruce man with a trim, pointed beard, a pipe clenched tight between his teeth. The lighting of the Tree by the President of the United States was the big issue for him. No one had the right to take that away from him. The hall vibrated with the stomp of feet, echoed with the repeated yells of the sign-waving National Christmas Tree faction, all in concord with the pipe smoker's righteous affirmation.

Sterrett had no help from Progg, no help from McMinn. They didn't care. It was easy for them, but Sterrett was there representing the client, and he would get Hell from Mr. Jorrigo and from Sir Simon. The Greek Dustman liked to have the public on his side, pure vanity, but it was also a way of spreading round the responsibility. That was democracy's great boon to businessmen.

"Okay, okay," Sterrett began. He had to invent something, invent something convincing, a whopper of a lie, if only to silence the droning and interminable pontifications of the Tree Party's pipe-smoking spokesman. "We thought about this issue, yes we did. We're going to let the National Christmas Tree stand," the young attorney said. "As Mr. McMinn will show you," he went on, tacking McMinn to his rendering board with an obstinate look. "The Christmas tree will be given a more prominent stage than ever before, with its own mound of refuse on which to stand. So tourists and let's say, children of all ages will still be able to go to the Ellipse and enjoy themselves, Christmas time."

"What about the stink?" one of the Tree Party complained. "I hardly think it's going to be inviting walking around with the smell and the stink and the pew."

"We want to recreate the natural beauty of the site. A bower, that's what the whole site will resemble, you know, a fragrant bower offering shade in summer and shelter in the fall," Sterrett said, getting back to his original material. "Instead of simply dumping waste, instead of soiling nature, we gently yield back to nature what came from nature in the form of the fundamental layer of an ecosystem that will offer nutrition to animals, to birds, to communities of plants and insects who will turn the site into a living habitat. Where once there was only grass, now there will arise hillocks full of the bug tussle of life. There will be birds to sing sweet lullabies and squirrels and…"

"Rats."

Sterrett mashed his lips together; this was what he feared, people not interested in a poetic description of the sanitary landfill as it might look if it were going to look the way the architect's rendering made it look, but interested in the facts. How to handle that, he wondered. He peered uncertainly into the crowd. "Rats?" he asked, dropping into his seat. "In what sense?"

"They're going to be rats, more of them than ever because of the garbage," one of the concerned residents said.

Celia raised her head out of her social networking and listened to the bad buzz about rodents. She pushed her tablet away from her and spoke up finally, projecting her voice to the audience, a voice of inescapable self-assurance, "I represent the Department of the Interior. The Interior was constituted in 1849, so it's been around for some time. The present Secretary of the Interior, Dr. Thomas Morrow, takes his role as custodian of America's natural resources seriously. He has approved the site. That should tell you something, shouldn't it?"

"It don't tell us anything about rats," another person shouted out. Rats, the crowd was getting agitated over the idea, hungry for an issue with bite.

"What about mice? They're worse than rats."

"Really, there's nothing to fear," Progg tried. "The Department of the Interior guarantees the area will be rat free. Shouldn't that be enough?"

"No. It's not enough," several people howled at her.

And now Celia Progg got to her feet, her foldout chair rattling as she pushed it away, and she went so far as to smile upon the tumultuous crowd, for she had seen the news reporter come tiptoeing in through the swinging doors of the auditorium, a reporter and a cameraman. The reporter, a young woman from a local network television station, advanced slowly down the side aisle, and the cameraman focused on the Melody Hogan attorney.

"The same care and methodical upkeep that goes into making our national parks safe and pest-free will be applied here, for whether it's a park or a landfill, we care. And we will work with Unfragrant Bin Systems to keep the landfill a model landfill. The other benefit I want to talk to you about today is that when this Yuletide comes round, my client, the Department of the Interior, will be putting up the biggest Christmas tree ever."

"Yeah? Well what kind of tree?" someone demanded.

"Oh, I think pine," Celia Progg said.

Someone else said, "Fir is better than pine."

"My client," Celia began. "My client, the Department of the Interior, has asked Steven Spielberg himself to design the lights and the display for the National Christmas Tree this year, and the president and his wife will be there, his children of course, both of them, but the surprise is, the big surprise is that the president's dog will be the one to light the tree. With his paw. He will be dressed in a green thunder coat like a cuddly, unshaven elf."

The Xmas Tree people were smitten. The idea was too cute to resist. They put aside their fear of rats and applauded. But one of the environmentalists decided it was time to make her point of view heard. She stood up and spoke with such frighteningly well-mannered respect and honesty that she was in danger of not being understood by anyone. She delivered what amounted to a highly informed lecture on the dangers of landfills. She concluded what she had to say, asking pointedly, "What about PCB seepage? PCBs are fatal to trees but also to animals, and people, too. Isn't that something we should worry about?"

"No, seepage isn't an issue," Sterrett said, jumping back into the arena, happy at last to be able to put to use the reading he'd done. "We use a nonpermeable plastic lining made of nondegradable polymicron fiber. Polymicron fiber, by the way, can withstand a pressure of up to nine atmospheres per square inch, one atmosphere is 14.7 pounds per square inch, so do the math, and you'll see this lining is one tough customer. There will be a double lining at the bottom of the site and a single sheet at each subsequent layer of trash. This lining can also withstand extreme temperatures and is guaranteed by the manufacturer."

"Polymicron?" the woman said. "That's an even worse pollutant than most PCBs. It leeches over time, right into the ground."

"Sir Simon Psora uses it in all his fills and has never recorded a single problem."

Curtis Bayard didn't want to go on the record for or against the sanitary landfill, certainly not on television. He'd made a speech about the issue in the District Council. His speech left each party in the discussion convinced he was on their side. But the vote to approve the project remained tied. Curtis Bayard had abstained. He was too intelligent a man to come to a final decision without a lot of hand-wringing.

"I have to get a clearer picture here," Councilman Bayard said, addressing the Guiteau and Garfield attorney. "What for instance do your studies say will be the impact of this project both uh, during construction and uh, during full operation on tourism? What about, you know, all those people, the tourists and the rest who want to enjoy the park? The District gets more than half of its revenue from these sorts of tourists. What will be the impact there?"

Sterrett didn't have to think one second about that. Its impact was going to be negative. People didn't drive across country, people didn't fly a thousand miles with their kids to see a trash dump spewing forth foul odors. They could see that at home. They came to Washington to bask in museums. They came to dance to the tour guide's pipe through groves of beech and sacred groves of oak. But Sterrett was getting good at answers. He said, "Tourism won't be affected in the least."

"I'm glad of that," Councilman Bayard said. "But I'm not yet convinced that this will be good overall for Washington, and by that you know, I'm talking about the District of Columbia where people live. Please convince me."

Sterrett was quiet a moment, gathering the forces of oratory within him, and he remained sitting. He felt convinced he was a natural speaker when it came to politics. He fixed the District politician, all the while conscious of the cameraman and of the microphone the news reporter was holding out to him. This was a chance like few others. He envisioned himself someday, surrounded by klieg lights and television cameras, making a stand on the federal courthouse steps, demanding fair play on behalf of his beleaguered client. Or perhaps he'd be making his moves on the floor as a young congressman. He stood up then, affecting a magisterial tone.

"I for one, was born in this city," he boomed. "This is my city and I care about it as much if not more than any of you. I can assure you Mr. Bayard, no one will notice that the landfill is being built until it is built. Every aspect of the disposal methodology has been made secure. Any eventual groundwater pollution has been shown in several scientific studies to amount to less than one percent of one percent."

That was another lie. There had been no study. But it sounded good and it sounded convincing and no one rose to challenge him and he went on. "The total costs of building and operating at the Ellipse will be handled by the Unfragrant Bin Systems. Of course the landfill will base its corporate headquarters here in the District and will therefore pay District taxes."

Lie again, that was one hundred and ten percent another lie. Sterrett had himself, only a week ago, compiled the paperwork so that Sir Simon could incorporate the landfill management and development companies in pro-business Delaware, and they would be owned by a partnership ultimately based in Liechtenstein. But he had no feeling of nausea, no, he was not just stomach, but guts too as his boss would say. More, he felt he'd worked as hard as any manual laborer in the last few minutes, digging himself with great skill and ardor out of the hole he was in, for lying was work.

He had lied, and lied to people who trusted his word, yet he had lied genially, convincingly here at this public meeting. He had done it and it didn't feel bad at all, a revelation that you could lie, even with a news camera in the room, and people would believe you. Lying was powerful. It gave a man supremacy over others.

"So you see, we believe and believe strongly in this landfill, not because it will bring us a profit. It might and then again it might not. Let the market determine that. The market will determine that. No, we believe strongly in this landfill because it is what Washington needs, what America calls for, a modern, scientifically approved, aesthetically attractive garbage dump. The Nation's capital will be the first world capital to bring the future of waste management into the present, and do so to everyone's benefit. For the wealth this site will generate in terms of jobs and investment opportunities will be spread around," the young attorney affirmed, and he peered round the room, trying to make eye contact with as many people as he could, radiating sincerity.

"It will help to improve rather than to harm the conditions of working men and women, people like me for instance who in fact reside and daily work in this fine city of ours." He paused. He felt tipsy from so much rhetoric and had to steady himself, leaning forward, both hands on the table. He gave Curtis Bayard a solemn look. "That's our notion of recycling at the Unfragrant Bin Systems. You can either be a part of that or not, Mr. Councilman."

It was boldly spoken and there was a hush in the auditorium, followed by a smattering of applause. The National Christmas Tree people and the softball players were fairly convinced by what they'd heard, but it had gotten that warm in the school's auditorium that even clapping hands, that most American of gestures, required way too much energy. Sterrett lifted his heart to what applause there was, and in that moment felt his own importance right down to the heel of his shoes. That was the purpose of work, to give a man attitude.

The elderly black woman in the back of the hall stood up. "But what about the trees? I don't mean that darn Christmas tree, but the real trees, the living trees, oak and maple, that shade the site?" She had a strong, unwavering voice. Her husband tried to shush her, but she spoke clear as a bell. "In case you don't know it, we need trees, and the birds, what about them?"

"The landfill will certainly see seagulls…"

"I mean songbirds, young man. Without trees to nest in where will the songbirds go? The cardinal, hermit thrush, and the meadowlark."

"If you feel so strongly about the goddamn meadowlarks," Sterrett shouted suddenly, "then why don't you buy the park yourself and give us a break?"

"You poor man," the woman said as her husband pulled her down, got her back into her chair. "You don't even know how to live."

"Do we have any other questions concerning the landfill?" Celia stepped in to say. "That's what we're here for, to answer your concerns about this landfill. And not about birds or trees."

There were no real questions in the air, some shrill voices trying to be heard, mostly the softballers. Celia glanced at her electronic notebook and told the gathering, one and all, "If you have serious questions to ask, or if you want to follow the progress of construction at the landfill, you can always visit our site. Let me give you the address." That got everyone concentrated. Thumbs began working cellphones and Blackberries, pads and netbooks. She repeated the address, staring full on at the reporter and her news camera.

"But, hey," one of the university students said with an air of having thought about the thing for at least half an hour. "Won't it be a big hole in the ground for the first couple months? I mean what's that all about?"

"The solution is we'll put a decorative fence all around the site," Ian McMinn, AIA, offered. "With a decorative fence, you won't ever notice we're digging."

The spokesman for the National Christmas Tree people was bowled over. He moved his pipe to the other side of his mouth and said, "Yes, I have to admit, a decorative fence would be rather nice."

"It went well, I think. What do you think?"

They were walking to Ian McMinn's car, parked on the school's kickball court. McMinn was carrying the large foam-board rendering awkwardly under his arm. He said, "It went very well. They really liked the drawing." A beep-beep sounded, and the trunk of his car flew open.

"I think we can steal an extra half acre along the 17th Street side," Ian McMinn was saying, careful to lay the rendering of the site flat in his trunk, tucking it in an old blanket. "I have that in the new plans, but I decided not to show it in this drawing. I thought it would just cause confusion."

"You did right, not saying a word," Celia agreed.

"We're going to have to mention it eventually," Sterrett offered.

"Mention what?" Curtis Bayard asked as he cantered over to them. He and Ron Lenzini had been talking. Lenzini was satisfied, and Bayard was satisfied too, the project had the public's support. "That nonsense about the president's dog lighting the tree?"

"It was supposed to be a secret," Celia answered in all honesty.

"Well, listen," Curtis said. "We do appreciate your coming down and talking to us. I wanted you all to know that."

Celia shook hands with the ward councilman. "The landfill has legs," she told him firmly. "I think it's going to be good for Washington, good for the District, too."

"The District is always glad to be a willing partner in whatever endeavor is good for the District," Curtis Bayard answered.

McMinn closed his trunk, did a little hop getting into his car, to show how much in a hurry he was. "I have to go back to the office. I'll send you those new drawings, Celia. All right?"

Sterrett stood moping around a moment. "I'm glad to have met you, sir," he said to Bayard.

"You did a fine job in there," Curtis told him. "I've rarely seen a hearing start off so badly and end so fine."

"Well, uh, thanks, sir," Sterrett answered in a hesitant, slightly imbecile way, feeling ashamed all at once. He knew that it was ridiculous to feel that way, but he did. One thing Sterrett's father hated was lies. Berwick had died in a hygienic bed at Walter Reed because of lies, government lies about depleted uranium. "I did my best…but…" No, he had not done his best; he'd simply done what was expected of him. "I hope, uh, we can move forward and, uh…"

"My job now," Curtis Bayard went on. "Inform the City Council and the mayor that this landfill is definitely in the District's interests. To give the green light."

Sterrett swelled up his cheeks, fingers to his lips, and whistled down a taxicab. A brown and beige Victor Company cab, its clever motto printed on the door, "ViCo where you want to go," pulled to the curb. The corner of M and 25th was where. He tossed his briefcase onto the backseat and got in. Ensconced in the back of the taxicab, he began to think. But not for long. He peered out the window and saw unexpected scenery. They were headed for Memorial Bridge, for Arlington, Virginia.

"Do you understand where I'm going?"

The cabby dropped his arm out the window in a languorous gesture. He was a man in his mid-fifties and maybe that explained his look of truculent boredom. Sterrett fell back into his seat. He was either too polite or it was the fault of his voice. He wasn't stern enough or tough enough when he spoke. Some people had their cabdriver take them right to where they wanted to go.

"If you were a real cabdriver, I'd be there by now. Stop. Stop here."

He was in the shadow of the Lincoln Memorial and the Vietnam Veterans. He got out and paid the cabby, a "go to hell" the only tip, words on the tip of his tongue. He made his way tramping along the edge of the Mall, swinging his briefcase like any tourist. He felt uneasy, sweaty under the high, gold-hatted sun, but really he'd proved himself well beyond his own expectations. Celia Progg saw it. She'd be sure to tell Jorrigo, and the word would get spread around, Groves had quieted an angry, fruitcake mob.

The old Groves would have cut right across the Mall to the Old Inebriate Grill and would have slapped himself on the back with any number of ice-cold beers. But the new Groves wasn't lucky enough to have that point of reference anymore. The new Groves had to think of himself, his name and reputation, and then there was Anne Marie. She would surely let him know he was letting her down if he went and got drunk.

He dropped his feet along Constitution Avenue, the big feet, intrepid feet, the dynamic extremities of a successful and dynamic attorney. Behind him, rising out of reclaimed swampland was the Washington Monument. It stood on a mound of earth, bleach-white like a reliquary bone. It had proved useful, Sterrett thought, and he recalled his speech about the Monument at the big meeting with the Melody Hogan attorneys, what seemed now like eons ago. DeMurphy was still working for the firm then, and Anne Marie nothing more than a rival attorney. But it was true, there was that line, the murkier stone. It was true, that murkier stone marked a failure of will before oncoming events.

Sterrett walked to the corner of Constitution, ready to cross the avenue. He cocked his head, where did he find himself, but standing opposite that 50-acre oval of grass and some trees, called the Ellipse. He hadn't been there, on foot, since years back. He'd gone there one Christmas Day to see the tree Ronald Reagan had lighted, a big blue and silver tree. Now he wanted to have a look-see, something a lawyer rarely did, take a look at the actual substance of what he was negotiating over. He wanted to see what the fuss was about.

But first he went up 17th Street to E Street, where he found a convenience store open, an Orange-U-Glad store. He went into the store and bought a bottle of imported beer, one bottle. There were only a few people about, a low-level bureaucrat buying cigarettes. Sterrett hung out in front of the store, drinking some beer out of the brown paper bag. Then he headed for the Ellipse.

He went back across 17th street and through the trees. There were pigeons on the grassy lawn, pigeons scattered in the grass, alarm, alarm. Sterrett watched them flop into the sky as he approached, pigeons making a wide turn to come back to the same spot, always coming back to the exact same spot. He thought that worth smiling at.

The Ellipse was mostly sunlit. It was surrounded by trees, many of them more than a century old. There was the statue dedicated to the Boy Scouts back among the trees, he'd forgotten about that, and the sandstone zero mile marker at the very north point of the site. Bleachers filled one side of the broad, oval expanse of grass, and the other side was full of parked cars, mostly staffers at the White House and

Treasury. Out in the middle of the Ellipse, some kids were running around pulling on a kite. It was a green space that announced itself, "For the Public Good."

Sterrett walked around, turned his eyes to the open sky. It made feeling the way he was feeling less of a burden, the open sky. He sat down on a park bench. He glanced up the lawn at the bluff brow of the White House. He was in truth disappointed. The Ellipse wasn't much of a park. It was weedy, badly maintained, and it was neither useful in embellishing the view to the Executive Mansion nor did it impact in any awesome way on the view across the Mall to the river. It was simply a green space with some shade. This was what he was pouring out his hours for, what he was working for, to transform that part of the Mall into something that could be used.

"Better knock down all these trees first," Sterrett blustered.

But he couldn't take much comfort in sarcasm. His sense of humor had changed along with much else about him. He sat forward on the bench, clutching the bottle of imported beer. He took a drink. He tried just breathing and not thinking. He liked the way the sun rested among the trees. The black woman in the auditorium was right. What was there more beautiful than a tree, durable and lofty, its blind, burrowing roots, its reaching limbs, nothing was more beautiful, that was the hands down answer.

Sterrett had read enough as a teenager, in high school and in college, of novels and poetry to know that there was a way to be that had nothing to do with sitting at his desk working, a way more vital, like the way a tree stood in a field. He knew that the tree had an importance to him. But it was knowledge that didn't fit in.

He drank from the paper bag. He put the mouth of the bottle to his lips and drank. A dribble of cold beer ran to his chin. He wiped it dry, pawing his chin roughly. What did fit in was the knowledge that he was a part of a conspiracy to deceive, knowing what he knew about Sir Simon and his lab technicians, knowing how much of the landfill was rotten, how badly it was going to smell. But up until then Sterrett had been as much a victim of that rancid deception as anyone else.

Now and for the first time in his life, he himself had lied, not to other lawyers, what might be considered reasonable, permissible lies, but to people not otherwise professionally prepared for lies. He had made a speech at the hearing, had willingly, boisterously deceived the public for personal advantage. So what, he thought. He'd done it, and no lightning bolt fell out of the heavens to cut him down. If anything he would garner blessings, prayers of gratitude from the client. The blessed Groves.

CHAPTER ELEVEN

The weather continued the way the weather did, in a circular pattern, turning on itself, moving forward by moving roundabout. The rain clouds that battened on the Northeast were finally being pushed out over the Atlantic by the Canadian breezes. But it was July, never a dry month in Washington, and the clouds circled round one more time, moving south, and now rain soaked the cornfields of Montgomery County, churned across Meridian Hill Park, washing the dust from the leaves, whitening the air above the Tidal Basin.

Celia Progg met Vincent Jorrigo at Union Station. She was carrying a large umbrella. Vince was so intent, he came up the platform looking almost depraved, his neck out, his eyes darting round him. He had the money. The Bitch, that was his only thought. He forgot to kiss her, to kiss Celia, putting out his hand like a rank stoopnagle. She had to reach up and kiss him. They got into her car and made round the circle, good-man Columbus rising alongside them in his stone toga.

"What's in that briefcase?" Celia asked him, seeing the tender way Vince held the battered briefcase Wilbur had given him. "It looks as though it was tossed out the window of a passing train."

"Toiletries."

"Money in it?"

"My shaver, a toothbrush," Vince said. He didn't want lectures on his gambling, and he didn't want to be burdened by the woman's anxieties over his gambling, not on the eve of the Bitch. Celia knew what was in the briefcase, but he was letting her know he wasn't going to compromise himself by confiding in her. "A magazine."

"Which magazine?"

"*Regardie's*. An old copy."

"It's got to be an old copy," Celia agreed. "You're pathetic."

She went on to fill him in. There was good news, the District was going to approve the sanitary landfill, and the protests had melted away, and it was in large part due to the efforts of Jorrigo's law associate, Sterrett Emerson Groves.

"He did a good job. I was impressed."

"Good."

The director of the Bureau of Land Management, Antonia Segreen, hadn't even read through the latest version of the ground lease, she was that ready to sign it and get the landfill underway. Both Congress and the administration had put their thumbs high in the rubbishy air, "go for it."

"Signing's for the end of the month, if all goes well," Celia said as she drove down 15th Street, heading for the Washington marina. "You have to ask Sir Simon when he can be in town. Segreen will adjust her schedule around his needs."

"Won't be in town. I told you, he's a total loss, mentally. The only one he'll talk to is Groves. His son the Kid will fly in. I'll call him and let him know," Vince answered.

"You could have called these last few days," Celia said. "Once."

He grinned. "Well, I did call you once."

"Yes, for your chauffeur," Celia said. She swung past the fish vendors on Maine Avenue, and then she pulled up to the forecourt in front of the Tahoga Yacht Club. They waited a minute in the car. She could tell Vince was in that mood, like a turtle, when he pulled himself into his shell.

"You want me to come on board tonight?" she asked him.

"Not tonight," he said. Lucky in love was bad luck for cards. Vince didn't want to have anything to do with her until after the Bitch game. He'd even send her off angry if it were in his power to do so. Win or lose, everything was focused on the Bitch.

"Give me a hug, will you?" Celia said.

He reached over and hugged the woman, hugged her hard, and she held onto him. She nestled her head between his head and shoulder, and kissed him. She let him go.

"I won't say 'good luck.' I know you hate that."

Stepping into the rain, no hat, no umbrella, Vincent Jorrigo burst into a run, holding the briefcase over his head, his small travel bag slung upon his shoulder. He went through the marina gates, and when the security guard stopped him, he barked out his name. The guard nodded. Vince went down to pier number four, slip 29, where he found his boat, the *Arabella*, riding the tide as surely as ever. In the rain the moldy film that ran round the waist of the boat was distinctly visible, but it didn't faze Vince in the least. He lay in his bunk in the darkened cabin of the *Arabella*, feeling much too serene.

Seven o'clock in the evening the next day, a Sunday, Vince was on Independence Avenue. It had rained a brief rain that morning, and he had the top up and was at the wheel of his car heading towards RFK Stadium, to the southeast of Washington. His car was an old model British sports car, its maple-wood luxury never dated. Vince seldom used his car. Most of the time the car was in the garage of the Guiteau Building and some of the time it was in the shop. No other car was its equal when it was tuned and running smooth. But there was a lot of humidity in the air that evening, and the car's 2.0-liter engine hiccupped, but Vince was after all a mule-head. He was going to get where he was going no matter what.

The battered brown briefcase was there on the seat next to him, not belted in, but looking quite safe. It was always important that money be kept safe. He had his stake, $30,000 and another $50,000, enough to buy more chips and keep playing. That was the Bitch, you had to keep playing.

There was little traffic, and he accelerated up the avenue, going through a light that shrieked red near the Botanical Gardens. He looked up in his mirror, but there was no cop hurtling after him and no flash of a camera. His face in the rearview was a face that was perhaps too ethnic. The mouth, the nose, broad features, too common to appeal to the elite, to the Caste, nothing he could do about that. It was nature.

His name too, he disliked it, had always disliked it, not Vince or Vincent, that was fine, it was from the Latin and meant "winner, conqueror." But his name, Vincente Jorrigo, of Portuguese origin, not American at all. As a youth he had wanted something more like Skywalker or Callahan in a last name, or best of all something like Shaft. He used to carry business cards he'd made for himself using a brown crayon and pieces of paper he cut out, "Vincent Shaft, Can You Dig It!" He knew what every child knew, no one messed with Shaft.

At 3rd Street, Vince made a left-hand turn from Independence onto East Capitol Street. He did feel good. He did believe in his fate, and his fate that evening was going to be to win. He would win, even though there was no reasonable expectation on his part that he would come out a winner. He saw with both eyes open that he was being reckless going to the Bitch with borrowed money, with so much borrowed money and on such terms, but he cared not a hoot. More, it made him angry that he was still reasoning that way. Fortune despised the weak-hearted man. He was going to win. He was going to foment nothing but good luck in his life from here on in.

Nothing changed a man's life like winning the Bitch. The Bitch was Frank Mavis's baby. He'd inherited it from another man whose name was Frank, Frank Wallach, taking it over when Wallach went on to serve time in North Carolina for a drug violation. Wallach himself had inherited the game from still another Frank, Frank Harding, who'd ended his days abruptly in a gun battle with a bunch of Georgia state patrolmen. Frank Harding had started the game on coming home from the war in Korea. Every Bitch Master being named Frank, that was surely no more than a coincidence. But it was spooky enough that Frank Mavis had already designated a younger colleague, a non-Frank, Scott Dunkirk, as his successor. Dunkirk was learning the ropes, working Caesar's in Atlantic City.

What made the Bitch particular, that was what made it worth inheriting. Harding had crafted the Bitch to be like any wife, full of arbitrary rules. One thing was the stakes. It was a no-limit game, no-limit to the amount of money wagered and no-limit on the times a player could raise. Another was the wild card. Every third round of play, a joker was introduced into the deck for one complete round.

Frank Mavis, known as Half Price, was a retired investment analyst formerly with the Simpson Archer Brokerage Company of Birmingham, Alabama. He hosted a number of poker games in any given town, rolling on through the country like an old-fashioned knife sharpener or pot tinker, rolling north-south as the season urged. He and his several nephews and his niece served the players and guaranteed the safety of the venue, both against the criminal element and against the police. Only six players were ever invited to play at a time, the names left to the discretion of Mavis's local contacts. There were no gate-crashers. Gatecrashers were dealt with speedily. Half Price's oldest nephew was always heavily armed.

"Smack is Back" was spray-painted on an overflowing dumpster, but Vince wasn't lost. He knew the street led out to the D.C. Armory and the parking lots surrounding the old Redskins stadium. Vince looked at his watch. He was going to get there early. There was still light in the sky, but inside the car, there was already the feel of dark-ness.

There were only a few cars parked in the lot. Mavis's large Road Quest motorhome sat off on its own. From the antenna of the mo-torhome a faded Confederate flag rose to each lethargic puff of air from the Anacostia River. The flag gave the Road Quest that perfect look of an operations center deep in hostile country. Vince parked in front and got out of his car. He squinted up at the flag, grimaced. One of Mavis's nephews came striding up to him. He took a piece of note-paper out of his shirt pocket, a ball-point pen from under the rim of his ball cap.

"Who you?"

"I'm Vince."

The nephew grinned. He was the second oldest nephew, a thor-ough type, and he checked that name off his list of six names. He glanced at the attorney's car. He shook his head. "Look what kind of shit ass convertible you got."

"Don't judge a book by its cover."

"I meant it like, in a good sense. One of those sports cars like that, it's always cool. I was barely born yet. But shit. That car's simple."

Vince agreed in a doubtful way it was simple, and then carrying the briefcase, headed the two steps up.

"Welcome on board," the girl said, opening the door to the trailer. She indicated herself. "My name's Vera. How you today?"

She wore denim shorts and a halter top that was really nothing more than a large silk scarf knotted around her neck and low across the back, obviously not wearing anything that Vince considered lingerie, which was fine. He was there to focus on the cards. The girl guided him to where the round gaming table was. One of the men at the table waved to see Vince.

"Bought yourself a new briefcase?" Curveball, Dr. Clarence Dunne, D.D.S. asked, batting his eyes at the battered brown briefcase. There could be nothing like friends at the Bitch, and Curveball wanted to put a tolerable distance between them. "Goes with that old car of yours."

"New isn't always better," Vince said. He moved around carefully, keeping the briefcase high against his chest.

The Road Quest revealed itself homey inside, if not spacious, and though there wasn't much walking-around room, where did a gambler need to walk, nowhere was the answer. To the john. The colors inside were restful, light browns, beige, and off-white. The ceiling high, the walls were wood-paneled, and the floor was wood parquet, the seats soft leather. Better than a hotel room, there was nothing extraneous, no pay-per-view television. No nosey-parker bellhop at the door knocking.

Half Price, wasn't in yet. He was eating at his favorite restaurant in D.C., Duke Zeibert's, and the people at the table were shuffling cards, playing with their cellphones, waiting for the Bitch to start up. Half Price always kept players waiting. He felt it was a way for them to understand better the principle of time. Card players thought they had forever, so let them get a feel of what forever was like was the idea.

Already seated at the table, Leonard Between Dogs waved to Vince Jorrigo. "Plant yourself beside me," Leonard B. said in a jovial way. "Last time you brought me luck."

One of Mavis's nephews stood at the sink opening one liquor bottle after another. When he saw the attorney look round him questioningly, the nephew went and got the man a chair from the back where the bedroom was. He held up until the attorney pointed, and then the nephew set the chair down next to the "Frost of the Plains" Indian. Vince sat down, swinging the briefcase under the table. He asked for a vodka martini with ice. Leonard B. offered him a cigar.

"Cuban, won't stain your teeth," the poet said, passing a corona to the attorney.

The dentist, Curveball, made his own comment, "You two lovebirds or what?"

About ten minutes later the network news anchor, Sky King, arrived. He paused in the cramped doorway, dressed in a checked sports jacket. He had on a pale blue polo shirt, and his pants were designer blue jeans bought in Hong Kong. What he hoped the others would notice however was his tan. He had a rugged, outdoorsy air, like a weekend rancher, and the tan was the confirmation of just how rugged he was. But no one even looked at him, and he sat down to the right of Curveball and said, "Boys, it's hot outside."

"You want a drink?" Vera asked him, and he told her a Jack Daniels with ice and a little lemon. Right away he took out a cigarette and lit up with a gold lighter. The crisp tobacco withered to ash between his fingers as he took a long puff. He looked across the table at Vince. "Did you see the latest movie by Spike Lee, Vince?"

"No," Vince said, always surprised when people treated him like he was an expert on things African American, movies by Lee, books by Walker, the politics of Colin Powell. "I didn't even know he had a movie out."

"You should go," Sky King went on. "A real thoughtful piece of work."

"Who goes to movies anymore?" Leonard Between Dogs put in. "Except I mean, children."

"Unless you have children."

"Mine are all grown, thank god."

"Hey, when's your uncle getting here?" Curveball asked Vera.

The players began getting hunkered down round the table. Each man had his own talisman, his personal good-luck piece, his own bit of juju. It was key that the talisman or magic ritual remain obscure to the others, and for instance Curveball went so far as to perform distracting business that was however not the real clue to his luck.

Vince too had a ritual he went through, and he went through it now, conscious that his fear of his losing streak continuing had put the yellow in his eyes. He didn't want the others to see. He knew Curveball had seen it, and he didn't want the others to know how much strain he was under, how desperate he was to make the night his. He took extra care in completing his little routine. He didn't want anything to disturb him, so he gave all his concentration to doing what he always did before a poker game.

Vince had already unbuttoned one button of his shirtsleeve and was moving on to the next stage when the motorhome shook, tilted slightly, and in came a young man, lifted through the narrow door by two of Half Price's nephews. The man's wheelchair followed, folded up. The young man, known as Stagecoach, gave orders even as he lay slumped in one of the nephews' arms. He had the wheelchair set up at the card table and told the two youths how to drop him down into his seat. He never let go one single expression of self-pity or anger, even when one of the younger nephews made known with grunts his dislike for taking orders from a cripple.

Stagecoach was not a famous figure, either nationally or regionally, like the poet and the news anchor. He was not a multimillionaire like the dentist. Nor was he a highly paid and renowned professional like the attorney. He was not yet thirty, the youngest player there. His face was unnaturally taut, cross-hatched with livid scar tissue, and there was a large divot of flesh taken away from the upper corner of his mouth. It was not a happy face, though the plastic surgeons had tried their best to give the young man a devil-may-care expression.

He introduced himself to the others, using only his nickname. A young Marine Corps officer, a captain twice decorated, a veteran of Afghanistan, he was called Stagecoach. The other players had heard something about him already or, like Vince and Curveball, had once before sat down at the green table with him. He was a fairly taciturn young man, and he had powerful, very swift-moving hands, clean hands surprisingly small and untouched by any scar or blemish.

Stagecoach had gone into Afghanistan in 2003 and had stayed there more than five years, before the last of his injuries took him out of combat forever. He'd learned to do two things well in Afghanistan: speak Pashto and gamble. He wasn't necessarily a great card player in terms of points, but he had the psychology of wagering down pat. He brought his own seat with him and sat in his wheelchair at the table, a red and gold "1st Marines Rule" sticker on the backrest.

Shortly after, the politician from the Lone Star state, Roger Simmers, stepped into the camper, the sixth player. Simmers was known around gambling tables as the Little Cardinal on account of his moral rhetoric in Congress. He had all the charm of a man who had no vices. One vice, gambling, and to prove he was not enjoying himself at his one vice, he played cards, sneering the whole time.

Born in a small town in Virginia, Simmers moved to big old Texas as a teenager and made his stand there, getting his hands dirty for a couple years working thankless jobs and getting to know his way around the state. Bald-faced hypocrisy was his saving grace, and so he became a politician. As a politician, eight years in the House, six and now six more in the Senate, he had the balls to espouse not just less government, but no government at all.

He came in and went right up to the sink. He had the one nephew pop him a beer. He patted the nephew on the shoulder and gave him five dollars. Senator Simmers was not blind to the value of good tips, that was trickle down in action.

"Roger, how are you?" Sky King said to the politician.

"Thanks for asking." Simmers turned to the Guiteau and Garfield attorney. He queried in his deep baritone, "How's that garbage dump on the Mall coming for you? Think it's going to happen for real?" He shook his head. "Sooner going to see Lyndon Baines Johnson in bronze down there."

"Good evening to you too, Senator," the attorney said.

Half Price finally arrived. He carried a big white bag with him, the logo of the Smithsonian Institute on it, presents inside for his family. He went to the back and got cleaned up. He came out refreshed, looking relaxed in a pair of shorts and a big, loose-fitting polo shirt. He was thin, almost bony with a hard, chiseled face and as little hair on his head as a man could have and still be said to have hair. He wore a pair of steel-rimmed glasses, and he looked more the role of a disgruntled supermarket employee than a professional gambler.

"You gentlemen ready to stop yammering and play some cards?" he asked. He himself wasn't there that evening to play poker. He didn't like to play the Bitch. He was there to make sure everything went by the book, and he knew the book better than anyone, from Hoyle to Scarne.

Most of the time Half Price would sit quietly in his chair at the table, watching the players to make sure there was no cheating or such going on. If he had a comment to make, he made it, sometimes using his hands to get the point across, sometimes, very rarely raising his voice. He had a booming, scathing voice and a willingness, known to everyone, to become unstoppably violent. Now Half Price sat down and motioned to one of his nephews to collect the $30,000 in cash, the opening stake, from each of the players.

The money was dropped into a cardboard file box. The box was marked "The Bank" in magic marker, and the nephew slid the box under Half Price's chair. That done, the nephew, the oldest one, Half Price's youngest brother's boy, distributed chips. Half Price liked routine round the poker table, said what he always said starting a game where there were high stakes in play. He rubbed his hands together. "Okay let's dance this fiesta."

Vince completed the fourth and final step in his propitious rite to the Goddess of Fortune. He took his cigar and put it next to the lighter his ex-wife had given him. The lighter was sterling silver with his initials on it. He put the cigar and the lighter to his right hand, lined up in perfect parallel. It was the only time he smoked a cigar, playing cards, and he never smoked more than one cigar per game. Leonard Between Dogs knew it and always brought one cigar extra for the attorney whenever they played the same venue. That was part of the poet's own ritual.

Normally the attorney waited until he won his first really big pot before he lit up, and that was most often around the midpoint in the game when the others were beginning to lag, beginning to play stale. For Vince Jorrigo had this advantage that he was a player for the distance, and his luck and skill came stronger on the further he went with the cards.

They were playing seven card stud. Vince was not normally fond of seven card stud, but Stagecoach liked it and everyone deferred to him out of respect. That ended with Vince winning. He won with three jacks, taking in a substantial amount of money. It had happened with such divine swiftness that the attorney hesitated hauling his chips to him. He was on top of the Bitch from the outset, that's the way it looked. It made him dizzy to be up there, dominating the cards that way.

Vera came and stood near him, fragrant and sweet. She rested her hand on the back of his chair, that was her ritual. Half Price leaned in to watch. He could see. He knew. Vince was being suckered in by his own winning. Half Price had a collector's sensibility and what he saw was a classic, and it moved him to see it.

Vince then did the worst thing he could do, and let himself go, let himself believe in his own luck. Thinking as though he'd already won the Bitch, he cut his corona, and lit up, his eyes crossing slightly as he watched the cigar's flame jump high. Soon after he was out of rhythm and started to play sloppily. His chips went tumbling into the pot and when he reached out before him for another stack, the tips of his fingers tingled in the empty air.

He was sanguine however, and he crouched low, head going under the table and he snapped open the briefcase. He took out several packets of bills, $20,000 in all. He turned in his seat and said smoothly to Vera, "Honey, will you give that to your uncle."

Simmers, the Little Cardinal, couldn't help snickering, "My aces clip your wings, huh, Vince?"

"Give him the chips," Half Price told his nephew, and when the twenty-year-old finished counting out the chips, the game continued.

Half Price had noticed it, everyone, almost everyone there had it in for Vince. He wondered whether it was because he was a lawyer they were abusive of him, or was it something racial, that could be, though poker players were by and large a pretty accepting bunch. He himself was ready to bet good money Vince was going to be the big loser that evening.

They played another round. There was some close betting. Pairs seemed to dominate, even as a couple players kept trying for straights. Then they took a break. It was midnight and they were all hungry, all grown grumpy. One of the nephews opened the door to let in some fresh air. Vera made sandwiches, and a big salad. Plates were passed out, and the eating was pretty good. Mavis's niece knew from experience poker players liked to stay light. But she knew too, how much they relied on contented stomachs to get through the night. Everyone complimented her.

Sky King finished his ham sandwich in one gulp. He went outside to stretch his legs, have a smoke. The Little Cardinal joined him, wanting to talk about next November's elections, what the secrets were for getting better coverage. Sky King however never talked the news business at poker games. But he was easy going about it and he told the politician, one secret was fluffy hair. The camera went to fluffy hair every time.

One of the nephews, the second oldest, came up from the shadows where he'd been reconnoitering with a pair of binoculars. It was now dark in the sky, and the parking lot was a checkerboard of deep shadow and harsh bright light. The nephew gave the politician and the news anchor a kind of salute as though they were all soldiers in the same fight and went on into the motorhome. He went over to his Uncle Frank and informed him there was a car parked not too far away. It had driven up with the lights off. It had two men inside. The nephew and his uncle talked what to do. Half Price weighed the possibilities. He told his nephew to check the tags to see whether it was a federal agency car or an unmarked District police car. It would be bad if the car turned out to be neither.

Vince sat at the table. He sat hunched over the table, plucking at his earlobe. A couple times he reached out and took a feel of the blackened cigar. The cigar had been his undoing. He wanted to yell, "fuck you" at the corona, but of course he kept silent, kept everything within him. The attorney associated having emotion with failure, that was to say a man suffered feelings when he lost something or failed to do something correctly. At all other times, a man, a lawyer especially was in a natural state of equipoise, like a well-balanced steelyard. But now as he was counting his few chips left, his steelyard was veering wildly.

He was down close to $50,000. A very strong fear came to him that all he had worked for, everything he'd been able to save from the wreck of his divorce, from years practicing the law, that was to say, his good name, his eminence in the city, all of that was in jeopardy. He was risking that, ready to sacrifice everything for the Bitch, and that was who he was, and he felt it keenly.

Curveball looked over at his old friend. "Not your night," he said. "Accept it for once."

"You're just a little too much of a smart ass, Clarence."

Words that had a strong effect on the dentist whose practice was suffering, losing patients. He threw down what was left of his turkey sandwich, a jet of mayonnaise flitting against his chin. He used the back of his hand to wipe his face clean, said, "You don't know a thing about it. You got to push the banana cart. Push it on down the street, if you want to sell bananas. You got to be smart if you want to make money."

The attorney allowed himself a shrug. He himself did not have a particularly worshipful attitude towards money. He was at heart hostile to money's allure, with a deep suspicion, natural to those born poor, of money's power to do good. Money per se wasn't the issue for the attorney.

"The worst thing for me," he said. "Is my good name, to lose that, and not be able to play this game."

Sky King came in. "It's hot," he said for the umpteenth time, savoring the complaint. He sat down at the table. The Marine Corps officer sat apart from the others, his wheelchair rolled to one side of the tightly spaced camper. He was reading, his head buried in a paperback book. It bugged the news anchor. He could ask him so many topical questions, soldiers right at the heart of the national struggle. The news anchor tried to get the soldier's attention, but no dice. Stagecoach was total concentration, reading for real.

Simmers came back inside, too. Being a politician, he was easily influenced, and now, convinced of what Sky King had told him, he was busy with his hair. He was quite proud of the few white strands he had left, and he wanted them to fluff up. He was busy with his hair and he didn't look where he was going and he knocked his knee against the wheelchair. "Da-a-arn it," he cried. "Keep that ungodly contraption under the table."

Half Price raised an eyebrow. He liked to have a name politician at the table. Win or lose, a politician always brought influence with him, a glow of legitimacy, too. But he couldn't let a politician think he was too important to behave. Half Price gave the Senate member a severe look and said, "I'm the only one can get angry round here. Do you want to see that? You want to see me get fucking angry?"

This time the game was played with the joker inserted into the deck. The Bitch had that particular quality that it changed in intensity. Professional players who could calculate what cards had been dealt out based solely on what they had in their own hand, were left flummoxed with a joker in the pack. The first hand was always a disaster. Chips were lost and cash went into the box under Half Price's chair and the box was as full as an Easter basket.

The second oldest nephew had come in from the parking lot to tell Half Price the car sitting outside was a federal car and they were Treasury Department tags. Half Price laughed, pleased. That was what he liked about Washington, the protection an enterprise needed could be had at the taxpayer's expense.

Around two a.m., Sky King began to lose steam, his chips whittled down to nothing, and he couldn't help it, he'd lost all the money he came with, dropping a total of about $160,000. He got up. He dabbed his face with a red bandana from his pocket. But he didn't look hot, and he didn't let his being tired or disappointed show more than it had to. He had that cowboy's air of a long ride to nowhere stoically undertaken. He took his leave cordially, turning at the door to say, "Goodnight from all of me to all of you."

Half Price smiled. One of his nephews got up and led the network news anchor out to his car. The man was groggy, that was clear, and the nephew made sure he had his safety belt on sitting behind the wheel.

"This means from now on, you're each of you free to cash out anytime," Half Price said, adding "FYI, there's about $600,000 total chips in play."

The Bitch got started again. Vince had some good cards, but no one would see him, then he had three jacks and he bet $10,000. The Little Cardinal was convinced he was bluffing and raised him another $10,000. Curveball saw the pot, $20,000. He too was sure the attorney was bluffing. Stagecoach folded.

"I'm out," he said.

"Two minutes," Vince said, handling his pile of chips thought-fully. Half Price got up from his seat. He had one of his nephews pour out some vodka. He told the nephew to fill the glass with ice. He went personally and put the vodka down beside the attorney, getting a peep through his round steel rims at the man's cards, keeping his face re-markably relaxed, to the point of having no active expression at all.

"What must be." Vince pushed his chips to the center of the table. He was going to see the $10,000 raise. "Must be."

The Little Cardinal guessed the attorney was putting on that act because he had jacks, three jacks, that was how Vince played, liked to win with jacks, and he personally was holding onto three queens. The politician laid down his three queens. He was a member of the Senate and he didn't gloat, senators never gloated. He certainly tried hard not to gloat after Curveball tossed his cards away with a lusty expletive and Vince laid down, beside his three jacks, well, nothing else, having nothing else.

Then they played a stretch of unexciting and humdrum hands, and once again the joker came into the deck. It was getting on to dawn and energies levels sagged. To the east, over the flat hills of Capitol Heights, a change was coming. The black of night was changing to blue, all the shades of blue across the treetops, and the motorhome itself was filled with blue drifting smoke from the cigars and cigarettes, and it began to be the worse too, for the funk of tense, edgy bodies.

Suddenly everything was on the table, a mountain of money. It was the poet's doing, he had the best hand he'd had all night and he kept raising. The poet had been gliding along as poets will do, making headway lackadaisically, and he'd put together a nice pile that way. Now Leonard B. came back to raise the pot again.

Stagecoach saw the raise. He said to the attorney, "You in?"

The young officer's face was enough to make any man want to look away. But Vince didn't look away. He kicked open the briefcase under his seat. He reached down and took out $30,000, leaving the battered brown briefcase empty. He put the cash on the table.

"I'm in," he said resolutely, pushing what chips he had left against his pile of neatly wrapped one hundred dollar bills. He had a clear idea of the cards each player was holding. He was confident Stagecoach was holding a pair at best. Did Vince remember there was a dancing, bell-capped jolly in the deck, perhaps not.

Stagecoach made the showdown with two tens.

"Well, that's mine then. It looks like it's all mine." Vince had a pair of jacks. Always jacks. A pair of jacks. "Jacks beat tens," he said.

"Bad luck for you." Stagecoach smiled a broad smile, like a teenager, all teeth and eyes twinkling, and he dropped the other cards he'd been holding, two sevens and the joker. He placed the three cards down, the joker alongside the two tens. "Full. I win."

"The hell you do," the poet said beatifically. "I win."

He tossed out his three kings, two nines. Then he repeated it, "I win." Felt a strange sensation saying that to a U.S. Army officer, "I win" being words a Native American seldom got to speak to the U.S. military. He reiterated the phrase out of sheer delight, "I win."

"Wait a minute," Vince mumbled. "Wait, please."

Slowly he pushed up from the table and bowled along in his shoes as he made for one of the curtained windows of the motorhome. He pushed aside the curtains and pressed his head to the glass, but he didn't take in the vista as much as he simply stared at the outside. His eyes shined. He wiped his eyes with the back of his hand. He felt like falling, not so much dizzy anymore as that he wanted to let go of all the things holding him upright.

The others were perplexed. Vince hadn't bothered to turn over his other three cards. His hand remained where it was, close to the edge of the mountain of chips. No one moved, except that Half Price got up and was standing over Vince's three undisclosed cards. "A Dead man's hand?" he muttered, speculatively. "May I?"

"Don't touch those cards," Leonard Between Dogs said. "He's folded."

"No, I haven't folded. I said wait." Vince in one bound was back at the table. He flipped the three final cards over. "Poker." Four jacks in their pressed suits stood grinning at the other players. "Poker. Poker."

No, he'd not been fond of it at all, losing was shameful, a shameful relaxation really, a reprehensible letting go of responsibility. It took him winning to make him realize how far down into personal degradation he'd gone. Now he had won, and won quite big. That was delight, that was vindication. He went ahead and pulled the Bitch to him.

"That's it. Time's past," Half Price said. "It's certainly been one of those nights. A good night. That was a show and a half, wasn't it?"

"I'd like to continue," the Little Cardinal, Simmers protested. "I was beginning to win back my losses."

"So who are you going to play with?" Half Price said to him frostily.

"No, you cannot complain about this night," Dr. Dunne said.

"Well, it's unfair to me," Simmers groused. "I'm thirsty." He snapped his fingers, and Vera poured him out some scotch, a couple soft cubes of ice in a tumbler. She sat in the chair vacated by the new anchor and held the bottle of Auld Reekie in her lap in case the senator wanted more.

The dentist was busy counting his chips. His eyes kept darting over to the lawyer sunk down in a chair. It was an amazing comeback. Blacks had that ability he observed to himself, amazing quality. It was only a shame he was a lawyer, that rankled everybody poorer than an attorney.

Stagecoach was vexed by his rather dramatic loss. He wheeled himself free of the baize-covered table and knocked around the trailer, going over to Vince, spitting out all his animus, "Playing poker, he who makes the boldest move wins. But fuck the man who relies on blind luck."

Leonard Between Dogs on the other hand was not shaken one way or the other. Playing cards was something so different from writing poetry that whatever the outcome he was sure to enjoy himself. He told the others, in his usual tongue-in-cheek way, "I'm glad the drinks were free."

It was morning, and Vera prepared coffee in the small kitchen behind the playing area. The nephews bumped into each other cleaning up. They threw out empty liquor bottles and emptied ashtrays. Vince was sitting quietly composed in one of the comfortable swivel chairs at the front of the Road Quest. The box came out from under Half Price, and he began the process of toting up the final balance, using a calculator and a clean sheet of paper.

Vince's chips and the cash sat where he'd left them on the table, in a poorly organized pile all to one side. It was easier for Half Price to add up the other men's chips and subtract that sum from the record of the total chips paid out. The dentist helped him. Then when they were done, Frank Mavis rose up from the table. He took off his glasses and rubbed his eyes, doing the math always a strain. He told each player what he had coming. The losers were Sky King and Stagecoach. Sky King had paid for each new pile; Stagecoach had borrowed from the bank, buying more chips.

The latter drained his cup of coffee. Then he wheeled himself, using both hands, over to Frank Mavis. Mavis let him go with a signed IOU, had no problem with that. Stagecoach was a Marine and as such was perfectly honest and trustworthy even when it came to money. Plus, despite his disability, he was an officer with the promise of a wonderful career at the Pentagon, and to a man like Mavis that was worth money in the bank right there.

Stagecoach said good-bye. In a harsh voice, he asked to be forgiven for being such lousy company. Two of the nephews came up and helped him out of the motorhome. They accompanied him to his specially fitted van, and the driver who'd been working for him for about a year, got him inside using a lift mechanism. The mechanism wasn't quick. Stagecoach sat waiting pretty much helpless for longer than he liked. The nephews stopped halfway back to the motorhome. They wanted to see how he did it, got into the van. It was all kind of funny for them, though they didn't laugh out loud or anything. They thought he was stupid, losing his legs like that for nothing. Stagecoach was about the same age as the oldest of Frank Mavis's nephews.

Inside, Simmers was sucking on his scotch. He'd come out even, but that wasn't the way for a righteous man, to break even. The righteous man enriched himself. In any case, he was nervous and he kept touching his hair. His hair was course and unmanageable, and the Texas politician kept trying to brush it up into something fleecy and light, only making it worse. He was unable to keep his hands still, and he said to himself, "No, got to stop."

Vince nodded. "I know it. I been there. You want to stop, but you can't help it. I been there."

"I'm not talking about that."

Roger Simmers let his hair alone. He sat slumped back against the wall, with a headache coming on, the tension he'd accumulated flowing in full tide through his bloodstream. But he was slowly gaining control over his mood, and his resentment found, through a carefully trained defense mechanism, its proper focus, how he'd get back at the attorney. He said sharply, "By the way, Vincent, let me tell you, if you think a garbage dump on the Mall is a good idea, it's a hideous idea. I personally will make sure, I'll do whatever it takes to block and obstruct…"

Mavis yawned, yawned again. Glanced over at the Little Cardinal to see if he got the hint. Then he motioned to Vera to make sure the man got the hint. Vera took the politician by the hand and said, "Come on with me. Let's go outside. I need a cigarette. Do you have a light?"

"I expected to be given a chance to win my money back," Senator Simmers insisted. He pushed Vera out of his way. He looked around at the others. The deprecating words and images in his head couldn't find a decent tongue. He bolted out of the motorhome. He got into his car and drove off the stadium lot. Lost and gone, but not forever.

"What's wrong with him?" Vera asked.

"Aw, he's going to learn," Frank Mavis said, expressing neither discontent nor disgust. It came natural, a frown so bland as to be in the end a simple judgment. "He's going to learn to be more polite one day."

He went over then, a spare man with a light stubble covering his face, lingering close to the lawyer. He'd crunched the numbers. There was cash waiting for Vince Jorrigo, $570,000. "That includes Stagecoach, what he owes me. I took the cash to cover that out of my own pocket, what was my percentage."

"Listen I don't know if it's going to fit, you know in my briefcase."

"No, it'll fit. I'll do it. I know how to do it. It'll take a while, that's all. Relax meantime."

"Some vodka?" Vince asked Vera, getting up from his easy chair.

"Sure," Vera said. She poured him a glass from the bottle of Russian, and then poured out Auld Reekie, scotch whisky for her uncle, a glass for the dentist who now joined them and a glass, just a hem of whisky for herself.

"Cheers," she said to the men.

Mavis said, "Cheers to you, sweetheart."

He put the back of his hand to his mouth and suppressed a yawn. "I'm going to kick you guys out when I'm done with this."

"Health," Vince said, still a little overwhelmed at what happened, a little surprised to have won, and won so much. What he needed was to make sacrifice, kill some small bird, immolate the fatted heart of some beast, open his own vein if need be, pour blood on Dame Fortune's altar in absolute gratitude. He was a winner, and nothing could harm him. His bad streak had been more than a streak; it had been a long deathly anguish.

Now he'd won almost ten times what he'd borrowed. It was a rebirth, an absolute rebirth. Vince had finally put behind him the whole win-lose state of being. He was born again, and risen above that endless, miserable, up and down struggle, he believed he was as close to feeling truly godlike feelings as an earthly man could be. That was the sensation that electrified his heart, he was in paradise.

Curveball went over to his host. "Thanks for the evening, Frankie."

"He seems to take it pretty good, all this money," Mavis answered, still stacking the packets of bills, row after row, carefully lining the battered brown briefcase. "I'd be raw-assed naked by now, running round my motorhome, singing halleluiahs. You know?"

"He's got no idea, Frank," Dr. Dunne replied. "The important thing to bear in mind is never to bluff against him." He gave the man a firm handshake and then skipped down the steps to his car. "I'll call you in the week."

"I'll be here another few days."

The dentist got into his car and pulled out of the parking lot, going too fast over a speed bump, and his headlights jerked high, like a so-long.

"No, I did that one thing that no poker player should ever do," Vince was saying to himself. His beatific feeling unabated, he moved on to thinking in a serenely detached way about the game, thinking through each hand he'd played. It was a luxury, sure, but Vince could afford to do it. "I was stuck in the same strategy. Those damn Jacks. It could have cost me. I see that now."

Frank Mavis cleared his throat. "Here I'm done, almost done. No, Vince, it's an honor for me. You played as good as I've ever seen." It was a lot of money and it was taking the man a couple minutes. When the briefcase was full, he closed it up, snapped the gold snaps closed, and handed the battered-up briefcase to the attorney. "Take care of that." There was an embarrassed moment between the two men. Vince turned through the door of the Road Quest motorhome.

"Thanks," he said.

"When I'm back in town, call me. You're always welcome."

It sounded perfunctory. Mavis didn't mean it that way. He didn't have to kiss ass to anybody. A gambler like Vincent Jorrigo was always welcome, not for the same reason someone like Senator Simmers might be, but because Jorrigo's was a story Frank Mavis could tell, could elaborate on, the type of gambler other gamblers wanted to see in action. Will he bust or will he make it, that was the draw of a gambler like Jorrigo. That was what his reputation from now on would be made of, that question. The Bitch loved a guy like him.

Crossing the parking lot, Vince did a little two-step. The nephews went with him, just in case. They stood by him as he got into his sporty two-seater. He had some of his winnings in his pocket and he gave each of the nephews five hundred dollars as a tip. They took it in stride.

"Be cool," the second oldest nephew said, and he stayed to watch the attorney drive off the lot. He could see it, he could tell, wise beyond his years, though the lawyer was happy, it wouldn't last. The second oldest nephew knew, some people had to keep playing, even when they had all the happiness in the world, for they were consumed by desire. That was what defined them, and when the high wore off from their latest big win, they returned to the table. The nephew saw it. He saw Vince had a desire greater than the rational desire for money. It was a desire like love.

CHAPTER TWELVE

The Russian word for him was *goopy*. Dinah Solatoff, busy curling her thick brown hair round and round her finger, watched him from the shadows. She knew the Russian because that was her background, her grandparents spoke the language and though her parents didn't want their children to know it, the children picked up a few choice terms just hanging around. *Goopy* she knew meant "stupid" from how many times her grandmother said it to her father. That's what the boy was.

The hour was late, well past midnight, another workday about to dawn. She'd gotten up to go to the bathroom, unusually, for it was only an hour since she'd gone to bed. She'd gone to bed, exhausted. She'd been to a national Elks Order dinner at the Commodore Hotel on 16th Street. Her escort for the evening had insisted she accompany him for after-hour drinks in the bar with a group of horned altruists from Duluth.

Her escort, Representative Bill Coote, had gotten a little tipsy in the bar. Driving her back to her house on S Street, he was full of compliments on how she'd handled herself with the Elks. He went so far as to tell her she'd make a fine politician. Dinah thanked him and told him "no thanks," she was glad to be a regular citizen. They kissed goodnight, each expecting a busy day the next day.

Now Dinah was at her window, feeling like she couldn't sleep despite how tired she was, and again she muttered the word, *goopy*. She spotted him by chance, having gone to the window simply out of boredom, simply to squinny at the night, and she saw him race by, saw him race by twice already. How many times had he raced by her house like that, she wondered, how many nights. It was the silliest thing she'd ever seen.

The lights in the bedroom were off. The light from the street lamp outside fanned across the ceiling, leaving the bulk of the room safely in the shadows. Dinah stood at the window in a too big T-shirt with the logo of the Minnesota Wild printed on it. The window was shut tight; the air conditioner was on and going full blast, an icy bulwark against Washington's swampy temperature. Dinah waited and watched, knowing that in a minute or so, he'd reappear, a tall young man on a bicycle, always on a bike.

And here he was, coming down the hill from Glover Park, coasting to a stop in front of her house. He put one foot down on the roadway and leaned into his bike, his chest touching the handlebars. He stared up at her window. He didn't wear a helmet, and his short, straight-up hair gave him a brazen look. Dinah was careful to step forward only enough so that if he were really alert he might see her.

He was dressed in his suit and tie, come from drinking she guessed. He lingered there in the street for a number of minutes, not seeing her, not moving except to drop his head low from time to time, as though tired, as though ready to give up. Then he mounted his bike. Dinah crouched forward. Forget the bicycle, she said softly. Come knock at my door, come in. She wanted him to knock. If he knocked she'd be down the stairs in no time. Knock, she urged as he took off up S Street. Come in, she said.

Presumably, he made a left turn at 37th Street and went uphill, doing a circuit of the Burleith neighborhood, developing his leg muscles, nothing else. She'd been watching him now for half an hour. He'd gone round four times. Each time he stopped and stared at her window. It was late and her window was dark, but if he really wanted her, if he wanted to be with her as much as she wanted to be with him, then all he had to do was put the bicycle down and walk up the walkway and knock on the door. There was a bed waiting for him, a desiring bosom. Why didn't he simply knock, she asked herself.

More than a month had gone by since they'd been together the very last time, that night they'd hooked up at Warty's, the week before the Dubuffet Gala. She'd treated him shoddily at the gala, and she'd continued to ignore his calls and messages, and she had gone out of her way to ignore him too when they met around the office. There was no point to their talking. Things had changed, and she couldn't talk back the time.

She had her congressman for one thing. They saw each other almost every day. Bill Coote was a charmer. He liked people. He liked the admiration people sent his way when he appeared in public with a young girl on his arm. No one in Washington made reference to his wife and his children; his children were grown, living on their own, his wife was parked in Mankato, living in a roomy mansion, and rarely came south to D.C. There were few men luckier than he, people said it to his face, and Coote beamed. They were right. But it was not luck. It was all in doing the day's work.

That was Bill's philosophy, each man doing his own business. It was something life had taught him, and it was the most he had to teach others, and he boosted it to Dinah constantly. Each man had to pursue his own interests, living willfully for himself; a politician had the added obligation that he had to pursue the interests of his constituency. That was what gave a politician a superior nobility others lacked, that obligation, seeing it through. That was why Bill Coote was known as the "Lion of the Longworth Building," on account of his lion-hearted philosophy, bending others' wills to his, and bending other nations to America's power. Roar, Lion, roar.

A day, a week, a month could go by slowly or it could go by quickly. Einstein proved it, but it didn't take an Einstein to feel it true. When she was in the beginning stages of a relationship, Dinah found that time was like a pig with wings, how miraculously it flew. Her first month with the congressman involved so many heady moments, had gone by with such haste that it left her absolutely no space to reflect. She was hardly ever alone for one thing. Bill took her out every night their first week together, to show her off as he confessed, dinner at the Capitol Grille, at the Palm, lunch at the Willard.

Dinah criticized that lifestyle from a dietary point of view. Bill minimized her criticism, saying a paunch, a fat belly, was proof to the common voters that he was a man like them. A thin politician was always a little suspect.

Not only eating, not only sex and lying in bed after, not just that, they did many other things together. Junkets, he called them, they went with other members of congress on junkets, to Tokyo one time. Bill Coote was the chair of the Ways and Means Committee, which apparently had great clout. Some of the junkets were fun, most times they were all business, and Dinah ended up in a hotel room alone, reading magazines, which she hated. She hated having to act as though she were enjoying herself on these junkets. Few of the other congressmen brought their wives, and Dinah didn't want to socialize with the other women they did bring along, women like her, but not like her.

The point was they were rarely alone together, sitting down together with time to talk and share their thoughts, away from the business of politics, away from the commerce between them of sex. Bill's thoughts were all about taxes and immigration and executive overreach. He told Dinah he loved her. That was all he had to say on the subject of what he was feeling. He didn't care what she felt, to know about that, and one time when she asked, what if she loved someone else, Bill gave her his deep-thinking stare and then said, "Do your day's work, the rest will take care of itself."

The other thing that irked her was he hadn't done what he'd promised. He kept promising to introduce her to the head of the Corcoran's Art School, but he never got around to it. Dinah in any case had begun to lose interest in architecture and painting and all that. Being around a politician was frustrating, but infectious too, and politics was intriguing in and of itself. While she may have been willing, ready and willing to compromise on her most intimate sentiments, her feelings, she was beginning to draw the line on what she thought politically.

She didn't agree with him that the sitting president was un-American. They discussed it, or rather Bill listened indulgently, and in the end they each held to their contrasting opinions. Dinah asked him what it was the president advocated that was so far unlike what the Republicans advocated, and Bill couldn't tell her, not in a few words. He got worked up and started in on a tangled explanation. Dinah suspected that it was simply because the president wasn't white, that was the real problem.

Like all real Republicans, Bill was tolerant of dissent. He understood, even shared some of Dinah's unease about one or two of his fellow legislators. Some went too far, he conceded, and were just plain unpleasant to be around. He let her off the hook, understandable that she might be reluctant to go to a cocktail party for retired Congressman John Fringuelli, formerly the leader of the anti-immigration conservatives on the Hill and now a major lobbyist for the biogenetics industry. But he was nigh unforgiving, and he made it known in loud language that he was, when she wouldn't go to a dinner in honor of a former president. She explained to Bill her workload, the Orange-U-Glad merger, but that only made Bill Coote more adamant, incredulous that she would think there was something more important than Bush.

And he went out of his way to rail against Guiteau and Garfield as a firm, and in particular he had a grievance with its managing senior partner Vincent Jorrigo. This and that and the other thing, he complained at Jorrigo's unprofessional behavior. It angered Dinah. She liked Vince Jorrigo, thought him certainly a better-looking man, smarter too than her congressman. Again she suspected the real problem was Jorrigo was mixed race. Dinah saw that her friend Barbara was right, lawyers and politicians, they were all racists at heart.

And Dinah liked being direct and she liked being frank, and during the argument over Guiteau and Garfield, she told Bill Coote, called him that, a racist. He was shocked. He assured her he was not prejudiced in any way against blacks, or against any other race or ethnic group, any religious or sexual persuasion of any kind, and he claimed innocence if it appeared he was.

The girl coolly called him to the carpet, what was the problem, if it wasn't the color of his skin. Vincent Jorrigo was an excellent attorney, Bill admitted. He'd misspoke. He apologized. That revealed to Dinah a weakness, Bill's fundamental distaste for any unpleasant confrontation with a woman. It was why he stayed married, even though he hardly ever saw his wife. He didn't have the guts to ask for a divorce.

For marriage had begun to interest Dinah, as a feature of her long-term plans, a future component to her overall desire for property. Her own dropout parents had not ever gotten married, and that had always unsettled her. But for the time being she only talked with Bill about eventually moving in with him; that was not a bad idea, a compromise really, all he was capable of she was sure.

There was an apartment in the English basement of his house on the Hill, and she could move her things in there and in that way, he'd know where she was and he could see her when he liked. That was his prime objective, having her available when he wanted; that sense of control was gratifying to him. For her part, Dinah thought, well, maybe she would do it anyway, and at least she would have a place of her own, free of drunk, loser college students. It was something she was considering.

Dinah pushed away from the window. She looked at her wristwatch, one thirty. In another five minutes, Sterrett would pass by on his bicycle. She was sure he had another two or three circumnavigations in him before giving up. It was all right, that he was only a lawyer. That he would have to work all the time and be well-off but never rich. She'd been so obsessed with her own poverty and her own squalid, rural, hippie past. There was nothing at all wrong with an ordinary existence, working the way others worked in the middle-class mold. Being bourgeois was her parents' hang-up, not hers. There were plenty of middle-class property owners, that was what put America ahead of the rest of the world.

Dinah left her room and went down the hallway. Her one housemate was asleep in the room at the foot of the stairs. Her door was open and a lamp was on, and Dinah could see the G.U. student sprawled out in her underclothes on the bare mattress, snoring. Dinah pulled the door closed and then went down the stairs. She opened the front door and stood there waiting. When Sterrett came by again, she'd run out to him, that was her decision. But that wasn't what she wanted either. She wasn't going to make that move, no. It had to come from him. She wanted him to come to her.

He appeared on schedule, his blond hair a little more flattened down than the last time he'd come biking past the house. "Goopy," she muttered. She watched as he braked. He put one foot down in the roadway. Did he see her, she wondered. She took a step out from the shadows of the doorway. The stoop was cold, its bricks slick with dew. She took a careful step back.

Siren sounds and a Metropolitan Police Department car came screeching up from Reservoir Road and two Secret Service cruisers arrived from 37th Street. The cars converged in the middle of S Street and surrounded the young attorney on his bicycle. A woman was first out, coming from the Metropolitan Police car. She slid her baton into its steel loop and started over to the attorney. The Secret Service types waited a moment and then drove off, first one cruiser and then the other, fish to fry elsewhere.

Dinah moved back into the house, griping the door open just a crack, and she peered out, her eyes wrinkling sharply. She could hear their voices, the cop's and Sterrett's too, rising and falling in an edgy duet over the static crackle from the dispatch radio.

"Uh sir, will you step away from that bicycle," the police officer said. "Just step away from the bike."

"Why? It's a bicycle."

"Can I see some ID please?"

"I'm an attorney."

"Will you please step away from the bike? And will you show me some ID?" the cop repeated, and now she put her right hand on her holster.

Sterrett did as he was told.

"Take your license out of the billfold," the woman said. "I'll be back and you stay put right there."

Dinah couldn't help it, and she moaned a little as her heart sank. The boy was lost in a world of his own, and he was unable to disentangle himself. Goopy for sure, goopy in triplicate. She couldn't watch anymore and she shut the door, went back up the stairs and into her bedroom. But the temptation was too great and she ended up at the window again. She couldn't get enough of him and his antics. There he was, waiting for the cop to return with his documents, standing looking up at the house, his bicycle lying at the curb. Could he see her, she wondered, or did he need glasses; she was standing flush at the window.

The police officer came back and handed him something along with his driver's license, a pink ticket, for what, Dinah couldn't imagine. She wanted to be there next to him, to hear what he said. But he didn't say anything. He stared at the ticket, staring at it stupidly. When the cop car was finally out of sight, Sterrett spat out a few hard words. Dinah watched then as the boy crammed the fine into his jacket pocket and picked up his bike, made for home. He made for home. Suddenly Dinah felt the stupid one.

She didn't feel like going back to bed after that. She went to the kitchen and had a bowl of cereal and a couple spoonsful of yogurt. She went into the living room and she tried to watch some television with the volume down low in the hopes it would put her to sleep. The flickering images only annoyed her, so dressed only in her big, floppy T-shirt and her underwear, slipping on a pair of flip-flops, she went out the door, to walk abroad in the new morning. Already among the trees, thin gold bedizened the highest branches.

Dinah would have preferred the illusion that she was free and in charge emotionally, and that she had a say in how she felt and about whom. But somehow it didn't seem to be that way. She knew for instance that Bill Coote was wrong for her, and yet she needed him. The politician gave her a sense of self-confidence she wasn't sure she could feel without him.

No, she thought, she was glad that things had happened the way they had with Sterrett. She was glad of her choices even if she didn't like the way they made her feel sometimes. It was a way for her to see into herself, to magnify her sorrow until it spilled over into her work, giving her the energy she needed to concentrate on working as hard as she could.

She went around the block a couple times, sorting these ideas out. She ran into one other person, no one else on the street. She walked past a middle-aged man walking his dog. The man carried a plastic bag in which he collected what his Airedale produced. Dinah tried not to laugh, watching the man kneel down to pick up the animal's plop; the man's expression was not one of distaste, as Dinah expected. The man patted the dog affectionately and said, "Good dog."

It brought to mind the doting smile on Ruth Laine's face when Bahman Trunkajar finally agreed to the 400-page contract by which Orange-U-Glad Corp. of North America, the holding company for Orange-U-Glad Stores Inc., bought out the controlling shares of High Leaf Bakeries of Golden, Colorado. Trunkajar was there with the CEO of Orange-U-Glad, in the conference room on the seventh floor of the Guiteau Building. There was unexpected resistance from Trunkajar. Ruth Laine got up and made a very personal declaration, her vision of what the deal meant on a national level. It meant low prices and flakey pastry for everyone.

Dinah walked past the entrance to Georgetown University Hospital, went round the corner, back to her house, thinking yes, she was thrilled to have been there, that was an experience that drama. She'd been brought in to help Corny Klocker with the documents that needed signing. Bahman Trunkajar made the whole room sweat with his last-minute stand, trying to save his company and the greater part of his kitchen workers. High Leaf had been baking in the same town, the same building, for more than a hundred years. The deal was for the baking formulas and the brands, in particular for the best-selling Ugly Alice Cupcakes, and the takeover meant moving the company headquarters to Delaware City, Delaware, moving the actual baking to some forlorn place in China. It was all being done to save the high cost of union labor. Trunkajar made a speech, save the town, save jobs, save Colorado's work force, put that in writing.

What made Bahman Trunkajar unclench was Ruth Laine's offer of an additional couple of million dollars in exit bonus over and above what was already on the table. Orange-U-Glad was no petty operation. Orange-U-Glad as Ms. Laine herself said, was interested in the lowest price, yes, but also in the winningest price. That was the part of her work Dinah liked the most, witnessing grown-up men and women get dazed and feverish over large amounts of money.

Back in her bedroom, under the covers, seeking to get an hour's sleep before she had to get up and go in to work, Dinah asked herself what her best price was. She'd heard the rumor, knew there was pressure on Bill to clean up his image. He was running in the next year's elections against a Democrat ready to grab at anything to discredit the Honorable Bill Coote. One of Bill's AAs who had made friends with Dinah told her that the congressman's campaign manager had warned the congressman to change his ways. Even though Minnesota was not a state easily shocked, still the blatant speciousness of Bill Coote parading around with a hot young mistress while running a campaign based on "making good sense for the family" would not be lost on the good people of his district.

Rather than waiting for something drastic to happen, Dinah very calmly refined her plans. She'd seek her price, ask some favor from the politician in return for clearing out at the end of the summer, returning to Idaho without making a fuss. She had no intention of making trouble for him. He'd been good to her and she was more than willing to take that at face value.

She was beginning to feel she'd had enough of Washington. She saw that the town's strength, its diabolical strength lay in drawing people to it, giving them little in return, other than the astounding promise that Washington was indeed the Shining City on the Hill. But in Garcia at night, with the Milky Way as close as the highway out to Boise, Dinah could see the Shining City was infinitely everywhere, a city in the sky. She missed that. That's what she wanted to do, go home. Maybe find a job in Sun Valley to start with.

She'd have to admit defeat. If she returned home, she would be admitting that her plans were a bust. She would have to give up on the idea of wealth and power and glittering cocktail parties. She didn't like that. It made her curse very softly lying there under the covers. It was giving up on her plans, but sometimes it was the best thing to do, to give up. It was easy to stay foolish, even easier to stay hungry in the world as it was. Sometimes you had to be smart too, and sometimes you had to swallow your pride. Dinah knew it took a courageous heart to yield to the facts. When she returned home there would be people, her parents especially, who would gloat.

"To heck with them," she said closing her eyes tight.

The problem was she really did enjoy the work she was doing. Being a secretary at a law firm engaged the totality of her personality, forced her to eat humble pie at times, but gave her the right too, to be as bossy as she wished. Partners who marched around trailing clouds of glory faltered pathetically when they had to make a color copy of some document, quailed when having to make a simple doctor's appointment. It was an unsurpassable privilege to see how much fragility and anguish there was in the daily lives of prosperous lawyers, jittery egos always on the verge of snapping. Secretaries were protected from snapping by their apparent insignificance.

As it happened, a couple days later Dinah's boss, Corny Klocker, kind of snapped. He'd culled a substantial fee for arranging the sale of High Leaf Bakeries, and the client had paid in full right away, and the success of the whole merger thing rose like a bubble to the lawyer's head. He came into the office and the first thing he did was to wrap his arms around Patty Johnson and give her a shockingly mushy kiss full on the lips. Then while she reeled around and stammered out sententious phrases on sexual harassment in the office place, Klocker wrote her a check for $30,000, her bonus for having encouraged him day in and day out, when he was in anguish, worrying that the merger would not go through.

Klocker hadn't forgotten his paralegals or his secretary either. He gave the girls, each one a big fat bonus. Gravy, as he called it, good gravy.

"This is for you," he told Dinah, standing at her desk. He handed her the envelope with several thousand dollars in it. "Go shopping. Take the rest of the day and go where you will. You need new clothes."

"Shoes mostly," the secretary agreed.

"And after shopping, go out with your boy-friend. Treat him to something expensive."

It wasn't something Dinah was going to correct him over. She let Corny Klocker assume she had a boyfriend like every other young secretary, some twenty-year-old just getting started in the world. She told Mr. Klocker she still had some work to do, but he was insistent, and she felt she really needed a break, and so she cleaned up her desk and went by taxi to the Galleria mall for an afternoon's shopping.

The Galleria shopping mall at the northwestern end of the city was not what Dinah considered a real place. It could have been any-where, and even its green plants in their fake stone planters sent their taproots into limbo. The Galleria was simply a place built to keep man-made loneliness at a distance and make a dime at one and the same time. It was full of movement, full of light without shadow, full of an indefinite din along concourses that led to other concourses that led to fast-food courts. But the important thing was, there were shops.

She went to a small boutique and looked around but she didn't see anything she liked. The clothes there were put together for women who wanted to be noticed for their good taste, and that meant bland colors and square designs. A few other places, and then she went over to the big store that anchored the mall, and there she saw a dress she really liked. It was kicky and fresh. She tried on several other dresses and looked at some purses, wandered the store over and bought a pair of shoes with some of her bonus cash.

On her way out, right beyond the magic counters of perfume and makeup, just as she stepped onto the darker marble of the Galleria's main corridor, someone came up to her. It was a man in a blue coat. He told her to stop. She tried walking faster, and for a moment, she was sure she'd heard mistakenly. A hand clutched her arm. She was made to turn around. The blue-coated security guard walked her past the salesgirls in white tunics standing at the makeover counter. They gave Dinah contemptuous glances. The guard took her down a cor-ridor and then to a room at the back of the store and sat her down to wait for his boss.

His boss had on the same coarse blue jacket. The man's nametag read, "J. Ferguson, Chief of Security." He was in his thirties, a meticulously groomed man with a stoical manner. He asked what she'd taken, and the first man showed him the dress that he'd found balled up under Dinah's blouse. The security chief didn't think much of it, until the man showed him the price tag. Then Ferguson handcuffed her and took her to another, even smaller room and left her there alone, after taking from her her purse and the shopping bag with the shoes in it. No one asked her what her name was. They left her where she was, and Dinah kept her head up and her eyes shot up from time to time to the camera posted in a high corner of the small room.

She began to feel sick with nervousness. She stood up and knocked with her knee against the locked door of the room. The first security guard came over and peered through a small window in the door. He scowled at her, not out of maliciousness, but simply from ignorance. She was a thief, and you scowled at thieves.

"Can I have a glass of water, please?" she shouted. The man went away without a word. Dinah went into a corner of the room, right under the closed-circuit camera. She leaned forward and threw up. There wasn't much, part of the sandwich she'd had for lunch and what little breakfast she'd had, mostly yogurt, but she felt better doing it.

She was taken by surprise when Congressman Bill Coote came to the door of her little room, and she really expected him to urge the store she'd stolen from to throw the book at her. He was after all not only a family first candidate, but also a well-known exponent of law and order, tougher laws, merciless on crumby criminals.

The security chief had gone through Dinah's purse. He found her driver's license and found and read and reread a note Congressman William Coote had written on his House of Representatives stationery reminding Dinah how sexy she was and that they had a dinner to go to at the Australian Embassy on Thursday. Ferguson was not dissatisfied with the pay at the Galleria shopping mall. It was just that he aspired to a better and more prestigious position elsewhere, and he thought getting a place on the U.S. Capitol Police wouldn't be half bad. So he'd been careful to telephone the congressman's office and ask them if they knew a Dinah Solatoff.

The congressman's office told the security chief that the person in question was a personal friend of the congressman. So Ferguson thought it wise to tell them what had befallen the congressman's friend, and in little more than an hour's time the congressman himself was there at the mall. He'd come in his own car. He'd driven across town going out Massachusetts Avenue. There had been traffic around Dupont Circle and that was why when he arrived, he apologized to the chief of security for being late.

Riding home in Bill Coote's car, Dinah kept her mouth shut. She didn't care to thank him for smoothing over everything with the security chief and with the store's manager. She even cried to keep from having to say anything. But the politician was unusually smug, and he said to her, "Don't worry about it. That's why I'm here."

"I'm not worried," she said.

"You should be," Bill Coote answered. "I didn't know you had a record."

"I never told you?"

"No, you never told me."

"I intended to."

He took her to his place. He lived on Capitol Hill in a three-story row house on F Street facing a park. Beyond the trees was the overpass for the Southeast Freeway, and on the other side of the freeway was one the city's poorer neighborhoods, lots of low-income housing, the kind of neighborhood a congressman would not be caught dead in unless it was for votes. William Coote didn't need the votes of the Washingtonians who lived on the other side of the freeway, and they went ignored, except when there was an outburst of crime.

There were a few stone steps leading up to his house, which was brick painted gray with a red door, tidy outside, a little messy inside. It was as though Bill Coote had set up everything the way he wanted the first day he'd moved in, and then never changed a thing. He lived like a bachelor. His wife and kids stayed there only briefly when there was a need for the image thing to work, otherwise, like the residents of southwest Washington, they went ignored. They stayed home in Minnesota.

The living room was cozy, crammed with furniture, crammed with personal items, the regimental pennon from his stint in the Army, a foot-sized marzipan effigy of Ronald Reagan, a soft-sided football signed by the 2000 Vikings. His bookshelf was full to groaning with copies of his first autobiography, *From Swan Lake I can See the Hill*, for like all good and conscientious Washingtonians, Coote had been sure to write a book, largely unread.

There were citations and awards and degrees. There were photographs too, showing 1st Lt. Bill Coote tall and valiant with his Fire Team in Iraq in 1991, Coote with President Nixon at the latter's house in Saddle River, Coote with President G.W. Bush, Coote with all the notables he'd ever met, the way Wild Bill Hickok would have had, all the scalps he'd cut on the warpath. One of the biggest photos however showed the congressman relaxing with his daughter at her graduation from Wellesley.

Dinah stopped at that photo. It was taken before she'd entered the picture, and it showed Bill Coote beaming to beat the band.

"I should have stayed where I was," she said.

"Let's look at it from a different angle," Bill said. "If you stayed where you were, I would have been involved anyway. I mean sooner or later, right?"

He put her in a rattan chair in the garden and gave her an iced tea to drink. Dinah's wrists hurt from the handcuffs, and she took an ice cube out of the glass and ran it back and forth over her bruised skin.

"Maybe we've been together too long," Bill Coote said. "Getting too used to each other. That happens."

"What does that mean?" Dinah said.

The politician went back into his house. The garden was surrounded by high walls. It had a patch of grass the size of a beach towel dominated by a birch tree whose shade reached over to the brick patio, just reached to where Dinah was sitting. There was a rusting portable gas grill in one corner and a garden hose rolled up like a bright green snake.

"No, it means maybe I've taken you for granted," Bill said, coming out into the garden, a bottle of beer in one hand. He sat down next to her in a chair he brought out from the kitchen.

"You've given me a lot," the girl answered. "You've done a lot for me. I'm grateful for that."

"I've taken care of you. I've taken good care of you."

"I'm not a child. But I am grateful. I think I've shown that."

"If I turn you over to the police, well, shoplifting is considered a serious offense, and you do have a record," Bill Coote said. He sat back in his chair. He rested his chin on his chest, looking pleased with himself. Smirking into his beer.

"That was back in Idaho," Dinah said. She winced as she touched the most sensitive part of her wrist with the softening ice. "I was a kid. I went through the whole detention scene. I didn't think you wanted to hear about it." The ice cube slipped around in Dinah's fingers.

"Today they let you go at my request. They can have you arrested any time."

"So?"

"Now you're going to do what I want, or else I kick you out of my life, kick your ass right behind bars."

The girl was in a condition to react several ways. She still had a little stomach upset, so she could easily have thrown up at that. She could cry, because she certainly felt like crying for real, a whole river of tears. But she thought of her mother, decked out in long beads with her dirty hair, her badly wrinkled, but sunny face, a face that beamed lovingly through an occasional, mental fog. Dinah spoke with much the same highfalutin tone her mother would have used, saying to Bill Coote, "So what do I care?"

"Let's get married," Bill declared, flying up from his chair. "That's what." He took some beer. "Let's get married."

"That's not what I expected you to say. Not at all."

Bill strode over to her, dropped to one knee and explained it to her. Almost losing her to jail made him aware of how precious she was to him. It was clear she needed him, even if she didn't love him. Need was all. He knew she needed him, and that was all he cared about, that she would be by his side.

"What about your wife?"

"Oh, I can get a divorce, that's easy to arrange. It's done, consider it done." Bill leapt to his feet. He walked up and down the small patio, his face flushed with the exertion of declaring his love to the girl. "My wife, she'll agree to a divorce if I give her the settlement she wants. She knows how to pursue her own self-interests pretty good. That's pretty much all she's ever done. She's as unlike you as I can imagine."

"No, but what about, you know, this is emotional extortion, isn't it?"

"It's an opportunity, is what it is, Dinah," Bill Coote said. "I would have asked you anyway."

"Yeah? You would have?" Dinah paddled round the idea. It was too unexpected and it was therefore almost impossible for her to focus on it and defend herself from it. "What about your image, your campaign for re-election next year?"

"That's what worries you? You been around me too long." Bill Coote took on a deep look, rationalizing his choice. "No, times have changed. I think a divorce and then getting remarried, well, my constituency will find that the common touch, that I'm a man like the rest. Draw the young people to me. I think it's a definite plus in these times. The gossip will bump up my name recognition."

"What about love?" Dinah asked, still trying to absorb her overall surprise. She'd really expected to be tossed back to the authorities. She expected to see Ferguson and his blue coats again. She had that rank fear of imprisonment that made actually going to prison, getting it over with, almost a relief. "Don't you think how I feel is important?"

"Am I that fortunate? I know I'm not," Bill confessed. "I know you're not in love with me. That's more than okay, I'm a lovable man when there's an issue at stake, otherwise probably not. But I can live without love, I'm sure. Enough with the questions. Marry me. Be on my side."

"It's not about sides, is it?"

"Of course it is. I'll be on yours," Bill answered.

Dinah put her drink down on the bricks. She wiped her wrist with the handkerchief she'd used to cry into on the way back from the Galleria mall. The handkerchief left her wrist as moist as it was before she wiped it, and she stuffed the hankie into her empty glass. She believed that Coote was being sincere, gone sentimental as older men so often did.

"Here's what I want you to give me then," she said. She pressed her hands together. "Yes. I want you to propose to me. Not now, not now. But in as real a way, as romantic a way as you can possibly manage. I want you to surprise me, take me out…It doesn't matter where, Bill. A romantic setting. You choose one. But I want a real engagement ring, a big fat diamond. Also then a wedding ring. The wedding ring can be simple gold. You understand?"

Bill Coote was going to have the prettiest young wife on Capitol Hill. More, he knew Dinah, and felt she was as ambitious as he was, and he was sure of his choice. As always he relied on his instincts and they never failed him.

"A church wedding...I want that, you know."

Dinah put all her hope into that idea, a church wedding, that would make up for all her disappointments and all her sorrow over love and all her confusion, too. A wedding with bells and flowers and every-one dressed the way she wanted them, that would not be so bad, and she touched the corner of her eye and said it again so that Bill would comprehend her, knowing full well that a woman had to repeat herself often when speaking to a man, "A wedding in church."

"Hold on, that's out. I've had a church wedding, it don't bring good luck to me. I've got that part planned. The Mayor of Minneapolis will marry us. He's a Democrat so if the thing goes wrong we can blame him."

"You have no choice in this, Bill, it's what the bride wants, counts. I want a wedding in church. Let's see, the National Cathedral, huh, why not? With a choir, too. And all the guests I want. My parents from Idaho, all their freaked-out friends. No expenses barred. A reception at the Four Georges. Also lots and lots of flowers. I love flowers."

"You can have flowers," Bill said hastily. "All right."

He went over to his small strip of grass. The late afternoon was looming up among the clouds, beautiful, serenely in step with all the best hopes of Man. He decided after he was done with Dinah, he'd zip out to Avenel and chase nine quick holes. He practiced a couple golf swings with the empty beer bottle. The girl was right, he thought, better in church, a wedding like the royals, it never failed to add glamour to a man's name, that kind of glamour the voters understood.

"And someone to sing," the girl added. "At the wedding ceremony."

"You're pushing your luck."

"T-Red. I love him. You know, for the reception dinner, too? You have pull."

"I know people, yes," Bill admitted. "I hate to use them for a wedding singer."

"You want to marry me?" Dinah asked. "That's part of the deal."

And suddenly she'd gotten what she'd planned to get, and it had been easy, as easy as stealing Slim Jims from an Orange-U-Glad store.

CHAPTER THIRTEEN

*G*amblers had an advantage over everyone else. Their world was totally comprehensible, unlike Hawking's, unlike God's. Gamblers knew there was no guarantee they'd always have the same luck. They lived honestly with that simple and alarming truth and didn't need the hokum of laws and social niceties to warm the heart. They had the rules of poker and that was all they needed. Feeling safe was something a gambler avoided, knowing there was no winning except in taking risk.

Vincent Jorrigo, however, pretended for about a week or so that he didn't exist in that world, in the steep mountain land of the gambler, the land of win or lose. He pretended he lived in the flattened-out world of the happy consumer. He used his winnings from the Bitch to buy a couple trinkets for Celia Progg, a tennis bracelet, dangling, sparkling earrings to match, and several bags full of colorful lingerie.

Despite the presents, Celia reproved him for his broken promise. She assumed the money came from playing cards, and he told her it did. He didn't tell her much more than that. He didn't tell her how much he'd won or how special a win it was. He left the Bitch out of it.

He bought some pricey articles for his two teenage daughters. He didn't know exactly what they liked anymore, but he figured it didn't matter. He got a little of everything, electronic devices, some silver jewelry, chic little blouses Celia helped him pick out. He wrapped the gifts up in bubble wrap and put a card, "From Dad" inside and sent the package UPS. It was the message that counted.

He bought for himself too, a clothes renewal. Took his double-breasted blazer, took his charcoal suit, his blue suit, and went to the stern of the *Arabella* and spread those old suits out one by one on the chop, let the flood take them away. Then he went to Britches and bought himself a couple three new suits, all of them made of the softest flannel nap, tailor made and ready in a few days. He went to another shop in Georgetown and bought shoes handmade in an obscure hill town in Italy. That was the one consumer indulgence that gave him real pleasure, clothes.

He gave his British-made sports car a thorough tune-up at a garage that specialized in old British sports cars, and it was like tuning a Stradivarius what it cost him. He turned his attention to his cabin cruiser, making an appointment with the marina to have *Arabella*'s engines overhauled, her hull painted. He paid off the loan on the boat too, and to celebrate that, bought himself a new captain's cap with lots of braid, at $60 the least expensive purchase item for that week.

Then one evening he got into his new blue suit, knotted his French silk bow tie. Slapped on a really expensive aftershave, and seeing himself in the mirror, found he looked fly. Took Celia out to dinner. He took her to the most fashionable and exclusive restaurant in Washington, the River Club. He didn't do it to impress her. She didn't need impressing as much as she needed to feel he appreciated all she did for him, and that was why he did it, to thank her, a happy meal with champagne and grilled snails sautéed in white truffle, breast of cactus wren with tortilla stuffing, lemon soufflé dessert. Since both of them were fed up playing coy, the meal was quickly followed by sex, a weekend of sex on his boat. Then a couple of days later, Vince bought himself a ticket to Las Vegas.

He was on a winning streak, and it was his intention to play out his streak for all it was worth, wanting to push his luck a little. He wanted to see what would happen if he used the Bitch money to win even more money than he'd already won. Test how much winning he could stand, how solid his nerves were. He tried explaining some of it to Celia Progg; she thought he was going through a crazy and degrading midlife crisis and she didn't want to have anything more to do with him.

Before leaving town, Vince called his law associate into the Outhouse. Guiteau and Garfield harbored plenty of wise counselors, sages, men of learning, and all of them prominent lawyers, too. But Vince didn't feel at his ease with any of them, not with Corny Klocker in

Mergers and Acquisitions, not with Cliff Lemberger over in tax law. No, Vincent wanted to talk to Groves.

A relationship of sorts had grown up between the two men, one which neither man was quite aware of. Alike in that they kept a part of themselves well apart from others, Jorrigo and Groves didn't reflect on the existence of this relationship, or think about it in any way, and that was what made it stronger and more complicit, its unexamined nature.

Vince wasn't interested in being around for the signing of the ground lease, scheduled for that next Monday. He had no intention of participating in anything as public as an official signing. In any case, he hoped to be several thousand miles farther to the west of Washington the day of the signing. He planned to be in the Best Vestal Hotel in downtown Las Vegas. He planned to leave that weekend.

He met with the young associate and told him he was going to entrust Kid Psora to him when the Kid came into town. Vince had decided Sterrett was going to represent the firm at the signing of the ground lease on Monday. Sterrett objected; he wasn't important enough. Vince told him his past actions had proved he was important, and had proved he was capable, more than enough, and he would represent the firm, period. It was a big responsibility, and Sterrett was flattered to handle it all, kudos and limelight and the promise of partnership. The sanitary landfill was now a big item, very cool.

It was hailed on CNBC as a number one example of the public sector working in harmony with the private, and on Fox as the proof that the way to go was a gradual privatization of all federal lands. The *Post* editorial praised the White House, its taking responsibility the way every citizen should, for the garbage it generated, the president proving that he was not a "NIMBY." The Senate called it Progress, the House, America's Future, and the mayor of Washington, D.C. went so far as to propose another sanitary landfill, to go where the Tidal Basin was.

The signing was scheduled for Monday morning, July 26, in the Department of the Interior's main building on C Street. The Interior's main building took up a whole city block. It was not a menacing structure however, cold and lowering the way modern bureaucratic offices were, or in any way arid or pretentious. It was a building with a plain, lived-in look to it, a building that seemed to say, "it is sweet and glorious to work for one's country."

The director of the Bureau of Land Management had a suite of offices that overlooked Rawlins Park. The signing took place in the small conference room. Thick, bound copies of the ground lease for the Ellipse were placed on the dark oak wood table. At the center of the table was a carafe of water and some glasses. The water was tap water. Arrayed around the carpeted room were the blue and white, bison seal flags of the Department of the Interior. The curtains were drawn and the harsh sunlight came through with a muted heat.

Sir Simon Psora was not there. He sent Director Segreen a note, he couldn't come, other obligations, so sorry. His son, Kid Psora, was acting in his stead, with power of attorney and all that. The Kid was trying to keep the waste management colossus, Unfragrant Bin Systems, from being sabotaged by his father. His father was looting the company's assets piece by piece and the son was busy trying to check him at every move. Kid Psora had tried to see his father to reason with him in person in Monte Carlo, where Sir Simon now rented a private estate. But Psora the son couldn't get close enough to his father to talk to him, the funk was too great, body odor far outweighing filial love.

Old Sir Simon sat in the pool most of the day, but even though it was an outdoor pool, the stink was way too strong for any normal person to stand. Sir Simon floated in his own waste and had garbage from the surrounding villas thrown into the now turbid water of the pool. Kid Psora spoke to his father from a balcony above the pool, and though he kept a heavily perfumed handkerchief to his face, that was as close as he could get, and the conversation was all desultory shouts. They agreed that the landfill in Washington had to go forward, that was all they agreed upon, and Kid Psora told his father he was going to America to take care of it. All right, Sir Simon yelled back, happy as a clam in his big bath of filth.

A contemporary, global-style entrepreneur, the Kid was involved in a whole range of businesses and was also a film producer and the owner of a string of hotels in Hungary and Slovakia, but it was as the CFO and vice president of Unfragrant Bin Systems that he actually made his money. It was in the role of president and chairman of that company that he saw his future. He'd flown into Washington that same day from Paris, having come up from the Riviera. He was tanned and dressed in a sharkskin suit that reeked of patchouli.

The signing itself was a very brief ceremony. The lead attorneys present, Celia Progg for Melody Hogan and Sterrett Emerson Groves for Guiteau and Garfield, asked their respective clients if they were ready to sign. The clients acknowledged that they were indeed at that time and at that place apt and ready to sign. The attorneys then turned back the pages of the lease, and Kid Psora and Antonia Segreen, sitting facing each other at a table, signed and initialed, here, there, everywhere they had to.

The scratching of pens was the only sound in the room for about a minute and a half, everyone else standing round the table, silent, attentive, hovering the way people hovered in Washington. Two original copies were signed, and the lawyers affixed their own signatures as witnesses and Director Segreen's secretary was brought in to serve as a witness as well.

After the lease was signed, there was an exchange of pens, Kid Psora giving Director Segreen the pen he'd signed with, a gold-nib fountain pen that had Unfragrant Bin's logo on it, and Segreen, hers, which was an official "Dept. of the Interior" ballpoint. There was an awkward interim, some bowing and scraping on the part of the lesser bureaucrats from the Interior. A bottle of domestic brand champagne was uncorked and poured into plastic flutes. When the champagne splashed out of her glass onto the floor, Antonia Segreen cried, "Whoopsy."

Then there was the photo op. An official Department of the Interior photographer came along and snapped jolly images of Antonia Segreen and Kid Psora shaking hands against the blue backdrop of Department of the Interior flags. There were photos of the lawyers shaking hands too, Groves and Celia Progg. The signing went into the annals of the administration's official acts and everyone was happy that after months and months and months of struggle and worry, the sanitary landfill at the Ellipse was a reality.

Sterrett Emerson Groves, Esquire, of Guiteau and Garfield was in seventh heaven. His was a major professional win, the kind of thing that made a man feel he had a prodigious reason to exist on the earth, a professional success of the most exalted, the most substantial kind. That afternoon, Vincent Jorrigo called Groves from the Best Vestal in Las Vegas and showered the young associate with praise. He promised him a bonus, he'd worked so hard and handled things so perfectly well, a little extra money out of the winnings Vince was going to bring home with him.

That Friday, Sterrett decided to celebrate the signing of the lease with Anne Marie Smith. He took her to the Kennedy Center. He had Suzy get him tickets, hard to find, for *The Trail of Broken Contracts, the Musical,* a work based on the verse play by Leonard Between Dogs. It was something he knew she'd like, and that was why he did it. The old Sterrett would simply have gone out and gotten drunk with his chumlings. The new Sterrett paid for seats in the box tier, two center seats, the best seats in the house.

The first act of the musical was all about the promises, in the form of signed treaties and legal contracts, made with the Cheyenne and Santee by the U.S. government. The protagonist was a Cheyenne chief named Wolf Robe. He was a Bowstring warrior who had chosen to turn lawyer, and the song he sang when he renounced his power shield and sacred arrows to go to law school and get his law degree, put on his power tie, that song was the emotional highlight of the first act.

Wolf Robe ended his bittersweet solo to loud applause. The applause rose from the orchestra, clapping sweeping up, overwhelming Anne Marie and Sterrett like wind-tossed leaves. They applauded too, exchanging looks, yes the first act was terrific, funny, and inspiring one and the same time. The curtain came down and the house lights came on and the Eisenhower Theatre was jammed with men and women making for the bar.

"You want something to drink?"

Anne Marie shook her head. "I have to go to the bathroom," she said.

"I'll come with you."

"The line's going to be horrendous."

Sterrett took her down the red-carpeted steps of the Grand Foyer. He told her, "Come on, I'll show you a trick." He led her by the hand through the Hall of Nations and then down the stairs that led to the garage. On the first landing of the stairwell there were bathrooms, no line, no crowd.

"Will you wait for me?"

"I'm going to get myself a glass of wine. Just one. I'll meet you under the Kennedy bust."

"'Cashew' later, then," Anne Marie said with a wink.

The noise across the gory carpet of the foyer rose to the hall's immense crystal chandeliers. People pushed and squeezed around him, trying to reach the bar, where they were selling plastic cups of wine for ten dollars, big chocolate chip cookies for five. Sterrett went over to the tall windows with his wine. Across the center's terrace was the shadowy tangle of Mason's Island and beyond that the lights of Rosslyn. Sterrett had his cellphone out. He dialed Dinah's cell and was listening to the phone ring, when Dinah answered. He said, "Remember me?"

It was put in a snide way. They ran into each other every day practically, at the office. Daily she ignored him.

"Yes?"

"I wanted to talk to you. Where are you?"

She was silent, silent for a long while, and then she said, "I don't want to see you."

"Let me come over later. Let's be together tonight."

She wasn't going to give in. "No," she replied. "To be happy, you have to choose. I've chosen."

"I choose to be happy tonight with you. Let me come over, Rover."

"No. You're drunk. Please stop calling me."

He closed his cellphone and slipped it into his jacket. He wasn't drunk, not at least on the watery chardonnay the Kennedy Center sold. He was cherishing in himself that ineffable self-satisfaction that marked a true Washington lawyer, that magic feeling of being on top of the world, implacably cool, and unbeatably manful. He had registered one success after another at the office in the last two weeks. Sterrett began to think in terms exclusively of himself, of the power he had, especially over women. The power a man had over women, in Washington was the one sure sign of having real power.

Sterrett knew he could get Dinah to see him, to be with him; he was working on her and it was only a matter of time. Women liked to be courted and they liked a man who was bold and unrelenting. Dinah and Anne Marie, a successful, hard-working man like himself, he knew, always had at least two women in play in his life. Two women gave him the leverage to disregard any given feeling one of the two women might have, while encouraging them both to keep having them, for him.

Anne Marie stole up to him. He was standing at the window, looking out at the flowing darkness of the river. She stole up to him and whispered into his ear, "The River of Swans. Remember?"

"There you are," he said.

"Yes, here I am."

Anne Marie's attitude had changed after the signing of the ground lease. She had been there at the Interior Department along with Celia Progg. Sterrett was the sole representative from Guiteau and Garfield, and it had impressed Anne Marie. She had always considered Sterrett a little lazy, and in that respect ineffectual, but in a good and quite pleasingly manageable way, a handsome but somewhat mediocre attorney. Now she felt the need to defer to him a little. She realized of the two of them, he was the one who might reach the heights first.

"Come on," he said to her. "Let's get back before the bell."

"I wanted to take a look from the terrace."

"Don't have time," Sterrett said.

They returned to their seats. Sterrett knew she was enthusiastic for Between Dogs's work; it was a satire, with very little of reality to it. But satire was the new thing, and Anne Marie had read about the genre in *Vanity Fair*. Sterrett himself was left unimpressed by the story, Wolf Robe representing himself as the plaintiff, suing Secretary of War Belknap for breaking a real estate contract, the sale of the Black Hills. From the trial room scenes, it was clear Leonard Between Dogs had no idea what really happened in a court of law. The love interest, the Statue of Freedom was even more far-fetched, a living statue gliding down off the Capitol's dome to coo and nuzzle with an Indian chief, impossible. The only saving factor was the music, a kind of folk-rock score with lots of strings, drums, and horns.

They were sitting, waiting for the lights to go down, for the curtain to rise. Anne Marie reached out and gripped his hand firmly in hers. She wanted to keep him close to her. She wanted him to know he made the difference in her life. Since she'd been with Sterrett, she'd been able to wean herself off the various mood-altering pills she was taking. That was a major change in her life, flushing the Tlaxcalin tablets down the john. She was feeling calm and totally able to sleep, as long as she had Sterrett beside her.

"By the way, I wanted to tell you, the Secretary of the Interior? Seems he's such a nervous Nellie, he wants the honor to go to him, you know, inaugurate the site? And not to dear Antonia. Can you believe that? The creep. He didn't do anything to get this deal done and he wants to take all the credit."

"He's the boss, isn't he?"

"It's not right."

The Department of the Interior had been granted "adequate time" by the terms of the lease contract to enable the removal of the various Park Service installations at the Ellipse in preparation for the landfill, and "adequate time" was open to some interpretation. Secretary Morrow met with Director Segreen the day after the signing, told her to inform Capital Landfill Development that it would take as much as three months to get the Ellipse in "broom clean" order before handing it over to Sir Simon and his backhoes. The real issue was a personal one. It took Celia a little time to figure that out, to figure out what was needed. She met with the Secretary of the Interior and discovered that Tom Morrow felt left out. In all the hullaballoo over Segreen, people had stopped thinking about him.

Anne Marie told Sterrett all this while the crowd settled in below them. She told him in a chatty way, to show that her office was busy, had issues.

"So it's easily enough resolved, isn't it?" Sterrett responded, re-reading what he'd already read of the program, who wrote the score, who designed the scenery, who sang the part of Wolf Robe. "Let him dig the first shovelful at the groundbreaking."

"Of course," Anne Marie replied. "But it's not fair. Antonia did all the work. And it may not be enough to make him happy."

The concert hall darkened. The curtain came up and the second act began with a rather weepy Wolf Robe seeking forgiveness of the Statue of Freedom for having doubted her charms. Anne Marie leaned forward in her seat. She took Sterrett's hand and placed it against her beating heart so he could feel how agitated she was, the Cheyenne chief at risk of losing love, when love was what he most needed.

The real worriment, what made Sterrett edgy, what depressed him despite the success of the signing was Senator Roger Simmers, who was having a tantrum not unlike Morrow's. The difference was Republican Senator Simmers was not answerable to the president of the United States. Whereas the Republican leadership in both the House and the Senate was unresisting, thinking that a garbage dump behind the White House seemed appropriate in so far as a Democrat was living there. Simmers simply refused to go along. Congress gave its approval, Simmers publically objected. He gave no reason, saying a man, a truly free man didn't have to give a reason.

The chairman of the Senate's Appropriations subcommittee for waste management, Howard Rudnick, told Simmers what he'd told the press, the landfill was America doing what it took to make American trash work for America. It was progress, pure and simple. Rudnick had originally spoken out against the landfill. But he was not up for re-election for another two years and didn't want to be bothered any more about that issue. Rudnick had gone on the public record against the sanitary landfill, and then gone on the public record for it, and that was all he intended to do about it.

Senator Simmers had called Guiteau and Garfield that very morning, trying to reach Vincent Jorrigo. In the end he spoke to Sterrett Emerson Groves. He growled into the phone and told Groves in no uncertain terms that he planned to go to the Justice Department. He planned to ask for an investigation into the signing of the ground lease with the Department of the Interior. He claimed Vincent Jorrigo had used bribes on behalf of the client, had corrupted the incorruptible Segreen. The signing was a sham, he said. He was going to call for an indictment of the Secretary of the Interior and of the director of the Bureau of Land Management.

Sterrett defended the landfill on the phone. He told Senator Simmers that the lease was signed and nothing could change that. The one problem from Sterrett's point of view was that he suspected the Texas senator had got it right. Having gone down to the Ellipse and seen the site, he couldn't imagine how anyone would think it a wonderful idea to put a malodorous landfill there, without having been given a sizable incentive to do so. Sterrett was now afraid Simmers's shot in the dark would end up laying bare an ugly truth.

And who could blame Sterrett for being anxious, and who could blame him on the other hand for keeping quiet about what he knew. The landfill, like all great projects, was a chance at pork for everybody. Sterrett too wanted to rise with the others to that slightly fantastic sphere of power where people respected you more, the more you got away with.

He knew all about the shadow company in Liechtenstein, an illegal way of keeping accounts out of the IRS's hands. He'd drawn up the documentation, and he'd spoken on the phone to the very respectable lawyer in Vaduz who was doing all the paperwork on that end. No one seemed in the least concerned about conducting business that way, in an unethical, illegal way, not his boss, not Anne Marie's boss either. It was the purpose of his being a lawyer, to make sure these acts were doable.

Fight them. And lose. Join them, Sterrett thought, get on the band wagon and win. He should be smart, try to learn from his nation's leaders. But he felt that by joining them in their dishonest acts, by following his nation's business leaders in doing whatever it took for profit's sake, by following men like Sir Simon, he was going to lose something of himself, not just his innocence and candor, but his freedom to act as a man. He was giving up his moral freedom. Knowing that he was willing to do it and that he was already doing it, this knowledge gave Sterrett a permitted sense of contempt for those around him.

Even though tempted, he didn't discuss these considerations with Anne Marie. He assumed she would be shocked out of her socks to know what he knew about how the people involved with the sanitary landfill did business. He clammed up, because anyway Anne Marie might end up shocking him. The only one he could confront frankly with these worries was Vincent Jorrigo. He'd have to wait for the man's return from Las Vegas.

The third and final act of *The Trail of Broken Contracts, the Musical*, was an unexpected relief. No waterworks, it was full of joyous song, full of exhilarating ghost dancing. Wolf Robe was assaulted, injured but not killed by Belknap's legal assistant, the unsavory Colonel Chivington. After fighting off Chivington and his group of pistol-packing bluecoats, Wolf Robe rediscovered his warrior nature, celebrating that discovery in a moving duet with the Statue of Freedom. The warrior-plaintiff emerged triumphant, and he was awarded by the jury chorus both the undying love of Freedom and an indemnity that included a wish list of mountain states.

"I find his work just terrific, terrific, really," Anne Marie said. "Celia knows him practically by heart. Can you believe it?"

"I thought it was kind of second rate."

They filled the silence between them going home with talk about what they'd just seen. Anne Marie sat behind the wheel of her utility vehicle and drove without her usual élan. That was due to the fact that the musical had moved her to think about the plight of the American Indian. She had never considered the Indian much. They had casinos and they had their reservations, large tracts of land where they could do whatever they wanted. She felt sorry that wasn't enough to make them happy.

"But we can't give them Montana and the Dakotas. Colorado? I mean, my goodness, Aspen's there. What next, we return Manhattan to the whoever?"

"I tell you one state I'd give away, Texas. I'd call Mexico City and ask the Mexicans to take back Dallas and Houston and whatever else they want."

"No, you wouldn't."

"I hate Texas," Sterrett groused. "They're the mafia here in Washington. I go for my guns when I hear the word 'Texas.' Fucking Texicans."

"Please, Sterrett, watch your language."

"Okay, all right. But I would."

They drove on, going up Wisconsin Avenue, passing as it happened the Lucky Key. His chumlings, how long had it been, Sterrett wondered, vexed. They had probably already forgotten him, cops forgot easily. The strippers, he missed the skinny ones, with their bleary smiles, most of all. He thought about asking Anne Marie to stop, if not at the Lucky Key, at least along the way home, at the Austin Grill for margaritas or the Zebra Room for beers. He looked over at her, so tiny behind the wheel, both hands grip-on. He realized Anne Marie was not someone he wanted to drink with. Didn't know whether that was a good or a bad thing, but could not imagine the two of them sitting in a booth and enjoying the fuzzle.

They turned right, off Wisconsin Avenue and onto Newark Street. Anne Marie's house was the gray one on the left. It was surrounded by other large houses, well-cared-for houses, immersed in green lawns and spacious gardens. They were country estates still within the borders of the city, houses that seemed to say, "All things are good to the good."

Anne Marie rolled up the driveway and threw the vehicle into park. Sterrett was out first. He undid his tie, stood at the foot of the walkway waiting for the girl, and he undid his shirt collar, too. Lightning bugs filled the air. Sterrett swung out, trying to catch one. Anne Marie laughed giddy laughter to watch him. Then she came up and put her arm around his waist and together they went up the brick walkway to the porch.

There was a mulberry tree overhanging the walkway, and the sour smell of the fallen berries crushed underfoot came to them as they went up the steps to the front door. Sterrett hadn't slept in his own bed in his own apartment for an entire week. On the other hand, it was true, on summer nights, Anne Marie's place was more comfortable, and it had that swimming pool.

She had the key in her hand. Sterrett came up behind her and placed a kiss on her neck. But when she turned round to reciprocate, kiss for a kiss, he pushed on through the open door.

"How about a swim?" he asked.

First she was annoyed. Then she stood in the doorway and gave him an injured look. She said, "You only like me for my pool."

"You have something to get off your chest?"

"I enjoy being with you, Sterrett, is that such a burden to you?" she asked wretchedly, coming into the house, tossing her purse down on a side table in the living room. "You're my whole life. Why don't you understand that? All I want from you, and I don't think it's a lot, really, but all I want is a little tenderness from time to time. I know you're capable of it. Don't be afraid of showing your emotions."

"Emotions fade. Love fades, you know, especially after a couple years being married," the boy said, experiencing one of those moments when he liked being mean, thinking it rendered him more of a realist. "I've seen it happen. Success remains. Money remains."

"You think money's that important?"

"You know the answer, Annie. You don't have to think about it 'cause it's always been given to you. But think about it. Suffering in the world, where would it be if everyone had enough money?" Sterrett brandished the evening's Playbill, which he still held rolled up in his grip. "Shit, wasn't that the point of tonight? I mean if those Indians had had enough buying power, they wouldn't have needed to go on the damn warpath, if the gold in those hills, which was theirs, had been theirs to keep. They could have bought the fucking warpath."

"What an ugly thing to say to me," Anne Marie told him, and she began crying. She fell onto the sofa and began crying. She folded up on the sofa, her hands to her eyes, and salt tears squirted like sea spray from between her fingers.

"I'm sorry," Sterrett said, standing over her, not sure how a seemingly pleasant evening had gotten away from them so speedily. It was a pattern, happiness followed quickly by tears. Tears, by apologies. He himself felt a tear form in his eye as he said, "I am sorry, really."

Anne Marie stirred, moving deeper into the cushions, moving away from him. "That's a lie. You're not."

"I am. I'm tired of hurting you."

"Be quiet. You're bored with me, that's what you mean," the girl said. "It's my fault. I'm a boring person, really, I know it. I don't want to go on…don't want your misery on my hands. I'm sorry, I'm the one."

"Misery? Do I seem miserable? Look at me."

"Yes, you're unhappy here."

"No, I'm not. Come on, I'm just overtired. It's been a long day."

"Except the pool. You like that. I have a pool. That's why you stay with me. That's the first thing when you come home, the pool."

"No, it's more than that."

He was feeling an asshole for being who he was. He didn't love Ann Marie, and yet that wasn't the whole truth of their situation. He didn't have the guts to face the whole situation and admit it to himself, that he was a long time needing someone to feel anchored to.

"I can't go on without you," Sterrett had to confess in that moment. He began crying, too. "I'm so tired of all this trying to make it on my own crap. I can't go on alone. I can't."

Anne Marie pushed herself up from the sofa. Her face was soft from crying, her body pliant with emotion, and she grabbed him round the neck and they made love standing in the middle of the living room. Then they went to bed. Instead of sleeping they lay in bed and talked. Anne Marie told Sterrett all her secrets, told him about her relationship with her parents, about the first time she had sex, and about an aborted pregnancy. She talked so much about these things, talking well into the night that Sterrett realized what he had to do. He suggested they think about getting engaged.

The next day, Saturday, they slept until the sun came dashing through the windows. They had morning sex, and then slept some more. That was real luxury for an attorney, to sleep late, and late meant ten o'clock. They had breakfast on the patio by the pool. Their conversation was mostly about how much butter went on the toast, how much milk was too much milk in the coffee. Sterrett took a swim afterwards. He was a beautiful swimmer, and Anne Marie sat down in one of the deck chairs and watched him with real pleasure, his long arms, long legs slashing through the water.

Now that they were about to get engaged, Sterrett felt the pool was half his, and after he did about ten laps, he flopped down on the inflatable raft they had and floated in the cool chlorine. He emptied his mind of all negative thoughts. He listened to the cicadas, their whirring high up in the trees, a sound he imagined was the way Mexican mornings sounded.

Anne Marie sat with her sunglasses on and chattered away about how he had to go meet her parents. That was how Washington mornings sounded, people always talking. She was onto their new priority as a couple, meet the parents, bring the relationship into the next circle of conformity. Sterrett didn't regret proposing their getting engaged because he didn't really believe they would.

Anne Marie, one month was all it had taken for her to believe their future was a ring, a cake, and children, and she was doing it for him, zealous in her desire to make him happy, thinking too, she got her way over the man at last, a definite victory. Yet Sterrett had no real desire to surrender his stupid and bitter little heart to her, or yield up his pride, his lazy self to the making of a family just at a time in his life when he was becoming an attorney of some importance. He had no real desire to live a life of togetherness with her. He had no wish to be happy the way she wanted him to be happy.

He couldn't be straightforward about it. He was afraid to tell her he didn't love her, and knew he would regret it if he did tell her. The risk was that he would not tell her until it was too late to tell her. He felt even more ashamed then, for he knew he wouldn't tell her, at least not until the end of the summer.

He let himself drift to the middle of the swimming pool. Anne Marie was telling him all about how her parents, John and Theresa Smith, lived in Grand Rapids, Michigan. They lived in Grand Rapids the way people lived in Topeka or Tampa, Tucson or Spokane he supposed, but Anne Marie seemed to imply they lived better on the banks of the Grand River than anyone lived anywhere else.

"It's the kind of place, oh what can I say? It's there and you think this is what America should be, this is the kind of city that puts the glow in 'hometown.'"

She got up and came and sat over by the deep end of the pool, with her legs in the water. She told him how it was growing up in Grand Rapids, how she was an only child and how her parents spoiled her. She thought then to ask him that most fatal question, wanting to know about his parents, now that she'd spent an hour going on about hers.

"All I know is your father was in the Army."

Sterrett called to mind his father, Berwick, sharp and trim, his grinning face bloated by cancer, as though he had been trapped too long underwater. Colonel Berwick Groves, his beginning, the reason he was there. He was there because Berwick Groves had been. He was there because Berwick had left him there.

"My father ignored me, that's all I feel about that."

He had to explain it to her. Anne Marie was appalled by that concept and by that sentiment, a father ignoring his child, impossible.

"Berwick was happiest in uniform, on a mission, and home was a place that was a duress assignment to him," Sterrett said, stirring the water so that he floated away from her. "He was always pushing himself, even when he appeared to be relaxing, because if the Colonel relaxed, he was sure someone would stick it to him. I felt sorry for him. He never did learn his own worth as a man."

"But he must have loved you very much anyway," she tried. "I mean he did his duty because that was what his country asked of him, but does that mean he didn't love you? I don't think so."

"No, I think one day my father looked at me and said, 'he's too much loved.' And from then on I was on my own," Sterrett replied.

And he hit on something that made how he'd always felt towards life very understandable. One day, his father had simply decided not to love him so much. Being an officer in the Army, he imposed that order on Sterrett's mother as well. They both chose not to give him so much love. He was to stand on his own without too strong a dependence on overt affection.

Sterrett didn't know whether it was to protect him from suffering too much. Or whether it was done to protect the Colonel from having to feel more than responsibility for someone not under his official command. Perhaps his father, from his experiences fighting to defend freedom knew that love weakened a man's instincts, that it made the heart weary, vulnerable, and he was concerned they'd smother Sterrett if they loved him too much, stunt his growth as a man. Sterrett just remembered that one day his parents stopped; in particular Berwick judged it time to stop giving him hugs and kisses. They stopped showing him how much they cared for him. One day it stopped.

"And your mom?"

"What about her? She lives in Florida. In Ft. Pierce, about half a mile from the sea. She never wants to see Washington, D.C. again and being a woman of high principle, I don't think she ever will."

"What's her name? I don't even know your mom's name."

"Brenda," Sterrett said. She was left behind, like Sterrett's sisters, not just ignored but left behind. He told her how his mother always loved music. She was always making up little songs to sing. He remembered coming home after elementary school on base, and his mother singing these songs of hers. She'd tried to get a job in a local club at one point, but her voice was too shrill for her to be any kind of professional. Sterrett found her singing in hushed tones over the dirty dishes one time, her hands sunk motionless among the suds, singing to her husband, to Berwick as though he were there with her, and not thousands of miles away pursuing Iraqi tanks across a charred desert.

Anne Marie began to sniffle. She sat at the side of the pool and waved to him to come over. She read into the common story of his life, tragedy. He didn't want to dwell on these things, while she did. He had suffered them and grown out of them, and was unwilling to have syrupy emotions drizzled over the past as though the past was a pile of pancakes.

When Anne Marie told him that they'd have to go together to Florida and visit his mother, Sterrett simply slipped off the raft. He let his body slip into the water and he let himself sink, sinking with his eyes closed to the bottom of the pool. Anne Marie probably thought he was drowning down there. He heard a splash and opened his eyes; she'd jumped in. Sterrett guffawed underwater and almost did drown it was so hilarious, Anne Marie coming to save him. But he couldn't drown even if he'd wanted to. In a couple hours, he had to go and meet his boss at National Airport, Jorrigo returning from his prolonged stay in Las Vegas, Nevada.

Anne Marie insisted on driving him to the airport. She was feeling very tender toward him, very protective, and he decided to take advantage of that, instead of resisting it all the time. They went out across the river and down the parkway, past Arlington Cemetery, Saturday's traffic surprisingly light. Sterrett almost made the mistake of telling Anne Marie that was where Colonel Berwick Groves was buried, and he was worried she would think to ask to go see the grave. He hadn't been to his father's grave for almost a year, and he had no desire to go there now to moon over a bitter gravestone.

They pulled round to the main air terminal. Sterrett insisted that she drop him off at the curb. He had a few things he had to discuss with his boss and they were confidential matters regarding a client. Anne Marie sat huddled in her big, fat utility vehicle looking as though she was about to cry again. She clicked her fingernails, clicking them loudly.

"One of these days," she told him. "You'll let me into your life. That's all I ask. Let me into your life."

Vince Jorrigo was coming into Reagan National Airport, a connecting flight from Memphis. On the arrivals board in Terminal B his plane showed up on time. Sterrett stood near the gate. He glanced at his reflection in a display window, pretending for a moment to be interested in the ad for cheap flights to Pittsburgh. A small pimple of misgiving shined on the tip of his nose.

He checked his watch again. Looked at the arrivals board. Yells burst through the concourse. People started coming out the gate. They were tired, eyes narrowed as though they'd had too much sun, limbs stiff. A very few however were relaxed-looking despite the hours in sway high over the continent. Vince was one of these. He came off the plane easily like he were walking back from the roulette wheel, and dressed in a loud linen shirt and loose khaki pants, with his hair combed down, held in place by a ton of gel, his appearance had as little of Washington in it as possible.

"Mr. Jorrigo." Sterrett came up to him and smiled, happy to see his boss at last returned.

"If you want to be useful carry this." Vince handed a shoulder bag to Groves who hesitated for a second, then took hold of the leather bag, holding it by the straps. It was light for how big it was, practically empty.

"Don't you have any other baggage?" The young attorney pointed to the baggage claim area.

"I don't have other baggage, no."

They drifted away from the gate, down the hall toward the doors of the airport terminal. They walked side by side and came out to the taxi stand. Vince seemed detached. But Sterrett was pleased that whatever had happened to him in Las Vegas, the man was still a man to be reckoned with, and that was reassuring.

"What are you looking at?" the senior partner asked.

"No, I'm just glad to see you, sir."

"You did a good job getting the thing signed. That's done. Good."

A brown and beige ViCo taxicab pulled up, moving very slowly, rising from the taxi stand to stop alongside of the two attorneys. The cabby leaned across the seat. His expression was suspicious, uncertain, was this a fare or not.

"I'm going to Maine Avenue," Vince said.

"I wanted to talk about something," Sterrett said.

"Come on, then, we'll talk on the way into town."

Sterrett sat back in the taxicab with his legs crossed and his back straight, his chin raised to the reviving breeze that came through the window. He told his boss all the things that had happened, careful to keep his voice low. There was the good news, which Vince already knew, the signing, the date for the groundbreaking set, the extensive and favorable news coverage. There was the bad news, and this Sterrett practically whispered, about Simmers. He told him the meat of his telephone conversation with Senator Simmers.

"Justice Department," Sterrett repeated. "That's what he told me he was going to do. I believe he will do it, sir."

"He's running for president. He wants a donation to his campaign."

"I don't think so." Sterrett lowered his head and sighed. "A donation?" he asked. "How do you mean?"

"He's not going to drag a Democratic Justice Department into the picture to spoil the fun, and gain what? You always have to think what is he going to gain, when you're dealing with a legislator."

"Yes sir, my idea is that's your idea of what he thinks."

"Groves. Please. Don't worry about it. Simmers is looking for money for his campaign and he thinks he can get us to give it to him. So maybe the firm'll make him a donation if he leaves the Mall alone. Can we move on?"

"That's not a donation, Mr. Jorrigo. That's more like a bribe."

"And yet the word 'bribe' comes from the Middle French *brimber, un bribe*," Vince argued for the sake of arguing. "A crumb of bread, to beg a crumb from the Master's table, so it has a pardonably meek origin."

"Well what are we going to do about it?"

"Please stop it, Groves." Vince gave his associate a severe look over the rim of his Ray-Bans and added, "If you'll let me, I can still handle things, you know."

They crossed out of Virginia, going over the 14th Street Bridge. The Potomac was a filmy, fast-running surface of a pale tobacco color. Anne Marie was right about that as about so much else. The River of Swans might have been a gentler, more inspiring waterway once, but in Sterrett's time it had acquired properties killer to any who embraced it. Every year capsized canoeists were pulled vomiting to the shore, and from time to time, off-balance anglers disappeared in the undertow, reappearing days later inert and bloated down by the bay.

The cab drifted along going up 14th Street. Sterrett crossed his arms upon his chest and looked down along the crease of his pants.

He studied the senior partner, pretending not to, saw he was a changed man, changed in his priorities perhaps. Sterrett thought of himself then, passed his hand across the silk vector of his tie. It was a perfectly elegant tie, regimental stripes in respectable colors. Anne Marie had picked it out for him. It was a tie of the sort he'd once sworn never to wear so that it was tangible proof, he had changed too. He bent his nose to his underarm. He could no longer distinguish himself from the others, because rationally speaking, objectively speaking, he smelled no different.

"So how was Las Vegas?"

Vince crossed his legs and sat up, so that he was balanced on the very edge of the backseat of the taxicab. Sterrett was unsure whether to button up or say something more. The senior partner looked precarious, perched like that.

"How was it?" Sterrett repeated.

Vince turned and grinned at the associate. "I lost everything."

CHAPTER FOURTEEN

A few days passed. It was the beginning of the next week. The landfill was moving quickly to groundbreaking. Kid Psora had a construction company, Wall Structural of New Jersey, ready to come in with its dozers, its hard-hatted crew champing at the bit to excavate. The engineers stood by rubbing their hands as hungrily as if they were all there to extract something of great worth from the ground—coal, diamonds, ancient treasure—when all they were about was the digging out of perfectly fertile earth, of no value to anyone in the modern world.

Kid Psora was staying at the Four Georges Hotel in Georgetown and had a big sedan to get him around town. He had some friends to see. Parties to go to and be seen at, money to spend, spending more and more money so that the landfill would have to earn more. Above all, he had the stench in his nostrils of his father, Sir Simon, wallowing around in the pool at Monte Carlo, a dreariness he needed to purge at all costs.

Sir Simon Psora, no pity for him, though, no. He knew what was going on. He was nuts, but he was unrelentingly manipulative, too. He had his money to move around, and he was going to do it, and he had young Sterrett Emerson Groves helping him. Waiting for the landfill to begin development, he contrived to stay in his grimy pool in his rented villa, and that was it, felt safest there, didn't want to budge. He kept to the pool, intermixed man and garbage, almost the whole day. He had a phone of course, and he called Groves at least once a day. He was full of questions. He was full of instructions, and he put pressure on the attorney. They talked about Vaduz. That's what the Greek

Dustman was most anxious about, Vaduz, and the profit-taking at the sanitary landfill.

A date had been set for the groundbreaking at the sanitary landfill, Sterrett's doing, that Friday, the 6th of August. Though he coordinated the thing working closely with Celia Progg and her office, though he met with a whole array of people, most of the work done towards making the ceremony a success, was Sterrett sitting alone at his desk.

The old Sterrett, and how he longed for the old Sterrett, would have taken a couple hours off during the height of the day to go have a drink. But the new Sterrett, and how he hated that one, contented himself with coffee and conscientiousness. He had ground out too many hours of his life on the Ellipse not to see the groundbreaking realized.

The groundbreaking, no sooner was that word out than Washingtonians boasted not of a brand new federal building or a stadium brimming with the latest in spectator comfort or some sublimely heart-rending war memorial, but of the sanitary landfill on the Ellipse. Not everyone knew where or what the Ellipse was, but everyone wanted to be there. People who had planned all year to be away on that particular Friday, cancelled their plans, hoping to bear witness to an event their grandchildren would one day seek knowledge of. The cry was in every lug in town, the Groundbreaking resounding high and low through the streets, streets both narrow and wide.

Official celebratory preparations were already underway. The popular country-folk band Rock No Water was scheduled to perform with a special guest musician. The Quinn brothers, notoriously hard-hearted lobbyists, were going to give their famed interpretive reading of *Winnie the Pooh*. There were to be speeches by Kid Psora and by the director of the Bureau of Land Management, and Ellen Berman, the banker, was going to speak to making money, refuse the next big investment. No less a personage than the Secretary of the Interior would turn the first shovel. Success was in the air. There were tears in the air, too. Women's tears, and the tears of human men as well, tears of sorrow, tears of joy, for Washington was nothing if not an excitable town.

Vince Jorrigo had been given twenty-four hours to make good his debt. His dear old lender, his college buddy, his fellow alum, Ray Wilbur called that Monday, Vince's first day back in his office to tell him he was giving him another day, interest compounded, then he would lay the hammer down. But he wasn't going to send muscle, no, that wasn't Wilbur's way. He told Vince he was sending another lawyer into town to collect what was owed, Louis Shackley. Shackley would arrive Tuesday morning expecting what Vince owed or know the reason why. Shackley would call him.

Wilbur wasn't unpleasant about his friend's failure to pay his debt. He was very calm and solicitous. It was a situation that could be handled easily. His goal, Wilbur's one shining ambition, was to make Hidell Kennedy and Stone the biggest law firm in Creation, and if Jorrigo hadn't the money, Wilbur was prepared, was indeed eager to take over Guiteau and Garfield as per their verbal agreement.

Vince didn't say he didn't have the money. But he didn't have any money left. He'd gone to Las Vegas, and he'd played and won, and lost and won, and then in one hour at blackjack lost every farthing of all the cash money he had in his possession. A wild time though, his week in Las Vegas, he'd had the best time he'd had in years and he came back to Washington feeling refreshed. He'd gambled hard, and had lost, but he'd lived his lusty, tumultuous dream to its fullest, and that was the point to being alive. He wasn't going to make excuses for the way he was.

There was that one problem with the way he was; he owed Wilbur money, and the amount of his debt augmented daily. Just sitting there thinking about it, sitting at his desk trying to come up with a way to pay that amount back, the amount he owed grew by twenty and eight-tenths percent. Vince was no accountant but he didn't have to be, Wilbur was keeping account and Wilbur told him what he owed.

He had no real options. Money had never been easy for him. If he didn't have it, if he did, whatever, there was always a problem with it. He wasn't a lawyer for the money. He was a lawyer for the sake of the struggle to be the best lawyer possible, the happiness that struggle gave him. Now the possibility that he could continue that struggle was in jeopardy.

Only the excellent pressing of his suit kept him from sobbing with sudden emotion, the fear he had of losing his firm. But the Guiteau and Garfield attorney knew there was always a maneuver in any situation, and he was sure the money could be had if one was willing enough. He sat, resting the *Arabella* against his belly, cupping its sterling silver frame in both hands, making a deep, churlish sound using his lips. It was the sound the boat's Johnson Marine engines made at full throttle.

It spooked Kimmie to see him sitting there like that. She peeked in from time to time, too scared to disturb him.

Vince thought about trying to access Sir Simon's line of credit, the Capital Landfill Development Partnership's $9 million over at the Consolidated Bank, but he needed someone at Unfragrant Bin Systems to countersign for that. He thought about trying to get into one of his wife's bank accounts, and that too was fraught and full of difficulties. That was what started him thinking as hard as he ever had. He had to get his hands on lots of money and he had to do it in two days' time. He sat at his desk for hours. He stood at his window, sat on the sill, stared out across the street and up into the twilight. Then came an answer.

To the purpose of bettering the lot of the poor and the grossly disadvantaged, the people in the street as it were, Guiteau and Garfield had established a legal aid fund. This LAF money was to provide a philanthropic reserve for the special client who hadn't the resources to pay for legal representation, but whose case had merit nonetheless. Merit meant it was not just a winnable case, but a case that would bring money and fame to the law firm.

Each partner contributed on a quarterly basis to the legal aid fund according to his earnings. At the end of the year, the unused portion of the LAF was redistributed to the partners. For bookkeeping purposes, that money resulted as a carry-over charity loss accredited back to the firm at the beginning of the next fiscal year, rather than as capital paid out. Thus it worked to distribute tax-free money to the individual partners, a bit of legerdemain put together by the firm's certified public accountants, clever men and women over in a building in Tysons Corner.

The LAF was in a managed investment account at the Dalecarlia Bank that, year to date, amounted to more than $3,000,000. Of course the fund had never been used for the purposes of representing an indigent client. No indigent client had ever been found whose case had merit because no such client ever bothered to present himself at the firm's client reception area on the seventh floor of the Guiteau Building, and certainly none of the partners at Guiteau and Garfield had ever bothered to look for a client off the street who might need the kind of legal representation that Guiteau and Garfield offered.

As in many things, doing something crooked, it was best to act without delay, and that same morning after wasting time, screwing around in his office worrying, Vince drove out to the Spring Valley branch of the Dalecarlia Bank. It was a small branch, a beige carpet, modular furnishings, one teller, a woman, under Plexiglas and on the wall the picture of a lake. A plastic banner floated over the customer service area, "Do you want your Money at a touch of your computer screen?" Vince had been banking there for years.

It was a question of persuading the bank manager to clear a withdrawal from the partnership's investment without going through the accountants. Vince told the manager there was a certain urgency, as the blighted individual in question was in desperate need of a lawyer. The manager, a truly dove-like soul, told him he'd try to be as obliging as possible. The best way was if the bank issued a draft on the firm's investment account to Mr. Jorrigo's private account in the same bank. It was a process that would require some paperwork, a signature here and there, and patience. But it was entirely possible that the cash would be ready for use by next Tuesday morning around nine o'clock.

Tuesday, Sterrett sheered into Lemke's Dairy looking for them, the associates from the fourth floor. He knew where they sat because they always sat at the same table, back in the corner of the restaurant, the same round table. He was matted with sweat, and his hair clung flat to his brow, giving him the look of a young Caesar. He felt like a young Caesar. He had come along and made the Ellipse happen and he had seen to the signing and now he was in triumphant charge of the groundbreaking, and it was an important event, he knew he'd organized well.

He sat down with the other associates without deigning to say a single word to them. The other associates peered round at him. For one thing, he had on a regular power tie of a blood red color. For another, he no longer had an odor of armpits about him. He used an expensive deodorant, Musk Ah! and smelled awesome. Too, Groves seemed to the other associates, bigger, physically bigger. It was as though he were on steroids. It was difficult for the others to look at him, for looking at him they wanted to smile, out of happiness, that's the feeling he exuded, energy and light. It was attractive, and it was intimidating.

Hugo Humphrey drummed up some courage, and then said, "How's it going, Sterrett?" He tried to keep his tone plucky. "Who you showing off for?"

"Not for you," Groves replied.

Barbara, their waitress, appeared, a young girl with outlandish eyeglasses and teased-out hair. She put the associates at their ease, and they looked up at her like little children, as though she were there to save them from that terrible demigod, Groves. "Who has what?" she asked them.

"The waffles are mine," Hugo said and the plate came down before him.

"And the eggs are for you?" she said to Bird Mallet. "Isn't that right?"

He nodded and Barbara dished out the plates, one for Walt Gdyap, too. Barbara rested her hipbone against the table as she said to the new arrival. "What about you, hon'?" She opened her order pad and brought the nubbin of a pencil out from among the tufts of her hair. She looked down at Sterrett. "What do you say?"

"I'll have the breakfast-burger with an order of bacon."

"The breakfast-burger comes with a big slice of honey-cured Virginia ham," the waitress said. "You want the bacon instead of the ham?"

"I want both." Sterrett stopped the waitress as she started back to the kitchen. He pulled her to him, holding her by the wrist. "And look, I want a cup of coffee. Not that crap from the pot that's been sitting around the hot-pad two hours. Fresh-brewed. Do you understand?"

"I'll check on it right away," Barbara said gently. She headed off, the lacey strings of her apron dancing along behind her.

"I like her," Hugo told Sterrett. "So you should please treat her with respect."

Sterrett turned to his colleague. He said, "Who cares?"

They ate breakfast pretty much in silence after that, that shut them up. It was apparent to them that the happiness Sterrett was enjoying was of the purely selfish kind, and its energy derived from a taking away. Its felicity was in having what others did not. It made the others grow naturally broody, and jealous, he was so thoroughly delighted to be who he was.

The door to the eatery swung open. Ed Lemke clicked his dentures as Kimmie came hurrying in, a flash of heel, her hair like a black veil a-swish down her back. She hesitated, afraid she might have made a mistake coming there. Studied the room from under her bangs, scouting out the associates.

"Over here," Bird Mallet rose in his chair. "Kim, we're over here."

"I'm in something of a rush," she said. "Can I squeeze in here?"

"You can have a cup of coffee with your friends," Walt Gdyap told her. Everyone liked the senior partner's receptionist; she was normally so shy.

"I'm here for you, Sterrett."

Sterrett lifted himself out of his breakfast-burger. He clutched his fork to his breast and asked her, "Me?" He crunched up his face, as though it were impossible anyone should bother him at breakfast. "Me?"

"For you. Yes, I'm here for you."

Kimmie reached over and took his fork from his hand and tasted some of his breakfast, which was thick, greasy layers of ham and bacon topped with one fried egg, all resting on a thin hamburger patty which itself rested cushy on an open sesame seed bun. She said, "So much cholesterol." She stabbed at his plate. "Once a week? Twice? How many times do you eat meat?"

"Most of the time I eat beans," Sterrett bristled. "As if it's any of your business."

"An industry of waste has grown up around you," Kimmie said as she ate what was on the fork. She cut into another serving. "Laying waste entire forests, destroying the natural resources, and using up our water, our fuel, all to bring ground beef to your table. Resources that you, the young lawyer rob from the rest of us."

The other associates looked on, gawking in surprise as the girl stabbed at Sterrett's plate. They feared for her, a mere secretary clowning with the celebrated and puissant Groves. But Kimmie seemed to like it, teasing Sterrett like that, getting his dander up. She did it with such sweetness that Sterrett himself couldn't stop her as she ate the last helping of his breakfast-burger.

"Anyway, Mr. Jorrigo wants very much to talk to you." Kimmie wiped her lips on a napkin and stood up from the table.

"Can't you see I'm trying to eat breakfast?"

"You're done with breakfast," the secretary answered credibly. "He's waiting, you know?"

Hugo Humphrey couldn't help himself. He practically choked with laughter. He told Groves, "I hope no one ever speechifies the dickens out of me like that." He patted his eyes. "Boy, that was fun."

Sterrett delved into his trousers and yanked out a ten dollar bill. He tossed the money onto the table. He pretended that getting up, his foot got entangled in his chair, and he fell hard against Hugo Humphrey. He used his elbow to steady himself, digging his elbow into Hugo Humphrey's shoulder.

"Excuse me," was all he said.

The other attorney thought to react, but he was a cautious soul and anyway at that point the waitress, Barbara, came up. She told them, "I made a fresh pot." She showed Sterrett the steaming Sunbeam in her hand. "You're not staying any longer?"

"It's bye-bye to an asshole," Hugo said. "That's all."

Sterrett ignored that. But only because he saw himself so clearly then. He was slowly but surely turning into Jacques DeMurphy.

It was a two and a half block walk round to the Outhouse. Kimmie Albright, in her light-blue dress moved quickly, out ahead of Sterrett so that he had to make like a steam engine and chug and chug to catch up to her. He put out his hand. Kimmie turned. She said, "Sorry to disturb you at breakfast."

"No, I don't care."

"Don't be angry, Sterrett. I don't know what came over me. I didn't have breakfast."

"Hah, neither did I."

Kimmie tossed her head side to side so that her long black hair settled straight upon her back. She grew very serious, "I'm worried about Mr. Jorrigo."

They started walking at a slower pace, turning down 24th Street, a street full of shade, full of shadows. "I'm worried," she repeated.

"What kind of worried, about what?"

"I don't know. Not worried, scared." She wrapped her arm around the associate's. "He sits in his office all day and doesn't do anything, Sterrett."

"He's relaxing. Let him relax, that's what old guys do."

"Relaxing? No. Today, for instance, he went rushing off. He went rushing off early this morning just as I came in. Now he just called and told me to tell you to wait for him to return. Something important, but I can't imagine what." She held her wrist out. "Yes, he should be back in about twenty minutes."

"So I'll wait."

Kimmie stopped at the door to the Outhouse. She rested against the door, as though to open it, but didn't open it. "Sterrett, your tie," she said, reaching out to him, dragging her fingernail along the associate's chest. "It's not even a little bit repellent."

"It's new."

"Something not quite you about you. You've turned into a lawyer with a capital 'L,' haven't you? And yet you still have these lines of kindness, here around your eyes. That hasn't changed."

"Really?"

The girl tugged at him. She led him through, pushing the door open and going on into the office. "Rely on that kindness. Don't let it get lost."

He gave her a funny look, a little bit confused. He told her, "I have to decide whether to get engaged or not. I have to decide soon."

"Oh that's wonderful, Sterrett." She clapped her hands together lightly. "To Anne Marie? Oh, that's the best news I've heard."

"Probably my choice is going to be to dump her."

It was meanly said, and it evinced a sorrowful look from the secretary as she got behind her desk. She told Sterrett to wait, Vincent Jorrigo would be in, any minute, and she took the opportunity to frown at the young associate a little more. Well, Sterrett was mean, that was all there was to it, the kindness thing was simply the receptionist's imagination, and he was becoming gratuitously mean, more so every day.

"Now let me get organized…Two minutes…" Vincent Jorrigo said, rushing up the stairs into his office. He was agitated and had that stale look too much stress gave one. "Two minutes to get organized." He waved at a chair. "Need coffee? I'm glad you're here on time today, Groves."

"I came from breakfast," Sterrett answered, following the senior partner into the office. He went over to one of the wing-backed chairs, but he did not sit. With the windows open, it was hot and oppressive as always, and he noticed a bumblebee was shrieking its last, spinning on its furred back in a corner.

"Breakfast, Groves?" Vince huffed. "I've been up since 6 o'clock."

"Is that why you wanted to meet with me, sir?" Sterrett asked. "To tell me what time you got up this morning?"

"No, you're right," Vince said simply. He had no desire to waste time arguing. "Look, this is important to me, Groves."

He was carrying his old briefcase around. He limped a little going over to the desk because his foot hurt from how much he'd used the clutch and the brake driving back from the Dalecarlia Bank. He'd come up from Spring Valley, pushing the Brit sports car, not sweating the small stuff, feeling the road fly beneath him like a magic carpet ride, right up to the door of the Outhouse.

Now Vince stood in the office, very quietly. A curling lock of hair hung at his temple. He put the briefcase down on the floor and leaned stiffly over the desk. The thought came to him looking at the photograph on his desk, at his boat the *Arabella*, that he could just leave, and with the weekend ahead of him, and with the LAF money in the briefcase, he could make for the Islands, where for a couple two, three years he could live like a king.

Instead, he began to explain to the associate what it was he wanted the associate to do, wanting to communicate to the associate the immediate gravity of the thing. Like everyone, he wanted to be understood. But Vince realized the impossibility of putting into words the complexity of his mood. He made his most basic appeal, hoping that would work one more time.

"I told you once before didn't I, Groves? You're the one I trust."

The word "trust" always preceded some sort of imposition or other. Trust was the overture to his getting screwed. Sterrett said, "What do you want from me?"

"Meet with someone today. That's what I want. Has to be done today."

"Today?"

"Today as in now." Vince looked at his watch. "Meet a man, Louis Shackley, at the Old Inebriate Grill, at eleven o'clock. That gives you plenty of time, more than an hour. So let's get going." Then embarrassed to be so brusque when in truth it was a huge favor he was asking of the associate, nothing in the way of legal work, he added, "Can we succeed by ourselves alone? The answer, Groves, the clear answer is, we cannot." He glanced away to the windows. He pretended to be interested in something going on outside. He was trying specifically not to think about Ray Wilbur. He'd tried for weeks not to think about him and had done it pretty successfully. "The key is sacrifice."

Vince came round his desk. He brought the battered brown briefcase over to Sterrett, who was standing steely-eyed by the chair. He came over and dropped the briefcase at the associate's feet. "I'm asking you a favor."

Sterrett touched the briefcase with the toe of his shoe. Then he bent low and tapped it with his knuckles. The briefcase was battered-looking, the brown leather scarred and the threads of the handle coming undone. But when he grabbed it, lifted it up, he saw it had an important feel, a uniform weight, but not like a contract, not at all, more chunky.

"You're to take this briefcase to Mr. Louis Shackley, he'll be waiting..."

"What's in here? Can I see what's inside?"

"It's locked and it's none of your business what's inside."

Not all the money he'd withdrawn from the firm's legal aid fund that morning was inside the briefcase; some of the money, $100,000, Vince had the bank manager put in a separate envelope. That folded brown manila envelope now bulged in the inner pocket of his buttoned-up jacket. Vince planned to try Atlantic City this time, take the $100,000 and escape to Harrah's or to Bally's, use that money to make back the money he'd taken from the fund. He was sure he could do it. There were no guarantees. He wanted a clean break from debt, but it was all up to the cards.

"Take it, hold on to it, and then give it to Louis Shackley. After that come back to the office. I'll be waiting for your call. That's all I'm asking. Give me a call when it's done."

"Who is this Shackley?"

"He's a lawyer, Groves, a lawyer like you, well, and he works for Hidell Kennedy and Stone. I've never met him, but he's a lawyer, so you'll recognize him, or he'll recognize you. All you have to do is give it to him, stand in front of the Grill. I'll be obliged to you in a very big way." He caught the look in the associate's eye, and went on to say, "I can't go myself. I have to stay here." He didn't have a real reason not to go and meet with Shackley himself, except that he preferred to let the associate do that work. He made a show of anguish, his anguish, hoping that would do the trick. "I have to hold down the fort here at the Outhouse."

"What fort?" Sterrett wasn't in a sympathetic mood. It was clear to him, and he didn't have any trouble thinking the thing through. Success had given Sterrett an unusual perspicacity as to the motives of the people around him. Vince needed the sanitary landfill to go ahead and would do whatever was required to make sure it would go ahead. "It's a bribe, isn't it?"

"It's not a bribe," Vince said in a raised voice. "I'm not asking you to do something that will create problems for you, Groves. I value you too much. You're the only one I trust. This is an awfully delicate situation, you have no idea, Groves, no idea, so, please." He was getting carried away, letting frustration wrestle from him his card player's calm. "Please don't start that goddamn bribe thing again."

Sterrett went on, "It's for the landfill, isn't it?" Principals never acted for themselves. Senator Roger Simmers was using this guy Shackley, Jorrigo was using him to handle the money. "To pay off Senator Simmers."

"No one cares what Simmers has to say so he says whatever he wants. Don't worry about him. This has absolutely nothing to do with the goddamned landfill."

"What the hell," Sterrett said. He himself had lied and he had done it easily, and now he was sure he was being lied to. He assumed Jorrigo wanted to maintain total deniability in the affair if things went askew. Maintaining deniability was important in Washington circles. It was just that Sterrett thought he should be allowed in on the scheme, trusted for real.

"I don't want to be engaged in an activity wherein I could be found guilty according to the code of law, of that which is known as 'particepes criminis,'" Sterrett said. "I don't want to be involved in that wherein which I am party to what a prevailing authority might consider that which I have been party to as unlawful." He grew sullen. "This is not why I became a lawyer."

"None of us have become what we set out to become," Vince cried. He lurched up his office to the open window, turned his eyes to the clouded sky. "I've come closer than most people. Pretty close. I deserve your loyalty in this."

"I think I deserve a choice in this," Sterrett countered obstinately.

But he himself knew that wasn't the real problem, freedom of choice. He could simply turn around and walk out the office if he wanted freedom of choice. The problem was Sterrett, too, wanted the sanitary landfill to succeed. He had to admit it. He couldn't be a hypocrite about it. Despite all his disgust at the lies and the manipulation of public opinion, Sterrett, too, wanted the landfill at the Ellipse to get dug. He could actually say for the first time in his life, he'd worked hard, working on the landfill through all its phases, in negotiation and community discussion, at the signing and now preparing for the groundbreaking. Sterrett had put his hard, grinding, predatory self forward and people admired him for it, and he might even get rich from it.

"Choice, Groves, requires an open mind," Vince was saying. He turned back into the office. "I'm saying please. Please do this for me, Groves…I need this done."

Sterrett had to admit it, he liked the feeling of success. Now he'd been put in success's way. It was his one big chance and he couldn't afford to flinch. He felt he was under an obligation of loyalty to the senior partner. Nothing like a strong desire for success to make a man feel obligated. So he came back into the office and reached down, clenched his fist round the handle of the battered briefcase. "I still think this stinks," he said.

Vince then said the right words. "Just do it."

The case bumped and bumped again against the backside of his knee as Groves came down the narrow staircase. He barely gave Kimmie Albright a glance as he hiked out the door of the Outhouse, onto the sidewalk. He didn't have time to go back to his office. Walking normally, in a relaxed and normal stride, it would take him thirty minutes to get to the corner of 15th and G Streets where the Grill was. But he didn't feel normal, and he walked, letting his long legs stretch out, his feet heavy across the pavement.

He came up to Washington Circle, stopped at the corner opposite the hospital, George Washington University Hospital, where a pink thing, slippery and first drawing breath, he had been born. He put the briefcase down between his feet. He would have liked to go and talk to someone, but he knew there was no one who could help him. He had to rely on himself. That was the purpose of the work he was doing, to make him feel that way, alone. But he was tired of himself, always himself.

Sterrett stuck out his wrist and looked at the time, half past ten. No, he couldn't be a lawyer like every other lawyer, happy to be a heedless part of the practice and make money. He couldn't live an ordinary life, not for trying. There was always something to baffle him, someone to make him have to take a look at himself and cry out, "what in the hell am I doing." It was always other people who made him unhappy.

The associate had no choice but to clutch his cargo and carry on, continuing down Pennsylvania Avenue. He straightened his shoulders as he crossed to the wide pedestrian area in front of the White House grounds to show he was proud, to show he was defiant too, a good citizen despite the briefcase. Summer-school students were hurling a Frisbee around, using all of the old roadbed as a playing field, forcing Sterrett up onto the sidewalk.

One of the uniformed Secret Service guards eyeballed the battered brown briefcase as Sterrett passed the entrance gate. Farther down the avenue, past the snapshot vendor with his cardboard cutout of the sitting president, the balloon man was pandering his fistful of taut twine. "Make the children happy," he sang out. "Make the little ones happy. When the little ones are happy, everyone is happy…"

Sterrett strolled to the corner of Pennsylvania and 15th, 15th Street a part of Washington's official parade route, with three lanes going south to Constitution avenue, and three lanes going north into McPherson Square. There was always plenty of sunlight down the six lanes and always a breeze blowing up from the river. Sterrett crossed to the corner of 15th and G. He was looking for someone who might be Shackley. He wandered down the sidewalk, stared at a sparrow bathing furiously in the dust at the base of a tree, then turned to look over at the Treasury Building.

"You dropped something."

Sterrett looked behind him and up along the sidewalk.

"Dropped your shine."

A gaunt black man with restless eyes was at the ready on a bench, chamois-cloth in hand. He pointed his buff chammy at Sterrett's ox-blood Churches. Sit down here, waved the chammy, in a good-natured way. Sterrett studied his foot in its size 12 wingtips, the refined and resolute foot of a refined and resolute attorney.

"All you need is a good shine." The man was bent over another man's shoe, working hard with his chammy. He said, "Here, I'll be done with this gentleman in a minute. You better be next. Look at those shoes."

Sterrett's shoes were in fact scuffed, and he had some time to kill, early to his appointment and the other lawyer nowhere in sight. When the other customer got up, Sterrett sat down. He settled back on the bench. He cradled the briefcase in his lap and put his right foot up on the metal template.

"Lot of hard walking on these shoes," the shoeshine man said. "About time you came by."

The bench was shaded by a tree, and behind the bench was constant traffic. Sterrett was cautious. He hunched forward and tried the briefcase, flipping up the two gold snaps. It was unlocked. He gave the inside a peek. The strong, soapy smell of freshly minted money filled his nostrils. Sterrett slapped the case shut. "I knew it," he groaned. "Knew. It."

He'd seen enough in movies, read enough in the papers to know that the money could only be one thing, the usual Washington bribe, just what he'd thought. Vince Jorrigo had lied to him. That didn't wound his pride as much as the fact that the senior partner hadn't even bothered to lock the briefcase. He simply trusted the associate not to open the briefcase, trusted thoroughly in Sterrett's goodness.

The shoeshine worked steadily. He was quick and nimble, and when he was done, he cracked his chammy cloth against the toe of the associate's shoe. Sterrett stood up. He checked the bills in his wallet, and gave the shoeshine man a twenty. The shoeshine started in making change, counting out one dollar bills.

"You keep it," Sterrett said, giving him back two of the bills, and the man was already trying out, 'You dropped something' on another customer.

Sterrett lingered there, his eyes dropping to admire his reborn leather. Then he pulled the briefcase to him, felt its docile heft in his grip. To discover that it was indeed money inside, well, that was mind-blowing. He wasn't sure what to do next, and he thought, what he was ordered to do, do that, always a good move when any other decision was too hard to come by.

Sterrett tried to recoup the bored attitude proper to a gofer so that Shackley would recognize him. He walked toward the Old Inebriate Grill, its brassy facade grabbing a hold of a number of lobbyists getting out of a limousine. Sterrett jostled by them and then rushed up into the sunlight at the corner. Standing across the street, in front of the Treasury Building, waiting, looking somewhat bored himself, was a short, muscle-bound man in a seersucker suit. He strained at Sterrett Emerson Groves with bulging eyeballs. The young associate blushed. He switched the briefcase to his left hand. Took a stance, legs apart. Shackley, that had to be him. The man came charging across the intersection, right up to the curb. He came right up to Groves the moment he saw in the young man an uncertain desire to recognize and be recognized.

"From Guiteau and Garfield? How you doing?"

"You're from Hidell Kennedy and Stone?"

"That's me." The man glanced quickly round him and reached out for the briefcase. "Looks heavy."

Sterrett didn't budge. Punch the seersucker's lights out. Then he'd have some peace. Parading up the avenue, peace, love, and happiness, that's what he was thinking. "This is a bribe, isn't it?" he asked.

"That briefcase, hand it to me, now," Shackley said.

"You represent Senator Roger Simmers."

"I'm here from New York," Shackley answered. "I'm here from New York." He caught hold of the case, pulled it to him. "The money is for me."

It occurred to Sterrett then that the whole thing was very simple, what he'd learned from his mother rather than from his father, not fight, flight. Take flight for a change. He didn't reason it through, didn't have to. He reached out and yanked the battered brown briefcase back, out of Shackley's hand. He turned and pressed on down the street. The HKS attorney howled, "Where do you think you're going?"

Sterrett was going with the flow. He could hear as he went briskly past the Grill, past the jeweler's shop on the corner, Shackley charging after him. Glutei squeezed tight. His face in close at Sterrett, teeth gnash, gnash, as he came alongside. He hissed into Groves's ear, "If you don't hand that over right now…"

It was a lot of money inside. Even in Washington, even for a top-notch lawyer come down from New York City, that amount would be hard to explain to the cop on the beat. Shackley reached out. Sterrett dodged him, high-stepped it down a side street, the briefcase in the crook of his arm like a pigskin.

He ran solid, in the lead going through the Willard Hotel's court-yard where a decorative fountain gushed water everywhere but into its basin, and where there was a spread of tables for a pastry shop, people sitting, writing postcards. Sterrett slipped on the pavement and he tumbled against one of the tables, spilling a cup of coffee onto the lap of a high-strung, thirty-something woman in pearls.

The woman jumped up and shuddered, "Look what have you done to my Chanel."

Shackley pushed the woman out of his way and chased on after Groves. Not a snail's pace. Each man in pretty good shape, lawyers second to none in time spent jogging, Sterrett running across Freedom Plaza, pigeons taking to the blue, Shackley beating up at his heels. Teenagers held their skateboards to their tattooed chests, watching the two men run past, heading toward the U.S. Capitol on its plain-Joe Hill. Sterrett shed his tie. Louis Shackley his shoes, a hopping pace as he slipped off one shoe and hurled it at the young attorney, then a hop and a skip as he took off the other shoe too, a strong arm, but a bad aim. The shoe sailed past Groves and hit a man visiting from Canada, knocking him back into his wife's lap.

Sterrett's arm began to ache, and he shifted the documents case to his left arm, his head down bullish, his eyes fixed on the movement of his legs across the pavement, one foot up, one foot down, his brains all in his feet. And in that sense, he was enjoying himself.

They crossed street after street, cars pulling up violently around them, drivers yelling, the sound in their ears of horns blasting. Epi-thets, but no stopping for them. Police by the District Courthouse turned their heads, hands on their guns. Then hardly any people, the pavement straight and hard, the two men running side by side, not for the money in the briefcase anymore, but running solely out of pride. To be the last to give up. The Nike way both men lived. When Sterrett realized this, not thinking it through as much as feeling it, he slowed down. Louis Shackley went sprinting ahead, chest out, arms and legs like a swooshing swastika, leaving the air damp behind him.

Then with Shackley grinning to be winning, Sterrett flagged down a taxicab, jumped in even as the HKS attorney turned, two hundred feet of pavement too late, shambled forward, sank to his knees, hands outstretched as though to seize at last, the battered leather case, even as Sterrett leaned out the window of the taxi, and waved. A tear of rage in Louis Shackley's eye.

Sterrett wasn't sure why he'd done it. Sitting in the backseat of the cab, he realized that whether he was sure or not, the fact was, he'd done it. He clicked the locks of the briefcase, and slowly tipped the lid back. He stared at the top layer of bills, and sifted through to the bottom. There were five rows of eight packets per row, four layers thick; the case was thick with one hundred dollar bills wrapped in packets of fifty, wrapped and bound. Sterrett did some elementary multiplication. He closed the briefcase. He glanced away, his blue eyes blurring from the sudden emotion, all that cash.

The cabby glanced into his mirror. A big smile was the outward sign of the buzzy thrill Sterrett was feeling with that briefcase on his lap, a big splash of green against his heart, hope and light and the promise of every immediate wish fulfilled. That was what he was feeling in that very moment and he keened to it, leaning his face to the inrush of air from the open window of the cab, holding back the impulse to roar out in his excitement. He held back his excitement, and when the cabby asked him for the tenth time, Sterrett gave the man the address of the Guiteau Building, gave it out in a determined voice. He would bring the money back to Jorrigo.

When they came to the Guiteau Building, Sterrett got a twenty out of his wallet and handed it to the cabby. It was an eight dollar ride and the cabby took his time counting out the change. Sterrett stood at the curb watching him, and then realized it didn't matter, what was twelve dollars, he was in a rush. He spoke garbled, inadequately communicative words at the cabby, left him with the rest of the twenty, and walked off, up the sidewalk.

He pushed through the doors of the Guiteau Building. He was heading for his office, his office first, and then he'd call Vince Jorrigo, tell him he had his money. It was lunchtime, and the elevator coming down to the lobby was packed. The elevator going up to the offices was empty. Sterrett was alone in the elevator, but he rode it squeezed into a corner. He got off at his floor. Suzy was in her cubicle. She was fanning herself with a magazine.

"The air-conditioning doesn't work," his secretary explained.

"Here I am," Sterrett announced, coming up to her, panting heavily. "Mr. Jorrigo ask for me?"

"No one has asked for anyone."

"I'm going into my office."

"It's a steam bath in your office."

Sterrett went into his office. He was secure, snug, and unassailable in his office. He set the briefcase down on his desk. A man at his desk. He imagined himself in the National Gallery, a piece of performance art, and that would be the title of the work, "A Man at His Desk." It would be a significant piece of art for once.

It was hotter than normal in his drab, cramped, puking little office; a feeble amount of air, and that tepid, came out of the vents. He removed his jacket and hung it up on the coatrack in the corner. His shirt was sticking to him in damp spots. He sniffed at his armpits. But he didn't smell stinky in the least despite all the running he'd done. The deodorant Anne Marie bought him really worked.

He dropped into his chair. It was an old swivel chair, a worn-out office chair that gave the young attorney's backside little support. He thought, take a few dollars from the briefcase to purchase something really luxurious, the kind of plush and enormous wing-backed chair, easy on the tush, he imagined Donald Trump sat in. Sterrett sat back, looked out his window. The vertical-standing sun had set the steel flagpole on the roof of the National Retirees Building alight like a match.

He swung his knees under his desk. He could hear people shuffling round, going to lunch, some few coming back from their early lunch. There was conversation and laughter down the hallway. All these people busily occupied with the day's routine, doing over and over again what they always did, thinking that was life. It made him feel sorry for them. It made him realize he was just like that, no different, every day the same thing, always returning to the same place, the same place.

"What the hell," he said. He reached for the telephone. He dialed the Outhouse number, his eyes on the briefcase. He hated talking on the phone and he hated having to talk to Vincent Jorrigo. He didn't want to hear the man ask questions he couldn't answer. He slapped the phone down before anyone could answer. Let them come to me, he thought. Let others make the effort.

The briefcase, sitting there on top of his desk had something of a historic look, as though it had come from another era. It was certainly more than twenty years old. Perhaps it was the briefcase Jorrigo had first used, practicing law. Most lawyers had a closet full of old beat-up briefcases they no longer wanted to be seen carrying around, but didn't have the heart to throw away, briefcases good for a rainy day.

Money good for a rainy day, the bribe, and where had the money come from, Sterrett wondered, from the firm, or from Jorrigo's pocket. He knew his boss was scrupulously professional, so he guessed that since the bribe was to advance a client's cause, it had to have come from some general fund. Perhaps Guiteau and Garfield had a "blacked out account," a secret fund for bribes and such illegal niceties. Giving the money back to Vince Jorrigo would not make Sterrett any less of a participant in what was essentially punishable behavior.

The thing to do would be to take the briefcase back down the street to the Justice Department. Go to the Justice Department before the Justice Department came to him. But Vince Jorrigo, Louis Shackley, they were reputable members of a powerful professional class, and Roger Simmers was an exalted and preeminent member of Congress, and Sterrett was just Sterrett, an associate, a man with no name. He suspected he'd be the one who would end up looking the guilty party if he took the briefcase to the government.

Even if he didn't get charged with bribery, even if he didn't get disbarred for violating client confidentiality, Sterrett was screwed as a lawyer. No client worth his salt would ever hire a lawyer so rigorously high-principled as to go to the feds.

But he felt he should confide in someone, share the burden just in case. He couldn't call Dinah, that was out. Anyway, she didn't answer when she saw his number. He couldn't call Anne Marie because Anne Marie was someone it was impossible to confide in without feeling condemned from the start.

He thought, strangely enough of his father, Col. Berwick Groves. They had always been honest with each other even in the midst of sharp disagreement, even if it seemed they were unfeeling towards each other. Berwick, a man Sterrett could still picture clearly, with his sly grin and his rousing voice coming out of that toughened, boozer's body, the way he carried himself, always a jaunty figure. For the first time in years, Sterrett wished his father was still around.

One of his chumlings, as it happened Sterrett had Gooch's number on his cellphone, and he reached into his jacket pocket. He was sure Gooch, a veteran police officer, would be able to tell him what the best approach was. They could meet at the Lucky Key. He scrolled through his numbers. But before he could call anyone, the phone began to vibrate and of its own accord sent into the air a hip-hop jingle, so that the young attorney, spooked, dropped the phone to the floor. It continued ringing there underneath his desk. Sterrett crouched down and retrieved it. Anne Marie was calling. He had no intention of answering. But he knew, soon after getting no answer, she'd send him a message. There it was, "Sweetheart, how are you? I'm in the middle of a meeting and it's chaos. I'm your fangirl. Miss you." The message was garnished with keystroke characters, a zippy emoticon.

Sterrett held the cellphone away from him, stared blankly at the display. He didn't really need to confide in anyone. Why volunteer information, he said to himself, never volunteer. He had the money, and the purpose of money was, it made being alone easier. He didn't want anyone to confide in. A selfish life was the only way to be when you had money. Dinah herself had hinted at that truth. He decided to wait and see what happened.

He switched his cellphone off. He reached over to the coat rack and dropped the phone into his jacket pocket. He was going to keep quiet for the time being. Now he found that he was tired, physically tired, the tension, the running. He'd had nothing to eat since breakfast, and he was beginning to droop. He let inertia take over, and he folded his arms on the briefcase and put his head down and took a snooze.

He woke, not quite sure where he was. He woke with a little kick, thinking he was still running from the Hidell Kennedy and Stone attorney. He sat up. The briefcase was still there. He grazed his fingers along its scruffy leather. He looked around him. Everything seemed normal. He'd carried off $800,000 in cash money, that was the only breathtaking thing going on.

If anyone was coming after him, well, they were taking their time. It was two o'clock, already three hours since he'd snatched the briefcase back from Shackley. Sterrett reckoned no one was going to send the law after him, no, not at all. Vince Jorrigo wouldn't. The guy Shackley wouldn't. He wasn't worried about that any more. He was enough of a Washingtonian to know the law served to go after criminals, not after other Washingtonians.

He saw, saw clearly. Justice was blind, but greed was a hundred-eyed. It was his money. If no one came after him, the money in the battered brown briefcase was his. He'd wait a little more, and if after waiting, nothing happened, that was proof that he could get away with it. Getting away with it was as good a justification for keeping the money as any.

So now he came out of his office carrying the briefcase. He looked a bit frazzled, that was all. It was the middle of the afternoon, and Suzy was working hard at her computer. He said good-bye to her. She was too busy to see him leave, too busy to hear him. He went on down the hallway past the telephones that rang, the voices up long corridors and the sweet hush, hush of lawyers doing their thing. The elevator heaved up to meet him. Jostled him to the lobby, the greased cables clattering down the shaft. "Piso Mojado" was propped up across the floor; the small plastic sign in bright yellow showed a man falling on his butt. Sterrett Emerson Groves found the warning timely. His money would keep him from any fall.

CHAPTER FIFTEEN

" **C**ome here, brother." A man was resting on a pair of crutches at the beginning of the wide bridge across Rock Creek. As Vincent Jorrigo went by, the man called out, "Don't run off. Let me ask you this. Why did Marion Barry go to Philadelphia? Can't be too hard even for a fancy nigger like you."

Vince stopped in his tracks.

"Why did Marion Barry go to Philadelphia?" the man repeated, shifting his weight, leaning forward on one of the crutches.

"I really don't know."

"Went to Philadelphia to get the crack out of the Liberty Bell," the man said. He looked at the attorney with a kind of apathetic good humor. Then he put his hand out.

Vince showed he got the joke, smiled, and walked on. He was in too much distress to dwell on the thing, but "nigger," that word had startled him. He forgot sometimes. It didn't make him angry. It was something far out in left field for what he had going on in his life that particular Tuesday afternoon, but it sent his heart throbbing in his chest, throbbing painfully. He hurried up the avenue, away from the Guiteau Building looming behind him like an unfriendly headland. If he was going to have a heart attack he didn't want it to be in front of his building. He didn't want anyone to see him vulnerable or sick.

He took out his cellphone and tried to reach Groves for the second time. He'd waited and waited for Groves to call him, but it never happened. Things had gone decidedly wrong, and Vince wanted to get as far away as he could from the Outhouse, in case. He was halfway across the Rock Creek bridge and he called Groves at his office, where the associate's secretary, Suzy, acted surprised. She had seen him come in, but she hadn't seen Groves leave. But he must have left for the day; he wasn't anywhere in the office.

Vince tried the associate at his apartment, and then at his cell-phone number. But there was no answer. No message to leave a message, and no beep, not a peep, nothing. A global industry had grown up around the simple fact of cell communication, and Vince was sure there were people in the world who successfully reached their party, but he was not one of them, not at that moment. He slapped his phone shut and dropped it in his pocket.

No, he was not having a heart attack; the pain was passing. He felt it passing. He rested a moment against the bridge's smooth, granite balustrade, let the pain ebb away. He should have gone personally to meet Louis Shackley instead of sending Groves, but he had been too embarrassed to go. He trusted Groves to do what he was told, and it amazed him to think that his career might be put in jeopardy by that youth's misplaced scruples.

It was past two o'clock, and Vince wanted a drink of something stronger than Pepto-Bismol. Once over the Rock Creek bridge and into Georgetown, he found no dearth of watering holes to duck into. He was not familiar with most of the bars however and had to go by instinct, and he ended up at a bar owned by a client, Nathan's. He had the bartender fix him a vodka tonic. He slapped open his cellphone. Held it unsteadily in his unsteady hand, called Celia. He was into his second drink when she came along.

"You look terrible," she said as she joined him at a table near the windows.

"Groves didn't deliver the briefcase."

"What briefcase?"

"Let me tell you."

Vince regaled her with the truth concerning the battered brown briefcase, some of which Celia had already guessed at, his winning with money borrowed from a loan shark in New York. She'd guessed about that, of course, that he'd borrowed the money. She knew money was what he brought back with him from New York City. He told her about Wilbur, and he told her about his time in Vegas, not quite the full story, leaving out the fact that he'd lost everything. He let her assume he'd won in Vegas. He left out the most important information, that the money in the briefcase was not his, not winnings, and not borrowed from Wilbur either, but money he'd stolen from his firm's legal aid fund.

And he left out of the story as well, and wisely perhaps, the $100,000 he'd put aside from those same stolen funds, money squirrelled away in the wall safe at the Outhouse, money to play poker with. He did tell Celia about sending Groves, that yes, about Louis Shackley too, Shackley, Wilbur's man come to collect what was owed. Celia listened. She ordered a wine spritzer and listened. From time to time, by way of interjection she exclaimed, "You're not serious, are you?"

"Whatever Groves is up to, I'm the one, me, understand? I'm the one who's going to look responsible."

"You are responsible, Vince."

"This didn't work out the way I planned, that's all."

"Did you call Wilbur?"

"The only person I called was you."

And the only one who'd called him so far was Louis Shackley. The Hidell Kennedy and Stone attorney was so upset that the first thing he did was to get a train heading back to New York City. It was the first time anything like what had happened had happened to him, and he wanted to get back to his home ground, to the safety of Manhattan. He regained his composure by the time the Metroliner pulled into Baltimore. He got off there, hurried out of the train station, and hired a taxi to take him all the way back to D.C. He got dropped off at the Mayflower Hotel, and it was from the bar at the hotel that he called the only number he had, calling Vince Jorrigo's cellphone number.

But Shackley was unable or unwilling to give the Guiteau and Garfield attorney a clear picture of what had happened beyond the fact that the law associate had run off with the money. He was not threatening on the phone, perplexed rather, fearful too, and he wanted to know whether it was intended as a provocation, if so to what end, something personal perhaps. But Vince told him no, there was no desire on his part to do aught but liquidate his debt.

"I don't think he's eager to tell Wilbur he didn't collect the money. It sounds too improbable what Groves did."

For all his being hard-boiled, Louis Shackley was merely a lawyer, and not so fearless a customer. That was why he'd called Jorrigo, to see if the situation could be set aright without going back to Wilbur. Shackley didn't want to go back to Wilbur empty-handed. Vince Jorrigo told Shackley it was none of his doing. It was all Groves's initiative, and he didn't have any idea what the associate was up to. Shackley insisted he wanted the briefcase.

"And you left it like that?"

"I asked him to give me time to sort this out, to talk to him." Vince touched his earlobe, plucking at it. "I can't reach that fucking bastard," he said with unusual vehemence. He started in on Groves. He used language that Celia had never heard him use before, describing just how unreliable the associate turned out to be.

"Each of us has had to face a dilemma like this," Celia explained when her turn came. "When our professional life clashes with our personal conduct. We've each gone on. It's the going on, the doing what has to be done, well, that's what unites us, makes one out of us, as lawyers."

"And how does that help me? The situation I'm in?"

Vince kept quiet about the legal aid fund because that was his business. He felt no remorse for having embezzled those funds. It was something he had a right to do at a firm he had built up from nothing and whose partners owed everything to his savvy as a promoter and his talent in a court of law. In any case, it would take time for the other partners to discover the embezzlement, and well before then, he'd have won back at cards all that he'd taken.

"I don't know what Groves is up to," Vince said. "You see, I couldn't tell him it was money I owed, that I owed it to a loan shark. He thinks too highly of me for me to tell him that. He seemed convinced it was a bribe, that I was trying to bribe a U.S. senator..."

"You're afraid of what?" Celia asked. "You think Groves went to the authorities?"

"That's what's driving me crazy."

They had an early dinner in the bar, veal cutlets with string potatoes, some red wine. They watched the passersby along M Street, tourists with shopping bags and paper cups of ice cream. Talked little, only to comment on the Bordeaux, its first sip peppery on the palate. Vince had his cellphone out on the table but it didn't ring, not once. He tried Groves a couple more times, to no effect.

While they sat in Nathan's, by and by, clouds came in and the sky grew dark, shutting like a lid over the city. Vince stretched his hand out as they came out onto the street. Thick drops filled the air. Then on the coattails of a rushing wind, a heavy downpour lashed the ville. It turned the buildings gray. It made the cars that slewed by bubble colorfully. The two attorneys ran close to the walls, at the edge of the downpour. They ran up M Street, ran and ran, a man and a woman running together in the rain.

They ran until they got to the garage where Celia had parked her car. Her solution was to take Vince home with her. He would hide out there, in her house, out of Wilbur's reach. For that was Vince's most rational fear, thinking it over, that Wilbur would come after him, harm him in some way. He worried too, that the whole mess would impact on the groundbreaking, and Celia agreed, they both agreed that whatever else, nothing should be allowed to screw up the groundbreaking.

Celia told him she would make a few telephone calls and everything would be taken care of. That was all Vince wanted to hear. He was afraid of consequences, but he didn't seem to give a hoot about all that money disappearing, part of it what Celia assumed he'd won gambling in Las Vegas. She could see he was tired of the whole business, and she drew her own conclusions from that. She knew all he wanted was some peace and quiet.

Another $800,000 or even $1,000,000 was not the core of what Raymond Wilbur lived for. Wilbur lived to make Hidell Kennedy and Stone a power all its own, something Celia Progg knew well. From that perspective the debt was an exiguous loss. Wilbur didn't want Jorrigo to pay him back; he was glad to have a perfect excuse to go into action. He owed a debt of thanks to Progg, who was heads-up in calling him that very evening, collaborating with him to everyone's benefit.

Indeed without wasting time, informed he had a clear field, Wilbur that next morning, Wednesday, went on to make Cornelius Klocker an offer. If Klocker left Guiteau and Garfield within the next twenty-four hours, he would be the new executive managing partner of Mergers and Acquisitions at HKS's London office. The offer included a house in the London suburb of Cobham, an office with a sweeping view of St. James Park, and one year's free laundry service.

Corny Klocker didn't hesitate. London was at the heart of the global "M and A" industry. Deborah Takahashi and the other principal "M and A" attorneys went over to Hidell Kennedy and Stone, too. It happened so quickly that only Patty Johnson was left to keep the lights on, on the sixth floor.

Wilbur had been trying for months to lure Corny Klocker away, but he was loathe to make any predatory attempt with Jorrigo hanging around; he respected too much Jorrigo's capacity to defend himself and his firm no matter what the loan arrangements had been. Now with Guiteau and Garfield's senior managing partner hiding out at Celia's house in Great Falls, Virginia, the New York attorney was able to start his takeover of the entire firm, its clients, its assets. That was Ray Wilbur's refined strategy. Hiring away the firm's best people, Wilbur then prepared to put his own people in place at Guiteau and Garfield, doing it to show other Washington lawyers he was not there combing doll's hair, but was dead serious about coming to town.

It was important, however, as Celia pointed out to Wilbur when they talked on the telephone, that the groundbreaking at the Mall not be put to risk. Too much was at stake for everyone. The president of the United States himself had put considerable pressure on the Department of the Interior and on Antonia Segreen of the Bureau of Land Management to hold the groundbreaking as scheduled, no matter what the weather, which was threatening wet and stormy.

But the "Prez" had no need to worry. Overnight Wednesday it would rain a little more, then by Thursday morning hardy northern breezes would come in and sweep the storm clouds out over the Atlantic. By Friday, Washington would once again glow majestic and true along the contours of its parkland, that was Bob Ryan's forecast. The Mall would be ready, watched over by the august figures of Jefferson, of Lincoln, surrounded by beech and oak and noble pine, ready and waiting to be plowed under in the name of sound waste management.

Dinah was going to be there on the arm of her prospective husband, Congressman Bill Coote. His divorce was in the works, and he was preparing to present himself in the media as a chivalrous type of modern politician, ready to do right by his lover as well as by his wife. But Dinah Solatoff had no intention of marrying Bill Coote. She had everything ready. She was going to go with him to the Mall but then slip away, slip into a cab, and then take a plane home to Idaho.

At the house on S Street, Dinah had one bag packed, another ready to fill with dresses and shoes, lying on the floor. She had purchased her ticket too, an American Airlines flight for early Sunday morning. With all the connections, it would get her to Boise by the afternoon. She'd be back where she'd started from, but what a relief to get away from Washington.

She planned to hang in town, in Boise looking for a job. She had some high school friends there she could contact. That was the neat thing about being young; there was always a start-over around the corner. Dinah was actually excited to be going back. Her first act would be to put on her running shoes and go for a jog along the river, breath real mountain air again. That was her plan, not shared with anyone, not even with Barbara. She wasn't going to say good-byes.

It was up in the air whether Celia Progg and Vincent Jorrigo would be at the Ellipse, for Vince had an image of Wilbur, eyes glowing like fox fire, coming after him. Celia encouraged that fear. She would be well remunerated for keeping Guiteau and Garfield's senior partner under wraps, and that was exactly what she did, keeping him happy and paranoid at her place. Vince was in fact far happier than he'd been in a long time, and Celia took all the credit.

Vince found he didn't miss the office. He didn't miss work, and he put aside poker, resisting the call of the cards. He felt he could stop struggling. It was a realization he had, sitting around with time to waste thinking, trust, his lack of trust in anything but chance, signified a distrust of himself. He'd been struggling against himself. He didn't need to win, and he didn't need to lose either. Celia gave him all he needed to feel good about himself, which was simply human warmth. The struggle was all an illusion. Winning, he realized, was important only to losers.

While Celia went to her desk at Melody Hogan, Vince spent most of his day lying around in his PJs reading the newspapers. He spent evenings lying around reading trashy novels, and Celia, in her silk teddy or in nothing at all, came to him and they had a little middle-aged sex, that kind of human warmth. He didn't have to lift a finger. Celia did everything for him, took care of him, made him feel more than a winner, special, made him feel he was someone very special. Special for who he was and not for what he did, he liked that. Too, he liked not knowing anything about what was going down at the firm or what was happening in Washington, and Celia was rigorous in keeping him uninformed.

Thomas Morrow, the Secretary of the Interior, would definitely be there at the groundbreaking. Hell, he was the groundbreaking, and he couldn't wait to get his hands on the golden digging tool and get his face in the news. If the rumors were true, Morrow was planning to leave the administration at the end of the year to become an executive vice president at Archer Daniels Midland. The groundbreaking would be his last chance to be in the public eye.

It was also rumored, and to be believed that the president, basically a man known for his unwillingness to put himself too much in the picture, would be watching from the south porch of the White House through a pair of Secret Service–issued binoculars. He too wanted to bear witness to that moment in history when in terms of the war on trash at least, he could say without fear of ridicule as his predecessor had said, "mission accomplished."

And indeed the sanitary landfill was being hailed as a new standard both for its display of great aesthetic sensibility towards its urban surroundings, the national monuments and such, and its exceptional viability in putting good earth to good use, as a servile and flattering article in *Time* magazine put it.

The bulldozers were poised, the hard hats ready. A preliminary hole had been dug and then filled back in to make the task of digging easier for Secretary Tom Morrow and the other dignitaries who had lined up to wield the golden shovel. The first ton of waste from a nearby federal office building sat in a big gold-painted truck, ready to be ceremonially dumped. Already down on the Mall, there was the pungent smell of garbage in.

The one person who as much as any other and certainly more than most could claim real credit for getting the thing done, Sterrett Emerson Groves, that one person planned absolutely not to be there. The groundbreaking, Sterrett had no intention of doing that. He had enough money in his possession to look himself in the mirror, to speak truth to himself and admit he felt ashamed of the work he'd done getting that landfill approved and signed, the Mall about to be dug up.

That, he assumed, was certainly not one of the announced purposes work served, to make a man feel shame, unless the work was poorly done. But where work was brought to a successful completion, completed as planned, that was often reason enough for doing the work, to complete it, so that the actual result of the work done, the end product was beyond ethical examination.

That was one of the advantages of having money without having to work for it, that a man could look to the end result, free of any corrupting means, free of employers and free of managers, free of proprietors, free of leaders and generals and their plans. The other great advantage, and Sterrett thought long and hard over this, more than an advantage, a privilege, was that lots of free money meant the end of having to work for a living. It meant time unrestricted by office hours, and time meant life.

Coming home to Newark Street, riding his bike up from the Guiteau Building, Sterrett collapsed on the sofa in the living room, sweaty, even a little stinky, wiped out from the accumulated tension of that busy Tuesday morning. He wasn't comfortable there in the living room. The couch there was an expensive couch and the chairs were covered in satin and not much use for sitting in. He took Jorrigo's battered brown briefcase with him into the den. That was a better place to thrash about with worry and sweat for thrill.

The den had originally been a larder and it was just off the dining room, near the kitchen. It was a comfortable room with a high ceiling, cool in summer, and next to the pool it was the thing Sterrett liked best about Anne Marie and her house. It had a big oriental rug on the floor, and a metal tea wagon with a glass shelf, stocked with liquor bottles. There was a television, a CD player, a glass side table with photographs of Anne Marie's astonishingly rich family, and over by the sofa, a reading lamp shaped like a drooping, long-stemmed flower. The room was mostly books, lined top to bottom with books, all the books Anne Marie had ever read in her life, and she'd read almost all of them through and through.

The books gave way to a window that looked out upon the window of the house next door. The curtains in the window of the house next door were of a heavy material, dark green. Sterrett could see angles of furniture and sometimes a cat came and sat in the window, a fluffy Persian. He never saw any people during the day. That was the way the upper middle-class lived. They were never seen, but you knew they were there.

He pulled up an armchair for the briefcase, a comfy chair in which it could nestle its battered bottom quietly and among flower-patterned cushions. The briefcase sat opened, sometimes closed, never all the way closed; there was always a glimpse possible, a salacious peek from where he sat, of the money's green bosom. Sterrett himself lounged on the small cloth couch, a do-it-yourself Ikea product facing the armchair in which the briefcase sat. He spent the rest of the day almost entirely in the den with the briefcase, overcome from time to time by an urge to hug the briefcase.

He slept a little, woke up, tried to get up, and felt too lazy to bother. He stared at the briefcase, pondered what it meant, the bribe, its implications. Vince Jorrigo had probably been doing business that way for some time, greasing palms to win suits. Sterrett began imaging the whole firm did business that way, all of the city. That was it, Washington the kickback kingdom, from private contractors to public servants.

He had a moment when he was tempted to go on Facebook with a photo of the briefcase and its contents, "look what I stole." But he reasoned Facebook was for people who took no real pride in who they were. He was full of pride, having done something he guessed few others had had the courage to do. He'd acted instinctively to prevent "favorable opportunity money" from circulating. And the most efficient way he had found to do that was to keep it for himself, "the buck stops here" with a twist. When he got tired of feeling cynical, he tried watching television.

Around five o'clock in the evening, it got inauspiciously dark. Sterrett turned off the television. He pushed up from the couch and looked out the window. Thick drops stained the sky. Then it began raining in all seriousness. Sterrett went over to the tea cart and poured himself some rum. He went to the kitchen with a sterling silver ice bucket and came back with the bucket full. He dropped a couple cubes into his glass. He stood, face turned to the window. The rain wasn't a softly falling rain. It wasn't a sloppy, country downpour. It was a piercing, lashing tropical rain that seemed to sweep upwards from the ground, confusing the starlings nestled under the eaves of the house next door.

He poured himself another rum, since that was the only real liquor left, the other bottles full of things like peach brandy and B&B, undrinkable potions Anne Marie liked to have for guests. He sat down on the sofa, got up again, and drifted over to the window. He was feeling idle, as though waiting before some trial he had to undergo.

The oppressive sense of his own solitude made him want to break something. He was tired of inanimate objects. He rattled the tea tray, tossed a cushion around, then he sat back down on the sofa. "Calm down," he said. "Relax."

It was a new situation for him, and he believed the only way to deal with it was to be pragmatic, see what worked. If they pursued him, then he was in the wrong, and he would give up the money. If no one came after him in the next few days, then Sterrett would be smart about it. But he was pretty sure that no one was going to come after him. He knew too much, and they'd not do a thing to him, who knew so much about how they did business. Maybe they'd even welcome him to the next higher-up circle of flimflam.

He'd earned the money with his own head, with his own feet, work no one could reprove him for. He supposed he would feel some guilt, some sense of having acted against the rules, but no man was free of those feelings. No matter how virtuous he behaved, the know-ing, insightful man knew there was always something he would live to regret. It was unavoidable. Feeling regret, feeling guilt those were ways of keeping nearer to one's self.

Anne Marie came home from Melody Hogan as she usually did, around eight o'clock in the evening. She looked for him and was surprised to find Sterrett sitting in the den.

"What are you doing here in the dark like some kind of thief?" she asked. "You just get home or what?"

She saw he had his suit on, but no tie and he was in his stocking feet. She looked for his shoes. They were lying over by the tea wagon. Anne Marie went and picked them up and put them side by side on the floor next to the sofa. She knelt down close to Sterrett. He had a worn-out look, like some switch within him had been left on too long. He had a glass in his hand with a thimbleful of amber liquid in it and some ice and she was worried, sure he was drunk. He hadn't got-ten drunk since they'd been going together, and she took his getting drunk as a sign she'd let him down somehow. She wanted to talk to him about it.

"It's raining," Sterrett said distractedly.

"No, it stopped now." Anne Marie tried to kiss him, but he jerked away from her. "What's wrong?" she asked. "Are you angry at me for something?"

"I'm nothing," he answered. The whole effort, the morning spent running from Shackley, the afternoon spent trying to make up his mind, all of it, had emptied him of every bit of interest in the people around him. But he still had enough sense to put a smile on his feeling empty, so as to avoid any protracted discussion about it, which in the end would make him feel emptier than before. "I'm tired is all."

"If I did do something to hurt your feelings, it was because I was in such a rush this morning."

She was so caring, so gratuitously contrite that he decided why not, and he was going to tell her about the briefcase, about his adventure, his run-in with Louis Shackley. He sat up and looked her in the eyes. "So why did you say before, I was like a thief?"

"Because you're here with the lights off, silly. Like you're hiding. Are you sure…You are a little drunk, aren't you?"

Sterrett sighed, "Oh, perhaps I am."

Once again he thought, tell her what happened to you today, but he squashed that impulse. He went on to say, "It's all this to-do, you know, and these very important people, I mean very important, well, they're arguing over who gets to have the golden spade first."

"It's really a digging trowel, honey." Anne Marie stood up.

"If there were two or three spades we'd be okay, but there's only one. That's it."

Anne Marie knew all about the digging controversy. Though it had been agreed Secretary Tom Morrow would break ground first, it still had to be settled whether next in line was Antonia Segreen or Kid Psora or even Ellen Berman, the banker. It was a question of protocol, that was the way it was in Washington, everyone demanding their due attention.

"Did you buy anything to eat? Did you stop at the Safeway?"

"I'm not going to answer any questions until I see my lawyer," Sterrett said, their usual joke.

"Well, I for one am hungry," Anne Marie responded. She went into the kitchen and made herself a salad with lettuce and tomatoes, a hardboiled egg, mayonnaise, and some crab meat and had a glass of white wine to wash it down with. She ate in silence, reading the newspaper, mostly the Style section, trying to catch up on movies and the theatre. As a special treat, for dessert she had a bowl of the ice cream from the freezer, vanilla, with a little honey drizzled over top. All the while she simply ignored Sterrett. It was what she did, thinking that by ignoring him, she was punishing him in the most effective way possible.

She dropped the dishes into the dishwasher. There were only a few dishes in the dishwasher, but she turned it on anyway, knowing that the noise the dishwasher made was one of the few things that really, really annoyed Sterrett. Then she went and peeked into the den.

He was sound asleep on the sofa, still dressed as though for the office. The glass of rum rested precariously on his tummy, one of the good glasses of cut-crystal Anne Marie's father had given her. Anne Marie took the glass out of his hand. Gently, she set it down on the tea wagon. She scanned the room. The reading lamp was on, the television off. Then she noticed the battered brown briefcase in the armchair, a briefcase she knew was not Sterrett's own. She stood over it, heart beating a little faster. She pursed her lips, full of a moment's suspicion, but concluded it was not the kind of briefcase a woman would carry.

She bent down to caress the case, gliding her hand over its roughened leather. It was a crack open. Anne Marie didn't make a move to open it all the way. Sterrett was totally exhausted and didn't stir from the sofa, sound asleep. The woman had a deft enough touch that she could have opened it all the way without waking him. It was rather that she felt it against her principles as a lawyer to pry into the papers of a lawyer from a rival firm even if the lawyer in question was her fiancé and had been acting suspiciously strange to boot.

She went over to Sterrett. Looking down at him she smiled, full of pride, knowing how much of himself he had put into making the trash dump at the Mall a reality. She knew too, how stressful it was to come to the end of a project, more stressful at the end perhaps than to be in the thick of it, working to achieve a concrete goal. She understood the drop in adrenalin, for a man, could be depressing. She forgave Sterrett his bearishness, his sleeping in his suit clothes there in the den. She gave him a goodnight kiss, her full lips smack on the air inches above his head. She turned off the light, and then went upstairs to bed.

The next day, Wednesday, Anne Marie had a meeting to attend in Baltimore and she left the house early. Sterrett stayed home. He got changed out of his suit and tie, got changed into the kind of clothes only the very rich were permitted to wear during the day, a pair of boxer shorts and an old T-shirt. He had never not gone into the office. He had never since his first day at Guiteau and Garfield skipped getting late to the office, not even for the sake of the Chinese influenza.

Even though he hated to do that kind of thing over the phone, he went into the living room and picked up the receiver, dialed his secretary Suzy. He informed her he wouldn't be coming, not coming in at all. Didn't want to discuss it. Was he sick, she wanted to know. A fever perhaps, Sterrett said. Suzy told him in a tone that was obviously sarcastic to take as many days as he needed to get better, that there wasn't anything much on his desk, only the groundbreaking, that was all.

"Mr. Psora has called twice, and that's just this morning."

"Sir Simon or the Kid?"

"The son," Suzy said.

"He's a jerk-off. Anyone call from Hidell Kennedy and Stone, some guy named Shackley call?"

"No Shackley," Suzy said. "But Mr. Jorrigo, he was looking for you yesterday afternoon."

"Don't care about that. You take a message," Sterrett told his secretary. "You tell people I'm too busy to deal with them."

"Someone's got to deal with them. Who for instance has the permits for the caterer's tents?" Suzy asked. "We need the permits."

"It's all on my desk," Sterrett said. "You deal with it."

He was excited about getting away with it, how easy it was. He blushed every time he thought about the money, snatching it away from Shackley, and having it, and no repercussions what so ever. Getting away with things wasn't something he was used to. He had always believed that every unethical or illegal act would be followed by an immediate and severe judgment. But this belief had been undergoing a persuasive erosion. He realized it now. It was even in the papers, the example of men and women of influence, bankers, brokers, college football players.

There had been no bolt from heaven for the lies he'd told the citizenry on behalf of the sanitary landfill, and no thunderbolt now that he'd absconded with the briefcase. Nothing prevented him from taking a plane to a faraway land if that was what he chose to do. He was ready to leave at the drop of a hat. He had no ties to anyone and he had no ties to anything other than to Washington, and being a born Washingtonian he knew that wherever he went he would take the city with him.

He had enough money to go where he wanted. Sure, if he were smarter, a better, smarter lawyer, he'd be content to work. Working hard, he'd become in his later years, a highly respected attorney, an influential member of the professional class that intimately served the ruling Caste, instead of being simply the way he was, which was to say merely human.

Everyone knew what human was. It meant of the flesh, weak, and vulnerable, and of a beating heart. Human was a lump of two-legged life of whatever color and whatever face. There was no dearth of examples of the human; if one went looking around, curiously poking one's nose out the window or simply turning to face a mirror, there was the human. It was the money that made the difference. In that sense he felt he deserved the cash. It was proof of his dominance over other human beings, his mind working so much more gainfully. That was the whole point of being a part of society, that one could feel dominant. It was the whole point of being a lawyer.

Thinking about these things, sitting in his boxer shorts in the den in the house on Newark Street was more important to him than anything else. He didn't want to go into work, and he didn't want to be among other people. The risk that he would sing out for joy was too great. Sterrett didn't need the company of others. He wanted to come to terms with himself by himself. The only person he wanted to talk to, he didn't want to talk to. He didn't want to talk to Dinah until he'd decided what he wanted to do with the rest of his life.

During the day, he roamed round the house on Newark Street. When he wasn't sitting in the den reading the *Post*, or thinking, he went from room to room. He noticed how tidy and very precise Anne Marie was. Even the rooms that weren't regularly used, the guest room to the front of the second floor, the bedroom in the basement, these were spotless rooms, models of home economy. Sterrett was amazed. Anne Marie didn't use a maid; she did it all herself. Her house was clean and in apple-pie order.

Those adjectives could apply to Anne Marie herself. She was above all warm-hearted for how intelligent and orderly she was. She didn't just love him in the careless way of most modern women, she cared for him and was minutely attentive, perhaps too much so. But it wasn't what he wanted. He didn't want to be cared for. Sterrett liked to be left alone. That was what he was used to and that was the problem, that he couldn't reciprocate and bring himself to care for Anne Marie. He lacked the energy, lacked the desire to see her happy. At times he resented her for trying so hard to make sure he was happy. Relax, he wanted to tell her to relax. But he kept quiet mostly.

Going from room to room, nosing into corners and closets, Sterrett took the briefcase with him, fascinated with the power the mothering cash generated, a physical warmth that came off the greenbacks. From time to time he opened the briefcase and caressed the packets of hundred dollar bills, high as a kite without drinking a drop, breathing in the down-to-earth smell of the money, savoring the solid loveliness of federal reserve notes all in a row. He took the briefcase into the bathroom with him. He wrapped it in a towel, careful not to let it get wet while he was taking a shower. Took it with him into the kitchen for lunch.

For lunch he made himself a sandwich, forging together ham and cheese, tomato and two slices of rye bread. The sandwich sat on a small china plate. Sterrett admired it, the balance of colors, pink showing against the ruffled perspective of green lettuce, dun yellow mustard contrasting with the bright yellow cheese, a blessing of the eponymous Earl of.

He took the sandwich and the briefcase with him into the living room, with a fresh bottle of beer. He sat down on the big sofa, doubling up the cushions, his feet up on the low Cherrywood coffee table. He rested the plate on his stomach, and he turned on the television. He went churning through the channels. He stopped at a Mexican soap opera, *Tres Mujeres*, playing on one of the Spanish-language channels. Mexico, that was the ticket. He could catch a plane. His revenge for all the time he'd wasted working would be that he would be his own man, doing what he wanted, having fun. He could go to Cancun where there were plenty of soused college girls he didn't have to get to know in a more than bodily way, and where he could put his professional life well behind him. Find his center outside of Washington.

The phone rang. He worried it might be Suzy looking for him with some problem concerning the groundbreaking, but it was Anne Marie on the line.

"I called and your secretary said you weren't in the office."

"I stayed home, Anne Marie. What is it?" He made the effort to keep his voice considerate. "Everything okay?"

"I'm fine, Sterrett. What about you, are you all right? What are you doing? Are you still in bed?"

He told her he was fine, but that he thought he deserved a day off, and what he did with his time was anyway, his business. He was eating lunch.

"Tonight there's a party, Kiki's giving a party and she invited us, she's dying to see you again. She's just down the block. We can go for a little while."

"Right. Well, no, I prefer staying home."

"I want to show off my fiancé," Anne Marie said firmly. "I tell people I have a fiancé, but no one believes me."

"I don't feel like it, that's all," Sterrett said. He looked at the battered brown briefcase. All that money, it gave him the power, the justification to be as rude as he wanted. "You go. They're your friends."

"I'm concerned for you, you know, that you work too much. You're becoming a hermit. You should be a part of the neighborhood. I want us to be a part of the neighborhood."

"No, I told you. No means no."

He hung up. He left his hand resting on the receiver. Deep in her heart, Anne Marie considered him a failure, pitied him. She was showing him the kind of loving sympathy one showed a man who failed to live well among his contemporaries. Sterrett smiled. That was the past. He had his briefcase with him and he was a changed man, and Anne Marie didn't know it yet.

Perhaps he could tell her after all. Bring Anne Marie in on the briefcase. Show her the money and see how she would react. At first she would resist. But all that money had its charm, and he would talk to her about it. They could go off on an extended vacation. Anne Marie loved travel, and they could go to Tahiti and they could go to South Africa. They were a couple and they could go wherever they wanted.

That night he slept in the den again. They argued about it. Anne Marie thought he was acting way too strange. She got close to hysterical, thinking she'd done something or that something was wrong with her, her fault if he was acting that way. She always blamed herself. Sterrett reassured her. He had this groundbreaking to worry about, a lot of pressure. Pressure was something Anne Marie could ken, but she found Sterrett strange in that he seemed positively frisky, not gloomy or uptight at all, and when he tried to have sex with her there on the small couch in the den, she pushed him back.

"I think you better see a doctor," she said getting to her feet, adjusting her bra, brushing a few filaments of her hair from her face. "I really do. Really."

"Because I want to have sex with you?" Sterrett asked.

"Because you're strange. You're not under who knows what kind of pressure, for heaven's sake, Sterrett." She pointed to the battered brown briefcase. "Who's is that? It's not yours."

He thought, yes, I'll tell her. He thought if he told her she'd be as excited as he was. But no, he knew Anne Marie, and she would be shocked. She was always shocked by the things he did when he acted in good faith with who he was.

"Who's briefcase is that, Sterrett?" she shouted. "Why is it always underfoot? That's all I'm saying."

"Important documents," he answered.

The next day was Thursday, the day before the groundbreaking ceremony. Sterrett pretended for Anne Marie's sake to go into work, but he merely took his bike round the block. He took his battered brown briefcase with him, strapped it to the light metal rack at the back of his Wind Wrangler. He cycled up Reno Road as far as Albemarle Street and then doubled back. He lingered at the top of Reno Road until he was sure Anne Marie's SUV was gone from the driveway.

It was at that point that Sterrett began to have some qualms over his own mental health. He realized he had become consumed with, and had become possessed by the briefcase. He wanted to prove to himself that he had control, control of himself and of his money, too. Because he had decided it was his money. So he wanted to try an experiment.

He closed the briefcase and set it down in the chair in the den. He covered the briefcase with some cushions. It wasn't quite hidden, but it wasn't immediately visible either. Then he left the house. He locked the door and went for a walk, his first walk alone since Tuesday, alone in the sense he didn't have the briefcase with him. He got as far as 36th Street, three blocks, before he had to hurry back, panicky with sweat, afraid someone had broken into the house and stolen the briefcase. He didn't try the experiment again. It was too nerve-wracking.

The remainder of the day, he was to be found in the den, always there in the den. He would go to the bathroom, and he would go into the kitchen for something to drink, for a snack, but he always returned to the den, always the den. He knew he had to come to some decision. The $800,000 was his money, yes, but he wanted to put it to its proper use before it was too late. Its proper use meant first of all putting it in a bank, getting it safely put away. But then what, he asked himself, what was to be done with his life.

He threw himself down on the sofa, arms and legs like he was impaled upon those soft, flowery cushions. He let his head flop back. He sighed, staring at the ceiling for a long time. Having fun was not enough of a purpose for all that money. All that money had to serve a greater purpose than simply not having to go into work anymore.

Work, he hated work. It meant nothing to him, so that having money or not having money made no difference other than in a practical way, eliminating work once and for all from his daily routine. Now he was asking himself what it was he really wanted out of life, and he realized it was love. He'd had to knock his head against it to learn it. It was a lesson that really amounted to an ecstatic revelation.

Love gave all that money he had resting on that chair a sense. Money was no good without a purpose. Being rich was no good; stealing was no good. Love had the power to justify what he'd done.

Work made people equal, and work kept Man with his worst impulses channeled, his biggest reward the fatty pleasures of conformity. Love was something else again. Love was not equal for everyone. Love was the enemy of the Law, the enemy of society, too intimate, too individual and selfish a thing. Justice was blind, but love had eyes to see and make its choice. Sterrett's dream was to do what he wanted, without any other consequence than his lover's happiness. To do that, and to see what happened doing that, that was Sterrett's purpose, to make Dinah happy.

"Well, that's the argument then," he said to himself.

He went looking for his cellphone. He had Dinah's number on his phone; he hadn't written it down. He dug around in the sofa, hand running between the cushions, but no luck. He found a quarter there among the usual crumbs, but no phone. He went through the house, living room, dining room, kitchen, bathroom, and bedroom, nothing, no soap. He tried calling himself, dialing up on the line phone, but his cell was turned off.

"Natch," he said, standing in the hallway, feeling angry at himself for being the way he was with telecommunications. Then he snapped his fingers and went hurrying up the stairs to the bedroom. The phone was in the jacket pocket of the suit he wore on Tuesday, the suit he'd slept in. He opened his closet and looked for it, pushing hangers back, but the suit, a gray pinstripe wasn't there. He shook his head and he let out a curse. Anne Marie was nothing if not fussy and exact. He was sure she'd put his suit in the hamper with the other clothing bound for the dry cleaners.

That hamper was in the extra bedroom. Sterrett went into the bedroom and burrowed through the hamper, tossing shirts and wool skirts to the floor until he found his jacket. The cellphone was where he'd left it, in the right hand pocket. He punched in the code, and the phone lit up, "let's go" it seemed to say. He tried calling her, Dinah Solatoff, on her cellphone, but like his, hers was always switched off. He tried her at Mergers and Acquisitions, but nobody answered the phone at Mergers and Acquisitions, everybody elsewhere.

He wanted to tell her. He had enough money in his grip to persuade her to love him, that was what he wanted more than anything in the entire world, to love her. That was why he'd taken a run with the money, not out of greed, out of love. Dinah was the one he hoped to see at the end of the day.

He decided to send her a text. He wrote, "You are the one I hope to see,

when the bartender throws me out, and the sidewalk lifts me up."

He hoped she understood what that message meant. That she would appreciate his desperate sense of humor. He hoped she'd read it.

Shortly after, his cellphone made a telltale noise, a text message received, and he assumed it was Dinah answering his text. But it was Anne Marie sending him a meaningful dispatch of her own. She was thinking of him at work, there during an important meeting with an important client, the Air Line Pilots Association. The message he got was brimming with exclamation points, "why don't you ever call me?!!" and a sorrowful emoticon.

That evening, Anne Marie came home early. She was more than just worried, she was frightened. She kept repeating it, she was frightened for him. She reminded Sterrett that she herself had been close to a breakdown, so she felt she knew what a breakdown looked like. She told Sterrett he was having one.

The temptation was too great. Sterrett was in too rough a mood. "One what?" he asked.

"Oh, stop that," she shrilled.

She marched back into the living room. He could hear her go through her routine, kicking off her shoes, going to the kitchen, opening the refrigerator for a soda. She came back into the living room and turned on the television to watch the well-known network news anchor doing his thing.

There was a lot going on, and she had the television going full blast. It had been a typical day, earthquakes in South America, volcanos in Asia, the president of the United States laughing off the mudslingers, and always, the alluring perfume of war. The weather, unsurprisingly humid for summer. Then there was the piece of news everyone knew about, the landfill in Washington, the scheduled groundbreaking ceremony, now of national importance. Anne Marie made a point of clicking to another station.

Sterrett knew she was waiting for him to apologize. That was her methodology, get him so pissed off that he went and said he was sorry for whatever it was he'd been doing that had made her want to badger him to an apology in the first place. He got up and appeared in the living room. He said, "You know how I feel about you. I don't mean to be the way I am. I'm sorry but I've been having a hard week. Remember how much has been going on at the firm? It's that I've been working hard, real hard."

It was a brief pleading made with Anne Marie not looking at him, pretending to be concentrated on the images gadding across the flat screen TV. It was a speech made with Sterrett's face gone as red as tomato juice. It was a hypocritical speech, an unbelievably duplicitous speech that like all hypocritical speeches delivered with apparent sincerity, worked.

They made love on the sofa. No volcano erupting, no earthquake, but it was sex of the very satisfying sort, that sort of useful lovemaking, a relaxation of the flesh, a turning off of the mind. He went and slept with her in the queen-sized bed on the second floor. He kept his eyes open through most of the night, and his ears alert, too, listening on the chance someone might break into the house and take the briefcase away.

Sterrett got up early, with the first sun. He padded around on very light feet, getting washed and shaved in the bathroom, getting dressed there, too. He put on his best dark gray suit, knotted the new power tie Anne Marie had given him, red Malaysian silk with tiny gold stars. As a last touch, he bathed his cheeks in Musk Ah! cologne. Then he went downstairs to nap for an hour on the big sofa in the living room, dressed and with the battered brown briefcase in his arms. He had his shoes off, that was all. When he woke, a couple hours later, he woke with a start.

Anne Marie was still upstairs. He could hear her moving around in the bathroom. He called up to her, "Good morning." She called down to him to make the coffee. She was happy because she was sure whatever had been bothering him had faded with the night. The proof was that she got a whiff of his aftershave in the bathroom and along the hallway, and she took that as a positive sign. He was going into work. The fact that he was going into work was a thankful sign that whatever it was that had been preying on his mind was not anymore.

"You have that groundbreaking today, right? Are you getting ready for that?" she asked from the top of the stairs. "You going to wear that tie I bought you?"

"Yes," Sterrett answered.

"Wish I could be there, so wonderful for you, sweetie. But I am so sorry. I told you, didn't I? I have this very important meeting this morning."

"That's all right," he shouted back.

"We'll celebrate our own selves after. We can order some food from Furin's and I'll invite… "

Sterrett didn't stick around to hear whom it was Anne Marie wanted to invite. He left the kitchen, exited the house. He didn't leave a personal note of explanation. He didn't have anything personal to tell the girl that she would understand. He went out on the porch of the house on Newark Street. Not that he knew exactly what he was going to do, but he decided to go like Twister move by move and see where he landed.

Sterrett started off without his bicycle, hitting the pavement swinging his briefcase without even realizing where he was headed. He did a turnaround and tramped right back up the steps to the porch, laughing at his foolish self all the way.

He set the briefcase down and mickied with the bike's lock, releasing the back wheel from the porch's wooden railing. Then he picked up the briefcase, strapped it to the rack over the back wheel, strapped it in secure. He clipped his trouser leg tight and carried the bicycle in his arms to the street.

CHAPTER SIXTEEN

*F*riday at last and the summer sky was a blue mum never going to fade. Washington was about to have one of those days that made the city seem truly capital, with no rival east to west, not spoor-ridden New York, not hayseed Los Angeles either.

Sterrett made the office in twelve minutes, gunning the road with the asphalt beneath him and the air hollow in his ears. The ride's unflagging excitement scattered to the winds the young attorney's nervous mood. He felt light winged as he swung round a slow-moving taxicab and blew through the crosswalk. Flabbergasted pedestrians, in harm's way, scrambled for the curb.

It was love that did it, the shape of his beloved's mouth, her earnest eyes, the haughty bounce of her hips. Sterrett didn't have any trouble thinking the thing through. Love had given him unusual perspicacity in making plans. Nothing stronger than love's power. He was going to use the techniques learned from Sir Simon Psora, too. Make his escape so complicated no one would have the will to follow him.

He had a valentine's full in the battered brown briefcase strapped to his bicycle. He was sure she would not say no to all that cash. He was sure she could not say no to him now. She was his one big emotion. The way he felt towards Dinah. They could run off together to some place out of the way. And if he got hurt, what he learned getting hurt would be easier to remember for the next time.

He parked his bicycle in front of the Guiteau Building. He draped the chain around a stop sign but didn't bother locking it. He took the briefcase in hand. The lobby was dead air and the elevator was empty. It was early Friday morning, but not so early that there should have been the kind of desert there was. On the fourth floor, it was like the hour before the cleaning crew arrived, the cubicles frozen in leaving time, coffee gone hard in a "Calvin and Hobbes" mug.

He came up the hallway, his feet clomp-clomping as noisily as possible down the carpet. He peered into one empty office after another. Craned round to look into one empty cubicle after another. Balloons from some secretary's party were still Scotch-taped to a partition. The balloons tilted low on their string, their thickening skin growing less and less festive. His own secretary was not at her desk. He tried a tentative, "Suzy?"

Then he crossed over to his office. He set the battered brown briefcase flat on his desk. But he was too agitated to sit down, and he went out to the men's room to piss away the feeling that now overcame him. It was a mistake coming in to the office, why had he done it, to say good-bye that's why. But there was no one there to say boo to.

The walls of the restroom resonated with the hum of fluorescents, and the flowing ceramic made him feel calm again. He had prepared himself for questions, and the fact that there was no one on the fourth floor, not one person, not even his lousy secretary to ask him where he'd been all week, was an absolute and total bummer.

But he kept to the decision he'd come to that morning. He went back to his office. He sat down at his desk. He pulled the briefcase to him and then placed it on the floor between his feet. He sat at his desk for several minutes. He opened the top drawer. There was his daily agenda for that year, a small, leather-bound book. He took the agenda out and leafed through it, staring at the forward planner section. There he had written out the personal goals for that year. Volunteer to feed the homeless, either during Easter or Christmas. Get his weight down to 185 pounds. Learn Chinese. Visit his mother in Florida. Find a girl, settle down. He tossed the agenda back into the drawer, too strange, looking back at that former untried self.

He turned his computer on, let it rev up. He pulled the keyboard close and began typing. He found himself being more methodical than usual, doing everything as though immersed in a hyper form of self-consciousness. He was to the point for once, three paragraphs. He printed out a draft copy. He read it over. He wanted to be sure there was no hint of bitterness or regret. He hoped the work he'd done at the firm was good work. A lawyer was not always able to judge the value of the work he did, its final worth to others.

He crumpled up the draft copy and chucked it into the wastebasket. He had to go through several more drafts until he got the result he wanted. He printed out a clean copy on good stationery, Sterrett Emerson Groves, Esquire, making the most of his letterhead.

He re-read the letter, staring at each word, feeling his eyeball feel its way across the heavy bond paper. It was because everything had to register clearly in his mind so he'd remember it long after. So that when he was on the beach in Mexico browning in the sun, feeling nostalgia for his hometown, he could explain to himself why he was there in Cancun.

He took a ballpoint pen from his Orioles mug. The letter had the right tone. He read it through again and again and was satisfied Mr. Jorrigo would understand. He signed the letter "Sterrett Groves," not his life he was signing away, merely his career. He was young enough that he could recover. He trusted in his education, in his strengths. He trusted in his talent with words.

Sterrett folded the letter in two, smoothed it flat, and stuffed it into a legal-sized envelope. He used the pen to address the envelope and then licked the gluey flap, sealing it. That was all the work he had to do for the day. He was done with his computer and he was done with his office. Leaving the battered briefcase for the moment where it was, he went out to his secretary's cubicle, taking the letter of resignation with him. It was well past nine o'clock. He tried calling out. He went up and down the hallway, yelling, "Suzy? Suzy?" But there was no one. He'd have to take his letter up to the receptionist himself, one more thing to do. He rode the elevator to the seventh floor, to the firm's client reception area. There was only one person there, sitting among the phones.

"Today's not a holiday is it?"

"I don't know. What do you think?" the receptionist answered. She was a natural blonde, naturally pretty in minimal makeup, but a little acid that morning. "Could it be everyone's leaving the firm?"

"Is Dinah Solatoff here by any chance?"

"Okay. The guys over in tax law, they're here if you want to talk to them. A couple of the others. Patty's here of course…and me."

"But Dinah? Over in Mergers and Acquisitions. Dinah Solatoff."

"I know who you mean. The ones who aren't leaving, they took the day off." The receptionist kept her eyes on him. She seemed to think him thick as a brick.

"So you think she's not here?"

"What did I just say?"

"This goes to Mr. Jorrigo." Sterrett handed her the envelope. "It's quite important. Why I want to be sure."

"I'll tear it to shreds the minute you turn your back. Satisfied?" the woman said, dropping the letter of leave-taking into the in-box. She added, "I know who you are. Do you even remember my name? You go ahead and guess. It's like the wife in *Ulysses*."

Sterrett shrugged. "Penelope?"

"I'm Molly? We spent a couple days together, then I never heard from you again."

"I'm sorry."

"Sorry?" Molly laughed. "It's our town's great strength, isn't it? Everyone's sorry." Then she reached out and gave Sterrett's hand a pinch. "Now we're evened," she said.

Sterrett did remember who the girl was. They'd dated what seemed like eons ago, around the time he'd first started working on the sanitary landfill. One weekend they'd gone to Annapolis together to watch the crabs swim. He'd meant to call her afterwards, but something else had come up. He remembered her interests included ballroom dancing. But he wanted the past and its shadows in the past.

He took the elevator back down to his office. The battered brief-case was where he'd left it, on the floor under his desk, a joyfully brimful bag of money treasure. Gripping the briefcase, he gave a last look around, then went out and wandered the fourth floor. He stopped at the Ebco fountain for water and decided to try Hugo Humphrey's door.

Their friendship had never gotten off the ground, but Sterrett had thought about it and he wanted to make peace. He knocked at the door, pushed the door open. A cockroach, big enough to have been a junior partner, came rushing out from under a desk. It fanned its antennae at Sterrett and then disappeared through a crack in the wall. Otherwise the room was empty.

Sterrett turned back into the hallway. No one to say good-bye to, except Neon Flores, his big, empty noggin sitting there on Suzy's desk. It was a moment of feeling sorry for the opportunities he'd lost, the companionship he'd failed at. A few salt streaks appeared on his face. But he shook that sentiment off. Only when he held his fate freely in his own hands and wasn't obliged to anyone would he allow himself feelings.

He made the elevators and went down to the lobby. He pushed through the revolving glass doors. He pulled his bike free of its chain and secured the briefcase to the rack. Then he was up on his wheels, feeling torquey to the max, speeding through red lights, speeding through traffic. The bicycle was giving its all, and its tires cried out happily, sending dust into the sky. He stunted close to car bumpers all the way out Pennsylvania Avenue.

Sterrett saw he had to keep focused on his goal. He was going to live his dream as if he was the only one who could live it. He and Di-nah together, see what happened. His one worry was that time would level out his feelings for her. His fear was that his feelings would run out at a much faster rate than the money would, and in a year, maybe two, he'd end up a man, and she'd be just another woman to him. He smiled at his silly cynicism. There were other things to worry over. He had to find the woman first.

All the roads that led to the city led to the White House. All the roads, from as far as the eye could see, and farther, over mountains and rivers, all roads brought the traveler to the doorstep of secular power, of power wielded by the chief executive who sat in the Oval Office.

The power to make peace, the power to make war, the power to enrich or impoverish a nation, to enrich or impoverish the world, resided there under that balustrade roof.

There was no power so great in the entire history of mankind, and yet the building that housed it seemed nothing more than a humdrum version of Graceland. That lack of pretension was on purpose, and the peculiarity of its inhabitant was that he, or she, could at times seem much less influential than a long dead Elvis. But the White House enjoyed an aura that radiated well beyond its century-old iron fence; that Friday morning, the entire Ellipse was cordoned off for the landfill's groundbreaking, as exclusive as any White House event, even though it was not an official White House event, but a private affair, paid for out of Unfragrant Bin's development budget.

Because it was an affair so thoroughly tinged with privilege, the people who were invited all of them came. They came to relax and make light of the world in the company of their peers. Kid Psora set out food tents on the wide lawn of the Ellipse offering everyone a chance to relax responsibly.

Music came from a low dais set up near the Zero Milestone. Strings flashed and feet stomped as Texas Senator Roger Simmers played his fiddle. He was against the landfill, but he couldn't resist a good party with a cause to scowl at. The other musicians chased along with the senator, the sweat beading up on their brows. The tune ended with raucous cheers.

"Let's do one more," Simmers said. "And then take a break. All right, boys?" Again fingers swooped and taut chords vibrated.

Rivaling the strains of "The Midnight Special," came laughter from around the barbecue set up by the caterer. The two Quinn brothers, natural gas lobbyists, were doing their version of "The House at Pooh Corner." It was a routine they performed at whatever party they were invited to.

The older Quinn was reading from a notebook, "'When she awoke in the morning, the first thing she saw was the President sitting in front of the looking-glass, looking at himself…"Hallo!" said Nancy Pelosi…"Hallo!" answered the President, 'I've found somebody just like me. I thought I was the only one of them.'"

The crowd round the barbecue was made up mostly of business leaders and hard-nosed real estate attorneys. The women were dressed in bad taste, but comfortably so, some in dazzling red culottes and sassy logo T-shirts. The men stood around in their blue blazers, khaki pants, and red neckties, imperturbable despite being stone drunk.

"'Nancy Pelosi got out of bed, and began to explain what a looking-glass was, but just as she was getting to the interesting part, the President said: "Excuse me a moment, but there's something climbing up your table," …'" The one Quinn peeked over at his younger brother who began a recognizable imitation of the president, the dude-like walk, the smile. The one Quinn then resumed, "'And with one loud Worra worra worra worra worra, he jumped at the end of the tablecloth, pulled it to the ground, and wrapped himself up in it three times, rolled to the other end of the room…'"

"Oh no, not rolled," someone cried as the younger Quinn threw himself down and rolled across the damp grass.

"Does it ever grow tiresome?" Vincent Jorrigo drawled. "Them?"

Celia Progg looked over her shoulder.

"They're a hot item at the Cato Institute."

Vince liked that about Celia. His feeling good about himself owed something to her ability to make him laugh at the world.

"What you want to do?" he said. "Something to eat?"

"Shall we get a little tipsy first? How about it?" Celia replied. She knew this was her window of opportunity, not to let it close, Vince there and vulnerable and willingly so, and she made a point of adding, "After the smoke clears on this landfill thing, what about you and me doing something just for us?"

"But away from D.C."

"You got it."

Vince fetched two flutes of Springfest champagne from the barman, and they went walking into the tall trees that edged the Ellipse, the two of them. They walked arm in arm away from the others. They weren't completely relaxed; they were professionals. But they were relaxed enough.

"When the smoke clears," Vince said, clinking glasses. "I might not have a law firm." He'd learned from Patty Johnson what was going on at the firm, Ray Wilbur and his crowd taking charge. He realized then he had nothing worse to fear. He realized there was nothing more he could do about Groves or the money and he came to the groundbreaking, accepting his fate and ready to try and enjoy himself.

"Firm or no firm," Celia said. "Here's to us. You and I, we shouldn't look back." She sipped her champagne. She made a sour face. "This stuff tastes horrible."

"What do you think a garbage man would serve except champagne that was garbage?" He took her hand, and Celia was happy to lean her head against his shoulder. The sun was warm on their faces. They stood together, close to the party's edge, two people tied by more than their profession, feeling that tie grow a little stronger.

"We have pancakes," one of the caterer's people was shouting, shopping noshes. He strode up and down in front of the side-order tent shouting, "We have French fries."

"It is a shame this park can't stay the way it is," Celia said.

"Where's the progress in that?" Vince wanted to know. Peering into Celia's eyes, he added, "It's not parks that are beautiful, it's the people in them." He went so far as to call her "darling" on the spot. They wandered around like that, hand in hand. That was the advantage to people over cards, there was no calculation necessary to achieve success, one kiss and a soft caress, a display of trust, these were enough to win with hearts.

They found themselves in a crowd. Some carried plastic plates loaded with potato salad. Some held clear plastic cups full of Springfest. Some held firmly to pizza. They were the empowered, the Caste, people of discretion and influence, and they were watching badminton, a game between the banker Ellen Berman and the architect Ian McMinn.

The architect had won the first game by one serve, after several tie-break settings. The second game and Berman was making her banker's comeback. The crowd, unruly at first, came to order as the game gained focus, and the only sound was the pu-twang of the racquets, the flutter of the shuttlecock as it was slapped back and forth over the net.

"Let's go," Ellen Berman said. She held her slender laminate racquet high, moving excitedly back and forth. "My serve."

With unexpected swiftness, she nailed the shuttlecock hard. The young architect couldn't get to it in time. Berman said, "My game, Ian. Too bad for you."

The architect flung his racquet, flung it to the ground. It was a boyish gesture; he was certainly not used to being made fun of. Ellen latched on to that right away. Her idea of courtship was to taunt a man into liking her. She laughed and pointed to the young architect, and said fondly, "Oh, Ian McMinn."

Her feet were hot, and Dinah slipped her flat-heeled shoes off, walked barefoot towards the refreshments tent. Halfway, she was accosted by a burly, bowlegged man in white ducks and a flashy Hawaiian shirt. He was wearing a war bonnet on his head. It was not a ceremonial bonnet of prized feathers, but a toy, the sort of fake Indian bonnet sold to children, with a small bow and the arrows with suction-cup points. He wore it knocked back from his forehead.

"Perfection of the life or of the art?" the man said to her. "Can't remember which."

"I'm sorry," Dinah asked. "What?"

"I chose one of them when I was young. But can't recall which." The man was no longer a young man to be sure, yet adolescence lingered in his sly glance. "It's the hors d'oeuvres make you thirsty, and then you drink," the man went on to say. "But these martinis..." He took a sip from the glass he was holding. Smacked his lips. "That's perfection either way." The man stuck his hand out. "Leonard Between Dogs. And you?"

"Dinah Solatoff. Pleased to meet you."

"I'm a poet. Heard of me?"

"I have too much work to do to read poetry." Right away, Dinah wished she could have taken those words back, seeing how the man reacted, watching his eyes grow pinched. She amended, "I like poetry. I do, but you know, when do I have the time?"

"But I know what you mean. Come on," Leonard B. said. "Let's go get you a martini."

Dinah let her path join with his. She felt in limbo really, no longer entirely in Washington, and not yet back home, but she was keeping as far away from Bill Coote as she could, for her heart was in limbo, too. She didn't want to argue anymore and she didn't want to get blubbery. As far as Congressman William Coote was concerned, she was going to try to behave herself, not burn all her bridges. She thought one day she might return to the city and get herself a political office, come back to Washington and change the way things were done. Coote for all his defects might prove a useful connection if in fact she did come back.

"It's a little early. I'd like something else," Dinah said.

"If you can drink a martini in the morning and still do business, then nothing's going to stop you. If you can't have one martini, then you're weak and you'll lose at whatever you do."

"I don't do business," was Dinah's retort.

"Neither do I," Leonard Between Dogs said. He passed her a glass of soda. "It was my imitation of people who do, do business." He tossed his head to brandish his toy feathers. He did it without a smile, though it seemed to Dinah a comical gesture and made her grin despite her mood.

"I'm a writer and I waste my time, you know, mocking myself," the poet was saying. "Like this." He reached up and pulled the atrociously fake bonnet into place. "Where you from?"

"I'm from Idaho." She leaned against Leonard B. for support as she put her shoes back on. The grass around the refreshments tent was soaked with dew and not adapted for going barefoot.

"Ah, a Westerner like me," he said, amused by her touch. He laughed. "A cowgirl? You were not made for this, this unfree life."

Dinah was about to protest, but she realized the poet was right. It was a startlingly simple idea, that she was not free to be herself in Washington. That was the reason she'd been afraid of facing another person honestly, because she couldn't do it the way she'd been used to back home. She'd been too hard on herself; the city constrained one and all to cheat their desires.

When the famed Washington poet turned round for a refill on his drink, Dinah took that opportunity to sneak off. She saw Bill Coote among a crowd of men in suits. He was too busy talking to notice her. That was a relief; she wanted to walk away clean, without a word, leaving her congressman guessing. She still wanted to catch sight of Sterrett Emerson Groves before she left. She had come to apologize to him for the rough way she'd treated him. She was sure if he were any place, he would be at the groundbreaking and she wanted him to know she wasn't an ungrateful type of person. One kiss from him, that's all Dinah wanted, a way to bring her stay in Washington to a pardonable close.

The gold spade that Secretary Thomas Morrow was to use at the groundbreaking was not a spade, and it was not a shovel. Though some called it a spade and some called it a shovel, it was a gardener's trowel, and it was not gold. It was an amalgam of inexpensive metals with a wooden handle, a small, plain trowel bought at an Orange-U-Glad store and spray-painted with gold acrylic by an artistically skilled paralegal from Melody Hogan. It looked convincingly solid, as inviting a garden tool as there ever was.

At a given signal, well into the morning event, an Unfragrant Bin flunky came up with the gardener's trowel, carrying it on a red satin cushion. People came over from the badminton court and from the refreshments tent. They gathered round the dais, and the musicians put down their instruments. Kid Psora and Secretary Thomas Morrow joined Director Segreen and Ellen Berman already there at the clearing where the groundbreaking was to take place. The guests applauded when they saw the trowel, and they yelled a boozy "Huzzah." It was a special moment and they cried, "Huzzah" again.

Before the tool was actually sunk into the earth and the first clod turned, Antonia Segreen, the director of the Bureau of Land Management, began to speak, speaking in a loud, lively voice, "I've worked with Sir Simon Psora and gotten to know him, working together on a project that my bureau is proud to sponsor, the Landfill at the Ellipse, and I think this year will be a special year. The Ellipse offers a remarkable opportunity for all of us. What do you folks think?"

There was applause and there were untiring cheers, too.

"Trash will have a future in our national parks. The Landfill at the Ellipse will be one of this nation's leading sites. I think we owe Sir Simon Psora, today represented by his son, a big round of applause, our thanks for his vision in making this model sanitary landfill a reality."

Segreen, her eyes hooded so that the exhilaration she felt would remain undetected, bathed her soul in the clapping hands.

"Who can say?" Segreen continued. "Look around you. Who can say they're from Washington? Who can say, I was born in the Nation's Capital?" She paused, and lifted her head. "No, I think it's safe to say, we are all of us from other places. But few of us would deny that this, this City on the Hill has now become our real home. I'll make no bones about it, I love Washington, and that's a fact."

Director Segreen dropped the microphone to her chest, looked around her, people nodding, smiling, too moved to applaud. "But now I'll pass the mike to Sir Simon's son and let him say a few words."

Kid Psora took up the microphone, his smooth operator's voice amplified across the lawn. First he turned to Segreen and Ellen Berman and said, "Thank you ladies. Thank you. A super job." Then he began, "I was born in a townhouse in London, a hideously enormous townhouse." Everyone laughed at that, even though it was not meant as a joke. "But my dear father, Sir Simon was born in a world that I believe it's safe to say no longer exists. You Americans might put it that he came from 'east of here,' from a rather grim little fishing village on the coast of the island of Cyprus. I say, trash is the future, and the future of trash is waste management. I'm looking out upon you on this marvelous day, and my father, who can't be here, would want each and every one of you to know how highly he esteems your constant friendship and warm regard for him."

There was loud, smitten applause, applause that Kid Psora tried to interrupt with a certain modesty, but then Secretary Thomas Morrow came hurrying up. He twisted the microphone out of Psora's hand. The microphone was not a toy; it was not for kids. Dr. Morrow glanced over at Director Segreen; it was not for women either. The microphone was a man's tool, like the shovel.

"I want to stop, I want to stop Mr. Psora before he says something that makes everyone think he's running for office." Then Tom Morrow announced, "In a few minutes, in my role as Secretary of the Department of the Interior, I'm going to have the honor of inaugurating this landfill." He cleared his throat. "I'm going to reach down into this ground and dig. Digging the ground, that's what made America great, what made this continent, made it the best home of Freedom, so okay, all together now, let's sing 'The Star-Spangled Banner.'"

Heads bent back as the jubilant anthem burst upon the sky.

Sterrett pedaled like all get out the last few hundred yards, turning down 17th Street. He looked up, men in uniform, guarding the sidewalk. He nodded at them. One of the men nodded back. He cut behind the Old Executive Office Building only to run into Unfragrant Bin's security guards. He flung his bike down and hurried up with the briefcase in hand. Since his name was on the guest list, Sterrett was allowed onto the Ellipse. He made his way to the clearing where the Secretary of the Interior, Dr. Thomas Morrow, was getting down to business with the golden trowel.

Dinah was nowhere to be seen, but Sterrett recognized many of the faces there, Jorrigo and others from Guiteau and Garfield. He recognized a few high-ranking government officials, too, and lawyers from other firms, their necks stretching out of sweat-stained collars, all clamoring for a better view.

Sterrett moved his shoulders to decamp the scene, to go and find the girl, desperate to find her, but his feet were planted in the ground, his eyes wouldn't leave the crowd. Not to have seen it before, the way to be was to do what came the hardest. Make it something to get drunk over later on. He walked, swinging the briefcase, batting at knees and hacking at backsides to get through. When he got to the clearing, his damp face was instarred with a smile.

It was hot, the sun laboring into the sky. The handle of the garden tool was already slick with perspiration, but the Secretary stooped, ready to break his bit of ground. The associate came on with the briefcase, and Tom Morrow stumbled back, swatting at him with the trowel. Sterrett held the battered briefcase high over his head so that everyone could see it. He opened the case, turned it upside down. He shook and shook it, thousands of one hundred dollar bills in neatly wrapped packets tumbling plop, plop onto the rich earth.

He dropped the empty case and looked around him, stared at the gathered lawyers and politicians as though to ask them something, but decided to keep his mouth shut, and pushing through, exited the crush of people. All attention was focused on the money. It was clear that the groundbreaking ceremony couldn't continue as scheduled until the pile was removed. It was too much in the way.

Crows in the branches went caw-caw. The rushing-river sound of the cars down Constitution Avenue could be heard across the Ellipse. Impotence overcame the onlookers. No one dared speak. Who would dare to be seen to be the first to approach all that money? To seem interested, to reveal to others even the slightest hint of greed would have been too much. People stared at the big pile of money, with a breathless disgust, galvanized.

Bills, some of the wrappers broken in the fall to the ground, took to the air on a faint breeze off the Potomac. They fluttered up among the skirts of the trees, then fell back among the crowd, hundred dollar bills blown gently into the faces of the empowered, falling on their stiffened shoulders, falling like ash among the countless feet that shuffled round the pile. Hundred dollar bills blowing onto the grounds of the White House, blown up the south lawn, so that…

Sterrett moved on shaky legs. He moved slowly, straying from tree to tree, heading away from the groundbreaking. He felt his going away would be easier if he unburdened himself of all his anger, and he was about to let out a raging shout. Instead he bumbled forth a pirouette, spinning round to stare.

Dinah was bored and tired and irritated. She had come to see Sterrett and she hadn't seen him. She held up a moment standing among some parked cars at the edge of the Ellipse, trying to decide where the best place was to catch a taxi back to S Street. Out of the corner of her eye, she caught sight of the boy, and Sterrett, thrilled to see her waiting there for him, lurched towards her. And when they opened their eyes again, breaking away from their long kiss, it was just the two of them, in a place full of sunlight.

Sterrett began to explain to Dinah what he'd done and why. But she stopped him and told him, "Forget the stupid things I said. Once you have the person you love, all you need is, well, the person you love."

They crossed an open field going home. Dinah could see an airplane make its course westward over the trees, silver wings banked against the sky. She stopped and watched the plane grow smaller. Sterrett lingered ahead of her, then came back to impress a kiss upon her cheek. "I'm the luckiest," he said. "The luckiest man ever."

"And I," she boasted as she turned in his arms, "I am the happiest, the happiest woman of all."

Sterrett drew her closer. He said, as he cinched her about the waist, "We are, Dinah. We are the two happiest people in the world."

The End

ABOUT THE AUTHOR

The author, Paul J. Hammond, is a native Washingtonian, born at George Washington University Hospital on Washington Circle. He attended Anthony Hyde Elementary School, St. Albans School, and Kenyon College, where he graduated with honors. He has worked variously as a trade consultant, a real estate developer, and an R/T officer on a cruise ship. He is married to Alessandra Bosa of Merano and spends his time between Italy and the USA, writing and guiding scuba divers round the rocks to see the bright barracuda.

ABOUT THE FISH

KCM Publishing
a division of KCM Digital Media, LLC

9 781939 961358